This book is dedicated to
Edith Phillips
with affection and appreciation

DON'T MISS ONE MOMENT OF
ALEXANDRA RIPLEY'S
FROM FIELDS OF GOLD

❦

"RICH, METICULOUSLY RESEARCHED HISTORICAL DETAIL . . . an odyssey of discovery about the South, the harsh business world, power, individual worth, and matters of the heart."
—*Newport News Daily Press*

"THE AUTHOR WHO BROUGHT RHETT AND SCARLETT BACK TOGETHER RETURNS WITH ANOTHER LUSH ROMANCE SET IN THE OLD SOUTH. . . . Ripley's knowledge of the period, her shrewd delineation of character, and her storyteller's gift combine to make this a warming entertainment for a long winter's night." —*West Coast Review of Books*

"A POWERFUL STORY. . . . Ms. Ripley writes strong characters with a need for power, wealth, and love. You will enjoy this story." —*Rendezvous*

"ALEXANDRA RIPLEY HAS AGAIN CAPTURED A BELIEVABLE AND INTERESTING MICROCOSM OF THE SOUTH FOLLOWING THE CIVIL WAR. . . . FAST-MOVING AND EASY TO READ, and enough like an antebellum version of *Cinderella* to warm the hearts of readers who grew up reading—and believing in—the happy-ever-after ending to stories."
—*Baton Rouge Magazine*

"IN FRANCESCA, RIPLEY CREATES A CHARACTER YOU'LL NEVER FORGET."
—*Los Angeles Features Syndicate*

Also by Alexandra Ripley

Scarlett: The Sequel to Margaret Mitchell's
Gone With the Wind
Charleston
On Leaving Charleston
New Orleans Legacy
The Time Returns

Published by
WARNER BOOKS

FROM FIELDS
OF GOLD

ALEXANDRA
RIPLEY

WARNER
VISION

A Time Warner Company

WARNER BOOKS EDITION

Cover design by Diane Lugar
Hand lettering by Carl Dellacroce
Cover illustration by Ron Finger

Warner Vision is a trademark of Warner Books, Inc.

Warner Books, Inc
1271 Avenue of the Americas
New York, NY 10020

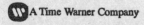 A Time Warner Company

Printed in the United States of America

Originally published in hardcover by Warner Books.

First Printed in Paperback: January, 1996

10 9 8 7 6 5 4 3 2 1

FROM FIELDS
OF GOLD

24 August, 1875

Chapter One

THE WAGON WAS MADE OF WOOD, long since weathered to a mottled gray. It had high sides, a plank seat in front, and four tall wheels with rusty iron rims and spokes that still showed small patches of red paint. It was an all-purpose farm wagon, sturdy and utilitarian, with no pretensions to beauty except for the red paint patches that hinted at a long-ago outburst of high spirits or optimism.

It was like most of the other farm wagons in the Piedmont, the central area of North Carolina.

So was the heavy-shouldered, short-legged dun horse that pulled it. Strong, well maintained, unbeautiful.

The boy who was handling the reins must have been the author of the red-painted spokes. His tanned and freckled face had an eager, energetic expression; his eyes were startling—a clear definite blue the color of a summer sky on a sunny day. They seemed to look at the world straight on, and to like what they saw.

His name was Nathaniel Richardson. Most people called

him Nate. He was eighteen years old and the recognized head of the family in the wagon, in spite of his youth.

His mother sat beside him on the plank seat; his brother sat on her other side.

Mary Richardson looked much older than her forty-four years. Most farm women did; it was a hard life of early marriage, childbearing, and never-ending work. Mary was small in stature, made smaller by stooped shoulders that thrust her wrinkled face forward in an aggressive pose. On this late summer day, however, she looked more anticipatory than aggressive. She was wearing her best dress, a serviceable black gabardine with a white lace collar, and her Sunday-go-to-meeting hat, a shiny black straw with a broad grosgrain ribbon that made a bow in front on the brim and a bow where it tied under her pointed chin. From time to time her large-knuckled hand patted the knee of the dark-suited young man beside her. He was her pride and joy, her elder son Gideon.

Gideon was unaware of his mother's affectionate pats. He was lost in thought. Even the excited chatter of the children behind him could not penetrate his concentration.

The rest of the Richardson family rode in the back of the wagon, along with boxes and baskets and barrels. Nate and Gideon's Uncle Joshua was a dour, thin man with a long dark beard streaked with gray and a wooden peg leg. His wife Alva was twenty-five years old and twenty-five years younger than Josh. Their children were the source of the high-pitched laughter and shouting. Micah was eight, Susan four, both of them towheaded like their mother, with the pale blue eyes of their father.

Josh turned the chill in his eyes on to his children, and their noisiness abated.

Nate called over his shoulder to them. "After this rise, it'll be downhill all the way. We're almost there."

"Don't you race this poor old horse down the hill, now, Nate," said his mother. "I don't want to end up a pile of splinters on the road."

Nate laughed. "Don't worry, Ma. Natchez doesn't have any

racing in him. Just hope he doesn't stop and go to sleep." He bent forward to look past her. "Like Gideon there," he said.

His mother shushed him. "Your brother's thinking about the words he's going to say."

Nate bit his lip to hide his smile. He could say the words himself by this time. Gideon had been practicing all week, standing on a stump near the barn.

At the crest of the hill, Nate pulled the horse to a stop. There was a breeze to be enjoyed. A faint sound of music rode on the breeze. His right foot began to tap.

He flicked the reins. "Gid-dup, Natchez. The Richardson family is going to Camp Meeting."

His Uncle Josh took charge of unloading the wagon. There were plenty of willing helpers, and Nate was glad to leave everything to them. Meeting was where he got to see friends he hadn't seen since the year before.

He spied the three Martin brothers on the edge of a crowd gathered near the bandstand. "Hey, Billy . . . Jim . . . Matt . . . what's the good word?" he shouted.

Only one of them looked at him. "How're you doing, Nate?" Jim waved, then turned away.

What was the attraction? Nate wondered. He went to see for himself, his shoulders making a hole between Jim and Matt.

The most beautiful girl in the world was sitting on a bench near the stand.

Nate was eighteen years old, vigorous, healthy—and virile. His body responded to the girl and his thoughts; he had to turn away and race to the cover of the pinewoods nearby. He prayed that nobody had seen the pointy shape in his pants. It was almost more than a man could bear, the way his privates had a will of their own.

Just put her right out of your head, he told himself. That one's trouble on two legs. But he couldn't erase the memory of the butter-yellow curls tumbling over her shoulders, or her big eyes, blue as cornflowers, or the full, high breasts beneath her prim, high-necked white shirtwaist. Her waist was tiny; he bet he could circle it easy with his two hands. Then he could move them, slide them up real slow and easy . . .

Nate groaned aloud.

He was no stranger to the pleasures of a woman's body. In fact, he'd had plenty of women, and they said they enjoyed him just as much as he enjoyed them. So why was this girl getting to him like this? She was against his number one rule: keep away from unmarried girls. They want to get married, and their daddies are real particular about it, too. He just knew this girl was unmarried; she had that look of expecting something and not knowing what it was. How he would love to teach her!

Oh, no, my friend. That's the trap.

Nate tried his best to think about the women he knew. There was Julie, at the Haw River Bridge country store. She was just as pretty, wasn't she? Or Millie, the one in the café at Mebane crossroads, or the other Millie on the road to Burlington. Or any one of many others.

Like most of the families at the Meeting, the Richardsons were tobacco farmers. But Nate had added a step to the process. He did not take his leaf to market the way most men did. Why sell it to some company that would shred it and pack it in little bags and sell each bag for as much money as they'd paid for twenty pounds of leaf?

His mother and Aunt Alva pounded the leaves and sifted the tobacco after it was cured and treated, then packed it in drawstring bags for Nate to sell. They had their own little paper label tag, just like the big companies. RICHARDSON'S RICH NORTH CAROLINA SMOKING TOBACCO. NONE RICHER. Nate was happy with how their brand was selling after only one season in the stores.

He'd been plenty nervous last year when he first set out on the road with his saddlebags full of the little pouches. But it hadn't been hard at all to get the country-store owners to buy a few just to try them out. All of them had a couple of dozen brands of smoking tobacco, and chewing tobacco, and snuff. Why not one more? And from a likable young fellow who'd grown it himself instead of one of the duded-up drummers who did the selling for the big-name brands like Bull Durham and Liggett & Myers. Lots of times they'd invite him to stop a while and take a drink or a meal or share a chaw. Nate always accepted, even though he didn't like the taste of tobacco, not after being in the field with it, and his Ma would throw a fit if she knew he was drinking liquor. But it was important to make friends.

More friends than he'd ever expected. It hadn't taken long for him to pick up on the messages he was getting from many of the storekeepers' wives. They were generally a lot younger than their husbands. Men had to make their way in the world and have a house and a livelihood to offer before they could marry, whereas a girl was thought ready for marriage and motherhood when she was fifteen. By the time she was eighteen or nineteen, she had a couple of children and a yen for something more exciting than cleaning and cooking and sewing and feeding chickens and babies. A half hour of fun in the house while her husband was over at the store—it did no harm to anybody. In fact, Nate liked to think, it made everybody's life a lot more cheerful. What man wouldn't rather have a wife who smiled and hummed a song than one who complained about how the housework tired her out?

As for him, Nate smiled and sang songs the whole time he was on the road. Hot sun, cold wind and rain, roads that filled your mouth with dust or bogged you in mud up to your boottops—it was all part of the adventure, because a road could go someplace you'd never been before, if that's what you were in the mood for. Or it could take you somewhere you knew you'd be welcome.

Whichever way he went, he was getting ahead. And that's what he had made up his mind to do. He wasn't going to be a farmer forever, not him. He was going to do something with his life. Something big.

And he would not be sidetracked by a girl, not even the prettiest girl he'd ever seen, or was ever likely to see.

Nate threw his shoulders back. He had made up his mind.

He'd avoid crowds, especially crowds of men. That way he probably wouldn't even see her again. Camp Meeting lasted three days, and he would have plenty of other things to keep him and his mind busy. This year for the first time they had a really famous preacher. Dan Gaskins was supposed to be able to make you feel the flames of hell licking at your heels. Maybe I'll even feel it, the Holy Spirit entering my soul. Maybe I'll be saved. It would make Ma happier than anything. Me, too.

Even if I don't succeed again this year, she won't be too let down. Gideon's going to preach, and I know he'll be good.

Nate's older brother had been away for five years, until the month before when he came back to the farm. At Trinity College he'd been one of the best; in the class at church, he'd risen to the role of class leader. Then he'd been asked to become an exhorter in an outreach church in Randolph County, near the college. He'd even preached a few times. He was a rising star in the Methodist Church, his mother said to everyone who'd stand still to listen. He had a true call. It was the dream she'd always had, and it was coming true, by the Grace of God. Nate was almost as proud of Gideon as their mother was. He'd always looked up to his older brother, always wished he could be as handsome as Gideon and as sure of what he was meant to do.

Now, with selling *Richardson's Rich*, he felt he was on the track. It wasn't as mighty a road as Gideon's, but Christ didn't call everybody. Besides, Nate liked it.

And he liked to sing. What was he doing, hanging around in the woods when he could hear the music from the afternoon service? He began to run toward it, already singing.

> *Rock of Ages, cleft for me . . .*

The hymns he loved so well led Nate to his undoing. That evening, the service was the best he'd ever heard. The Reverend Dan Gaskins was everything people had said he was. For a moment, when the Reverend's voice had thunder in it, and lightning was in his eyes, Nate felt the weight of his sins bowing him low, and he waited for the voice of God to call him to reckoning and salvation. It was not to be.

The preacher's voice suddenly became hushed; the huge tent and the hundreds in it were silent. "My brothers and sisters," said Gaskins softly, "I have a blessed moment from my life that I will paint for you in words, knowing that your loving hearts will give color to them. Picture, then, my beloved wife, suffering as all you mothers have suffered—you know better than I the full glory and agony of that pain—in the miraculous labor of bringing a new life, a new soul into this world. After the birth, she called me to her side, and I saw that her fragile body had not the strength to prevail. But the Holy Spirit was within her, and her dear face was shining with happiness, even as earthly life was departing from her. I wept, and I begged her to live, even though it was God's will that I lose her to a more perfect, eternal life where there is no suffering.

"She raised her hand, then, to quiet me. And for her sweet sake I was quiet, though my heart was clamorous with grief.

"Into the quiet came a sound, so small and weak that I doubted my hearing. And then my beloved wife breathed her last words. 'A gift,' she said, 'from heaven.'

"And I saw the miracle with my own eyes, the miracle of life even in the midst of death, for calling to me at that very moment was my baby daughter, whose name is Lily, because the day of her birth was Easter Sunday, and the beauty of lilies was all around.

"I have asked her to greet you now and to testify to the wonder of God's love for each of you. He is here, waiting to grant you that gift. You have only to open your hearts to it and to him."

Dan Gaskins stepped to one side. From the shadows behind stepped a vision of loveliness. An indrawn breath of astonishment swept the crowd, and tear-stained faces smiled with uncomplicated happiness at the sight.

The small figure was clothed in a plain white robe with

long sleeves, and folds of fabric that hung straight from the shoulder to the floor. It had no ornamentation, except the gleaming long locks of Lily's golden hair and the beauty of her perfectly oval face, with skin as fair as buttermilk and eyes as blue as sapphires.

"She looks like an angel," whispered Gideon into Nate's ear.

"Yes," was all that he could say. There was a heaviness in his heart, and a soaring excitement. He could not escape. He could not deny. He was lost to sense and reason. He was captive to love.

Lily held out her arms, as if she were embracing the whole congregation. She began to sing, and her soprano voice was as pure and beautiful as her face.

> *I love to tell the story*
> *Of unseen things above*
> *Of Jesus and his glory*
> *Of Jesus and his love.*
> *I love to tell the story*
> *Because I know it's true.*
> *It satisfies my longings*
> *As nothing else can do.*
>
> *I love to tell the story;*
> *More wonderful it seems*
> *Than all the golden fancies*
> *Of all our golden dreams.*
> *I love to tell the story;*
> *It did so much for me.*
> *And that is just the reason*
> *I tell it now to thee.*

Nate slumped on the bench. Who was he to dare think of even talking to an angel? But he had to see her, talk to her, touch her, to see if she was real. This was Friday. There were two more days of Camp Meeting. He had to find a way.

On Saturday he jostled for position amid the dozens of young men who gathered wherever Lily appeared. She was kind to them all, bestowing her smiles evenly and listening to each one who pushed forward for a few words, with her full attention, her rosy plump lips slightly parted. The glimpse of her tiny white teeth and pink tongue nearly drove Nate mad.

But he wouldn't make a fool of himself the way the others were doing, offering to bring her lemonade, asking if she needed an escort to the hymn singing or the prayer meeting or whatever was happening next.

True, she accepted the lemonade, and she allowed herself to be escorted, but the entire pack of admirers was around her even when she was walking with her hand tucked in the elbow of only one.

Nate had to be alone with her. He had to. So he remained on the edges, unable to stay away, but too proud to act like the rest of them. He hoped his face didn't look as stupid as theirs, like they'd been hit with a shovel between the eyes.

He was very much afraid it did.

His mother berated him when he took his place next to her Saturday evening. "You're late," she said, "and at the service where your brother's going to speak, too. Where did you get to? I haven't laid eyes on you the whole day, and there were things for you to do."

"I'm sorry, Ma," he mumbled, but he did not look into her angry eyes. He was watching the platform, wondering if Lily was going to sing again.

He tried to listen to the Reverend Gaskins' sermon, but he heard not one word. Last night she had sung immediately after.

But not tonight. Instead, Gideon came forward to exhort. It was a tradition of the church. After the sermon on a text from the Bible, a layman would comment, expanding on the sermon's message, bringing it closer to people like himself, in a way that the traveling preacher was unable to do, because he wasn't one of them.

Mary Richardson could not suppress a sigh of satisfaction at the sight of her tall, handsome son standing up on the platform. Gideon's new suit was dark, his white shirt immaculate, his blue tie perfectly knotted. She had trimmed his dark hair herself that morning, and watched carefully, at his request, to be sure that he trimmed his neat beard evenly. He looked wonderful, like a scholar and Godly man should look. She settled herself comfortably. This was the crowning moment of her life.

She felt Nate's bulk beside her, but she didn't look at him. She knew what she'd see, and she didn't want to see it. His hair was mouse brown and always shaggy. Even she with her scissors couldn't tame it. He was freckled like a bird's egg, too, and too stubborn to wear a decent beard to hide some of the freckles, at least. He'd never grow as tall as Gideon, or be as handsome as Gideon, or as gifted as Gideon. About the only thing she could say for Nate was that he didn't mind hard work, and he kept himself real clean. He always smelled of soap, and at least that was next to Godliness.

Gideon began to speak, and her heart panicked. You couldn't hear him.

But after a few phrases, his voice strengthened. Then it grew, until it rolled powerfully over the watchful heads in front of him. His mother sighed happily again.

Nate heard his brother's voice, and he was impressed. He hadn't known Gideon could sound like that. The words didn't matter; Nate knew them by heart anyway. His eyes roved over the rows of people until he saw Lily up front, her face lifted toward his brother. Maybe she didn't know Gideon was his brother; maybe she'd be impressed; or, maybe being a preacher's daughter, she was only interested in preachers, not their brothers. Nate felt as if a fist had hit him in the chest.

No, there was no point being jealous of his own brother. Gideon was old—twenty-five already—and he only cared about his church work. He paid no attention to girls, never had, since he went to Trinity. He hadn't been anywhere around Lily, either. Nate could name every single one who'd been there, and how close to her, and what each one had said and what she'd said back to him. . . .

When he congratulated Gideon after the service was over, his praise and pride were from the heart. Then he got out of the way so their mother could strut around on the arm of her preacher son, accepting everyone's admiration for him.

Nate looked for Lily, but she was nowhere to be seen. He went to bed. No sense joining up with his old friends. They were all enemies, now that they were rivals. He couldn't stand the sight of them.

Sunday morning he was so frantic that he cut himself when he shaved.

His Aunt Alva laughed gently when she saw him going to the breakfast tent. "Come here and let me wash your chin, it's got fresh blood on it. Poor Nate. I've never seen such misery in all my born days. Why didn't you just cut your throat and be done with it?"

"Does it show so much, Alva?"

"I'm afraid so, honey." Her voice was kind, her touch very light when she cleaned him up. Nate wanted to kiss her for being so easy on him. Alva was the most comforting person he'd ever known, and he loved her. It was Alva who had shown him the way men and women were together, who had taught him how to please a woman while he was pleasing himself. She had been his first love, when he was only thirteen and didn't know what his body was telling him, or what to do about it.

She had even taught him that the fierce love he had for her wasn't what he thought it was. "I'll kill Uncle Josh for treating you like he does," Nate swore when he saw the bruises on Alva's face. "Then you can marry me, and we'll be together all the time, and we'll be happy."

No, they wouldn't be, she told him, and she told him why. Like it or not, he was still a boy, and he should wait, and try out life in lots of ways, before he chained himself to a woman, any woman. Also, he would discover pretty soon that two bodies enjoying each other wasn't all there was in life. It was new to him now, but the newness would wear off, then it would grow old. "It's comfortable then, and I'll always be glad to welcome you to my bed, Nate, because I hand-trained you to do what I like to have done to me. But comfortable isn't the best it can be. It can be a lot more than that. And you shouldn't make do with anything less than the best. You don't have to. You're a man, and the world gives a man chances that a woman never gets."

Nate argued with her, promised that he'd never even think about anyone but her, much less look at another woman.

Alva was right, of course. She was only six years older, nineteen to his thirteen, but she had a woman's wisdom. Nate learned that as time went by.

Not many days after Alva talked to him, Nate's father left home. As soon as Gideon was enrolled at Trinity College, Ezekiel Richardson told his family that he was leaving. "I want some freedom before I die," he said. "You're the man of the house now, Nate. Gideon never could have done it, but you can."

After that, Nate was too busy to have much private time with Alva. He was too busy to have any private time for himself. His Uncle Josh would work, but with his wooden leg and his bad temper, he couldn't be the one to run the farm. Besides, half the land belonged to Nate's father, so now it was his. And it wasn't in his nature to hand over what was his. Josh didn't argue or complain. Responsibility wasn't anything he wanted.

The five years since then had gone by almost too quick to notice. Nate could hardly remember a time, now, when he hadn't been head of the family. He was a man, now, full grown. At least he had believed he was until Lily Gaskins made him feel as clumsy and foolish as a boy.

"I don't know what I'm going to do, Alva. Today is the last day of Meeting, and I'll go crazy if I have to leave here tomorrow without even meeting Lily and hearing her call me by name."

Alva held his chin steady in her hand while she looked

into his eyes. "She's not somebody's lonely wife, you know, Nate."

He stiffened; the suggestion that Lily might be like other women was offensive. "I know what she is, Alva, and what she isn't. I wouldn't hurt a hair on her head. I want her to be my wife."

Alva started to say something. She looked at Nate's face and stopped herself. Instead, she kissed his cheek and released his chin. "Come with me, Nate. The young girls are tending the little ones while the mothers have breakfast and a prayer meeting. It happens that Lily's got my Susan. I'll take her back, and you can take Lily for a walk."

"Oh, Alva, I—"

"Hush up, and come along. If you think too much, you'll get tongue-tied."

He was tongue-tied. Alva shooed the two of them off together so fast that Nate had barely time to say hello when he was presented to Lily. Walking beside her, he couldn't find any words at all. The nearness of her was paralyzing. She was even more beautiful close up, and she smelled like all the flowers in the world.

He headed for the pine woods where they wouldn't be seen. Lily went along without comment.

She stopped his walking by putting a hand on his arm. Nate caught his breath. "I know who you are, Nathaniel Richardson," she said.

"You do?" His head was swimming.

She tilted her head to one side and looked up at him through her lashes. "You're the fellow who took one look at me on Friday, then turned tail and ran. Now, that doesn't make a girl feel very happy. Tell me, am I such a horror to look at? You're doing the same thing now, racing along so I can hardly keep up with you."

"Oh, no!" He was shouting. "No," he said more quietly, "Miss Gaskins, you are the most beautiful girl in the world. I knew it the first time I looked at you."

She smiled. "That's better. Now, let's go into the trees

where there's some shade." She tucked her hand in the bend of his elbow. The top of her head barely reached past his shoulder. Nate felt ready to protect her from anything. He wondered how to tell her, if she would laugh. He'd kill himself if she laughed.

"You make me feel so safe and protected, Nathaniel—it's all right if I call you 'Nathaniel,' isn't it? 'Mr. Richardson' sounds like an old man. You'll have to call me 'Lily,' of course, if I'm going to be able to call you 'Nathaniel.' But not in front of people. My daddy would think you were being impertinent, and he'd thrash you to within an inch of your life." She hugged Nate's arm. "Oh, I do love breaking rules, don't you?" Her cheek rested against his arm when she looked up into his face.

Her parted pink lips were moist and inviting, her nearness intoxicating. Nate lost his head completely. He put a hand into her thick soft hair and cupped the back of her head with it. A swirl of perfume was released from her hair, and he breathed it in. This must be what it felt like to be drunk. Nothing mattered except what he was feeling, a dizzying rapture, heedless of anything except this instant. He could not speak, but he could show what he wanted to say. He pulled her to him and kissed her. Her lips were soft, her breath sweet, her breast warm and firm against his chest.

"No," Lily said, and the movement of her lips against his sent fire racing through him. But the word cut through the fire like a sword. He was a friend, how could he do this to her? He tore himself away from his heart's demand.

"Forgive me," he stammered. "No, that's asking too much. I'm the lowest of the low. You must despise me." He dropped on his knees and bent his head. "I'm not worthy to kiss the ground under your foot. But I love you so much. That's all the excuse I've got. I love you so much that it's made me crazy."

Lily poked him with the toe of her tiny boot. "Oh, do get up from there, Nathaniel. You'll get all dirty. And you're making both of us look foolish."

He raised his head then and looked up at her with eyes swimming in shameful tears. "Do you mean you forgive me?"

"Only if you get up."

Nate's heart pounded with joy. His ears rang with it. He picked up the hem of her skirt and kissed it. He had a smile in his eyes when he looked up again. "I heard that this is what a man's supposed to do when he proposes," he said. "When can I talk to your daddy about the wedding?"

Lily held out a hand to him. "Get up from there, Nathaniel. I'm not going to marry you, and you know it."

He forgot her hand when he leapt to his feet. "But you have to," he blurted. "I love you; I'll love you as long as I live."

She shook her head very slowly. "I'm flattered, Nathaniel, I truly am, and I thank you. But if I married every man who told me he loved me, the tabernacle tent wouldn't have room to hold the wedding in. That's just not enough for me, Nathaniel. Besides, I'm going to marry your brother."

"Gideon? You're betrothed to Gideon? He never said."

"He doesn't know it yet. My daddy says it'll be a good match. Gideon's got a real good future. The elders already have their eye on him."

Nate staggered back a step. He wouldn't believe what he was hearing.

"Don't look at me like that," said Lily sharply. "You're acting like a boy all of a sudden. Be sensible. I'm sixteen, Nathaniel, and I've been traveling with Daddy all my life. One church after another, one campground after another. It's time, it's past time I got married. I'm sick to death of staying at somebody else's house and having to be grateful for it. And I never want to see the inside of a tent again. I want a home and a yard full of flowers and a place to hang my dresses and leave them there."

"I can give you a home."

"What? A farmhouse with all the paint worn off? Nobody to talk to for miles around, and the big excitement of Camp Meeting once a year? No, thank you. I want a parsonage in a nice town with real stores, and people treating me special because I'm the preacher's wife. I want a pretty parasol to hold up over my head when I walk down the street, nodding to the right and to the left and knowing everybody's name."

He had no answer to that. "But—Gideon's not interested in marrying," he said in desperation.

Lily's lips curved in a secret smile. "I'll get him interested," she said. She stepped toward Nate. "Now you can kiss me one more time, for goodbye. And if you tell Gideon, I'll call you a liar. The truth is, I like you a lot more than your brother. I wish it was you that was the good match. I'm sure he doesn't kiss half as good as you. I liked it when you kissed me, Nathaniel. Do it again. Then we've got to go."

"No! Don't go." Nate's hands closed about her waist, as in his fantasies, and he lifted her to kiss her, long and hard. Her arms wrapped around him and held him tight. He could feel her tremble.

When the kiss was over, Nate still held her in the air. "Marry me, Lily. I promise you, I'm going to be a rich man someday. I'm going places."

He set her on her feet. "Marry me," he said again. Her kiss had demolished his self-control. He put his big hands on her breasts. "I love you," he groaned. His hands were on fire, and his body. Lily let out a little scream.

"Let me go. You're horrible." She began to cry.

Nate backed away. He was sick with shame and guilt. His hands had a life of their own. They had defiled the angel. And they wanted more. Nate made them into fists and hit the tree nearest him as hard as he could. Again and again. He felt Lily pulling on his arm, but he ignored her. When he began to smell the blood that was spattering from his hands, he stopped. He needed his hands to work with. Dimly, he heard Lily's footsteps running away.

He told his family he'd had to fight off a dog that attacked him. Alva bandaged him.

Later that day Gideon rushed up to his mother and announced that the Reverend Dan Gaskins himself had sent word that he wanted to talk to Gideon about starting a trial period as a traveling preacher. "I'll go with him everywhere he goes, Ma, and I'll learn from him. He'll coach me where I need help, Ma. I'm so honored I hardly know what to do."

Nate closed his eyes and his ears. He wanted to be dead.

Five years later

24 August, 1880

Chapter Two

CHESS SAW THE MAN AT A DISTANCE, walking toward her on the dusty road. He was a stranger, no doubt of that. Everyone knew everyone else in the countryside. A mighty uncomfortable stranger, too, wearing a dark suit in the baking heat, and a city hat dark and tight on his head. She bent her head so that the wide straw brim of her own hat shut out the blinding dazzle of the sun low in the sky. It made her feel better to see somebody who was even hotter and sweatier than she was. A rivulet of water ran down her neck.

She lifted her head, squinting. Who on earth could he be? Strangers were rare birds, especially strangers on foot. Even the poorest sharecropper had a wagon and a mule. He was closer now. She could make out the shape of the package he was carrying, only it wasn't a package, it was a doctor's bag. Had old Dr. Murchison brought in somebody to help him? Would be a blessing if he had. He was so old that Chess did most of the doctoring on the place herself. She could sew up a cut as well as he could, better in fact because at least she could see what she was doing, and Dr. Murchison's eyes were getting the milkiness of old age. She hoped to God he knew what he was doing when he mixed her mother's medicines.

Chess felt her shoulders sagging, and she straightened her spine. What was she wasting time like this for anyhow? The stranger was no business of hers, and it was getting late. Cleaning out the spring had taken longer than it should have, even with her standing there in the mud telling the workers what to do. Chess looked down at the filthy overalls and boots she was wearing. What she needed was a cool bath. And a hair wash. She had pushed her braids up under the hat, but she was sure mud had gotten in them somehow.

She slapped the reins against the mule's back. You're as lazy and good for nothing as every other creature on this Godforsaken place, she thought. Get me home, will you? I've still got ten thousand things to do today. The mule sped up for a few steps, then resumed its slow pace. Chess leaned forward and gave its rump a good wallop with a worn, once elegant riding crop. The wagon swayed and bounced behind the startled, running animal. Chess lifted her chin to feel the air moving past her flushed face.

The stranger-doctor was barefoot, she saw. His boot strings were knotted together and his boots strung around his neck. Some fine doctor he must be, Chess thought with contempt, if he can't even afford to resole his shoes. He'll fit in with old Murchison just fine. She hauled on the reins to slow the mule before turning in at the open, rusted gates.

As she turned, the stranger broke into a run. "Hey, mister!" he shouted. "Wait up, will you?"

Chess stopped. She turned on the board seat and watched the stranger run. His boots hit his chest in rhythm with the pounding of his feet. Small puffs of dust from the impact of the boots synchronized with the spurts of dust his feet kicked up. What energy he had. He definitely wasn't from this worn-out part of the world.

He wasn't even winded when he reached the wagon. "You're the first living soul I've seen in nearly an hour," he said, smiling. "Whereabouts is the Standish place? Have I passed it?"

Chess blinked. "This is Harefields," she said. She gestured with her crop. A crouching hare carved from stone topped the brick gatepost on each side of the entrance.

The stranger looked at the one nearest to him. Chess looked at him. He was clean-shaven, unlike most men she'd met, who took pride in their beards. It made him look like a boy. But he wasn't a boy at all. His shoulders were broad, and his heavily muscled arms strained the seams of his dust-covered dark coat. Dust also coated his sun-browned face and clotted in his dark eyebrows. His shirt had no collar, and the top button was undone. Chess could see his strong, grimy neck and the damp, dust-free circle that sweat had made at the hollow of it.

He turned back, looked at her and grinned. "Yep, folks told me to look for two big bunnies. How far to the house? Can I ride along with you?" Without waiting for an answer, he tossed his bag in the wagon bed beside the mud-caked shovels and stepped on a wheel spoke to reach the seat and sit next to Chess.

She was so astonished by his casual boldness that she was unable to speak for a moment.

Not so the stranger. "Hot and dry and a long walk from Richmond," he commented. He stretched, groaning, and then the smile vanished. "My gosh," he whispered, "you're not a mister at all." The smile came back. "I'm sorry, ma'am. From a distance—" He lifted his hat politely, then replaced it on his head, this time resting farther back. Chess stared at the angry red mark on his forehead, left by the tight hatband. Served him right. "Mister," indeed!

"Who are you and what do you want?" she said.

"My name's Nate. Nathaniel Richardson. I've come all the way from Alamance County, North Carolina to see Mr. Augustus Standish." He made the announcement as if he expected her to applaud, Chess thought, or as if he expected her not to know that North Carolina was only the next state south of where they were, in Virginia. What kind of fool did he take her for? And why was he showing her all his big white teeth in that wide grin?

"I reckon you take me for the worst kind of fool, ma'am," said Nate, "figuring you as a man and all." He shook his head slowly, making a rueful, apologetic face. "My Ma always tells me I jump first, then look to see where I'm likely to land."

But she did look more like a man than a woman in those overalls, Nate was thinking. Even up close, there wasn't much to show the difference. Chest just as flat and jaw just as hard, only small. If it hadn't been for the long braid of pale hair that was falling down from her hat, he could still have mistaken her for a skinny, sickly man, with those hollow cheeks and long, knife-thin nose. She sure was pale.

And she was mad, and she was the only person in sight, and he needed answers to some questions. So he had to sweet talk his way out of the mess he'd made.

He lifted the boots from around his neck. "Lucky I wasn't wearing these," he said. "I put my foot in my mouth, that's for sure, but at least it was only a foot." He smiled, encouraging her laughter.

But Chess was long out of the habit of laughing. "It's three miles to the house," she said, "and you seem to be riding with me already." She clucked to the mule and slapped the reins. Nate stopped smiling. She was sitting up straight as a board, her eyes staring straight ahead. He looked from side to side, thinking how to proceed. The land was well tended, he saw, although the fields obviously needed rain soon. Weathered shacks were located haphazardly, some distance from the track they were on. He spied children playing in some yards, and a woman unpinning washing from a line. Must be tenant farmers. Where were the men, he wondered.

Then he wondered aloud.

"They've all been at the spring, cleaning it out," Chess answered. "Now there'll be enough water to save the corn crop, even if the rain doesn't come." Nate glanced at her muddy boots. A lot of things made sense now. She had to do a man's work, because she didn't have a husband. You'd think there'd be a brother at least, but so many men had died fighting the Yankees in Virginia that women were doing all kinds of things now. Poor soul. No wonder she was so sour.

He shifted his weight on the seat, stretched his legs out ahead of him. It felt good to be off his feet, and close to his goal. Close. He leaned forward, eager to get there.

Nate was unaware of the effect he was having on his companion. Chess felt crowded. It wasn't so much his body that hemmed her in—he was not a very big man. She felt pressured by his vitality. Energy radiated from him. Heat. The mixed odor of sweat and dust and camphor, stirred into the air by his constant small motions, as if he were urging the wagon forward. His voice seemed louder than normal, his smile broader, his blue eyes wider and brighter. He upset her.

The world Chess lived in was not "worn out" as she thought. But the people and the land were tired. Tidewater Virginia, it was called. It was beautiful, gentle, flat country along the wide waters of the James River. Plantation country. A place of gracious living, extravagant wealth, extravagant beauty; of hospitality; of feasting and hunting and dancing and dueling; of dozens of softly walking slaves who gratified every desire.

Until war brought that life to a sudden, bloody conclusion. It had been fifteen years since the end of the war, and the wounds had not yet healed. No new patterns of life had emerged to replace the elegant patterns that were still remembered so well. Sadness lay over the land and hopelessness slowed the steps of the survivors. It was a world in limbo, a world of memories, a world of the past, not the present.

But this barefoot doctor was very much a man of the present. He was not a plantation man. It showed in his ill-fitting shoddy suit and his boldness and his refusal to be chagrined by her curt replies to his questions and her silences. She had never been around anyone like him. He was coarse, he was lower class, and it made no difference to him. He thought he was just fine. He was life and vitality amid the aftermath of death. It was frightening. And it stirred something in her, something smothered but struggling to live.

"Yes, ma'am," he was saying, "there's nothing like getting rain when it's needed to make a person feel good about life. Down in Alamance County last month, we were all pretty much in despair. Then the rains finally came and the world was a different place altogether." Nate waited for a response, but there was none.

"These stands of corn look plenty strong," he continued. "A little water's all they need to make a fine crop. You did the right thing, opening up the flow from the spring like you did."

Chess nodded, but didn't speak.

Nate looked ahead. The dusty, dry ruts seemed endless, but he knew they weren't. He was running out of time. He turned toward Chess. "Look here," he said, forcing a laugh. "I'm sorry if I got your back up, ma'am. I said so, and I mean it. I'd appreciate it if you'd put it right behind you and help me out some. Fact is, I never met this Mr. Standish, and I've heard some wild tales. You could set me straight about what's true and what's false. I don't want to end up with a mouth full of foot when I meet him, too."

Chess turned her head. Her face, Nate saw, was even paler than before. Her eyes looked pale, too. They were gray, made lighter by the dark circles that ringed them. He couldn't remember ever actually seeing gray eyes on anyone before, although he'd heard of them. They looked clear, like he was looking through them the way you could look through water. But he couldn't see what was behind them. He couldn't figure out what was going on in this pale, silent woman's head.

"What do you want to know?" she asked him.

She was talking. That was a start, anyhow. Nate bent his head in a confidential manner. "Is it a fact that this old Standish is as smart as they come? I heard that he can put together a bunch of wires and wheels and make them turn into a windlass that'll raise a bucket from a well without hardly touching it.

Or into a clock that doesn't need winding more than once a year. Or into a contraption that'll shell peas, or pick peas, or plant peas, or—for all I know—cook peas." His voice had risen steadily with excitement, and his cheeks flushed.

He crashed his big hands together. Chess was startled, but he didn't notice. "Some folks say that this old man can figure a way to solve any problem you put to him. What a thing that would be. They say he invents things, hatches out answers made of wheels and pulleys and pieces of rope. Nobody knows the half of what he's done, not even a hundredth. They say he's some kind of wizard. Is that so?" Nate's face was shiny with hope, his hands clenched together.

Chess could feel the energy vibrating in him, and the force that held the energy in check. She looked at his hands, then looked away quickly.

"He's an inventor, all right," she said, "but he's no wizard. He spent two years building a machine to make rain, and you see what became of that." That should calm him down some.

Nate shook his head vehemently. "You don't understand," he nearly shouted. "Nobody gets it right the first time, or every time. But to get it right just two or three times— just once, even—that's worth a man's whole life. To make something no one's ever made before, to dream up a thing that never was until you dreamed it up—" He broke off, unable to say what he was feeling.

Chess forgot her nervousness. "What are you trying to invent, Mr. Richardson?" Curiosity was stronger.

"That's not the way I am," he said. "I'm a doer, not a dreamer. But I wish—oh, nothing to that. I need to talk to this old Standish about a machine I heard about. Do you figure he'll be willing? I know he's crazy as a coot. Everybody says so. The whole family's peculiar, but I reckon you know all that. You probably know them all pretty well."

Chess nodded. "Hold tight," she said. "The barn is right up ahead, and this mule will start running pretty soon when it smells home."

Nate grabbed hold of the wagon's side just in time.

"Thanks for the warning," he laughed when he was safely on his feet in the barnyard. "Can I wash up at the pump before I go looking for the old man? I brought soap with me."

"Over there," said Chess, pointing.

While she unhitched the mule and wiped it down, she stole glances over its back. She gasped when Nate pulled his shirt over his head, threw it down near his feet and pumped vigorously. He leaned forward and held his head and shoulders under the heavy stream of water. His skin was shockingly white in contrast to his sun-browned face and forearms. It shone like wet silk in the water; the froth of soap sliding over it made Chess' fingers ache. She peeled off her gloves in sharp jerks. What was happening to her? She wanted to touch that wide back, feel those muscles moving against the palms of her hands. She wanted to smell his man smell again before he washed it all away, then she wanted to taste the soap on his skin with her mouth. This was all wrong; she was shocked. "You should be ashamed," she told herself. "Don't look at him, don't think those things."

But she could not look away. Chess had never seen a man's bare back. She had never been tempted to attach the fantasies of her private world to a real person. She was thirty years old, and she had never been held, never been kissed, never known anything about what happened between men and women except what she read in books. She was unprepared for the desires that were confusing and worrying her now. They were not mentioned in the pages by Dumas or Sir Walter Scott.

She felt faint when Nate Richardson stood and turned and she saw the mat of wet, glistening dark hair on his chest. She turned away.

By the time he was lacing up his boots, Chess had found an appearance of calm. She led him to the "inventing shed," conscious of his long shadow touching her shoulder and carpeting the path ahead of her. She could smell his soap and the starch in the shirt and collar he had taken from the doctor's bag.

She knocked briefly, then opened the door. "Caesar, it's me, Chess. I've brought someone to see you."

The man who came to the door had scanty white hair and a stoop. But his lined face was brightly youthful. "I'm close," he said, "I know I'm getting very close. Just a few adjustments—the flywheel has to be completely redone, but that's nothing—" He looked over her shoulder. "Who's this?"

"This is Nathaniel Richardson, sir, from North Carolina." Chess looked back at Nate. He was unnaturally stiff, like a wax image. She smiled briefly at him. "This 'crazy old coot' is my grandfather, Mr. Richardson. Augustus Standish." The quotation marks were underlined by her tone.

Nate flinched. Then he seemed to come to life. "I'm tasting leather," he said, and he chuckled deep in his throat. He put his hands on Chess' shoulders and moved her aside. "Mr. Standish, sir, I'm real honored to meet you. I'm here to talk about James Bonsack."

"Jimmy? Fine boy. Good family, I knew his daddy and granddaddy. Come in, young man, and tell me what's on your mind."

Nate closed the door behind him.

Chess was almost certain that he had winked at her. And her shoulders still held the touch of his hands. She ran for the house.

Chapter Three

THE LONG TWILIGHT OF SUMMER was thickening quickly when Mr. Standish and Nate came out of the workshop. Nate looked at the sky with a farmer's practiced eye and judged the time to be close to seven o'clock. He'd have to bed down in the woods beside the road and walk back to Richmond when it got light. Maybe there'd be some wagons going to the city and he could get a lift, not like today.

"Looks like you're benighted, Nate," the old gentleman said. "You'll have a meal and a bed here with the family."

"Thank you, sir," said Nate. Truth was, his empty stomach had been sending him messages for several hours. But he hadn't noticed until now. The models of Mr. Standish's inventions were fascinating, and so was the inventor's conversation. So much so that Nate was even able to forget his bitter disappointment for a while. Now the bitterness flowed acrid into his mouth, together with the sour taste of hunger. He had to force a semblance of cheerfulness. He felt like he'd rather crawl off someplace and howl at the moon.

So close, he'd come so close, and he'd lost. It was worse than he could ever have imagined. The machine invented by James Bonsack held the promise of a real revolution in the tobacco business; Nate had been hearing talk of it for months. He'd also heard that the machine had problems, that it might turn out to be all promise and no delivery. But—and much more exciting—there were tidbits of rumor about a crazy old man near Richmond who had invented a machine better than Bonsack's. And he'd done it before Bonsack had filed for a patent. No one knew anything definite; the rumors were most likely moonbeams and myth. But if they were true, and if he could find the old man and get hold of his patent, then Nate would have found the big chance he'd been waiting for and working for all these past five years.

Don't count on anything, he told himself. There probably isn't a machine at all, at least not a machine better than Bonsack's. There might not even be an old coot named Standish near Richmond. When something sounds too good to be true, it's generally because it's not true at all.

But he couldn't squash his hopes. Even when he was walking the long miles and hours from Richmond, his mind was making plans about how best to use the old man's machine and how to get the patent away from him.

Mr. Standish had shocked him over and over again. First, by welcoming him so warmly. A man from a little farm in the middle of North Carolina didn't expect to be treated that way by a man who owned a plantation so big that the gate was three miles from the house.

Then the old man had been interested in Nate's ideas and Nate's history and what Nate planned to do with his business and his future. Nate had talked to Mr. Standish like he'd never talked to anybody in his whole life. He'd told him things that he would have sworn he'd rather cut out his tongue than tell.

"I feel I know you now," Standish said then, "and I like you, Nate Richardson. I'll be glad to show you what you came to see."

Then he had lifted a box down from a shelf full of boxes. And from it he had taken an intricate wooden model about two feet long and two feet high. The pine wood was polished to a satin sheen; it looked like old gold. Miniature cogs meshed, miniature pulleys held tiny links of chain, small rubber belts and fabric runners moved soundlessly and smoothly at his touch on an activating wheel. It was a work of art.

It was all that Nate had hoped for, and more.

"Jimmy Bonsack?" said Mr. Standish, with a broad smile. "Oh, yes, I had lots of talks with Jimmy. I've known him since he was in pinafores. A smart boy, then and now. I told him his ideas were just fine, and they are. But I didn't tell him everything I know." The old man winked. "Like a cook we had once. She was glad to share her recipes, but somehow or other she always forgot to include one little thing, a pinch of pepper or whatever. And that made all the difference in the sauce."

"Did he see the model?" Nate asked. He wanted to be the only one.

"Of course he did. I'm a vain old man; I like to show off. Thank God the rheumatism's in my knees and not my fingers. I consider myself the best whittler since Grinling Gibbons."

The name meant nothing to Nate, but he understood Standish's pride. "You are, Mr. Standish, sir, and no doubt about it," he said sincerely. "Can I touch it?"

"Sorry, son, I have to say no. It's sturdy enough, but the trappings—all those chains and such—they are the very devil to get in place because they're so small. They'll slip right off if they're handled."

Nate was disappointed. His fingers itched to touch the smooth wood, turn the tiny wheels. Still, he hadn't come to play. He took a deep breath. "I don't know much about patents; I thought you had to send the model to that office."

"Oh, no, they'd rather you didn't. Then they might have to use their brains and figure it out. Thomas Jefferson could have done it in a minute, and in a minute more he'd have improved on it. That man was born to be an inventor; too bad he had to waste time being president. . . . Sorry, son, the old are easily sidetracked. You were asking about the patent office. They'd rather have drawings every time. Fools! They don't understand them any better, but they're easier to store away. That's the main reason I quit dealing with them. They told me my models took up too much room, to send only the pieces of paper."

Nate plucked words from Mr. Standish's irate speech. " 'Stopped dealing,' did you say 'stopped?' You mean you never got a patent?"

"Hell no!"

Nate felt poleaxed. He didn't dare let himself examine the shock, it was too great. And Augustus Standish was still talking as he reached down another box from the shelf. "Now, this one had an especially ticklish little problem to be solved. Archimedes himself might have had trouble with it. You see, the lever doesn't have enough clearance to lift the full load. What to do? I tried one thing, then one more, then twenty, thirty more after that. I was on the verge of giving up, when out of the blue . . ." Nate bent low to look at the model. He'd pick the scab of his failure later. For now, he was enthralled.

There were more than twenty empty boxes on the floor before Mr. Standish noticed the time.

He led the way to the house, a path through a thicket of bamboo. Nate stopped in his tracks when the path opened into a clearing and he saw the house ahead. It was indistinct in the growing dark, a huge shadow without form except for eight tremendous white columns taller than the trees on Nate's farm. They guarded the deep veranda. Hazy lights shone in windows far behind them. It looked, Nate thought, like the State Capital Building in Raleigh, a place he'd seen only a few times in his life, and never dared to enter.

"Come on in," said Augustus Standish.

He ushered Nate through a door in one side of the house and up a steep, narrow flight of stairs. "My daughter-in-law carries on something wicked if I'm late for dinner," he said, "so we'll have to hurry." They always dressed formally, he told Nate, another thing his daughter-in-law was particular about. He thought the suit that belonged to one of his grandsons would fit Nate well enough.

The sleeves and pants were too long. Mr. Standish produced pins and expertise, a shirt, collar, studs and cuff links and nimble fingers to arrange them. There was nothing he could do about shoes. "Just keep your boots under the table," he said, "and you'll do fine." Nate had to take his word for it; he felt like the dressed-up trick bear he'd seen once at the State Fair. But Mr. Standish looked plenty foolish too, he thought, and his clothes fit him. Besides, there was a mouth-watering smell in the air, and he needed food.

The dinner was an experience Nate never forgot.

The table was as long as his whole house, he figured, and the room so big that the walls were all but invisible in the shadows. The table was lit practically like daylight by two dozen candles—Nate counted—in tall shiny holders. But the brightest thing of all was the necklace on the lady at one end of the table. She was the daughter-in-law who made the old man so nervous. But she did not at all look like the kind of woman who'd throw fits and scream at you if you were late. She was beautiful, with pale silver-gold hair piled on her head in loose curls, one of them falling free along her throat just in front of her left ear. It reached down to her shoulder—her bare shoulder. Nate had never seen so much skin showing on a woman who was wearing clothes. Her red dress had big ruffled sleeves, and they looked like they had pulled the dress down to bare her shoulders and a great deal of her bosom. A very pretty bosom, too. It mounded slightly above the red lace on the edge of the dress. More red went around her neck, but this red was rubies, Nate was sure. It had to be. What else would have diamonds all around each red stone? He couldn't keep himself from wondering what something like that must be worth. Enough to build a factory or a mill, he'd bet. He thought of the high hopes he'd had when he came to the Standish place, and he wanted to bawl like a baby.

It's just 'cause I'm hungry, he told himself. How long would they have to sit here before some food got on the table?

"Mr. Richardson."

"Yes, ma'am?" Nate turned his attention to the glittering lady.

"Do you ride?"

"Whenever I can, ma'am." He still felt the heat of the Richmond road in his feet.

Mrs. Standish smiled. She had a lovely, face-lighting smile. "Excellent. You must stay until the next hunt. We'll give you a choice of mounts, of course. My elder son is Master of Hounds, he'll see that you have a good time."

Nate didn't know what she was talking about. For one thing, there was no sign of this son of hers. Nobody was at the table except him and the old man, the quiet woman he'd thought was a man, and the lady in the red dress.

"My daughter doesn't care for hunting at all," she was saying. "Such a pity I think, don't you? I always tell her she's making a mistake. Riding habits are so very becoming." She made a delicate, playful face, looking at the silent woman sitting next to the old man.

Was that her daughter? It looked more like the other way around. The daughter was drab and drawn and thin as a rail; even her hair looked more gray than silver, like the mother's. Maybe it was because it was skinned back tight in a knot on her neck, but Nate didn't think so. It looked gray, so did her skin. And she was wearing a gray dress, too. She had looked a lot better in overalls.

An elderly black man came to the table. He, too, was wearing a dinner suit. White gloves were on his hands; they held a big silver tray with silver bowls on it. Nate inhaled gratefully. Food at last. But not yet, he discovered. He watched the dinner ritual with incredulity.

Just to slow things down some more, the bowls weren't put on the table. The tray was held at Mrs. Standish's elbow, and she spooned something, Nate couldn't tell what, from each bowl onto her plate. Then the black man walked all the way over to the daughter so she could help herself. After that, he left the old man sitting there hungry while he went back around half the length of the table to hold the tray next to Nate. What a waste of time, thought Nate, I could have finished eating by now.

The food wasn't fancy, he was happy to see, and there was plenty of it. He helped himself to big mounds of spoonbread and black-eyed peas and a stew that looked a lot like rabbit. Then he dug in to the spoonbread, using the big spoon that was next to his plate.

"My favorite, Catherine," said Mr. Standish; "I do appreciate a stew. It's the only way my old teeth can handle venison." He smiled at his granddaughter. She returned his smile, and for an instant she resembled her mother.

"I always feel a little ambivalent about venison," Mrs. Standish said. "The deer are really such pretty creatures. I do love the taste, though. I just tell myself that this is one of the horrible beasts that eat all the lilies in spite of that high wall around the garden."

"Perhaps the lily bulbs give it a special flavor, Mama," said the quiet woman. "Then it's almost worth it to do without the flowers."

"Francesca, you do think the most amazing things sometimes. I can't imagine anything being more important than flowers." There was a wide blue and red bowl in the center of the ranks of candlesticks. It was filled with Queen Anne's Lace and sprays of ivy.

Nate concentrated on his food while the three Standishes talked. They ate slowly because they talked so much. He refilled his plate from the tray that was offered again, and he finished that, too, before the others had eaten half of their first helpings.

A full stomach made him feel much more sociable. He listened to the conversation and smiled agreeably at each speaker in turn. Mrs. Standish talked almost constantly, with little food passing her lips. She made no sense, as far as Nate could tell, but the others seemed to understand her perfectly. From time to time Nate glanced at the shadows, expecting to see the husband and sons she was talking about. But they didn't show up. He hoped they were away someplace and not just late. He'd hate to see the lady in a temper. If she frightened the old man, she'd likely scare him silly. She made him nervous already, he didn't know why.

All of a sudden she stood up. Mr. Standish and the daughter did, too. Nate hastily got to his feet.

"We'll leave you gentlemen to your cigars and brandy." The hand she held out to Nate was laden with rings. "Good evening, Mr. Richardson. We're delighted you've come to visit."

Nate reached out his hand, too. What was this about? Mrs. Standish's fingertips brushed his, then withdrew. When she walked away, he saw that she was wearing an old-fashioned hoop skirt. So was her daughter, who followed close behind.

"Sit down, Mr. Richardson," said the old man when the door closed. "I'm afraid I should have prepared you with more than a dress suit. Will you have a whiskey?"

"No, sir, I thank you."

"Well, I can use one. Maybe two. Catherine was particularly trying tonight. I knew when I saw the red dress that we'd have trouble. It's a sign of danger, just like a red flag." The black man appeared from the shadows with a decanter and two glasses. He quietly removed the plates from the table. "Thank you, Marcus," said Mr. Standish. "Have you got your decanter?"

"Yes, sir. By my bed." The black man chuckled as he left with the tray of china. "I'm going to sleep real well."

Mr. Standish had three drinks, not two, while he gave Nate "the explanation you're due."

"I had only one child," he said, "a son. For some reason no one could figure, my wife and I never were blessed again. Frank was enough, though. He was a strong child, and he grew to be a strong man. He gave us great happiness.

"His mother died—it was pleurisy—when Frank was at

the University. Maybe it was best; she would have broken her heart over Catherine. The marriage was so hasty and so far away. I heard about it after it was all over. Frank was doing his Grand Tour when he met her. He was only twenty-three years old. I guess that's about what you are, isn't it?" The old man didn't wait for an answer. He was looking into his glass.

"It was love at first sight, he said, a kind of madness. Frank lost all reason. He married her less than a week after he met her. The mayor of a little town in Switzerland performed the ceremony."

Nate thought about Lily. Lucky Frank. They'd been married almost four years now, Lily and Gideon, and it still hurt, he supposed it always would.

"It didn't really matter that Catherine was an adventuress with no background. She was a good wife to Frank, a good mother to the children, an excellent mistress of the plantation and a beautiful, brilliant hostess. The house parties at Hare-fields were famous, and the Christmas Ball was talked about almost until it was time for the next one. Most important, Frank never stopped loving her, and she made him happy.

"Not that there weren't problems, of course. Who ever heard of a life without problems?" The decanter clinked against the rim of the glass. "Catherine cried all the time after the first child was born. The doctor said that often occurred with new mothers. But when the second boy came so soon after, she had an attack of nerves that lasted for months. Luckily the doctor found a laudanum mixture that brought her out of it. She was always high strung. That mixture's been her salvation. Ned and Charles were good boys always, but boys make noise, and boys climb trees, fall out of them and break their arms or legs, and boys don't always do what they're told. It was hard on Catherine's nerves.

"When the boys were seven and eight, Frank took Catherine back to Europe. A second honeymoon, he called it. I always wondered if it wasn't really his plan to give the boys some growing room, without their mother's coddling. They had a good tutor, a young fellow who was smart as a whip and strong as an ox. He took no sass off them, but he didn't try to hold them down. Whatever Frank had in mind, it worked like a charm. When he and Catherine came home two years later, Ned was ten, Charles was nine, and more manly little boys you'll never see. They had a baby sister, too, born in Venice, and they doted on her from day one. So did I, and still do.

"Francesca. That's what Catherine named her, but I called her Chess right from the start. I don't like foreign frills. All of us called her Chess, somehow it suited her. Except Catherine. She liked Francesca, she said it was romantic.

"Whatever the name, she adored that baby. She'd always wanted a little girl to dress up, she said. They were a sight, the two of them in their pretty, ruffly frocks with their silver gilt hair shining. The boys were dark, like Frank, but Chess was the image of her mother. And she was the happiest child on earth, always laughing or singing, or both at the same time. She was smart, too. I taught her to play chess when she was only five. She loved the game, thought it was named after her. She loved everything—dogs, cats, horses, birds, flowers, trees, even the clouds in the sky. And she loved everybody, even her governess, who was hated by everyone else. With Chess, though, she was different woman. You could hear laughter from the classroom all day.

"The war stopped the laughter. The boys had just finished at the University, and they rode off with their daddy looking like the three musketeers. Charles died in the Wilderness, Ned at Gettysburg.

"Catherine couldn't believe they were gone. Even when they came home and were buried in the family plot, she kept looking for letters from them, fretting about how thoughtless they were because they weren't writing to say they were all right.

"She even complained to the Yankee officer who was in charge of the troops that came here. She blamed the Yankees for intercepting the mails.

"Some places on the river had it hard, but Harefields was hardly touched. Catherine invited the officers to dinner and charmed them out of their boots. So they kept their men in control. Except for the cattle and pigs and horses, we hardly lost anything. Until the day everything was lost.

"Frank was wounded four times, but never anything serious. He got invalided out from the siege at Petersburg for malaria and dysentery, not a bullet. He came home to get his strength back and then he was going to rejoin Lee. The more desperate things got, the more Frank believed in the Cause.

"He was almost well when we got the news that Lee had surrendered to Grant at Appomattox. I did a lot of swearing myself, but Frank didn't say a word. He polished his boots and brushed up his uniform himself. Polished the buttons, too. Then he went out to the graveyard where his sons were buried, their young lives sacrificed for the Confederate Cause. Frank ate his sidearm, his pistol.

"His head was only bloody pulp. We would never have known it was him except he was wearing his signet ring with the Standish coat of arms.

"Poor Chess, she was the one who found him. She woke up screaming in the middle of the night for weeks afterwards.

"Catherine never shed a tear. She closed her mind to it, just like she'd done with the boys. Only she shut out the whole thing, the war and all. As far as she's concerned, Fort Sumter never happened. It's still 1860, and the boys are at school and her husband's due home any minute. We all play the game. It keeps her happy. She may be the only truly happy person in the whole state of Virginia."

Augustus Standish pushed his chair away from the table. "Mr. Richardson, I thank you for your courtesy and your patience with an old man's maunderings. Now I fear I'll have to impose on you even further. I seem to have gotten rather drunk. I'd be grateful for your arm to lean on going up the stairs."

Nate jumped up. "I'd be honored, sir."

* * *

After he went to bed, Nate wished he had taken a drink with the old man. It might have helped him sleep. He was tired, but not the kind of tired he was used to. He should have walked back to Richmond; then he would have had the kind of fatigue he understood. Instead, he was worn out from too many new thoughts, too many things learned too fast.

He had automatically hated the planter aristocrats. His Uncle Josh had lost a leg fighting so they could keep their slaves. None of his people owned slaves, nor expected to. The Cause wasn't their cause at all.

But he couldn't hate Augustus Standish. He half-loved the old man, even if he had been too stubborn to take out the patent that would have meant everything to Nate. His only son was dead, and his grandsons, and yet the old man kept going, kept his farm going—no matter that it was called a plantation, it was just a farm with more acres—and he kept his ladies protected and safe from the world. He must be eighty if he was a day. How did he do it? Just sitting at that table every night listening to Mrs. Standish would be enough to drive Nate crazy. He couldn't do it.

He'd been told the gentry were soft. Well, not Mr. Standish. And not skinny old Chess, either, come to think of it. She had to sit at that table, too. And that lady was her mother. Nate thought of his own mother and felt fortunate. She was righteous, pious, and critical, and nothing ever pleased her. But she wasn't insane.

He decided he'd get her a present on his way home. She wouldn't like it, and she'd lecture him about spending the money foolishly, but it would make him feel good.

He'd leave at first light. He wanted to get away from this place.

"Mr. Richardson—" Chess Standish intercepted Nate on his way out the door. "There's some breakfast in the kitchen."

"Thank you, ma'am, but I think I'll just get going before the day heats up."

"All right, but come with me anyhow. You don't have to eat if you don't want to. I've got a business deal to offer. It won't take long to hear it." She was wearing gray again, a calico frock. Streaks of color stained her cheeks, bright against her colorless skin.

Nate had no choice but to follow her.

Chess held on to the back of a chair near the big table in the center of the brick-floored kitchen. It wobbled a bit on the uneven floor.

"Maybe you should sit down," she said, "though you don't have to if you'd rather not." Her voice fluted nervously.

"No, thanks." Nate said.

"So be it. What I have to say is simple and short. I talked to my grandfather last night after you went to bed, and I know what you want from us . . . from him. I've got it, Mr. Richardson. The patent. I've been sending in applications and his drawings for a long time, on the chance that one might turn out to be worth something. I gather this one is."

Nate let out a whoop. He couldn't believe his luck. "I'll say it is," he said. His smile made his jaws ache. "What do you want for it? I don't have much ready cash, but we can work out a so-much-every-year payment plan. My word's good, I can get testimonials for you."

Her knuckles shone white along the top of the chair back. "I want you to marry me, Mr. Richardson, to take me back to Alamance County, North Carolina with you. I want a husband and I want children. That's my price."

Chapter Four

THEY WERE MARRIED THAT MORNING in the small Episcopal church on the Richmond road. The minister was an old man, nearly as old as Augustus Standish. His swollen hands were careful with the silver chalice when he served their Communion. It bore the crest of a hare, above quartered ancient insignia. The first Standish in America had donated it in 1697.

Augustus Standish gave his granddaughter away. The minister's tiny elderly wife was second witness. Chess had changed into an ill-fitting blue cotton gown. The awkward drape of the bustle labeled it as a homemade makeover of an earlier style, even to Nate's untutored eye. A single strand of small pearls circled her neck. She held a bouquet of field flowers, and a veil of cobweb-delicate antique lace covered her head. Beneath it her jaw was rigid, but her lips trembled. Nate made his responses automatically. He was dazed.

They returned to the plantation the way they had come, in a hastily dusted shining black landaulet with seats of cracked red leather. It was drawn by a mule. Somehow the word had spread. When the bizarre equipage turned in at the rusted gates, they saw that the rutted drive was strewn with white blossoms of Queen Anne's Lace for its entire length. Dark-skinned men, women, and children were lined on each side. At sight of the carriage, they began to cheer.

"God bless, Miss Chess," they called out.

Chess began to cry.

"Stand up, child," said Augustus Standish, "let them see you for the last time." His voice was shaky.

Chess stood, her hand on his shoulder for steadying. She waved and smiled through her tears and called to each of them by name. "Goodbye, Julia . . . thank you, Pheemie . . . bless you, too, Perseus . . . take care of that new baby, Celia . . . goodbye Paula . . . Justice . . . Delphi . . . Sukie . . . James . . . Jason . . . Zanty . . . Agamemnon . . ."

"I've always been fond of the classics," Mr. Standish murmured to Nate. "I named most of them myself. Not the children, naturally. They came after emancipation."

"Goodbye, goodbye, goodbye . . ." Chess was weeping openly now.

Augustus Standish dried her face with his handkerchief after they alighted from the carriage. "Ave atque vale, Caesar," she said.

"Are you sure about this, Chess?"

She lifted her chin. "Sure," she said. Her eyes were frightened. She swallowed. "My sun hat is with my other things. Help me fold the veil, please, and put it away very gently."

"I will," her grandfather promised.

Nate eyed the canoe with trepidation. It was already loaded with the large valise Chess was taking, plus his doctor's bag, and the box containing the model of the invention that had brought him here. There was hardly room for him, none at all, that he could see, for Chess. His wife. The thought alarmed him even more than the fragile-looking craft. He held fast to the rickety dock and followed Mr. Standish's instructions as he stepped in and sat down. River water lapped dangerously near the gunwales when his weight was added to the load. He'd never been in a canoe, and he didn't like it at all. He closed his eyes when Chess stepped in, expecting to turn over or go under or both.

"Good," he heard her say from behind him, "we've caught the tide at its fullest." She was already in the canoe, although he hadn't felt it tip at all. He guessed it was a good thing that she was so thin. He opened his eyes just in time to see Mr. Standish waving to them from the short length of the sandy beach beneath the overhanging branches of the trees. The canoe had slid out into the current without his noticing; it was moving rapidly, carried by the river.

Nate waved to the old man. The motion caused a slight tipping, and water whirled across the toe of his boot. He grabbed the edge of his plank seat.

"Rest easy and don't make big, sudden movements," said his unseen wife. "I've been on the river a million times. Don't worry. You'll get used to it in a few minutes." Her gloved hands held the paddle in the water to direct their course. Nothing more was necessary, but she adjusted its angle repeatedly, glad to have something to think about, other than the wild gamble she had embarked on.

Her grandfather had told her that Nate Richardson was "sound." He had approved the marriage. Sorrowfully—he would rather she married a gentleman—but without hesitation. "You deserve a life of your own, my dear little Chess."

It was more than Chess had expected when she told him what she intended. Perhaps, she thought, he hadn't expected her to succeed. She had not expected it herself.

And yet, she had. Now, what would become of her?

She studied Nate's back and his terrible hat. She wished she could see his head. If I'm going to live with this man for the rest of my life, surely I'm entitled to know if he has a crown cowlick, she thought. The nonsensical workings of her own mind made her want to laugh, and to cry. Where was the hard realism she had learned at such cost? She needed it now. She had bought herself a husband, that was the truth of it. She was married—how impossible to believe—married to a boy, much younger than she, because he was the only chance she had and she was desperate.

She wondered if he hated her. She would if she were in his shoes. The patent had been like a gun held to his head.

But he could have said no and he had said yes, so he couldn't really hate her, could he? Not much, anyhow. He'd learn to like her, with any luck. She wouldn't nag, like some wives, and she'd work her fingers to the bone. Lord knows she knew how to work.

She knew other things, too, all the things that a young lady was taught in the days before the war. She could play the pianoforte rather well, embroider rather unevenly, paint an adequate landscape in watercolor, read Latin, speak French, do the minuet, ride sidesaddle, including jumps if they weren't too high. . . .

She dug the paddle into the river viciously. Oh, yes, she'd really need all those so-called accomplishments in North Carolina. He wasn't even a doctor, her grandfather said, only a red dirt farmer.

He ate his dinner with a spoon! How could she have married a man who didn't know enough to eat with a fork? Maybe she should go back right now.

To what? Drudgery and the pretense that the world had not changed, when it had really turned upside down. And cast her to one side.

No, that was unthinkable. She'd been right in the first place. Her husband was a good man, that's what "sound" meant. He wasn't dishonest or cruel. She would learn to know him, and she would like him. Love was something in books, it wasn't everyday reality. Liking was more durable.

Nate's broad back in the dark jacket looked as big and hard as a wall. It would be a luxury to have someone else around who was strong, who took responsibility. Not her, for a change.

A sudden unexpected memory filled her mind. That same back, bared, glistening with water and sliding soap. Yes! Yes, she wanted to know how it was with a husband and wife.

She wanted to be held, kissed even, and . . . whatever. She wanted to know whatever, wanted it very much. Surely he must know. Men knew that sort of thing, and he wasn't really a boy, he just looked so young because he had no whiskers.

Nate rubbed his chin. He had borrowed the old man's razor, but it hadn't done a very good job. Or more likely he hadn't done a very good job. His hand had shaken so much it was a wonder he didn't cut his throat.

Maybe he should have. What a lunatic thing to do. He'd married an old maid. A very old maid.

Worst of it was, she was a lady. She'd be about as much use on the farm as a cow without teats. Which, come to think of it, might be true, too, by the look of things.

But he had the patent. That's what he had to keep in mind. He'd gone after it and he'd gotten what he'd gone for. It was what he needed. A wife wasn't, but so what? She wanted babies, he could understand that. There was something in all women that made them want babies. He'd give her all the babies she could ever want. All he had to do was shut his eyes and think certain thoughts and nature would take care of the rest.

If only she was a regular woman instead of a lady. He didn't know anything about ladies, he'd never met one before.

Nate was no different from the other men of his time and place. He perceived a vast difference between ordinary females and the rare species known as ladies. It was a distinction also made by women, including many of those same ladies.

Southern men put their ladies on pedestals, thought of them as fragile, delicate, requiring shelter from harsh reality, including frank language and knowledge of the seamier aspects of life. They were to be worshiped and protected and guided, because they knew nothing about the real world and its ugliness.

Like Chess—what a name, no ordinary female would ever have a name like that, Nate thought. She's lived her whole life on that huge plantation, with darkies working for her and laying flowers on her path. She's used to being waited on and eating her supper out of silver bowls. She must have dressed up like a man in those overalls for some kind of a joke. No wonder she acted so strange in that wagon. Probably shamefaced to be seen by a stranger. Poor thing. I'll have to be sure to not mention it, ever.

His lips twitched. It had been funny. But he'd never say a word.

Not about her pitiful mother, either. Most likely he wasn't even supposed to know. And he'd have to keep silent about her daddy, too.

All of a sudden there were a lot of subjects he'd have to avoid. What was there left to talk about? He needed to come up with something cheerful. He thought for a long time. Then . . .

"The State Fair in Raleigh goes on for a whole week in October," he said over his shoulder. "It's cooler then, and the parade's really worth seeing."

"That's nice," she replied. "I'd like very much to see it. I've never been to a State Fair." Nate couldn't turn to see her face, but he could hear the stiff politeness.

He couldn't think of another thing to say. What did he have to offer a lady like her? A three room house and a pile of tobacco. She was going to repent the bargain she'd made quick enough. He'd have to get that patent in his name first thing.

"There's Richmond ahead," Chess said. "You can see the smoke from the factory stacks."

"You mean it? It took me nearly half a day to walk that road. How long have we been in this boat?"

"Almost an hour. We still have a while to go. The smoke shows up long before the city."

"That makes sense."

"Yes, I suppose it does." She coughed to clear the tightness from her throat. "The road you came on is nearly thirty miles, but the river gets from Harefields to Richmond in under twelve. That's why there'll be so many boats nearer to the city. All the commercial traffic . . ." Her voice trailed off.

"You know, it's real hard talking when you can't look somebody in the face," said Nate quickly and loudly. "I figure we can do our talking later. You're right about the canoe. I've gotten really easy with it. I think I'll just enjoy the rest of the ride."

"Good idea," she agreed at once. She thought that he'd been very tactful. He was nice. Why, she was already starting to like him.

Chess steered through a maze of shipping to a small-boat mooring at the base of Shockoe Slip. She'd brought her grandfather here many times. Because the tide was high, she was able to tie up without even stretching. It felt good to get off her knees and onto her feet and dry land.

"Hand the luggage up," she told Nate, "and I'll put it on the dock."

He lifted her bag, then his. "Be real careful, now, with this one." The box with the model in it was not very heavy, but it was very large.

"Got it," said Chess, "you can let go—watch out!"

But it was too late. Nate's hat was bobbing over the spot where he had plunged into the river.

When he surfaced, three grinning stevedores hauled him up onto the dock, sputtering and coughing. The phrase "mad as a wet hen" took on fresh meaning in Chess' mind. Quite a crowd had gathered, and there was a rumble of talk and laughter. She felt pity for Nate, and apprehension about the explosion that his scowling red face promised.

Then she felt an unaccustomed desire to laugh. His suit was shrinking. She watched in fascinated horror as the cheap material drew in. She could actually see the cuffs of the trousers moving slowly up his calves, the sleeves up his arms.

Nate scratched the itch he felt on one wrist. Then he looked at the sleeve. He stamped one foot, then the other, bent from the waist and stared at his socks. Chess discovered that she was holding her breath. People were pointing now, exclaiming aloud, "Look at that . . ."

Nate straightened up. His shoulders shrugged, straining the soggy fabric across them. He grinned at the crowd, at his rescuers, at Chess. "How about that?" he said. "I've been meaning to get taller, and it's finally happening." He threw his head back, and laughed loudly and without pretense.

Chess felt her own laughter fill her and spill over. It felt wonderful. It had been so many years since she had felt like laughing at anything.

It was at that moment that she fell in love with Nate Richardson, her husband, and gave him her full, eager heart, with no conditions and no reserve.

People were looking at them. Not just at Nate in his shrinking clothes, but at Chess, too. She did not know it, but her laughter was unique. It attracted attention. It began deep within her, then seemed to rise bubbling through the column of her throat, as champagne opened too quickly will surge spontaneously from the captivity of its bottle. There was pure joy, and joyful freedom, in her laugh. In addition, she made a sound within her laughter, a sound of happiness to be laughing. It was extraordinary, a kind of purring sound at the base of her throat and beneath the other laughing sound. It was as if delight distilled was resident inside her.

Nate was startled by it, and by the sudden change in her. She was still much too thin and pale. Her hair seemed lifeless and colorless. Her ill-fitting dress made her look even taller and thinner than she was.

But the wide smile that accompanied her laughter revealed lovely, white, even teeth, and the smile in her gray eyes made them darken and sparkle.

She looks alive, thought Nate, and before she looked like she was dead but walking around with her eyes open.

Nate did not know how right he was. Chess felt alive in a strange and wonderful way for the first time in her life.

So this was what the poets meant when they wrote of love.

Why didn't they simply say that all colors were brighter, that the raucous call of seagulls sounded like music, that every cobblestone underfoot looked like a giant, priceless black pearl, that every leaf on every tree had its own clear beautiful shape and texture, that one's feet wanted to dance, that the world was a place of infinite happy possibilities because Nathan Richardson inhabited it and found it funny and good.

Chapter Five

CHESS APPROACHED NATE with new confidence. She felt giddy from emotion, but she did not know how much it showed, therefore she felt safe. And there was something she could do to help him. "You'll have to get out of those clothes before they strangle you," she said calmly. "Come with me. A friend of my father's has offices in this building. You can dry out there. I'll ask a clerk to put the luggage somewhere safe."

Nate picked up the box with the model. "I'll hold on to this one. Let's go."

ALLEN AND GINTER was painted in tall letters on the wall of the building. Nate's eyes sparkled. He knew this was the largest cigarette company in the South. This was a place he very much wanted to visit. He followed Chess inside.

A gray-suited man looked at Nate with horror, at Chess with bewilderment. "Miss Standish?"

"Good morning, Mr. Grogan. We're on our way to Major Ginter."

Nate regarded his wife with new interest. She was as cool

as a cucumber, staring down a fellow who figured he was important, and proposing to see one of the biggest men in the tobacco business.

"He's not here, Miss Standish. He's taken the family to Saratoga."

"Oh bother! I forgot about the races. Well, just open his office for us, Mr. Grogan, and get hold of some hot coffee, please."

Now Nate was astounded. Grogan did exactly what he was told to do, as Chess continued to issue orders. An hour later Nate was dry, refreshed, and clad in the finest ready-made clothes Richmond had to offer.

Furthermore, he was inside Allen and Ginter's. "I'd like to see the factory workings while I'm here," he told his astonishing wife.

She smiled, astonishing him again by the difference it made to her face. "Mr. Grogan'll go home and kick his dog after today," she said. "I'll tell him to give you a blue-ribbon tour. Grandfather told me a little about you. You're spying, aren't you?"

He admitted it.

"What fun. Don't let him hustle you, or leave anything out. Major Ginter was in my father's regiment. I even call him 'Uncle Lewis,' though he's not. He's known me all my life."

Her expression became serious. "Before I call Mr. Grogan, I want to put some things straight. I told you I want babies, and that's true. But today taught me something new. I can be a real help to you, Nathan. I wish I knew enough to help you spy. You had your reason for marrying me—the patent. I'd like to think you haven't made a bad bargain. I want us to be partners. I can keep books and write business letters and lord it over clerks like Mr. Grogan. I can do a lot, if you'll let me."

Nate could hardly believe his luck. He held out his hand. "It's a deal. Shake, partner." This was an arrangement he could handle much better than marriage. He had hated school when he was a boy, and he hated record-keeping more than anything else about business. With him doing the dealing and her doing the impressing, there wasn't anyplace they couldn't go. Already they were on the way.

Chess relished the feel of his big, warm, callused hand on hers. But she didn't allow her fingers to linger or to cling. As long as he never suspected it, she could love him as much as she liked.

The relief on his face had not escaped her. He was glad to make their marriage all business. She would settle for it. No, more than that. It would be joyful for her if she could help him get what he wanted. It would be enough, she told herself, and, in the excited first moments of being in love, she believed it.

Nate was inside the factory for what seemed a long time to Chess. In fact, it was. When they left Allen & Ginter, Mr. Grogan drove them to the depot in his buggy, so that they wouldn't miss the southbound train.

Inside the station she asked Nate about his discoveries inside the factory, but he shook his head and frowned, saying that they must never talk about business unless they were alone in a private place. She looked at the people hurrying by, intent on their own business, and thought his caution was extremely foolish. However, they were hurrying, too, toward the gate for the train, and she was willing to put aside his venture in espionage. She hadn't been "on the cars," as Southerners always said, since she was a child, and she was excited by the ride to come.

It was quite different from what she remembered. The coach was stifling, the horsehair upholstery stuck her in the back right through her dress. Worst of all, the location of the car was exactly where hot cinders from the smokestack would fly into any open window; they were repeatedly raised and lowered by optimists and realists. It was maddening. So was the constant twang of tobacco juice into or near the spittoons at each end of the car. The smell made her feel ill.

"I hate tobacco," Nate muttered.

"But I thought that was your business."

He smiled. "I like business, and tobacco's all I know."

They got off at Weldon, a small town with a lovely little old brick depot. Chess gulped fresh air. She felt as if she'd been shut in a corner of hell for half eternity. The trip from Richmond had lasted just over three hours. It was 6:42 in the evening of her wedding day.

"Is this where you—we—live?" she asked Nate.

"We're only barely across the line from Virginia. There's a real long way to go yet. I figure we should walk up the street to the hotel and get some rest. The train for Raleigh's not till ten o'clock and you're worn out."

"What time is tomorrow's train to Raleigh?"

"Quarter to four."

Chess could see the big brick building, only two blocks away.

HOTEL.

The sign was huge.

She felt strangled with panic. This wasn't what she had expected for her wedding night. It wasn't supposed to be like this at all. She had dreamed of marriage, and she had tried to imagine what came after. But it was always romantic. She would bathe in cologne-scented water, and her hair would be fresh and shining and scented with cologne, too.

Not like this. Not tired and hot and grimy and smelly from the train.

She couldn't do it. She couldn't go to a hotel with a man, not even this man that she loved. She was too frightened.

"Ten o'clock?" Chess said. "That's not such a long time. I think we should go on. Don't you, really? After all, we've barely begun the journey, and it seems downright silly to stop before covering as many miles as possible."

Nate had never heard such panic and such artificiality in his life. He diagnosed the problem with no difficulty. Ladies were always scared and disgusted by anything as animal-like as sex. It was an accepted fact. He wasn't looking forward to the wedding night himself, but at least he didn't see it as something terrible. He almost patted her shoulder to calm her down, but he thought that might scare her even more.

"If you're not too worn out, that's the best idea. I'll get the tickets, and then I'd say it's time we got a meal."

"Oh, yes," Chess said. "I'm starving." Now that the consummation of the marriage was averted, she realized that she was, indeed, very hungry.

They ate heartily in the now-harmless hotel's dining room, making clumsy conversation about the food. Afterwards they walked, slowly, because Nate insisted on carrying the model with him everywhere. Weldon's Main Street was three blocks long. They strolled both sides of it, back and forth, three times. "I've had enough," Nate said then. "Let's go wait at the depot."

There were no benches, only an empty baggage truck in the graveled area in front of the station. The waiting room was locked; Nate put the model on the high wood-floored cart, then made a step with his two hands for Chess and boosted her up. He joined her, and they sat with their legs dangling over the edge. Side by side, but not too close.

Darkness was falling. They could see lamps and lanterns coming to life up ahead on Main Street. But the depot would stay dark and still until train-time neared. They might have been all alone in the world. There was no need to look at one another, no point to it in the darkness. The night was soft and warm and comfortable. "Tell me about the factory now," Chess said softly. She was feeling drowsy.

Nathan looked at the shadows that surrounded them. "Keep your voice down," he said. "I don't see anybody around, but you never know. . . ." His hushed words were confidential, intimate, as he talked about his discoveries. There was a series of huge rooms with row after row of tables where clever-fingered women put tobacco on rectangles of paper, rolled them, glued them, and placed them, once assembled, into cardboard boxes, which they stacked on trays. Men with hand-carts gathered the trays and removed them. He'd known that was how it worked, but he'd never seen it for himself. He couldn't have imagined how many cigarettes were turned out in as little as ten minutes' time. No wonder Allen and Ginter was the biggest cigarette company in America.

Chess was puzzled. Was that what he was so secretive about? Anybody could see that, if they bothered to ask, she told him. Major Ginter was very proud of his girls.

Nate nearly lost patience, but he kept his voice from rising. No, that wasn't all he was after. He wanted to find out—and he had—how many people it took to produce how many cigarettes. Also what kind of paper they used and what kind of glue. He hadn't simply stayed in the rolling room, he'd seen the receiving and shipping areas, too, and he'd spied and memorized the names of the suppliers.

"You know what this model is for, don't you?"

"Don't you, *Chess*." She sensed his irritation, met it with her own.

"What?"

"I have a name. I think you should use it. I intend to call you 'Nathan.' I know it's more proper for me to say 'Mr. Richardson,' but I prefer Christian names. It's easier, and it leaves me with something to call your father." She could hear her own voice, high-pitched and sarcastic. What had gone wrong? There had been such easy closeness there for a minute or two, and now they were snapping at each other. She wanted to stop it, stop herself, but she couldn't.

He nearly snarled his reply. "I don't have one, and you're not paying attention to what's important here."

"I'm sorry, Nathan. I will pay attention." Patience was heavy in her tone. "Yes, I know all about the model. Uncle Lewis asked grandfather to invent it. It makes cigarettes. There's a hopper for tobacco and spinners for a roll of paper and a pasting gadget and a knife at the end. The paper unrolls and streams out along a track under the hopper, with tobacco spreading a line on it. Then all the cogs and pulleys act to roll the paper around it in a long tube that shoots into the guillotine where the blade cuts cigarette lengths. Grandfather was very pleased with it. He said it made him feel like Robespierre. But he didn't send it to Uncle Lewis when it was finished."

"Why not? You mean it doesn't work?" Nate grabbed her arm and shook it. "It doesn't work?" He was almost shouting.

"Of course it works. Stop shaking my arm like that. But Grandfather said that it would take the place of all the roller-girls and he couldn't do that. They're all nice girls, you know, from families that really need the money they earn. And Uncle Lewis treats them well, too. They have dormitories to live in, and good meals, and time off to visit their families. What would become of them?

"Besides, Uncle Lewis wasn't all that upset. He doesn't think very much of machine-made cigarettes anyhow. If they were made, they'd be too cheap. Nobody would want them. Hand-rolled have more prestige. Grandfather says that ciga-rettes are cheap, hand-rolled or not. They're only one step above chewing tobacco. Only cigars are worth the trouble of smoking them."

Nate felt like his knees and elbows had filled with water. He was weak with relief. "Don't you ever scare me like that again," he said. "Your 'Uncle Lewis' with his factory and your grandfather with his couple of million acres are both wrong." His tone was cold and angry, but quiet again. "This country bumpkin from backwoods North Carolina is going to prove it. I'm going to make cigarettes, a thousand times as many as your fine 'Uncle,' and I'm going to make a fortune doing it. I can only pray God nobody beats me to it. Now— Chess—that's the big secret that you don't think is worth keeping secret. Let me tell you something. This Bonsack fellow's got another machine out there. People are talking about it, and somebody's going to use it. Maybe soon. I've got to be sooner. The man who gets going first is the man that's going to win. If anybody sees that model, or hears about my plan, they'll speed up their own plans. There ain't no gentlemen in the tobacco business these days. It's dog eat dog and rabbit punches and eyeball gouging till the best man

wins, and that means the toughest and the roughest. I mean
to be him." Nate's near-whisper vibrated with passion. It was
hot and mysterious in the darkness.

Chess had never been exposed to raw ambition or to power
or the driving desire for power. All of them were nakedly
evident in Nate's voice. He seemed to her to be somehow
inhuman, supernatural in the strength of his savage determination. She knew, without his saying it, that he would destroy
anything and anyone who got in his way. Including her. She
was frightened and thrilled.

This was a man, a man not a boy. He would never settle
for life as it came, he'd grab hold and wrestle it and take
what he wanted. No Tidewater melancholy, no yearning after
Lost Causes. Nathaniel Richardson was too alive for that, and
too strong.

Oh, she'd been so right to follow her instincts, to throw
herself into his world, at his side. Chess looked at the gaslit
street in the distance and wished desperately that they were
in the hotel, cursing herself silently for her cowardice. How
could she tell him? She couldn't, the words wouldn't come.

But she could say what she was feeling, in a way he'd
understand.

"You will be the one that wins, Nathan." She reached for
his hand. "You will, I know it." Her voice, even muted, rang
with a passion that matched his.

Nate's fingers tightened around hers. He'd never doubted
himself, but he'd never known anyone else who believed in
him. Until now. "Our secret?" he said, hoarse with unforeseen
emotion.

"Our secret," Chess agreed. His hand was firm and warm.
She could feel the heat of it through the thin leather of her
glove, and she wished that her skin was bare. "Tell me all
about it," she urged. "Why cigarettes? How did you know
about my grandfather?"

Nate was glad to have an opportunity to talk. Events had
moved so swiftly that he'd had no chance to savor the plea-

sures of his triumph. The cigarette machine was his, he'd accomplished the impossible, and now all the other impossibles were certain to be his, too.

"Well, it's like this . . ." he began.

Cigarettes were the coming thing, he was sure of it. Sure, most men still chewed, but plenty had switched to rolling themselves cigarettes instead. The country storekeepers that he sold his tobacco to were his source of information. They were all in Alamance County, the heart of bright leaf tobacco country, and tobacco money was what kept them going, so they noticed everything to do with it. Tobacco was what everybody talked about all the time, in all its manifestations. How good was the crop, how bad was the weather, how high or low were the prices at auction for the farmers who sold their leaf instead of processing it.

Up north cigarettes had pushed plug tobacco out of the way already. And the ready-made cigarette was halfway to pushing roll-your-owns right out of the picture. You could see how popular they were by the size of Major Ginter's operation. The factory foreman told him that they made and sold nearly 50 million cigarettes the year before—50 million! And up north nearly ten times that many were being rolled and sold by other companies. They could hardly make them fast enough to satisfy the demand for them.

And why was that? Because there weren't enough skilled rollers.

But a machine—a machine could do the work of a couple dozen rollers, maybe more. And it could work day and night without getting tired, like humans did. Her "Uncle Lewis" might say that people wouldn't want machine-mades, but he was nobody's fool. He'd offered a huge prize to any man who invented one—probably after her grandfather told him he couldn't do it.

How big a prize? Chess wanted to know.

Seventy-five thousand dollars.

The sum took her breath away. If only she'd known . . .

She felt like murdering Augustus Standish. His high principles had kept them poor when there might have been money enough to live like kings. Why, with all her work, seven days a week, fifty-two weeks a year, the best the plantation could clear was $300 to $500 a year. And that was eaten up by paying for Augustus Standish's manservant and her mother's maid and doctor bills and laudanum. They could have had a cook, and maids; they could have fixed the roof instead of just closing off the third floor; they could even have painted the house. . . .

But then Nathan would never have walked the road from Richmond. Chess sent up a silent prayer for forgiveness that she'd thought such harsh thoughts about her grandfather. What was Nathan saying? She shouldn't have let her mind wander that way; she didn't want to miss even one of his words.

He was talking again about Bonsack. Chess concentrated, pulling from her memory snatches of what he'd said while she was wool-gathering. From Roanoke, Virginia, that's what it was, and Nathan had met him in Danville, at a tobacco auction.

"So that's how your granddaddy's name came up," Nathan said. "I heard this James Bonsack bragging to a friend. He said he was sure he'd win the prize—he'd been fiddling with his machine for nearly four years already and it almost worked—but he was worried that old Mr. Standish might be doing the same thing.

"That's when I decided to go find this Mr. Standish for myself. If I could just get hold of his machine before Bonsack finished—"

"What would you have done?"

Nathan's laughter was quiet, but it filled the darkness around them. "I'd have fast-talked it out of him if I could, otherwise I'd offer to go shares in business."

"Not get the prize?"

Nate's hand closed in a fist, squeezing her fingers until it hurt. "What's a one-time pile of money when Allen and Ginter would have the machine? I think bigger than that—oh, Lord, I'm breaking your hand; I'm sorry, Chess." He opened his fingers to allow hers to escape.

"But it doesn't hurt at all," she lied. And she left her hand in his. "Tell me about tobacco," she said.

"It's the hardest thing in the world to grow," he answered. "Farmers call it the thirteen-month crop, because the work never stops. It's nasty stuff. Oozes a kind of tar that sticks to your skin and your clothes and your hair. You never feel clean again once you've been around tobacco.

"Don't bother asking why grow it. It makes more money on one acre than any other crop does on fifty. When you've got your green leaves in your curing barn, you watch them turn gold. That's the kind of crop it is—it makes gold."

Chess thought that was beautiful, like something from mythology. Just right for Nathan. For several minutes she sat quiet, aware of his closeness, of their two hands joined, of their shared secret. So this was what happiness was like—a heightened perception of everything, of the soft darkness, the dampness within the air, the movement of that air caused by Nathan's breathing. Happiness was being with him, loving him. Love. How strange and wonderful it was.

She turned her head to look at him, but it was too dark to see more than a vague outline of him, darker against the darkness. She wanted to hear his voice, in proof that he was really there.

"What will happen with Grandfather's machine now, Nathan? What's the rest of the secret?"

Strange, he thought, she must be able to read my mind. "I've been thinking about that," he said, "I mean, about how fast I can go now. I wish I had more money, I'd set up a factory tomorrow. But I don't, so the secret's got to stay hid while I work up to it. The first thing is to get room for a factory and power for the machine. I figure that the way to go is to find the right place and build a mill. Yes, that's the best."

As he talked, his voice became even more quiet, and Chess

knew that he was thinking aloud, probably not even aware of her presence, or of their clasped hands. A chill of disappointment ran through her. She wanted to be part of his plans, his dream.

But even this was more than she'd ever hoped to have. She was beside him, whether he was conscious of her or not. And she was, in fact, a vital part of his plans. She owned the patent. It bound them together. He couldn't make his dream come true without her.

"It'll have to be close to Durham," Nate mumbled. "The railhead's there for shipping, and the auctions and warehouses for supplies of leaf. But not too close. I don't want Blackwell's or Duke breathing down my neck. They just might be thinking cigarettes, too, and I'm not ready to fight them, not till I get going good. . . ."

Suddenly he turned toward Chess.

"It's going to work, Chess. It'll take a while but it's going to work. Do you believe me?"

"I believe you," she said. She had no idea what he was planning, but she knew he would succeed.

Nate chuckled. "I'm so full of the future I feel like a balloon. I'd probably bust if I didn't let it out some. I've never had anybody I could tell about it before. I guess your ear is pretty much black and blue from all my rambling on and on."

"I like it when you talk. Don't stop."

"I'm just about talked out."

"A little more. Please. Tell me about your family. Do you have brothers and sisters? Is your mother still living, or is she dead, too, like your father?" Chess wanted to ask if they would like her. She'd already made up her mind to like them, no matter what.

She sensed Nate's shrug. "My daddy's not dead, far as I know. He just moved on, 'bout ten years back, when I got old enough to take care of things. Ma is in fine fettle. She runs the farm and every critter on it, man or beast. My uncle, his name is Joshua Richardson, called Josh, he and his wife and children live on the place, in their own house."

"How many children?"

"Three living. Micah, he's thirteen, a grown man nearly. Susan, she's my pet, she's nearly ten years old now. And then there's Sally, the baby, she'll be two when summer's gone."

"What's their mother's name?"

"Alva. You'll like Alva. One of the sweetest-tempered women God ever made." He paused, took a deep breath. "You can't exactly say the same thing about Ma. She's going to take some getting used to."

Chess felt her heart grow heavy in her chest.

Nate spoke quickly, stumbling over his words. "She's a fine woman and a good Christian. She's a little set in her ways, that's all, and she don't care much for surprises. Just pay no mind if she uses the sharp edge of her tongue on you. She don't mean half what she says."

Worse and worse, Chess thought. I hope the aunt will help me. Or maybe—"Do you have any sisters, Nathan?"

"Only one. Mary's her name, just like Ma's."

Chess smiled into the darkness. But only briefly. "She married a man from Orange County," Nate said, "and they went all the way to Oregon to homestead. We got word after a year or so that they'd got there safe.

"I'm the only one at home still. My older brother, Gideon, he's a circuit rider."

"What's a circuit rider?"

"A preacher. He goes all around the district they give him, preaching in all the towns too small to have one. He's a good one, too, he can make you feel the hellfire nipping at your feet. He's working in Georgia now, way down in the southwest part."

"What church do youall belong to?"

"Methodist, of course. Everybody in North Carolina's Methodist, at least in our part of North Carolina. . . ." Nate's words trailed off, and he squeezed her hand gently. "That's where the trouble is, Chess. It's like this. Ma, she's a mighty God-fearing woman, she knows her Bible backwards and forwards. But she kind of figures that only Methodists are real Christians. Everybody else is a heathen or a papist."

Chess tried to laugh. "I guess I'll be one of the papists, in her eyes."

Nate's laughter was more convincing. "At least that's better than a heathen. I'm glad it doesn't bother you."

"Of course not." She was grateful for the darkness. "Tell me more about Gideon. Is he married?"

"Yes." Nate pushed away the pain that was strangling him. Why did she have to ask that? Why make him think about Lily, his brother's wife, and the commandment that he broke every minute of his life, wanting her for his own. Dear God, here he was married to an old woman, while Gideon had Lily in his bed whenever he returned from his circuit. Burning hatred scalded the moisture in his eyes. He hated her, this wife, and he hated his brother, and he hated himself most of all, for his weakness.

"Yes," he said again, "Gideon's married to a preacher's daughter. Lots of religion in the family."

Chess could hear his anguish. She thought she understood. His mother must prefer her other son and let Nathan know it. She sounded like a horrible woman. If only, Chess thought wildly, if only we could stay in Weldon, never go to Alamance County, wherever that was, never have to see his mother at all. I'd make it up to him, I'd love him so much that he'd never be sad again.

In the distance a train whistled, mocking her.

"That'll be the Raleigh train," Nate said. He was happy to have something to do, it helped him stop thinking. "I'll get your case, and then I'll help you down."

Two men came running from Main Street. They quarreled as they ran. "I told you to watch the time!" each shouted at the other.

The station's gas lamps came on bright, all doors opened, and the ticket window was manned when the locomotive hissed and squealed its way to a stop.

The car Nate and Chess entered was less than half full. People were sleeping on the makeshift couches that side-by-side seats provided. The lights were turned down low, and several windows were open to the fresh night air.

"Stretch out the best you can," said Nate. "Here, I'll make a pillow for your head." He took off his jacket and folded it.

"There's no need for that, Nathan. I'm hardly tired at all."

"Hush up and get some sleep. We've got a long ways to go yet." Nate arranged the jacket into a thick wad. His face did not show his regret at damaging the best garment he'd ever owned, nor was there any sign of the shock he'd felt when he saw the pale gaunt face of his new wife. While they'd been talking, he'd forgotten how very plain she was.

She was looking at him with such worry in her eyes that pity softened his heart. He grinned and patted his vest.

"Who do I owe for these clothes?" he asked. "And how much? I forgot to ask, and I'm probably going to regret asking now."

Chess returned his smile. She nestled her head into the lumpy pile that he'd made for her. "It's a wedding present from Uncle Lewis," she giggled. "I left him a thank you note with the bill. Good thing he doesn't know you're going to put him out of business." She was asleep within seconds. She'd had no sleep at all the night before.

Nate sat quietly in the dim railway car, smiling. She kept surprising him. He liked that. And when she smiled like she'd just done, she didn't look nearly so old.

The train reached Raleigh on schedule at 1:00 A.M. In spite of her rest, Chess was groggy with fatigue. She stumbled after Nate to the track for the next train they had to take. When it arrived in Hillsborough, the time was after three. For the first time ever, Nate spent money on a livery cab, even though the hotel was only a few blocks away.

Once there he deposited Chess on a bench in the big reception room while he carried the boxed model, then the bags, to their room. He put one arm around her waist to help her climb the stairs.

"Which valise is your nightshirt in?" he asked her. Chess staggered to it and removed her things. She'd helped herself to one of her mother's nightdresses. The heavy silk was slippery in her awkward grasp, and it nearly fell to the floor.

"Want some help with your corset strings?" Nate offered. Chess shook her head. Her corset, too, had been her mother's. The laced back was pulled to its tightest, but it was loose on Chess' thin body. The hooks in front were easy to undo. Nathan turned his back on her to give them both privacy. He took off his clothes, carefully hanging up his new suit and shirt. Then he washed. When he'd emptied and refilled the bowl, he turned to Chess, holding her towel out to her.

She was already in the bed and asleep. "Good," Nate sighed. He spread the clean towel carefully over the bowl of water to keep it fresh. Then he walked to the bed and got on it. "Chess, you ought to wake up now. This is going to hurt, and it would scare you more if you were sleeping and didn't know why you were hurting."

His words worked slowly into her consciousness, and she opened her eyes. His face was very close. She smiled. She liked having him close.

"Put your arms around my neck, honey, and hold on. It'll be real quick."

Chess did as she was told. She dimly felt him pushing up her nightdress and spreading her legs. Then she felt his weight on her and a piercing hot pain, and she screamed.

"Hush, honey, hush. It's all over. You've got yourself a husband. Now go back to sleep." The pain was gone, and so she did. Nate stared into the darkness until fatigue overcame his sorrow, and he slept.

She slept late the next morning. Nate brought a cup of sweet creamy coffee up to her after he finished his breakfast. He woke her, then put it in her hand. Chess blinked the sleep from her eyes. "Thank you," she said. What she wanted to say was that being wakened by him made her happier than she'd ever been, but she was overwhelmed by shyness.

"Do you remember what happened last night, Chess?"

She looked down into the cup and nodded.

"Well, I just wanted to tell you that the worst is over. It'll be easier from now on. Drink your coffee and then get dressed. We want to be on the road before it gets too hot. I'm going out to arrange for some kind of rig. I'll be back soon."

She blinked some more as she watched the door close behind him. Not to wake, as before. Now she was holding back tears.

What are you crying about? she berated herself silently while she removed her nightdress and folded it. What did you expect anyway?

Her suitcase was a tumbled mess. Chess rearranged the few things she'd brought from home. A dressing gown of patched and faded blue wool, three muslin chemises and step-ins, two petticoats, a calico dress, a dark brown ottoman skirt and a white linen blouse, gloves, lisle stockings, paisley shawl, boots, silver-backed comb, clothes brush and hair brush— her tears fell on the books she'd chosen so carefully from the shelves in the dusty library at Harefields. *Idylls of the King. The Three Musketeers. Sonnets from the Portuguese.* With them was her prayer book. Her initials were incised in faded gold letters on its ivory cover; inside her father had written *To my beloved daughter Francesca Augusta on the occasion of her confirmation.*

Chess wished very much that Nathan's mother had just gone off and left him when his father did.

She washed and dried her face, then her body. She was sore between her legs, but not very much so. Nothing about the mystery of marriage was very much, she decided.

Still, she was married, long after she'd given up hopes of it. And to Nathan, whom she loved. What did it matter that sexual congress was not a transcendent, transfiguring experience. Love was. Chess felt the giddiness again; her heartbeat was racing.

She dressed quickly, finished packing in only seconds. Nathan would be back by now, perhaps, and she wanted to see him more than she'd ever wanted anything in her life.

Chapter Six

"THE RIG I FOUND ain't much," Nate warned Chess when she came down the stairs.

He was a master of understatement. The "rig" was an old cart, listing perilously to the right, with an aged horse that seemed to be sleeping.

Chess didn't care. They'd be together on the sagging plank seat. She giggled like a girl. "I think it's wonderful," she said. "It will be an adventure."

Nate laughed. "You don't know the half of it," he told her. "The horse is blind in one eye."

"Let's hope it's the left one. That might balance things out."

He was still chuckling when he went into the hotel to get their luggage and pay the bill. He had to give her credit, she wasn't a complainer. In fact, she was even good company. It surprised him how good it was to have someone to talk to who was in on the secret. And, as for her looks and age, well there were younger ones alongside every road he traveled, and plenty of them were agreeable. People were going to laugh behind his back, but he could ignore it. He had more important things to worry about than what folks thought or even said.

Hillsborough was a beautiful old town with streets shady under the ancient trees that lined them. The late-summer heat was like a giant's fist when it hit them on the unshaded dusty road. It was not yet eight o'clock.

"I got some ham biscuits and a gallon of water from the hotel," Nate said. "They're in that burlap sack underneath the seat. You didn't have breakfast, so dig in. I'll want some water after a while."

She was hungry, and it amazed her. She'd been hungry at supper the night before, too. Being with Nathan must be magic; it had been years and years since she had felt like eating. She was always too tired to bother with food.

Or, perhaps she'd simply been unhappy and now happiness had restored her appetite. The ham was sweet and the biscuits were spread with honey butter.

"This is a feast, Nathan. Won't you have some?"

Nate shook his head. "I had about a dozen this morning." Lord, but that woman sure could put the food away. It hardly seemed possible a body could eat like that and be so skinny.

The horse moved at a slow, reluctant walk, but Nate made no effort to speed it up. It probably would have done no good, and besides, he wasn't all that anxious to face his family.

"Tell me about the mill, Nathan."

He looked at her, startled.

"You were kind of talking to yourself about it last night. While we were waiting at the depot," she added quickly.

Nate grimaced. "That's a bad habit I've got."

"It sure is, for a man with a secret. Don't fret; nobody heard you except me. Tell me about it. I've got a right to know. I'm your partner." She'd have to watch her tongue, too. She'd nearly said "wife."

Nate nodded, smiled. "Okay, here goes. The machine needs power to run it, and the business needs money to keep it going until it takes off. So I figure the way to put all that in one bundle is with a mill. I've got a little money saved—not much, but it should be enough. I'll find a piece of land near a good fast-running creek and build a gristmill. In the daytime I'll grind grain for people—for pay—and at night when no one's there to see what's going on, the mill wheel can drive the machine. I can put a mattress in the loft for sleeping."

He had let the reins go slack, engrossed in his plans. The horse stopped.

"We'll need a fireplace for cooking," Chess said as she reached over and twitched the reins.

Nate grabbed them up and flapped them on the horse's back. But it had already resumed its plodding walk.

"Don't talk crazy," he said. "That's no kind of life for you. It'll be rough going at first. You'll stay at the farm. When I start to make money, I'll build a house for us to live in."

Chess wanted to wail in misery. But she spoke quietly. "No," she said.

"What do you mean?"

"I mean no. No, I won't be left out, and no, that won't work. One person can't run a mill single-handed, and it takes two people to run the cigarette machine. Plus, you've got to sleep sometime."

A muscle in Nate's jaw jumped erratically. Chess couldn't stop staring at it. The beads of sweat in her eyebrows rolled into the corner of her eyes, salt stinging.

Nate's jaw relaxed. She would have wiped her eyes, but she was afraid he'd believe she was crying.

"You're right," Nate said. "I was figuring to hire a boy to help at the mill, but I can't let anybody see that machine. I'll put up some walls and make a real room in part of the loft. Do you know anything about milling?"

"Only what I've seen when I went to one. Do you?"

"Some. It can't be hard to do, though. The miller at the town we go to hasn't got the sense God gave a June bug."

Chess waited.

"I just forgot," Nate said after a few long minutes. "I've

been going it alone for a long time, and I've got to get used to having a partner."

She relaxed then. "Me, too," she said. "I shouldn't have grabbed the reins."

Nate shrugged. "I never even noticed." He turned his head and grinned at her, laughing at himself.

Chess felt as if she were floating above the splintery wagon seat. "Would you like some water?"

"Yes, ma'am, I sure would."

Chess was surprised by the number of wagons, buggies, riders on the road. Nate shouted greetings to them all, sometimes by name.

"Is there anybody you don't know?" Chess asked him.

"Lots. I hail them anyhow. It's likely I'll get to know them one of these days. There ain't that many folks in this part of the world."

"There are plenty on this road."

"Always. Hillsborough's the county seat for Orange County. Anytime there's any legal or political doings, they're in Hillsborough. We'll be turning off soon, toward Alamance. Things will quiet down then. I'll be glad to stop eating everybody's dust."

Chess drank some water. She'd be very glad herself. The dust hung in the air, so fine it took forever to settle. Her dark skirts were already filmed with gray. Where the earth was bare, it looked almost like the sandy ground in the Tidewater. But dirty. And there was no cool salt air from a wide river to offset the parching of dusty heat.

For the first time, she felt a sharp ache of homesickness. She had never been so far away in all her life.

She tipped the gallon jug again and gulped more water. Then she passed it to Nathan.

They stopped in the middle of the day and watered the horse at a small stream that ran through a grove of tall pines.

Chess and Nathan bathed their hot faces and necks, then drank the tepid water from cupped hands.

Nate stretched out on the cushiony fallen pine needles, while Chess sat with her back against a tree and fanned herself with her hat.

"We're about halfway there," said Nate. "If we had a decent horse, we'd be home by now."

"I don't mind. It's too hot to think about hurrying."

Nate's even breathing became deeper and slower. He was asleep.

Chess eased her way quietly, until she was at his side. Then she looked at him as she hadn't dared do before, with love naked in her eyes. He wasn't anything special to see—a healthy young man with a farmer's browned skin, freckles barely distinguishable. His brilliant blue eyes were closed, and he was almost like a stranger without them. But his lashes were thick, and long enough to make any woman envious. She hadn't noticed them before; now she studied each individual hair. Then she marveled at the intricate arcs of the inside of his ears. And she feasted her sight on the clear outline of his lips. Her mouth hungered for them.

Better go back to your tree, she told herself. And she obeyed.

Nate woke as easily as he had fallen asleep. He squinted at the sun through the boughs of the trees. "I slept too long," he said. "Now we'll have the sun in our eyes the rest of the way." Suddenly, and for the first time, he seemed uneasy. He cleared his throat.

"Um, I'm going to take a little walk back into the woods before we leave." He gestured to his left. "Would you like—" He waved his hand toward the right.

"I took a walk while you were asleep," Chess said. She concentrated her attention and her eyes on the process of putting her gloves on. They were dirty, but she was prepared for that; she had put another pair in her pocket. Just before they reached the farm, she would take off the soiled ones and replace them with the fresh ones before she met Nathan's family.

Her gloves were made of white kidskin; they were as thin and supple as silk. She had ten more pairs in her valise.

Chess had beautiful hands, thin and elegant. They were her one vanity. She knew she was plain, and too tall, too thin, too old. A gaunt, colorless drab. But her hands were beautiful, and she found that a comfort. She had been taking gloves from her mother's bureau drawers for years, to protect her hands whenever she had to work with them or expose them to dirt. The gloves were never missed. Her mother had them by the hundreds, and she never left the house.

"Ready?" Nate called. "I'll hitch up the racehorse, you fill up the jug with water."

Nate stopped the cart and jumped down. "I'll open the gate, then close it again after you drive him through. Pull up and wait for me."

Chess strained to see, but the sun was low and directly ahead. She couldn't see the farm at all, only a glare. She took up the reins Nathan had dropped and made encouraging sounds while she slapped the horse with them.

When Nate climbed up to his seat, she handed the reins to him, then shaded her eyes with her hands.

Then she busied herself, changing gloves. She had no wish to look again.

The Richardson farm was nothing more than a straggle of small, sagging weathered-gray wooden buildings along the edges of a single big field of dusty gray soil dotted with naked stalks and stubs that looked dead.

"We're home," said Nate.

"And just what am I supposed to make of these carryings on, Nate Richardson?" His mother was screeching like a barn owl. "You tell me you can't come to Camp Meeting—where your very own brother is the main preacher, mind you—

'cause you've got to go all the way to Richmond, Virginia on tobacco business and then you come back in a store bought suit that cost who knows how much with a woman I never seen before that you're calling your 'wife.' I got a good mind to push you out and bar the door."

The homecoming was not going well.

Chess was horrified. By the tiny woman with her loud voice and angry, wrinkled face, like every witch in every fairy tale. By the raw bleakness of this place that was going to be her home. Most of all by Nathan's attempts to placate his mother. Where was the man whose confidence and power had been so exciting?

She realized that she was trembling, and her weakness disgusted her. Why should she be frightened? She was an adult, not a child. Furthermore, she wasn't just anybody. She was a Standish of Harefields plantation.

Chess retreated into all the prejudices and snobberies she'd been taught as a child. They crowded her mind and stiffened her spine, so that when Nathan's mother approached her, Chess looked down her thin nose at Mary Richardson with icy hauteur.

"How old are you, girl?" demanded the old woman.

"Thirty." Chess threw the reply at her.

Mary Richardson smiled a satisfied smile. A momentary look of surprise washed over Nate's face "Seven years," gloated his mother. "Seven years older." Nate had thought it was more.

His mother turned to face Nate. She put her hands on her hips. "You always were all kinds of a no-'count fool, boy." Chess flew to his defense.

"Your son is a businessman, Mrs. Richardson," she said distinctly. "He married me to create a business partnership. I married him for the same reason. It has nothing to do with you, and no one invited your opinion."

Her tone was full of arrogance and contempt. Nate's mother was thunderstruck. In her world mothers held the power of absolute dictators. No one talked back, certainly not a daughter-in-law.

Nathan put his arm around his mother's shoulders to comfort her. "Thing is, Ma," he explained, "Chess is a Virginia lady."

His mother was in no way defeated. She shrugged off his embrace, whirling to confront Chess again. "Are you a Christian?" It was more an accusation than a question.

"I am."

"Do you go to services?"

"I do."

The old woman pounced. "What kind of services?"

"Episcopalian."

"Ha!" Nate's mother reeked superiority. She turned on her heel and marched to a rocking chair near the open door, where she seated herself like a reigning empress. "Hand me that pan of beans I was stringing, boy. I can't waste time with you and Chase. I've got work to do."

"It's 'Chess,' Ma, not 'Chase.'"

"Whatever it is, it's a heathen name."

Chess was fuming. But Nathan looked at her, rolled his eyes, then winked. Suddenly everything was all right. His mother was ludicrous.

Nate put the beans in his mother's lap. "I'm going to take Chess around the place and show her everything before it gets dark," he said. He gestured to Chess, and she scampered to join him in the open doorway.

"Got to give some food and water to the horse," he said in a loud voice. To Chess, he murmured, "I want to put the machine model where nobody can see it."

Those first few minutes set the pattern for Chess' life at the farm. Nathan was her refuge and protector from a situation that was infuriating and intolerable. Every evening, after a tasteless supper prepared by his mother, he led Chess to a

quiet, mossy clearing beside the shallow stream that mean-
dered through the pine woods behind the house.

He whittled deadfall branches, made small waterwheels,
and they waded in the cool, refreshing stream to try them out.
They talked about their secret plan for the gristmill until the
music of the night peepers reminded them that day was done
and it was time to go.

The long hot days were bearable, because Chess could
count on the evening to come. In every other respect, her life
was miserable.

On the first day she was there, she thought optimistically
that Nathan's aunt Alva would become her friend. Alva's
daughter Susan was sitting in the doorway, playing pat-a-cake
with her baby sister, and both of them seemed to like her at
once. Alva was different. She congratulated Nate, kissed Chess
on the cheek, but her eyes were hostile, and she made little
effort at conversation.

Later, when Chess met Alva's husband, Josh, and her son,
Micah, they said hello and immediately began talking to
Nathan about needing to repair the roof of the barn. Chess
might have been invisible.

There was no welcome for her in the Richardson family.
Nathan's mother put it into words: "There's no place for you
here, Chase. You'd do better to go back where you came
from."

"You know I can't do that. I'm wed to your son and 'thy
people shall be my people.' You do know the story of Ruth,
don't you, Miss Mary?"

Mary Richardson brought out the worst in Chess. Chess
learned quickly that it enraged the old woman when she quoted
the Bible to her, because it was a favored tool Mrs. Richardson
used. Also, Chess called her "Miss Mary," a Tidewater gentry
tradition, just to emphasize her own aristocratic heritage,
because Mary Richardson was subject to the universal Southern weakness for ancestor worship and aggrandizement.

They were the only weapons she had. Nathan kept well
away from the battle between the two women in his house.

He was busy with tobacco all day, coming home only to wash and eat dinner at noon and to wash again, then eat supper at six.

After supper, he took Chess to their place near the stream, and her hurts were healed. Until the next day.

The worst aspect of it all was that Mary Richardson was right. Chess admitted to herself that she didn't belong there. She had been in charge of a 10,000-acre plantation, but she knew nothing about how to manage a 40-acre farm. She had never milked a cow, or churned butter, or fed chickens or wrung their necks. Most of the food at Harefields was provided by the tenant farmers as part payment of rent. Chess knew how to prepare it, but Mary Richardson spurned her offer to cook.

"I ain't about to let you fix dinner for me and my boy. If you did as bad at that as everything else, we'd die from poison."

Mary's criticism was continuous. She was obviously enjoying herself, and in Chess' eyes, she gained monstrous proportions.

Even when Nathan took her to bed at night Chess thought she could hear Miss Mary's outraged muttering on the other side of the thin wall between the two rooms. She was sure Miss Mary could hear the creaks of the old iron bed and she was grateful that Nate performed his marital duty so quickly. Afterwards, he rolled off her and immediately fell asleep. She put her cheek against his strong bare back then and was comforted, thinking about their secret, and the mill where they would live together. Alone.

Chapter Seven

It was almost three weeks after their arrival at the farm that Nate made his announcement. He came in for dinner smelling strongly of soap, as usual, but instead of sitting down and wolfing his food, as usual, he made a *ta-ra-ta-ra* sound with his hand to his mouth as mock trumpet.

"Josh and I finished the grading this morning. I'll be going to Danville tomorrow with a couple hundred pounds of the prettiest, yellowest leaf you ever saw. Make out your want list, Ma, and don't stint. We should get top dollar for this crop." His wide smile was a sunny antidote to the steady rain that was falling outside.

"How long will we be there, Nathan?" Chess' smile was the equal of his. Oh, what joy to get away from this place. Nate sat down. "You can't go," he said. "Tobacco auction's no place for a lady."

Chess grabbed his arm. "Please," she said. "Nathan. Please. I'd like to go very, very much."

Mary Richardson put a plate of collard greens and pork

chops in front of Nate. "You heard him, Chase, you ain't invited," she said. "Get your plate and fill it up and eat some dinner for a change instead of picking at it."

"Nathan ... Please ..."

"Well ... all right. I guess you should see what drives the tobacco farmer. It's not a vacation, you know, just there and back as quick as we can."

She was smiling again. "Thank you, Nathan," she said quietly.

That afternoon she saw tobacco up close, for the first time. Nathan had shown her the storing barn, a small building full of huge yellow leaves hanging from narrow sticks that were laid across ranks of poles that rose to the ceiling. It looked like all of autumn compressed within walls; it smelled like nothing she'd ever known, musty and pungently sweet. Chess started to go to the center of the barn to give herself over to the intoxicating exotic strangeness of it, but Nathan kept her in the doorway. "That's our money for the future," he told her. "Don't break any of it." The dried golden leaves were fragile.

At the curing barn, she backed away as soon as Nate opened the door. The interior was ferociously hot. Ten mounds of charcoal dotted the floor, smoldering red in the darkness like huge monster eyes. The open door made a draft that rustled tobacco leaves that were suspended above the fires. Chess could just glimpse those closest to the door, then Nathan closed it. She was glad. Her hands had lifted automatically to cover her head. She had gone into a tenant's barn once and disturbed a huge colony of bats that were hanging there asleep. She'd had nightmare memories of their swooping, erratic flight for months afterwards.

Now two golden leaves were in her hands, placed there by her proud husband. She caressed them with her fingers, fascinated by their stretchy toughness and simultaneous thin fragility. "They're like beautiful yellow leather!" she exclaimed. "I wish I could make gloves out of them."

Nate snorted. "I doubt that," he said. "Feel the tar on your fingers."

He was right. Her hands had become sticky all over; they felt as if she would be glued to anything she might touch. "Take the leaves back," she said. "I want to wash my hands."

"Wait till the day's over," Nathan advised. "We'll all be handling 'baccy the whole afternoon."

"Not Chase." Mary Richardson had walked up behind them while they were talking. "She can watch over Alva's little one to keep it out of our way. Any fool can handle a baby."

Chess held a squirming Sally in her arms and watched what the others were doing. Oh, how she'd love to prove Miss Mary wrong.

Josh, Alva, Mary, and Susan were seated on a bench in the large room they called "the factory." It was attached to the storing barn, but it had its own entrance and its shed roof was much lower. Three windows on the north wall were open, as was the door, and the space was well lit and pleasantly cool. The rain had stopped, leaving the air refreshingly washed and fresh. It was almost possible to believe that autumn was on the way, even though September was often the hottest month of the year in the South.

The four of them worked with no waste effort, bending forward, taking up five or six leaves from the pile of tobacco in front of them, quickly arranging them into what Chess learned was called a "hand." She was mesmerized by the deft beauty of their actions. They stacked the leaves by tapping their stems against their knees, then rapidly pulled an additional leaf through curled fingers to flatten and fold it. Finally—faster than she could follow—they wrapped the collected stems with the extra leaf and tucked its tail in between the leaves of the bundle.

Miss Mary was right again. She couldn't do that. "Let's go, Sally," she whispered to the child.

She waited outside the factory just long enough to see what part Nathan played. In a short time, he and Micah emerged, carrying a long stick laden with the "hands" neatly arranged over it. They placed it carefully in the first of the notches in a framework that filled the big farm wagon they had put near the door. There were dozens more notches to be filled.

"We'll go sit on the step, Sally, and I'll read you a story. Would you like that?" Even if Sally wouldn't, Chess thought, I would. *Geraint and Enid* was much less foreign than dealing with tobacco. She held the child close until Sally protested. One day, she dreamed, I'll have a baby of my own. Nathan's baby.

It was dark when they left for Danville, the still darkness of the hour when the whole earth rested and all its creatures slept. Overhead the sky was black and infinite and lavish with stars. The moon was only a pale thin crescent near the horizon. The road was a dull silver line. The creak of harness and wheels was a comforting familiar sound in the hushed night. Chess could feel Nathan's warmth beside her; it banished the chill of the darkness.

The two of them were alone, on an island of their own making. This was like the time in Weldon depot. Unseen in the darkness, she could love him without caution. She felt weightless and free and girlish and joyful and safe. Happiness bubbled in her throat and she laughed her special laugh. Nate had forgotten how it made everyone around her feel good. She hadn't done much laughing at the farm. The tobacco was covered with pale canvas stretched over a hooped frame. "We must look like a huge ghost," Chess said. "Any farmer that's up will be scared half to death."

"Likely so," Nate chuckled, "but not by any ghost. He'll know that Nate Richardson's getting his leaf to market a full month or more before him."

"Is that good?"

"It is if you've got a load like this. The best lemon wrappers you'll ever see. The buyers will bid them up through the roof." Nathan was exuberant; he talked and talked about the wonder of the shrouded tobacco behind them. Chess could hardly keep up with the stream of words, so rapid was his speaking.

. . . Most farmers would have lost their crop this year, what with the drought all through May and June. But they'd hauled buckets of water from the creek half the day every day and the plants grew strong and straight. Then when the rains came in July, the tobacco was able to stand upright instead of being battered to the ground. . . . Yes, sir, he'd seen the fields of fellows he knew, and they were sorry sights. There'd be a shortage of good leaf, everybody'd been talking about it already for months, and that meant that good leaf would fetch a premium price. And this leaf wasn't just good, it was as near perfect as leaf ever got. Nearly a third of it was wrapper quality, the best, and the wrappers were lemon, to boot. He had to say it, Josh knew more about curing and grading than probably any man in all North Carolina. He could drive a body crazy, the way he hung on to the old ways of doing things and wouldn't try anything new, but when it came to curing, the old ways were the best ways, and Josh knew them like no other man could beat. . . .

. . . It was all in the temperature, see? How to get the barn heated to exactly ninety degrees, then a hundred ten, then on up to a hundred thirty and sometimes a hundred forty. And how long to stay at each number, and when to open the door to let some damp get back into the leaves and just when the fires needed more charcoal and when they had to be raked open to cool them down. Folks would tell you there was a set system, like some kind of science, but if that was so, then a lemon wrapper wouldn't be the rare thing it was. No, siree, it was near magic, that's what it was, the way Josh could tell what the curing ought to be.

"Why wrap lemons?" Chess slipped the question in when Nathan paused to catch his breath. She was astonished when he hugged her quickly with his right arm.

"Lord save us, Chess, I forget how much you don't know."

His voice was warm; the brief embrace was, too. She felt boneless from bliss, and she had to force her mind to pay attention to what he was saying.

Lemon was the color of the leaf. The best color; the other grades were called orange and mahogany. And wrappers were the best leaves, used as the outer wrapping around the shaped lumps of chewing tobacco that they called "plugs." Each and every plant produced eighteen leaves, at least that's what he and Josh had chosen. Some farmers let them grow as tall as twenty-four or even more, and some topped them off at only twelve. The bottom leaves got sandy from being on the ground; they were tougher, too. They were called "lugs" and they weren't worth much. Nor were the leaves at the very top, known as "tips." It was the leaves in the center that were the real crop. They had the best flavor. Usually they were shredded or pulverized to make smoking tobacco, so they were called "cutters," because they got cut up. The leaves in the very center, with cutters above and below, were the best of all. They were the wrappers. A man was lucky if he got two wrappers from a plant, because they had to be whole, with no tears, and no holes from tobacco worms feeding on them— those devils could chew up a leaf faster than a man could chew up a chop.

Add to that the fact that almost always the leaf cured up orange or mahogany. Then you might get some idea of what a wagonload of lemon wrappers really meant.

Chess felt that she'd learned enough about tobacco for now, thank you very much, but she didn't say so to Nathan. She would rather remember his embrace. But she loved him, and therefore anything to do with his life was fascinating to her, even his accounts of last year's harvest, and the year before that, and the intricacies of collecting seed from the plants and saving it for the following year, and the details of the discussions he'd had with Josh about a new system for heating the curing barn that a lot of people were talking about.

"If it's new, it's probably better, Chess. That's the thing about the time we're living in. People are coming up with new things, new ideas every day. There's even talk that this year at the State Fair there's going to be a demonstration of electricity. I mean the real electric light, not some game you play with a gadget to make your palms tingle. Last year I talked on the telephone to a friend who was so far away I couldn't even see him! It worked; the electric light works. The world's already a different place. Shoot, they've already got meat and vegetables in metal cans so they'll never go bad and you can have them whether they're in season or not. Next thing you know, it'll be milk and butter and who knows what else? I tell you, Chess, it's great to be alive in times like these."

"Yes it is." Her agreement came from her heart. It was great to be alive, especially right this minute, here with the man she loved. Her husband!

Her silk nightdress was in the valise at her feet, and she had washed her hair. If the tobacco sold for a very high price, she'd ask Nathan to buy her a small bottle of cologne. They'd be staying over at a hotel.

"Tell me about Danville," said Chess.

"It's a real city." Nate's voice rang with excitement. "I'd rather go to Danville than almost any place I can think of. They should have called it Tobaccotown, 'cause that's what it is. More tobacco is bought and sold there than anyplace, even Richmond. I can hardly credit that you don't know about Danville." He laughed. "Come to think of it, you especially should like Danville. It's across the line, in Virginia. I'm talking you back home, Chess."

Nate began to sing. His baritone voice was true and strong. "Carry me back . . . ,"

Chess joined in. ". . . to Old Virginny . . . ,"

Both of them knew only the first verse, so they sang it again and again, their voices blended, as the wagon moved slowly along the road and sunrise painted the sky ahead.

At midday they stopped to water the horses and to eat the food Chess had packed. The sun was hot, and the deeply rutted road threw dust up to coat their clothes and the inside of their throats.

"Only a couple more hours," Nate promised. "You can tell we're getting close."

All around the field where they were resting, Chess saw rocks painted in bright colors. BEST PRICES FOR TOBACCO . . . FAIR DEALS AT NEAL'S . . . FIRST OPENINGS. She'd seen similar messages for miles, blaring from rocks, from the sides of barns, sheds, even houses. "Those are the auction warehouses," Nate explained. "They're always battling each other to get the most business. I always use Big Star. Some of the fellows there know me." He stood up and began pacing with impatience. "Are you ready to go?"

"Ready, willing, and eager," Chess replied. "But you've got to promise me one more stop. I want to clean up some right before we go into the city."

"Good idea." He was already backing one of the horses into its harness.

"There!" Chess said, "Let's stop there." A patch of black-eyed susans was blooming beside a little pond to their left.

When they entered Danville, her straw hat sported a wreath of bright yellow flowers on its wide brim. She had replaced her dusty blue dress with a crisp white linen shirtwaist and dark skirt, and she was wearing clean white gloves.

"You look real fine," Nathan said, with an approving nod.

Her face became pink. It was very becoming.

Danville delighted her. It was an old town, in the foothills of the Blue Ridge Mountains. She knew only the flat world of Tidewater; hills were a new experience.

Thanks to tobacco, Danville had suffered none of the chaotic economic depression that disrupted most of the South after the Civil War. Nate drove the wagon along Main Street, past imposing houses in the latest styles, then block after block of stores, their windows piled high with enticing merchandise beside signs that said WELCOME TOBACCO GROWER. The unmistakable smell of cured leaf permeated the small thriving city.

For Chess, the best part of all was the wide rushing Dan River. On the cobblestoned street along its bank, the sweet water-smell was even stronger than the tobacco musk. She sniffed happily, her eyes closed.

"You look like a hunting hound dog," Nathan commented, but there was no criticism in his tone. Only an uncharacteristic nervousness.

He guided his horses into the covered driveway beside the huge brick Big Star warehouse. The scent of the river was lost; Chess opened her eyes.

Nathan was pale beneath his tan. They were there and soon he'd know the size of the jackpot he believed he would hit. Everything was riding on it. Only he knew how scant were the savings that he'd accumulated over years of hard work. The leaf behind him was lemon wrapper. He believed that. Josh had said so, and Josh should know. But the truth was, very few men had ever actually seen lemon wrapper. It was the ideal, the ultimate, the end-of-the-rainbow for a tobacco farmer.

He pulled the horses to a halt.

Warehousemen swarmed around the wagon to help him unload. "You want the baskets?" one shouted. "Ten cents' rent for the day."

"You bet I do," Nate bellowed. "This leaf's not going to touch the dirt on your floor. Wait till you see it, boys." He leapt from the seat and began to untie the canvas. His hands were trembling.

When they lifted the covering, the jabbering men fell silent. It was a tribute from men who spent their whole lives handling cured leaf.

Nate grinned. He put his hands in his pockets and lounged against the tail of the wagon, cock of the walk. He was no longer trembling. He watched the unloading with satisfaction greater than he'd ever known. The men were famous for their speed, but they were handling this load so carefully that their practiced motions were as slow as a baby's first steps. The hands were laid on the huge flat baskets in circles, stems pointing outward, layer upon layer. When it was done, all of them, Nate included, looked silently at the gleaming mounds in rapt admiration.

"You're Nate Richardson, ain't that right?" said a man with a sheaf of cardboard tags in his hand.

"That's me."

"This'll be your ticket for your wagon and team." The man scribbled on a numbered card, tore it in half, and gave Nate his receipt. He started to attach the other half to the wagon, then stopped, his hand in mid-air, when he saw Chess.

His hand leapt to his hat, removed it. " 'Evening, ma'am," he said.

"Good evening," she replied. "Will you tell Mr. Richardson that I'm ready to get down?"

Nate hastened to help her, although he had seen her alight by herself four times that day. He saw the glint of laughter in her eyes when he reached up for her, and he chuckled inwardly. Good for her. She knew exactly how to make these fellows toe the line.

"A couple with a load of lemon wrapper should be extended every courtesy," she murmured close to his ear.

The ticketer never knew why Nate Richardson "all of a sudden got that attack of belly-laughing."

The tobacco smell inside the warehouse almost overpowered Chess. The room was immense, with tall windows along two walls and huge skylights in the lofty ceiling. Sunlight poured through them onto closely spaced long rows of piled leaf, most of it unprotected by baskets.

"Less than half left," said Nate.

"I didn't know there was this much tobacco in the whole world," Chess whispered. She felt very ignorant.

"Stand over here by the back wall," Nate told her. "I'll go take care of the weighing and tagging, then walk around a little to check the action, then I'll be back." He strutted away.

Chess stared at the scene before her. There were lots of men around, but she saw no women at all. In the center of the room, a group of men were moving along a row of tobacco piles. One of them was singing a strange song she could not understand.

Nathan came back. "Cutter's selling at twelve and a half," he told her. "Last year it was fourteen." He looked worried. When he walked away he was no longer strutting.

Chess did arithmetic in her head. Say, ten cents a pound to make it easier, times the four hundred-and-some pounds in the wagon, that would be over forty dollars. It was a lot of money. You could furnish a whole house with that, right down to the best cookstove around. Or be dressed like a queen. Her good skirt and shirtwaist were the most extravagant purchase she'd made in her life, and together they had cost under a dollar. She'd be delirious with joy if any one of the crops at Harefields brought ten cents a pound, much less fourteen. No wonder people grew tobacco. That strange barn at the farm was packed with leaf. She was married to a rich man, and she'd never known it. How very pleasant.

"What are you smiling about?" Nathan was back. He was edgy and truculent.

His attention was caught by the entrance of his baskets, and Chess had no need to answer. She watched as Nathan's leaf was set down, then five piles of unbasketed leaf next to his. The comparison was shocking; the lemon wrapper seemed to draw all the color out of the other leaf. It looked dull brown.

"How about that," Nate said to himself. His eyes gleamed, and his face was lit by a wide grin he couldn't control. "How about that!"

During the next hour, Nate's baskets attracted an ever-increasing crowd. Whiskered farmers in faded overalls squatted or bent to feel the leaves, even sniff them. They moved aside for a man wearing a dark business suit and polished boots. He stood up when a second well-dressed man arrived, then a third. All of them, farmers and businessmen, wanted to talk to Nate. Chess watched from her discreetly shadowed viewpoint. Nathan looked so happy. And so handsome, she thought, even though she knew that in fact he was not. But he was so much neater than any of the others, even the businessmen. His Levi's were pale from long wearing, but they did not bag. And his blue shirt was buttoned all the way to the neck, not gaping open with undershirt showing like so many of the farmers. It made his eyes look bluer than ever. Most of all, he looked so clean. His shaved face and short sideburns were in dramatic contrast to the men around him. Chess fancied she could almost smell the soap he'd used at the pond outside of town. Her heart felt heavy with love for him, yet light, too, with the joy of it.

In the course of time she came close to understanding the auctioneer's rapid chanting. He was moving quickly along the long rows, coming nearer to Nathan's leaf. He sang, rather than spoke; the gibberish gradually sorted itself out, and she could hear that he was singing numbers. ". . . ah, a ten, and a ten and a quarter, *and* a half, I've got the half, now eleven, who'll give me the half, that's it eleven half, now twelve, last chance, twelve and a half, no, then *sold*, Blackwell's. Now what have we here? Ed Whitbread's cutter, two hundred sixty-three pounds, and do I tear ten, a ten and a half, and eleven, and a half . . ."

There was something breathtakingly exciting about the rise and fall of his voice and the punctuating explosion of "*sold!*"

From time to time he stopped chanting and spoke to the row of bidders facing him. "Now, gentlemen, we've got Charlie Henderson's leaf here. You all know Charlie, and you'll remember he's had his troubles lately, with his house burning to the ground and his youngest trapped in it. An extra half cent'll go a long ways toward getting a new roof for the Henderson family, and God'll bless you for it. Now we'll start at eleven . . . ah, eleven, 'leven, now 'leven and a half, and twelve . . ."

Another time, he reminded them that someone's tobacco was known for its quality, year after year, and no need to look at the leaf in the middle of the pile, even. Yet another pause was for a mention that Joe Wilson was still laid up with two broken legs and his sons had picked every leaf of his crop, 'though the oldest hadn't yet got any more whiskers than a peach.

Chess wished he'd stop being a newspaper and get on with his chanting. She wished people would stop fingering Nathan's leaf, too. By the time it was auctioned, it would be worn through.

Oh, get on with it, she begged silently. I'm afraid I'm going to jump out of my skin.

Chapter Eight

THE AUCTIONEER WAS ONLY three bundles away from Nathan's basket. Chess had clasped her hands together so tightly for so long that her gloves were slippery with sweat.

She could no longer see Nathan. He was somewhere in the silent crowd that had been growing steadily as the auction progressed. There were over 100 men now, all waiting for the sale of the lemon wrapper. Word had spread throughout Danville that something remarkable might just be about to happen.

"... *sold* ..."

"... *sold* ..."

"... *sold* ..."

It was time. Chess held her breath.

"Now, folks, this is the moment we've all been waiting for...."

Oh, *no*. No talking. Just sing your song and sell it. I can't bear this.

"... This here is maybe the finest leaf you'll ever see in

your lifetime. It's surely the finest I've seen in many and many a year. Nate Richardson's the grower. A lot of you know Nate, and those that didn't already know him will dang well know him from now on. One thing, though, I'll bet almost nobody knows is that Nate's gone and taken himself a bride. Now, gentlemen, when you're bidding, I want you to remember your own brides and what a constant and abiding joy they are in your lives. And what an expense. Let's have top dollar for Nate!"

Through the roar of laughter from the crowd Chess heard the song begin. ". . . Ah fourteen, and a half, and fifteen, and a half, and . . ."

When it was over, the cheering knocked starlings off their roosts in the high rafters. Squawks and flapping wings added to the din.

The lemon wrapper had *sold* for a record-breaking forty cents a pound.

Chess leaned against the wall, limp. Nathan shook hands, accepted congratulations, reeled from friendly slaps on the back.

The auction stopped altogether for nearly a half hour. Samuel Allen, the owner of the warehouse, had to call all his clerks from the office to help him disperse the crowd and get back to business.

He was perspiring heavily when he came over with Nathan, to be presented to her. He had his hat in his hand.

When he heard Chess' distinctive Tidewater accent, he bowed from the waist. His father, he said, had had the honor to serve in the Confederate Army under the command of the gentleman from Boxwood Plantation.

"Of course. You mean Mr. Archibald McIntosh," Chess said graciously. "When next I write to my people, I'll ask them to convey your regards."

Mr. Allen said that he hoped Mr. and Mrs. Richardson would allow him the privilege of providing them with a suite of rooms at the Planters' Hotel while they were in Danville. He would be most grateful and happy.

Nathan shook hands on it.

Allen grabbed up the small valises at Chess' feet. He insisted on carrying them himself across the floor to the office. There he consigned them to a clerk for delivery to the hotel. Then, with a flourish, he presented Nathan with the check that represented his proceeds. "Never forget, Mr. Richardson, that the Big Star Warehouse has the shortest waiting time in all Danville."

Nate assured Allen he'd remember.

"Mrs. Richardson, your servant, ma'am."

Chess offered her hand, for a handshake. She felt very friendly toward the man who had twice called her "Mrs. Richardson." It was the first time she'd been addressed that way, and she loved the sound of it.

Allen stammered his thanks.

As Nate and Chess walked along Main Street, they were stopped again and again by men who wanted to congratulate Nathan. She had only a moment to ask him about her cologne.

Sure thing, he told her, he was a rich man. She could have a quart of the stuff if that's what she wanted. But first let him get the check to the bank. He was afraid the ink might run and change the numbers. One hundred and sixty-two dollars and five cents. He'd never seen a number like that in his whole life. Not all at once.

The hotel manager himself escorted them to their rooms. Three of them. A sitting room with the latest thing in elaborately carved furniture; a bedroom with a China silk coverlet on the heavy mahogany-framed bed; a private marble-tiled bathroom with a geyser over a mahogany-encased tub, for hot water. He demonstrated its use and showed them the mechanism for the gaslit wall lamps.

When he finally left, Nate stood in the center of the sitting room with his arms outstretched.

"Them that has, gets," he said. He looked at Chess; she looked at him; they broke out laughing simultaneously.

It was the first chance they'd had to talk since the auction, and they chattered like magpies, comparing their reactions, reminding each other of what this person had said, that one had done, how another had looked.

Do you remember . . . did you see . . . how about when . . . I thought I'd keel over . . . I felt like screaming my head off . . . can you believe it? They relived every moment, every up and down, all the worry and all the thrills. Many times.

When they had talked themselves hoarse they went downstairs to the dining room for supper. They'd barely finished the soup when a nattily dressed young man approached their table and identified himself as a reporter for the Richmond *Dispatch*. He wanted Nathan's account of raising the tobacco that everyone was talking about.

"You're famous," Chess teased when they were back in their rooms.

"That puppy never saw a farm in his life. Did you see his feet? Spats! He'll get everything I told him all wrong."

But she could tell that he was very pleased to be famous. She was pleased, too. The reporter had promised to send a newspaper to Harefields. Her grandfather would be very, very happy.

Not as happy as she was. No other person in the world could ever be as happy as she was. This day, this night, was better than the best dream she'd ever had. Forever after she would think of this as her real wedding night. This was how it should be. Magic. The luxurious setting, the intoxicating excitement, the glory of sharing the most dramatic moment in Nathan's life.

Mrs. Richardson. She was Mrs. Nathaniel Richardson.

It was late when they went to bed. The big bathtub and the running hot and cold water provided a new, enthralling experience for them both. Nate was even more taken by it than Chess. He spent more than half an hour in the bathroom. She could hear the sound every time he added more hot water. When he emerged, wrapped in one of the big towels provided, his skin was vivid pink. "One day I'll have an outfit like that," he vowed. "It's better than a telephone and electric light put together."

Once in the deep warm water, Chess understood. She had perfumed her bath recklessly, and the billowing steam rising from it was sweet in her nostrils. She could have stayed there forever. But Nathan—her husband—was waiting for her. And this was her chosen wedding night.

She loosed her hair from its bun, lavished cologne on her hairbrush and pulled it through her long straight hair fifty times, ten times as many as usual. It felt soft under her hand. The silken nightdress felt soft against her skin. She opened the door and walked, barefoot and shy, to the bed.

"That stuff sure smells good," said Nathan. He was sitting in a chair near the window.

"It's nice when a lady has a rich husband," Chess murmured. She got into the bed.

"You know what's the best part, Chess?"

"No, what?"

"That was Dibrell who bought my leaf. He's the Danville man for Liggett & Myers. The fellow that hung in the longest, pushing him up, was Dick Reynolds' boy. I've sold to him before. But Mr. Dibrell, he's a lot choosier, 'cause Liggett and Myers is the biggest and the best. They're in every store in every town in every mile of this whole country. My wrapper might end up all the way out in California. How about that?"

How about me? She didn't say it aloud.

Nate got up and began to turn out the lights. The mechanism fascinated him.

"Come to bed, Nathan," Chess said. Then, quickly, "It's late."

When he climbed in, he pushed up her silken gown and lay his body on top of hers. She put her arms around his neck. His back was warm to her hands.

"That's right, honey, just hold on. This won't take long."

She opened her legs to welcome him.

Then he was in her body, close, so close. They were together, each one part of the other. She felt an urge to wrap her legs around his waist, to pull him deeper into her, to move her body with his, merging herself completely with him.

But it was over and Nate rolled away. Hug me, she wanted to cry. I loved it when you hugged me this morning. Kiss me. I want you to kiss me. Love me. I love you.

She folded her arms across her breasts and hugged herself. What she had was so much—being with him, being Mrs. Richardson—she should be satisfied with that. She *would* be satisfied. Asking for more would only drive him away. He'd lose all respect for her if he knew what she was thinking, what she was wanting. She disgusted herself.

Eventually Chess fell asleep.

Chapter Nine

DOING THE SHOPPING WAS FUN. They added candy to Alva's packages, and to Miss Mary's. "You don't have to be a child to have a sweet tooth," Nate said. He licked his lips.

When the grocer weighed the wheat flour he bragged that it was far and away the freshest and best there was. He went himself to the gristmill every week to fill his barrels. Nate and Chess looked at each other with unspoken secret significance.

Nate was still a celebrity. Everyone wanted to shake his hand, to ask him questions, to tell him stories of their own farming successes. It slowed down the shopping. So did the shopkeepers' efforts to sell them the most expensive items in the store. Some merchants even ran out of their shops and tried to entice them in.

"It'll be dark by the time we reach home," said Nate when finally they were on the road.

"It doesn't matter."

"No, it doesn't. That was some day."

"That was some leaf."

"Wasn't it, though?" And they began again to re-create the auction.

"I can hardly wait for the next one," said Chess. "I know it'll be a far cry from the lemon wrapper, but all the same it's very exciting. And your leaf will still be better than anyone else's. Maybe Mr. Allen will even treat us to the hotel again. Probably not a suite, but the regular rooms must be nice, too."

"Huh, don't fool yourself about that." Nate punctured her daydream quickly. Allen's warehouse took a four percent commission from the seller. He could have paid for the suite with half what Nate was paying him. But since Allen owned the hotel, too, it didn't even cost him that.

Then Nate went on to deflate all her happy expectations. They wouldn't be going back to Danville at all. "We don't sell the rest of the leaf. Why let Blackwell's or Duke or somebody like that get all the profit from manufacturing? We do it ourselves."

He described the process. After Josh and Micah cured the leaf to greater dryness, the women set things up on the tables in the factory room. On the first one Susan cut out the dried stem of the leaf and beat the leaf with a flail to break it up. On the second Alva ground the fragments into small particles with a big mortar and pestle. His mother was at the third table, forcing the tobacco through a wire sieve until it was "granulated."

In the evening they all sewed small drawstring bags and filled them with the processed tobacco.

"You mean *all* the women?"

"Of course. Josh and Micah have got to watch the curing temperatures. And they're plowing, too. The field's got to be turned and manured before it gets cold. The frosts work the soil over the winter."

Chess noticed that her hands had made themselves into fists. She could picture it already: she'd be all thumbs in the factory and Miss Mary would comment on it a hundred times a day. Nathan didn't have to tell her; she knew the others must have been doing this for years and years and were expert at it.

But Nathan did tell her. "The processing is a real push," he said. "There's over five thousand pounds of leaf, and I need a couple thousand bags every week to take out selling on the road. I cover four full counties until the roads get too bad to move on."

"You're gone all the time?" It was worse than she'd imagined.

"That's my job. That's where the money is. You can figure it for yourself. There's not much lemon wrapper in this world, and the rest brings fourteen cents a pound if you're lucky. So you process a pound, and then you divide up that pound into eight little bitty two-ounce sacks, and then you sell them for three cents apiece for the store to sell at five cents. That's business."

He had noticed the tight fists. "You don't need to worry none, Chess. You'll be busy enough. Alva's baby is turning into a real handful."

Nathan's voice was friendly, but his tolerant condescension was more than she could bear, after so many hopes had been ruined. She could not demand or expect his love, but she had a right to be respected. She beat one fist on her knee.

"You just listen to me for a minute, Nathan. I'm sick and tired of everybody looking down their noses at me because I didn't spend my life learning how to do things on a forty-acre tobacco farm.

"I'm not some kind of useless, helpless plantation flower. You were at Harefields once, for one dinner and a wedding, and you think you know all about it and all about me. You never bothered to wonder, did you, much less ask, what either one was really like. Well, I'm going to tell you, and I'll thank you to pay attention.

"I ran that place, all ten thousand acres and thirty-eight families of farmers, and I did a mighty good job, too. You want to know how I did it? With these two hands." Her white-gloved fingers waved in his startled face.

"Who do you think cooked that dinner you ate? I did. I cooked every scrap of food in that house. I got up before daylight to get the kitchen stove going right. Then I started breakfast and while it was cooking I cleaned the downstairs rooms. My mother's breakfast had to be put on a tray, my grandfather's in the dining room. Mine, too, because Augustus Standish always wanted sparkling conversation with his meals. That was only the beginning, because the servants had to eat, too. Oh, yes, we had servants. Two of them. One is my mother's personal maid. You saw Marcus, the other one. He's been grandfather's body servant since he was a boy. Marcus is broad-minded; he even takes on the butler's role and serves dinner at night. But he stands on his dignity any other time. He takes care of grandfather's clothes and grandfather's room. But I had to cook Marcus' meals. Diana's, too. That's Mother's maid. Diana was much too grand to eat with Marcus in the kitchen, though. No, I had to fix her a tray, three times a day.

"And it was up to me to fetch the trays. And the slop jars. And to come up with the money to pay their salaries every week of the year and to buy their clothes.

"I've got no quarrel with Marcus and Diana. Mother and Grandfather couldn't manage without servants, and I couldn't keep up the playacting without them. You saw my mother. She changes her clothes four times a day, with her hair done fresh every time. Inside her head it's still before the War. My father and brothers will be coming home tomorrow or the next day. She even manages not to notice that I'm a grown woman and not a girl. Only old, loving servants would go along with that, no matter how big the salary was. My quarrel's not with them, it's with you and your whole holier-than-thou and harder-working-than-thou family."

Nate pulled the wagon over to the side of the road. "Tell me the rest, then. Did you work in the fields, too?"

Chess shook her head. She couldn't speak for a minute, she was too emotional. No longer angry. Nathan wanted to listen; what a blessing. There'd never been anyone she could talk to, telling the truth about how her life really was. She had to play a game, even with her grandfather, and always with outsiders. The surface wasn't to be disturbed; everything was fine, everyone was happy.

She cleared her throat, eager to talk. "I didn't do farming, I did managing and planning. I visited every farm every day and heard people's troubles. I bought seed and distributed it, the same with fertilizer. Mules and plows and harrows and wagons were kept and kept up by me, and lent to the farms on a schedule I made. I watched the growing crops, nagged people into weeding or top-dressing or thinning or whatever they were being lazy about. Of course I fed and doctored the mules and mucked out the stables. When the crops came in I did the haggling and selling. Then I figured the shares due each of them and gave them their money. I did the bookkeeping every day because there were expenses they owed and deductions for the food and such they gave me.

"Three days a week I held school for the children. If there was a wedding, I lent the lace veil and provided the refreshments for the party."

Nate was flabbergasted. He'd seen the veil, after all. It looked like something for a princess. "They didn't need to wear your Momma's lace."

"My great-grandmother's, really." All of a sudden Chess laughed. "Don't be too shocked, Nathan, but, you see, I always felt like the Harefields people were all one family, including all of us at the big house. You never knew for sure in the old days. My father and my grandfather were likely responsible for a lot of the babies born in the slave quarters. Now they're grown up, and some of them might be tenant farmers at Harefields today."

Nate stared, slack-jawed. A lady shouldn't know anything about such things. And if, by accident, she did, she certainly shouldn't talk about them!

"Oh, stop catching flies, Nathan. Close your mouth. A child is the nosiest creature on earth. I overheard a lot of things I wasn't supposed to. There were twenty servants in the house when I was little, and they talked among themselves all the time."

His expression was a sight! Chess was glad she had shocked him. It certainly got his attention. She felt much better now that she had let her temper loose for a while. Since she didn't dare tell him she loved him, it helped a lot to holler when she was mad at him.

Then she remembered Miss Mary, who was mad all the time and let people know it. Nathan had a witch for a mother, he shouldn't have one for a wife, too.

"I'm sorry for yelling at you like that, Nathan. There was no excuse for it. I'm truly sorry."

He smiled at her. "Excuse is, I needed educating. Do you want to know what I learned? I learned that you know how to do the things I don't, like bookkeeping and managing workers. When we get the cigarette business going, we'll be the perfect partnership. The day I met you is turning out to be the luckiest day in my life."

Chess smiled her thanks. The words weren't the only thing; there was genuine admiration in Nathan's eyes. Respect, too, and she needed his respect, perhaps even more than his love.

Nate started the wagon moving again. As they drove he told her more about life on a tobacco farm in the autumn months. "About two weeks from now we go to Pleasant Grove for harvest festival. I think you'll have a good time. It's not Danville, mind you, but it's a nice little town. We get our mail there and do our blacksmithing and doctoring and such. Then, in October there's the State Fair in Raleigh. I sure would like to see that electric light. Might have to miss it, though, it all depends. While I'm on the road selling, I'll be looking for the right spot to build the mill on. Keep that under your hat, remember. I don't figure to tell the others until time comes to move.

"I'll make sure to get back to the farm the first week in November. November is hog-butchering time at our nearest neighbor's. Ol' Livvy Alderbrook keeps pigs, sells the little ones for money. Everybody goes to her butchering. There's

a pit for roasting, with her secret sauce painted on the meat,
and fiddlers, and a generous dose of homemade brew. There's
no party can touch it for a good time."

It sounded wonderful to Chess, all of it. There'd been no
social life at all at Harefields. With so much to look forward
to, she almost didn't mind going back to the farm and Miss
Mary. Almost. After all, she and Nathan would be leaving
one day soon. All he had to do was find the right place. He
had made enough money at the auction to buy land and put
up the mill. Add all the profits from the little sacks of tobacco
and he'd have plenty to build the cigarette machine and start
the business. They were really on their way.

She'd forgotten the rest of his family. When they got to
the farm everyone gathered at Miss Mary's to unload the
provisions from the wagon and share out the money from the
lemon wrapper.

It was only fair, Chess told herself. Josh really should get
half. He was the one who knew the secrets of curing.

Even when Nathan divided his half in half, to share with
his mother, Chess managed to see the justification. He did
live in her house and she did work in the factory and she
was, after all, his mother.

"That's fine, Nate," said Mary Richardson. "When we go
to the festival I'll buy a money order at the post office and
mail this to Gideon. He's got a new baby on the way, plus
his missionary work, too."

That was not fair. Gideon didn't work on the tobacco. And
Nathan looked as if the old woman had kicked him in the
ribs.

Chess had gotten a tablet and some envelopes in Danville.
She had a letter all ready to mail to her grandfather when she
climbed into the wagon for the ride to the harvest festival.
The letter was full of lies about Nathan's fine big farm, tree-
shaded lovely house and warm, welcoming family. Caesar
liked her to be cheerful.

Miss Mary was genuinely cheerful. At least as much as she ever could be. She had money to send to her favored son; and there might be a circuit rider there, with a real church service and hymn singing. There'd been one the year before.

Josh was almost agreeable, something Chess had believed was impossible. She thought that there might even be a small smile hiding in his thick, long Old Testament beard.

Micah and Susan were practically feverish with excitement. He bragged that he was going to beat all the other boys at wrestling; he'd grown three inches and a lot of muscle since last year. Susan rattled off a dozen names of other girls who'd be there, plus all the sights there'd be to see. They'd even had a monkey in a little red hat one year. And the parade was the "best thing in the whole world."

Alva and Nathan agreed with her. Pleasant Grove had a marching band, with all the trimmings, bright red uniforms and big bass drums and a leader who could turn cartwheels the whole length of the town.

They were almost there when the sign appeared. "Look at that," Nate exclaimed. A huge black bull was painted on the side of a big barn. Lettering beneath it read GENUINE SMOKING TOBACCO. ASK FOR THE BULL. NORTH CAROLINA'S OWN AND BEST.

"That's Blackwell's," he said. "All the way back here in the middle of nowhere. It's a regular plague. Seems like every single building on the main roads has got the Bull painted on it. Even some of the stores I sell to. Seems like the Bull's determined to get all the business. They've already got most of it." His face had lost its holiday look. But when they rounded the next curve, he began to laugh. The barn ahead had a different sign. PRO BONO PUBLICO, it said. THE BEST AND THAT'S NO BULL. Nate grinned. "Old Wash Duke's starting to give Blackwell a run for the money, looks like. What do you bet Buck's behind this?"

"Don't say things like 'bet,' Nate," his mother interjected. "Gambling's a sin."

Nate made a wry face and winked at Chess. She concealed her smile. She was sure now that it would be a good day.

It was a perfect day, Chess thought drowsily. There was all the excitement the others had promised, and that was grand. And there was a letter for her from her grandfather. But the best part was the people. They all knew who she was, naturally. News travels fast and far in the countryside. There was some staring at her gloves and pearls, but it was curious, not hostile. Everyone—farmers and townspeople alike—was friendly and welcoming to the newcomer from Virginia. Her head was stuffed with the names of her new friends.

First and foremost was the neighbor Nathan called "Ol' Livvy." Almost everyone referred to Lavinia Alderbrook that way, but not to her face. She never thought about how old she was, she told Chess, so why should she let anyone else remind her?

She looked as old as the hills, with face and hands as brown and wrinkled as dried apples. But her tall spare body was supple and straight, and her bright smile was all her "own, not storebought." She speculated that her strong teeth were a result of a good glug of home brew in her boiled coffee in the morning. She called it her "sweetener." "Or maybe, like some say, it's because I never married and had babies. I never needed none; I brought more than six score into the world with somebody else doing the labor." Ol' Livvy was a renowned midwife.

She took Chess under her wing the instant they met. "I'm glad Nate's got you," she said after an unabashed scrutiny. "I've always liked that boy, and he's been needing a strong woman that'll love him like he deserves. No young girl's going to have what it takes to make him a wife; she'd never have the sand to stand up to Mary Richardson. When that sour face of hers gets past bearing, come visit me, Chess. I'm just up the path after you cross the creek; you'll find it. It's a pretty little walk through the woods, hardly more than a mile."

Ol' Livvy was contemptuous of age, she approved of Chess, and she disliked Nathan's mother. It was only natural that Chess liked her better than all the rest.

I'll walk up and see her very soon, she promised herself. As soon as the rain stops. The festival's only flaw appeared at sundown, when the welcome clouds that had covered the sun all day suddenly opened and washed out the scheduled fireworks finale. It was a steady, chill rain, not a thunderstorm. Summer was definitely over.

And high time, too, most people thought. The heat had held on for too long.

They didn't know that the cold rain was the beginning of the worst winter in the memory of any living soul.

The following day Nate finished his breakfast and went over to the factory with his mother. He came back alone, carrying a pair of old saddlebags. "There's enough done to make up a load. I'll head out today to start selling. Make me up a packet of those good biscuits, will you, Chess? I'll get my razor and socks and such."

She had known he'd be leaving, but now that the moment had come, she wasn't ready for it. She mixed a batch of dough, rolled it out, and cut the biscuits. They were in the oven when Nate returned from the bedroom. The saddlebags hung over his shoulder. In his hand was a pistol. The smell of gun oil was sharp and greasy around him.

"What are you taking that for? I didn't even know you had one."

"I keep it locked up in a box so the little ones can't get to it. The only time I need it is when I'm selling. People know a drummer's got cash money on him."

Chess had an instant picture of ambush on a deserted back road. She said only, "Of course." Nathan had been making these trips for years; she had to believe he knew what he was doing.

"I hope you've got a whole panful cooking," he said. "Your biscuits are the best I ever ate. So's everything else. Things have really improved around here since you took over the cooking."

"Don't say that in front of your mother. She didn't want to let me, but with her working in the factory, she had to. She's not happy about it."

"Well, I sure am."

Chess opened the oven and slid the tray of biscuits out onto the door. She couldn't look at Nathan; she was afraid she might break down and beg him to be careful. A stupid thing to do. "There's other ways of cooking things beside boiling them to death with a slab of fatback for flavor," she said instead.

Nate laughed. He'd be back in a week or ten days if he could, he told her. If the storekeepers were reluctant to buy it could take a little longer. His voice dropped as he came close to her. "Or if I find the place for the mill. I've got my earnest money in the saddlebags if I get lucky."

Chess hurried to get the biscuits wrapped up. Now she was eager for him to leave.

Before many days had passed she was wishing with all her heart that she had gone with him, on foot if need be. She had never before known what it was to be truly lonely. Yes, Harefields was isolated, but nothing like this little farm in the middle of nowhere, North Carolina.

At Harefields she'd had her grandfather; and the tenant farmers were, at least, people to talk with and to care about. She had been important there, too, with important work to do.

On the Richardson farm, she was nobody. Worse than nobody, she was a disliked or despised outsider. With nothing useful to do.

Chess read and reread her books. She prepared increasingly complicated meals. She taught herself to milk the cow and wring a chicken's neck. She cried into her pillow, refusing to give Mary Richardson the satisfaction of knowing how miserable she was.

Chapter Ten

THE HORSE'S HOOVES SLIPPED on the film of ice that covered the road. Its front feet plunged into a hole, the icy water in it spattered up onto Nate's legs. His boots were sodden and no protection at all.

He scarcely noticed. The rest of him was equally wet and cold. Icy rain fell from the sky, from the needles of evergreens, from the rim of his pulpy felt hat. If he didn't get warmed up somehow, he was going to get frostbite. He had to stop.

There was a deserted shell of a house not far away, he knew. Everyone knew the Mullins place, it was haunted, they said. The whole family—ten of them—had disappeared. No one knew how, or why, or exactly when, except that it was a long time ago, when even his Daddy's daddy was little. They said that the food was still on the table and the quilts on the beds and the rifle on its pegs over the fireplace. But when a neighbor stopped in, there was no living creature in sight save for the mice gnawing at the stone-hard crusts of bread. Afterwards there was talk of moving lights in the windows, and strange sounds. Nobody went there ever, and the woods had reclaimed the land.

Nate shivered from the cold. And perhaps fear of ghosts. But he'd die for sure if he didn't find cover. He dismounted and led his horse through the thicket that surrounded the house. He was hungry and miserably cold and apprehensive. "Spooked" he would have said if he'd been his usual self, and he would have laughed it off. But he wasn't his usual self, he was profoundly depressed.

He had never felt this way before, not even when his Daddy just said good-bye and left. He'd been confident that he could take over and be the man of the family. He believed that he could do whatever he had to do, and make a good job of it, too. He'd always believed that, and he'd always been right.

When had he stopped believing? Why?

Nate could see what remained of the Mullins house. The roof had fallen in at one end, but the other looked safe, and it had most of its chimney left. He patted the horse's neck. "Come on, Natchez." There'd be room enough for both man and horse if he was lucky. Natchez's warmth would be welcome.

He was even luckier than he'd dared hope. Beneath the toppled roof there was dry wood. Shortly there was a big fire on the hearth, with his wet things drying in front of it. Nate took a loaf of bread from his saddlebag and a tin cup, which he filled with rainwater. He had already given Natchez oats from the same saddlebag. Steam was rising in the air above the horse's back, eddying gently in the weak air current stirred up by the fire's heat.

Nate stretched out on the floor after he ate. He propped his head on his saddle and stared into the changing colors of the life-saving flames.

Contemplation was a stranger to him. He had always been too busy to stop and think about what he was doing or what it might mean. And he did not have the vanity necessary for him to enjoy thinking about himself.

But now he could not sleep. He had to keep the fire going

to save his life. If he fell asleep, he might sleep forever. There was no way to pass the time and stay awake unless he kept his mind active.

Maybe he could think how to break out of the heavy hopelessness that bedeviled him. It frightened him much more than any chance of ghosts in the broken house.

But he couldn't locate where or when it had come over him, and thinking about it only made it worse.

He thought about his plan instead. It was the center of his world, and had been for a long time. Then, it's not going to work he thought, and plunged deeper into what he had named "the miseries."

The patent. He had the patent for the cigarette-making machine. It made him the luckiest man in all God's kingdom, didn't it? He'd think about that, and it would lift him out of the miseries.

The patent led him inevitably to Chess . . . a wife, when he wasn't ready to be married. A wife who was older than he, who looked even older than she was, who was a thorn in his mother's flesh, in his own. She was too fancy, with her gloves, and her nose in the air, and her Virginia way of talking. She was a burden that weighed him down.

She had no heart. He had agreed to give her children, and he did his duty, but there was no pleasure in it for either of them. Fine for her—she was a lady and everyone knew that ladies only put up with it. But he had always enjoyed sex. No, more than enjoyed. He loved it, the giving and taking of the bodies' sensations and pleasures. He truly liked women, with their different way of thinking and talking and looking at things. They made him happy, and he made them happy. He'd had a happy life, all in all.

Until he married. Why couldn't a regular country girl have owned the patent? Or, if it had to be a lady, why not a real young one? Then maybe he would have taken a chance at teaching her a few things. He wouldn't dare to suggest anything as unrefined as playful sex to Chess.

But a deal was a deal, and a man didn't go back on a deal.

Even Daddy. He'd stuck it out with Ma till Nate was old enough to take over before he walked away. Stuck on the farm, all those years, with no life but tobacco.

Nate hated it. The sick-sweet smell of it. The sticky tar that the plants put on your skin and in your hair and on your clothes. The never-ending work of planting and growing and harvesting and selling. Always at the mercy of weather and blight and worms.

The only way to break out was to manufacture. Others had done it. But it looked like he was too late. The stores would only take his little bags if he cut the price by a penny. "No demand for them," they said, not unless he advertised like The Bull. The same would likely hold for cigarettes too, and he'd never have the money for that.

How could he ever hope to beat the giants, like Blackwell's, or Allen and Ginter? "Uncle Lewis." How did he ever get mixed up with a woman who called the biggest tobacco man in Virginia "Uncle"? He wasn't in that league, never would be, not even if his plan worked perfectly. If that was what Chess expected, she was going to get a mighty big letdown.

What did she expect, anyhow? Partners—she said she wanted them to be partners. Partners in what? He'd never even find the land he needed to start the mill he'd promised her, much less succeed.

Round and round his thoughts went, pulling him deeper and deeper into a vortex of angry hopelessness. He fed the fire when it burned low, even though the thought of sleep without waking was a dangerous temptation at times.

When the cracks in the walls showed gray instead of black, he gathered up his warm dry clothes. But he couldn't dress without washing, and he went outside wearing only his boots, to find some ice to melt for water. The cold took his breath away. But at least the rain had stopped, and the wind that accompanied it.

He heard water somewhere. Moving water. He wouldn't have to melt ice after all. Nate slid and skittered over the ice-coated ground to a fast-running black-watered creek behind the house. It was so cold it burned his skin, but he splashed it all over his face and body. He'd rather burn than be dirty. Without washing, he still could feel the tobacco tar that had stuck to him all his life.

The fire roared up the chimney when he threw the last of the wood on it. Its warmth was good. So was the warm wool of his union suit. And the rest of his clothes.

But the best warmth, the life-renewing fire of determination and hope, had come from the aching-cold black water of the creek. Nate had been searching for weeks, searching for exactly what he had found by chance just when he was about to admit failure. The derelict property that no one wanted, the racing water that would not freeze.

"Thank you, Lord," he said, in simple, heartfelt prayer.

The miseries had vanished. He could see his way clear now. He was ready for the first step in his plan. After that— he'd do whatever he had to do.

He could hardly wait to tell Chess. She was the only one he could tell. She believed in his plans. She was his partner.

Chapter Eleven

"STOP WIGGLING, or we won't go at all," Chess said sternly to Sally. At least she believed she was being severe. The two-year-old was not impressed, but she became still. She wanted to go to Livvy Alderbrook's and play with the piglets. There were ten of them, just like her fingers. Chess had taught her. Sally allowed Chess to wrap her shawl close around them both.

Chess went to visit Ol' Livvy every time weather permitted, which wasn't often, maybe twice a week if she was lucky. It was an easy walk; the footpath was protected by trees from the full onslaught of the rain, and no deep puddles or thick mud formed.

Livvy was always glad to see them. She was a welcoming woman and her one-room cabin was a welcoming place. It was warmed by the iron cookstove and by the bright colors in the hooked rugs on the floor and "drunkard's path" patchwork quilt on the bed. And by Livvy's presence. Chess felt better the minute her foot crossed the threshold.

Two tiny black-and-white piglets were sleeping in a basket near the stove. Sally marched directly to it. "How did you know we were coming?" asked Chess.

"The rain let up more than an hour ago," said the old woman, smiling her prideful smile. "Fix us some coffee." Her hands were busy with the new rug she was making.

Chess filled two cups from the pot on the stove, added cream and sugar, plus a glug of sweetener to Livvy's. The filled cups were warm in her cold hands. She felt much better.

"No news about Nate?"

"No news." Chess gave Livvy her special cup, seated herself, and began to sip from her own. There was no need to say more. Livvy already knew how desperately worried she was. Nate had been away for three weeks; he'd said it would be one. The old woman made no foolish reassuring remarks; nothing was going to make Chess feel better except the sight of Nathan, unharmed and back home.

"Maybe you should teach me how to do hooking," she said. "I don't have anything to do aside from some cooking, and it's driving me crazy. I used to be so busy at the plantation I didn't have time to think. I'm no good at twiddling my thumbs."

Sally came to Livvy's side, pulled at her sleeve. "What is it, darling? Do you want your milk now?"

"Pigs," said Sally. She had a piglet under each small arm. One began to squeal. She squatted and released them to run across the floor, then she stood and held out her small fat hands toward the interested old woman. The thumbs were folded against her palms. "More pigs," she demanded.

Ol' Livvy laughed. With her free hand she caught the little girl around the middle and hugged her. "Ain't you the smart one, missy? Well, you be glad for what you got. That big old sow would tear me to bits if I took all her babies away. When it's time for you to go home we'll take these two back to their brothers and sisters and you can have a look at the whole batch. All right?"

Sally nodded, satisfied, then set off at a run to capture the piglets.

"There you are, Chess. That's what you can do. Teach Alva's girls. Micah wouldn't stand for it, but I know Susan would take to reading and writing like a duck to water. She's a sweet-natured child, and smart as paint."

"But, Livvy, Susan's going on ten years old. Hasn't she had any schooling at all?"

"Not a lick. Josh don't hold with it."

Chess was aghast. How could anybody be against learning? She had assumed that the Richardson children would have gone to school for a few years at least. Granted, it took a long time to go and come to and fro to Pleasant Grove, but country children did it. She knew that for a fact. Nathan had told her about riding behind his brother, bareback on a plow horse. Livvy must be mistaken. As tactfully as possible she pointed it out to the old woman.

Livvy scowled. "That's just what set Josh's mind against it, the old fool. He saw what schooling done to his brother. It was Gideon drove his daddy from home. Gideon and his schooling."

Chess' pulse quickened. At last, all about Gideon. Nathan's brother was an intriguing mystery. Miss Mary talked about him constantly. According to her, Gideon was perfection itself. Nathan wouldn't talk about him at all. She had asked him to tell her about his brother, but he'd said there wasn't anything special to tell. Gideon was a preacher, he'd been away for over five years, that was all there was to say.

It was the way in which he had said "that's all there is to say" that made her believe there was a great deal more. She sat quietly, ready to listen. Livvy finished her spiked coffee and picked up a scrap of wool. She wrapped it around the big, hooked bone needle, then put her left hand in position beneath the stretched burlap on the frame. Chess waited.

"I was just figuring backwards to recollect what year it was," Ol' Livvy said. Her voice had taken on a distinctive, somewhat distant tone, almost singsong. It was her storytelling voice.

"Ezekiel, he and Mary wed in 1846, that's more than thirty years ago now. She was a pretty little thing, just turned fifteen and real perky. She was Mary Oakes, from over near Reidsville, visiting a cousin in Pleasant Grove. Zeke was a good catch. He had his farm, and his brother Josh to help him farm it. Their folks was dead, but they was already grown men, Zeke twenty-five or more and Josh five years younger. Josh, he'd been married three years already—one of those love matches helped along by a daddy with a shotgun. He and Ellie had one child and another one on the way.

"Pretty soon Mary was in the family way herself. She and Ellie used to sashay up the path to show me their bellies and ask me questions about birthing. Not that Ellie didn't already know, but she didn't want to answer Mary herself, afraid of scaring her. Ellie had a bad time with hers.

"The second one was easier, like usual. It came at Christmastime, a pretty girl baby with cornsilk hair. Then, in January, Mary had hers, a boy that come out of the womb yelling to beat the band. Zeke said he'd never heard so much noise outside a revival tent.

"But that's not why Mary named the little fellow John Wesley. She was a pious girl from a real practicing Christian home. There was a full-time church in Reidsville.

"The next year Charles Wesley came to join his brother. Ellie had another one, too, but the poor mite was stillborn. And that December she died, right before Christmas. She never really recovered her strength after having that baby.

"Mary took Ellie's two in with her two. She was a loving mother to all four of them. And to the new ones. There was a girl, Mary, then Gideon, then another girl, Lucinda.

"That house was popping its nails out, with seven little ones inside. Zeke figured to build on another room.

"But before he got started, it wasn't needed no more. The

diphtheria came. It was a fearsome thing. Gideon was the only one made it through."

Chess gasped. She knew how fragile a child's life was; there had been many lost on the tenant farms at Harefields. But never six from one house.

Livvy continued. "Mary turned to God for comfort. And to Gideon. That baby was in her arms all the time. A year later she gave birth to another boy. She named him John Wesley, just like the first one, but more meaningful-like. She said it was her way of thanking the church for pulling her through the tragedy.

"She was still young, remember, only twenty-one years. Strong, too. Tiny as she was, she could do a man's worth of work in the field alongside Zeke and Josh. The next four years gave her four more children and the house was bulging again. Six she had now. But the specialest one was always Gideon. He was God's gift to her, she said.

"He was eleven when the War started. Nate was five, the youngest. Naturally Josh and Zeke went off to fight. Mary got the crop in, with neighbors helping out. Then, just after New Year's, Nate came beating on my door, crying. The children was all sick, he told me, and their Ma was just sitting in the corner, rocking and praying. Nate was choking something terrible, so I knew it was the whooping cough. I picked him up and ran like the wind. My legs were a lot younger then." Ol'Livvy searched through her scrap bag for red pieces.

"How many died?" whispered Chess.

"Half. Gideon nearly died, too, but he recovered. Mary said it was a miracle. She hardly even noticed that her little Mary and her other son were still alive, too. Those poor children hardly had any mother at all till Josh married Alva when he got back from the War in summer' sixty-five. She gave them as much loving as they'd take from her—Alva was a sweet girl, just fifteen years old. If the war hadn't killed so many she could have done a lot better than Josh. He was wounded in the stomach, it's a wonder he didn't die. The pain of it never left him, though; there's been no pleasure in living for him since that minie ball. Alva grew old faster than nature intended.

"Still, she did have the children for a comfort. Mary's two and her own when they came.

"There was no comfort anywhere for Ezekiel Richardson. By the time he come home Mary had turned crazy religious. It was all Gideon; he was the only thing she cared about. I've always speculated that she made Gideon a little crazy, too, telling him all the time about how God chose him from all the others to save from the diphtheria and then the whooping cough. He was thirteen when he experienced the rapture. That's what the Methodist Church preaches. If you truly believe that Jesus Christ died for you and that he will wash away your sins and be your Savior, then Christ will enter your heart and you'll feel the rapture of being one with God.

"It's something to hope and strive for, but not many ever feel it. Gideon did. Or he believed he did. Or he said he believed he did. Mary sure and certain believed it. Nothing would do but to give that boy the schooling it took to become a real, ordained preacher. She nagged after Zeke every minute of every day to plant more seed and grow more tobacco to pay for Gideon's room and board and books and bills and fine clothes. He finally got ordained, all right. Then Zeke just walked out. He gave her the only thing she wanted, half killing himself to do it, and then he gave Nate the only thing he had left, his half of the farm, and off he went to seek a little bit of happiness before he died. I pray he found some."

"What happened to him?"

"Nobody knows. Little Mary did the same thing. She left home as soon as she found a man to marry her and take her far away.

"Mary's brand of religion poisoned the air in that house. It's a wonder Nate's the way he is. He's a good and generous man. I credit Alva for keeping him from harm. And I pity Mary. But she's a hard woman to love, no matter what the

Bible tells us to do. She gives religion a bad name. In her it's all 'don't' and 'shalt not.' I don't like her, and I can't think of anybody else I'd say that about."

Ol' Livvy glanced over her shoulder. "Now there's a pretty picture for you," she said. Her storytelling voice was gone. Chess' eyes followed the direction of hers. Sally and the piglets were all asleep in the basket.

"You'd better get that baby home now, Chess," Livvy prodded. "The light's starting to fade."

"I know. You're right. Just tell me one more thing. What's Gideon's wife like?"

"Lily's as pretty as an angel. I don't know what she's like inside. Her daddy's a famous soul-saver, so she should be a good wife for a preacher. I only saw her two times, at Camp Meetings. She sings like an angel, too." The old woman smiled wickedly at Chess. "It has come to my notice that she don't exactly rush over this way to visit Mary much, nor send Gideon neither. Maybe there's a woman inside the angel outside."

Chess kissed Livvy's brown, wrinkled cheek. "Thank you," she said. "You kept me from worrying about Nathan all afternoon."

"Come back any time at all."

Sally slept quietly the whole way back to the house. Chess was thankful. She had a lot to think about.

One certain thing was that she had been unfair in her judgments of Nathan's family. Their tragic lives made her own past troubles seem insignificant. She had to be more tolerant, and nicer. Especially to Miss Mary. But she'd never forgive her for the way she had treated Nathan. Nor for the way she treated him now.

The following day while Sally was having her nap Chess walked over to the factory, where Alva and Susan were working with Miss Mary. She had made molasses cookies; they were still warm and soft in the basket she carried. Miss Mary had a sweet tooth, she knew.

She phrased her suggestion delicately. Instead of their sewing in two separate houses at night, they could all eat the supper she prepared at Miss Mary's. Josh and Micah, too. Then after supper they would all be together, so they could sew right where they were, and fill the bags there, too. That way Alva and Susan wouldn't have to spend time cooking; they'd be able to make and fill more bags.

After a delicious venison stew—with compliments to Micah the successful hunter—the sewing at Mary's house was companionable and relaxed. Chess put Sally in her bed to sleep, then returned from her room with *Idylls of the King*.

"Why don't I read aloud instead of to myself?" she said casually. "A story will ease the tedium."

Miss Mary objected. "Heathen stories. I won't be a party to this."

Alva and Susan said they'd love to hear a story.

Miss Mary stuffed wads of muslin in her ears.

Within a week, she was engrossed in the saga of King Arthur's knights and their quest for the Holy Grail.

And Susan was staying for an hour after her mother took Sally home, so that she could learn how to read stories all by herself.

Chess was grateful for Ol' Livvy's advice. Teaching, plus reading aloud, took up several hours every day.

But there were many others, and she worried more desperately all the time. It was November, and bitter, bitter cold. Anyone out on the road could die of exposure when darkness came and temperatures fell below zero.

If a thief had not already killed him for his horse and saddlebags.

Chapter Twelve

"CHESS, WHERE'S MA?"

"Oh, Nate. Thank God you're safe, I've been so worried—"

"Where's Ma, Chess?"

She was furious. He'd been gone more than a month, she'd been half crazy with worry, and that was all he could say? "She's in the factory, where else should she be?"

"Good! I've got so much to tell you, I'm fit to bust. Build up the fire and put some coffee on. I'll get Natchez to the barn and fed, then I'll be right back."

Chess had to sit down. Her knees were weak. He was alive. So alive. More than ever before. She'd never seen him so excited, not even in Danville. And he wanted to tell her about it. How could she have felt so angry?

He wanted coffee. And a bigger fire. She jumped up. He must be starving. There was an egg; one of the hens had forgotten it was winter. And she'd slice some bread, big thick slices, the way he liked it. There was some ham left on the bone, too. By the time he'd eaten that she could have grits cooked. . . .

The grits boiled down in the pan and scorched, but it didn't matter. Nate's hunger to talk was much greater than his hunger for food.

". . . After the seventh time I looked at a place and found out it wouldn't do, or the price was too high, I was about ready to give up, and I headed home. I was really discouraged. Then the rain came again and the wind and ice. I was going to freeze if I didn't find some kind of shelter. The only thing for miles around was this haunted house—hey, Chess, you don't believe in ghosts, do you? 'Course you don't, not with all your education. Well, it was that or nothing, so . . ."

She wanted to throw her arms around him, hold him, know by the feel of him that he was really back, and happy to be with her. But she urged him to talk. That was what he wanted.

". . . It's perfect. And it was cheap, on account of the haunted part, I bought a hundred acres. Thirty with the house, seventy on the other side of the creek. We'll build the mill there. The banks are plenty steep where it takes a turn, so a bridge'll be no problem. And the road goes right to Durham. Only five miles. It's better than I ever hoped. That's where it's all happening, Chess. Durham's grown ten times over in the past ten years. The Bull is there, and the Dukes, and the railroad. Some say Winston's growing faster, mostly Dick Reynolds, but that's way west, and to my way of thinking, we want to be right in the middle of the tobacco belt, not on the edge.

"We'll build the gristmill first, like we planned. There isn't another one close enough to cause trouble. Grinding corn will make up some money to live on while we're getting started. But the main thing is the mill wheel will give us power to drive the cigarette machine.

"Soon as sales are good enough, we'll build a factory and move the machine over to it. Then put in more machines . . ."

His eyes were surrounded by dark circles of fatigue. They filled suddenly with emotional tears.

"Oh, Chess, we're really going to do it. It's starting. No,

it's already started. I don't know if I can keep it to myself. I feel like yelling it to the world." Nate threw his head back and cupped his mouth with his chilblained hands.

"Watch out, world. We're on our way," he howled.

"Hush." She was laughing so hard she could hardly get the word out.

Nate grabbed her around the waist. Before she knew what was happening his strong arms lifted her high in the air. Then he spun around and around and around. When he put her down she was dizzy.

"Now you know how I feel. It's better than being drunk. Are you happy, Chess?"

"Oh, yes, yes, Nathan."

"I knew you would be. I kept that poor tired horse going all through the night. I just had to get home. I had to tell somebody or I would have blown up in a million pieces."

Suddenly his expression sobered. "It's still a secret, Chess. More secret than ever. Ma and Josh wouldn't understand, not in a million years. I don't want anybody ragging me. Not now. I'm too happy to have it ruined. I'm too tired to fight, too."

He brightened again. "Let me tell you about this lawyer fellow in Hillsborough. I had to hire me one just to find out how I could buy the land. The place was deserted, you see, so there wasn't anyone who owned it.

"Well, this Mr. Clarence Montgomery took me to the County Courthouse. No, that's not quite straight. He took me for five dollars in cash first, then he took me to the courthouse. It turns out that the state owns the land but the state never noticed it. So, good old Mr. Montgomery, he put his finger on the side of his nose, like this . . ." Nate imitated an archconspirator. ". . . and he said, 'A very interesting situation you've stumbled on, Mr. Richardson—' " Nate's lawyer voice rumbled deep in his chest.

"I'm not such a bumpkin that I didn't know what was coming. He was fixing to cut me out of the deal slick as a whistle.

"So I spoke up. Real country-like, as if I had hay in my teeth and stuffed between my ears, too. 'Do you reckon the ghosts'll make it cost more? I'd sure hate to pay for something I can't even see. There's nothing there except a bunch of noises in the nighttime.'

"He looked at me real sharp, to see if I was pulling his leg." Nate's eyes narrowed.

"So I looked at him real dumb." He widened them into blue vacancy. "The ghosts changed his mind real quick.

"He whizzed through a flock of papers, and four different offices, and the courtroom, complete with judge, in that one single day. Before it was good dark I was the owner of one hundred acres of prime land plus running water that nobody can 'divert by damming or other obstructions.' And it cost me exactly what I'd figured to put down for earnest money. Plus five dollars.

"Fifty cents an acre, Chess, can you credit it? A dream come true for only fifty cents—" Nate broke off at the sound of his mother's footsteps.

Mary Richardson sniffed the air inside the room as she came through the door. "Are you burning supper for some special reason, Chase?"

"I'm home, Ma."

"And high time, too. Alva and I nearly put our eyes out sewing so you'd have plenty of tobacco ready to sell, and you couldn't bother yourself to come get it. I suppose you went to that heathen State Fair instead."

"No, ma'am. Ice on the roads slowed me down."

Chess wanted to hit Nathan's mother with the grits-crusted pan she was holding. "Nathan was just heading off to bed, Miss Mary," she said. "I promised to wake him for supper." She put on a sweet smile. "We're having sweet potato pie for dessert tonight."

Miss Mary did not soften.

Not until Nate produced the mail he'd collected in Pleasant Grove. There was a letter for her from Gideon.

He and Lily were bringing the children to spend Christmas at the farm.

"Go to bed," Chess told Nathan. He looked ashen with exhaustion.

He loaded the other horse and left two days later. Natchez was too used up for any more hard traveling. Nathan hunched his shoulders against the cold and guided the heavily laden mare along the verges of the frozen road. The dead weeds were frozen, too, but they gave better purchase than the slick ice of the road.

It had been such a shock. He'd thought the entire packet of letters was for Chess. The top one was from Augustus Standish. The bottom one, too. It hadn't occurred to him to break the string tied about them and look in the middle.

It wouldn't have mattered anyhow. Gideon would still be coming for Christmas. With Lily and their children.

No. He wouldn't think about it. He would think about his hundred acres and the mill he was going to build there. It had made him so happy. For days and days he hadn't thought even once about Lily. He could do it again, he had to. He just had to concentrate. . . . Nate closed his eyes in a desperate effort to recapture his elation.

The mare skidded perilously, nearly unseating him. Nate pulled the reins gently. "Take it easy, Missy, just stop for a minute and catch your breath." He leaned forward to stroke her neck. "There, girl, it's all right. Nothing happened, no harm done. I know, it scared you. But it's over. No cause to tremble anymore. There, now, there . . ."

He had gone barely three miles before it began to get dark. He spent the night at the farm of a man he knew, sleeping in the barn near the warmth of the cows and horses. Just after midnight a whispered "Nate" woke him. He made love to the farmer's wife with an ardor that brought screams when she climaxed. Nate cried out loudly when he found release within her warmth. Let her husband hear. It didn't matter. A bullet would hurt so much less than the memory of Lily.

Chess waited to open her letters until after Nathan left. She hadn't wanted to waste even one second of the time with him, not even for news of home.

She smiled, then laughed quietly. Augustus Standish was just as drily amusing on paper as he was in person.

Scylla, he wrote, who was now the permanent cook, was even more determined to poison him than she had been the two weeks she had worked at Harefields when Chess had grippe. Now she was more subtle, Augustus Standish wrote admiringly. She was no longer mixing brown sugar into everything as she had done before. The astonishing effect of it on turnips was so memorable that he was quite convinced that he had mentioned it at the time. Presently the food was universally flavored with honey. Not clover honey, which would be remarkable enough when discovered clinging to an otherwise pedestrian rib of beef. No, Scylla had achieved an earth-shaking entomological discovery of a variety of bee that drew nectar from a species of thistle. So advanced was this magus of bees that it was able to incorporate actual spines of the host thistle into its honey for later deposit in the throats of those ingesting it. The sensation was, alas, indescribable by a pen as feeble in imagination as his. . . .

What a darling old humbug you are, Chess thought. She knew that Scylla was an excellent cook. She had begged lessons from her at the beginning of her own career at the stove, but she had never been able to equal Scylla's beef gravy.

The second letter was more prosaic. It commented on the rhapsodic reports Chess had sent in her letter to him, with a simple "Well Done." He might be congratulating her on her choice of husbands, or on her skill at dissembling.

She added the closely written sheets to the first letter she'd gotten from him. How long ago it seemed now, that warm joyful day at the Harvest Festival. Yet in fact it was barely more than a month ago.

What a peculiar thing was time. In some ways she felt as if she'd been here on the farm forever. In others she felt it was no more than a curious brief stop on a journey to another place as yet unknown.

I much prefer the latter, Chess decided. And it's accurate enough, except that I know the destination now. It's near Durham—wherever that might be—near a rushing stream and soon to be occupied by a gristmill with a cigarette machine.

Longing for Nathan hit her an unexpected blow. She wanted to be spun around in his arms again. How happy that little bit of time had been. There would be many more, she was sure of it. It was only because he was so totally exhausted that he had been so withdrawn and uncommunicative these last two days. Please, God, don't let him keep riding all through the bitter night again. Let him stop at some warm place for shelter.

Nathan came back to the farm three more times in November. For Chess his arrival was always the same: the cloud-covered skies became brighter, the confining shabby house turned into a cozy nest to hold her in happy closeness to him.

The initial joy did not last. Nathan was preoccupied; often he didn't even hear her when she spoke. And he ate almost nothing, although she tried to make each meal appetizing, despite the limited food supplies of winter.

"You're getting as picky as Chase," his mother complained. "If you don't watch out, you're going to get sick and you'll have only yourself to blame."

That was what Chess feared most, that he was ill. Nathan was a hearty eater, even when the food was much less appealing than the dishes she prepared. She had little appetite either, but that was normal for her. She couldn't remember a time when she had cared about eating. A few special occasions, mostly with Nathan, had been different, but by and large she didn't care whether she ate or not. At Harefields she had often skipped meals altogether except for a pretense, because she was at table with her grandfather.

That was fine for her, but not for him. He needed his strength for the long cold journey from store to store. When she watched him load the big packs of tobacco bags on the horse, her heart ached with worry. But she waved goodbye with a broad smile on her face. It was the only gift she could give him.

In December she broke down and pled with him. "Don't go back out there, please don't. There's no shame to staying. There's never been a winter like this, even Livvy Alderbrook says so. She couldn't even have her pig roast this year, for the first time ever."

"There's no shame, but there's no money either. It's my job to sell the sacks when they're finished." He wasn't even impatient with her. It was as if she were someone he barely knew.

Chess sobbed into her shoulder when Nathan left. He was carrying a shovel, walking ahead of the laden horse, leading Missy through the thick snowfall that had begun that morning.

She was afraid that she'd never see him again.

Ol' Livvy scolded her. "Didn't he say he'd be back to celebrate Christmas? Then he will. Nate Richardson's not a man who'll break his word."

"But suppose he gets caught in a storm? He could freeze to death trying to get here."

"Nate Richardson's too stubborn to die. He'll be here if he said he would."

Nate dismounted. There was another snowdrift blocking the road. He filled and arranged the feed bag over the mare's head, then unstrapped the shovel. He did not mind having to clear the way. A bright sun was warm on his shoulders. And the labor delayed him. He did not want to reach the farm. Gideon and Lily might already be there; Christmas was only two days off.

He stabbed the shovel into the sparkling white snow. There

was no getting out of it, he had to face his brother—and his brother's wife. He knew he could do it. A man found the strength to do whatever he had to do, or he was no kind of man at all.

Thing was, he didn't feel like a man. He was that boy again, at Camp Meeting, seeing the vision of the most beautiful girl in the world. Why did the memory have to be so clear? And—oh, God—why could his hands still feel her soft breasts and tiny waist. Nate groaned aloud. His lips were burning, as they had done, as hers had done against his.

How could he be in the room with her and not touch her, pull her body close to his, move his hands on her? His brother's wife.

How could he look Gideon in the eye, when he wanted to sin against him? How could he stop himself from hating his own brother when he saw Gideon's arm around Lily's waist?

Nate's heart called on God to witness that he didn't want this torment, these feelings. He couldn't help himself.

The shovel bit into the snow over and over again; then the way was open. Nate led the mare over the treacherous footing, removed the empty feed bag, reattached the shovel. For a long moment he rested against the warmth of Missy's flank. Then he mounted. There was no way to avoid seeing Lily and Gideon this time. He had managed to miss their wedding and their visit to Camp Meeting. But he had no excuse to stay away from his own home at Christmastime. It would make everyone wonder. He could not bear it if anyone guessed how he felt. The shame of it would kill him.

When Nate entered the farmhouse he saw the bent back of a man huddled by the fire. Steam rising from his frosted clothes blurred the outline of his head. At first Nate thought it was his brother. He forced his face into a smile. "How about sharing that heat, Bro?" he said.

The man turned. He was a stranger.

Chess ran into the room at the sound of Nathan's voice. "Welcome home. Get over in the warm, Nathan, and meet

Jim Monroe. Take off that wet coat and hat and hand them to me to dry by the stove. Yours, too, Mr. Monroe. You'll warm up faster without them."

She stood close to Nate. "Do hurry," she said in a low voice. "Your mother has taken to her bed and she won't let me comfort her at all. Mr. Monroe just got here a few minutes ago with a message that Gideon isn't coming because of the state of the roads.

"Oh, Nathan, it's pitiful. Miss Mary's been standing by the window off and on for days, breathing on the glass to make a peephole in the frost. Just watching for Gideon."

Chess did not mention that she had done the same, looking for him.

"Go on, Nathan. Shake hands quickly with our guest then go to your mother. I've already put the coffeepot on. I'll bring some in to you."

Nate was glad to comply. He felt so weak from relief that he needed to sit down, even if it was on the edge of his mother's bed. And he needed time to compose himself. He mustn't let it show that he thanked God that Gideon wasn't coming, with his family.

Jim Monroe stayed for the night, then for Christmas, then to help with the outdoor work in January. He was a widower in his forties, "with neither chick nor child," he said, and he was glad to do any work that needed doing in exchange for Mrs. Nate's good cooking and a pallet by the warm fire and the stories she read so pretty from her book.

The tobacco was, at last, all granulated and packed into the little sacks. Alva and Miss Mary were doing their piled-up darning instead of sewing the tiny bags. Chess read *Idylls of the King* again, while Susan looked over her shoulder, learning new words.

Nate didn't stay to listen. With Jim there to do his share of the work he'd been free to load the final 2,000 sacks and go back on the road to sell them.

"I'll go to the mill site, too," he told Chess in private. "I need to know what winter does to the road over there and if there's ice on the stream. If anybody questions why I'm gone so long, just speculate to them about how bad the roads must be."

"I don't need to. Anybody can see they must be worse than ever." Icy rain and sleet were covering December's thick snowfall with a sheet of ice. But the cold wasn't quite as crippling. She was less worried about Nathan. And she was enjoying Jim Monroe very much.

As Nate said with considerable admiration, Jim was a "champion cusser." Mary Richardson chastised him constantly about taking the Lord's name in vain. Every time, Jim promised to do better; every time, he failed. Chess found it all very entertaining.

Jim was a hard worker, too. Throughout January's short harsh days, anytime the sleet and rain stopped, he joined Josh and Micah in the backbreaking task of clearing and burning the area that was set aside for the seedbed of the new crop. The trees had been cut down and sawn into logs. Now the roots had to be dug out, then the land evened out, then the logs piled on a skid and set afire. In this way weed seed and insects in the freshly cleared land were killed. If more rain came the fires had to be rekindled when the skies cleared. After one small patch of land had been burned, the men dragged the skid to the next patch, with huge iron hooks, while Micah added more wood to the fire atop the skid.

The work was nearly completed when Nathan returned toward the end of January. He was in high spirits. "The days are getting longer, the roads are mostly mud mires with only a skim of ice, and I saw something that looked for all the world just like a robin over toward the county line." He joined in with the other men. In two more days, the seedbed burning was done. Another two days with hoes, then rakes, finished the job. The soil was loose and friable and ready.

Nate made a quick visit to Livvy Alderbrook's cabin. He returned with a jar of her home brew, which the men, including Micah, passed from hand to hand. The end of the job deserved a celebration.

Jim reluctantly mentioned that he guessed it was time for him to go. Unless, he added hopefully, Nate and Josh could use a damn good hand with the seeding or even plowing the goddamn frozen dirt in that Satan's hell of a field of theirs. He could scare the bejesus out of any thrice-cursed plow horses God sent.

"It couldn't be better, Chess." Nate was exultant. "Jim's like an angel sent from heaven. This means that I can start in on the mill right away. I have to get the seedbed planted. Josh and I are going to have words over that because there's a new wrinkle I heard about that he'll fight tooth and nail. But, shoot, that'll only take a day or two, and then I can light out for Orange County.

"You should see it, Chess. I spent two days and two nights over there. Walked over every inch. A hundred acres. That's enough trees to build a whole city with. And the stream—it races around that bend making the sweetest little rapids at the turn. The sound of them is like a song being sung.

"I found a whole outcropping of rocks, too. We'll have a foundation that'll be so solid a tribe of giants couldn't move it. A root cellar, too, and even an icehouse if we want one. My hands are itching to get started.

"Now this is what I'm going to do. I'll tell Ma that Jim's staying. Then get the seedbed planted. Then I'll face the showdown all at one time, get everybody together and let them know what we're planning.

"Not the whole plan, naturally. The cigarettes are our secret. It's enough to say I'm going to be a miller because I hate farming." His face was grim with the strength of the hatred.

Then he smiled, now alight with happiness. "I'm getting out, just like I wanted all my life. Great Godalmighty, it's wonderful."

"You can hire that Jim Monroe if you've got your mind made up to it, Nate," said Mary Richardson. Her voice was shrill. "But I won't share my roof with a blasphemer. If he stays, I go. It's him or me, you got to choose."

Chapter Thirteen

NATHAN STORMED FROM THE HOUSE. Chess didn't have to ask what had happened. Miss Mary's sharp pitch had cut through the door as if it were made of gauze.

Chess stepped in front of him. He raised his arm to shove her aside, pulled it back with obvious effort. "Get out of the way, Chess. I've got to go fire Jim Monroe while there's still daylight for traveling."

"Five minutes won't matter that much. Let's go into the factory room. Please, Nathan. We might be able to come up with something if we put our heads together."

It took considerably more than five minutes, but they succeeded.

More precisely, Chess succeeded. She convinced Nathan that he need not stay, that she and Susan together could do a man's work, Jim's work.

Once Nathan agreed that it was worth a try, the details fell into place. He'd take Jim to Livvy Alderbrook's place where he could lay low until Nate was ready to leave. Then he'd go with Nate to work on building the mill.

Chess would start riding to Pleasant Grove every week to mail a report on conditions at the farm. If Nate saw he was needed, he'd come back.

"And you'll send me a report, too. You can mail it when you go to fetch mine." She stared him down until he agreed.

You'd never know from looking at him that anything was going to happen, Chess thought. Nathan simply had to be apprehensive. His mother had carried on like a banshee about Jim Monroe. What was she going to do when Nathan announced that he was leaving the farm for good? The others, too. Josh would be terrible in wrath, she was certain.

But Nathan was actually smiling, even laughing at baby Sally's indignant struggles against her confinement in a tied-rag harness that attached her to a tree near—but not too near—the prepared seedbed.

He had already done the sowing. Chess had been fascinated by it. Tobacco seeds were so small; how could such a tiny speck grow into a plant with leaves bigger than a platter? "A tablespoon of seed is ten thousand plants," Susan told her, proud that she had a chance to teach her teacher something.

Nathan's graceful movement was mesmerizing. The seed had been mixed into a pouch of sand. His hand dipped into the pouch then swept in an arc as he walked the length of the seedbed, then returned on a parallel path, then back, then turn, walk, turn, walk, always with the dipping, casting, sowing. It was beautiful. She felt like applauding when he completed the route.

Josh had a pouch also. In spite of his peg leg, he performed the same elegant ritual, crossing the seedbed in a direction perpendicular to Nate's.

Chess then joined the others in a row at the edge of the bed. Slowly, so slowly, they placed their feet carefully, side to side, heel to toe-print for the length of the seeded bed. Then back, turn, tread, reverse, step, step, step.

Nathan laughed at Sally. They all did. It made the finicky task less tedious.

When it was over Chess' legs were trembling beneath her calico frock, and she wanted to sit, right where she was, although the ground outside the seedbed was still half frozen. She looked at Nathan, hoping for a compliment. Hadn't she just proved that she could do the job as well as Jim Monroe?

"Unloose that poor baby," he told her, "and take her with you to go make us a big pot of coffee. We'll deserve it after we do the manuring." Josh and Alva were already arranging smelly burlap pouches across their shoulders.

Chess returned with coffeepot, cups, spoon, sugar and cream in the tin dishpan. Sally trailed behind her, carrying a basket of heavily buttered and sugared bread slices.

Miss Mary, Alva, Susan, Josh, and Nathan were crossing the seedbed, tossing arcs of dry, powdery horse manure. Chess concentrated on tying Sally again while the little girl was distracted by a slice of sweet bread. Thank heaven she had missed the manuring. The smell didn't offend her. Harefields often reeked of it. But it would have meant wearing gloves and washing them would have been a real chore. . . .

No, she mustn't think like that. Hadn't she committed herself to working?

She ran to the house, ran back with her gloves. "Can I help?" she called to the others.

"You'd do it wrong," Miss Mary shouted back.

Subdued, Chess sat down by Sally. "If she's cross with me now, she's going to be really put out when she hears what Nathan has to say," she told the uncomprehending little girl.

"Hope you've got a good dinner cooking," Nate said. He was sitting with Sally on his knees, sharing his bread, enjoying his coffee. All of them were sitting on the ground at the edge of the seedbed.

"The hot coffee's real welcome, Chess," said Alva with one of her rare smiles. She had become much friendlier since Chess began teaching Susan to read.

Susan edged even closer to Chess. "You bake bread better than anybody," she whispered. She had developed a major case of heroine-worship. Chess liked it, she'd never been adored before.

Nathan had to murmur very close to Chess' ear to prevent Susan from overhearing. Chess liked that, too. His breath was warm on her cheek, his shoulder touched hers. "Feed Josh extra good," he said. "We'll be having a small ruction after dinner, and I want him as agreeable as he can be."

"Why not have dinner now?" She saw no need to be quiet. The way everyone had wolfed down the little bit she'd brought, they clearly were hungry.

"Because we're not done." Nate stretched the kinks out of his shoulders. "Come on, Miss Sally, back to your tree," he said.

As it turned out, Chess needed her gloves after all. The whole family, except for the squalling Sally, spread foot-high piles of spiky dried brushwood cuttings over the bed.

"To keep animals off," Alva explained when Chess asked the purpose. "Woods are full of fox and deer and raccoons and possum. They wander in the nighttime."

After serving up the thick rich stew she'd had cooking since morning, Chess learned that the brush had a second purpose.

"There's a new wrinkle I learned about from a Durham newspaper," Nathan said casually. "I aim to give it a try. You spread these big lengths of muslin cloth over the bed and stick it on the brush to hold it from blowing away. They call it 'canvas.' I don't know why, but the paper says it keeps away the fly."

"Dang foolishness," Josh said at once. "Ain't nothing on earth can keep you from losing a quarter of your seedlings to the fly. Always been that way, always will. You can sprinkle kerosene, might help some. But still you're going to have the fly as soon as the first green starts to show."

"I bought canvas, and we're going to spread it." Nate put his spoon down.

"The only thing that'll do is keep off the rain. Then you'll lose all of the crop instead of a quarter." Josh dropped his spoon on the table and took a knife from the bib pocket of his overalls. He tilted his chair back, removed a plug of tobacco from a pants pocket, cut a piece, and inserted it into his mouth. As his jaw began to move, he pushed his plate away. The stew was not yet half-eaten. His eyes never left Nate's.

"Seem to me—" said Micah. Josh raised a hand, and the boy was silenced. He finished his meal with his eyes on his plate, like the women. Chess couldn't eat at all. She wanted to look up, but the tension forbade it.

After a long time, when the gravy was congealed on Josh's stew, Nate pushed back his chair. "Let's go," he said.

Chess looked at him, then at Susan, then at Alva. Both of them were staring at Nathan. "Let's go, I'll do the dishes later," she said. She stood, smiled at Nate. He walked to the door and she followed, snatching her shawl from its peg.

The canvas covered the seedbed before sunset. Everyone helped place it, even Josh. Nathan made jokes about Sally's acrobatic attempts to free herself from her harness, and they all laughed. It was as if there had been no confrontation at all.

But Chess knew it would be up to her to keep the canvas in place once Nathan was gone. Still, maybe it wouldn't be so bad after all when he told them he was leaving, not if today was any guide. She could still feel the strength that had emanated from him, and the unyielding determination. She had sensed it before, that first night in the Weldon train station. It had excited her then, and it excited her now, even more. He would let nothing and nobody stand in his way. What a life they were going to have!

"You were a true partner there at the dinner table," he told her when they went to bed that night.

Chess was suffused with happiness. She even imagined that there was something different about the way he used her body, even though the coupling was as brief as always. She smiled in the darkness for a long time after he was asleep.

He woke her before dawn. "Hush," he whispered, "everything's all right. I got something I want to do, and I want you to do it with me. Wrap up warm and tiptoe out. I'll be by the door."

They went to the factory. The colorless part-light of moonset was eerie, and the cold bit through to the bone. Once inside, Nathan lit a kerosene lamp, gave it to Chess to hold. He dragged an ancient iron-bound trunk from the darkest corner into the center of the room.

"Lift up the light," he said. Chess heard the sound of a key in the lock. Then he raised the heavy lid. Inside, Augustus Standish's polished pine box shone golden in the light. Nate ran his palms across its surface. "Beautiful," he murmured.

He breathed deeply, then lifted the gleaming pine cube out and set it on the floor. "Knowing it was here all this time and not being able to see it—I was afraid maybe I'd made the whole thing up, that it wasn't here at all. I've been dreaming about this." He undid the brass latches, removed the lid. The model of Augustus' invention was revealed. Nate let out a sigh of delight so strong that it set one of the tiny cogwheels in motion, and a thin wooden shaft moved in an up and down stroke. "Magic!" he breathed. "It's like magic." The flame in the lantern was reflected in his eyes, the shape made irregular by unshed tears of emotion. Chess held her breath. She had never in her life seen such naked joy and love. To her, the model was only another of her grandfather's enthusiasms turned into something almost like a toy. To Nathan, it was something very different. Now she understood why he had kept the model secret and insisted that she tell no one about it. He couldn't talk about magic with his uncle. Josh had no confidence in Nate's ideas about anything. The others were much the same. They believed only what they had always believed, what they thought they knew. His vision of the future, of his future, of the magic waiting to be used—they wouldn't understand and so they would mock or spurn.

"I'll take care of it for you, Nathan," she said.

Her voice startled him, he was far away from the tiny shed. He brought himself down to earth. "There's something else in with it," he noticed. His big hand moved cautiously down beside the model to remove a shallow, large, polished walnut case. When he opened it, Chess all but shouted.

"That's mine," she said. "Grandfather made it for me. Hold the light, Nathan, and let me show you."

It was a chess set and board. She lifted out the pieces, one by one, turned them from side to side. "This is my father's face, see, on the king. My mother's the queen." Tears clogged her throat. "The knights are my brothers, and I'm here—in the rook—a maiden in the tower window. I was only ten when he made it for me. The bishops are Mr. Bondurant, the minister at the church, you remember him, and all the pawns are hares, because of the plantation being named Harefields.

"I didn't know he'd put that in. I haven't thanked him. What a dear, thoughtful old Caesar. I've got to write a letter at once. You can mail it for me." Chess had forgotten the model completely.

"Hold your horses," said Nate. He was all business. "Keep your playtoys out; I'm going to lock up, and you have to be sure that no one, I mean no one at all, gets in here." He was so angry that his hands shook, and his fingers were awkward. When he dropped the key that locked the chest, his clumsiness made him even angrier. How could Chess be so childish? The future, its possibilities and risks, was in the model, and all she cared about was some complicated, high-toned game that was a piece of the past. Her babbling reminiscences had broken into his dream, just when he had the means to reach it in his hands. He'd waited so long, the knowledge of the model always in his mind, waited and waited for the moment when he could look at it, touch it, examine its intricacies, taste the triumph of having it in his possession. She'd ruined it. She had shattered the moment, and for a hot, blinding instant he hated her.

But Nate put his anger aside; feelings got in the way of doing what needed to be done. "Watch where I'm going to hide the key," he ordered Chess. "There's money in the trunk, too, in case there's an emergency." He closed the lid on the pine box and then the top of the chest. His dream would have to wait. He wanted the moment to be perfect, and Chess had spoiled this one.

Chess made herself watch and remember the location of the key, but she used only the front of her mind. She was living inside herself, in a world of memories and mythology, a world where her handsome parents were king and queen of the big house parties, her dashing brothers rode their favorites among the forty spirited thoroughbreds in the stables, and a beloved and pampered little girl was taught to reason by playing an ancient game with her sternly indulgent grandfather.

Homesickness was like an iron weight on her heart. But you're homesick for twenty years ago, she told herself, not for working like a mule on a decrepit plantation of tenant farms. There's no bringing yesterdays back.

This is today, and I'm with the man I love, and we have a million tomorrows to think about. She smiled at Nathan. "I'll take good care of it for you," she promised again.

It was disappointing that he didn't respond. He must be thinking about the fuss his mother's going to make, she thought.

As it turned out, there was very little reaction to Nate's proclamation about leaving. Everyone was too thunderstruck.

He made his announcement, and then he was gone. On foot, with a sack on his back. Josh and Micah would need the horses for the farm.

Chess walked to the road with him. Perhaps, with no one looking, he would kiss her goodbye.

Jim Monroe was on the road, waiting for Nate. She waved to the two of them as they walked away.

At least there was a faint blur of pale green on the witch hazel bushes beside the road. Winter was over, no matter how cold it might be.

Chapter Fourteen

NATE AND JIM WALKED from the farm to Durham without stopping at the mill site. Before they could begin any work they needed tools, a mule, and a wagon for hauling. The trip took them more than a week. The welcome warming turned the roads into slippery miles of mud, with frequent sinks that were knee-deep. They accepted rides at first, but after the fifth time they helped a benefactor haul a stuck wagon out of a sink they decided that walking was "a damn sight easier, and hellish faster, too," as Jim put it.

A terrifying loud roaring noise frightened Jim so much that he tried to sprint to the protection of trees beside the road. His sprawling, howling skid and fall made Nate shout with laughter.

"Get up, man. That bellow should be music to your ears. Means we're almost there."

When they slogged into town, he showed Jim the origin of the noise. The Durham Bull was a huge beast, shiny black with brilliant red nostrils and glaring white eyeballs. It was fifteen feet high and twenty-five feet long, painted on sheets of iron that were bolted together, then bolted to the biggest building in the small city, the William T. Blackwell Tobacco Company. Jim was awestruck. No longer by the Bull, but by the home of the Bull. He'd never seen anything to match the grandeur of the five-storied, block-long brick factory. It stood on fifteen acres of fenced-in land right in the center of town. The location was appropriate. It was the heart of Durham's business and the reason for its astonishing growth from village to city.

The factory was the biggest in the world for processing smoking tobacco. What Nate and his family did in their lean-to room, the Bull multiplied by many thousands, using machinery operated by hired labor, for granulating, for packing into the tiny sacks, for boxing in wholesale lots, for transfer to the long loading dock beside the Bull's own railroad spur. *Bull Durham* was known and sold and smoked all over the world. Every day except Sunday 25,000 pounds of it left the mammoth factory.

Almost 500 factory workers led their lives according to the mechanical, steam-powered roar of the Bull at opening time, closing time, and noontime. The sound of it could be heard up to ten miles away. It was a suitable symbol for the brash, chest-thumping pride of Durham's inhabitants. In ten years it had grown from a muddy railroad stop with a population of 258 people and a main street with four shabby saloons to a bustling town—with muddy streets—of nearly 3,000, a square mile of factories, warehouses, bungalows, stores, mills, churches, and grand residences complete with turrets, cupolas, and wide porches. There were now seven saloons, but they were called barrooms.

It was typical of what was happening all over America, where business meant progress, and progress meant pride, and the old coastal cities no longer had a monopoly on commerce. Battle Creek, Michigan, was producing cold breakfast cereal ... Ravenna, Ohio, made oatmeal ... Indianapolis, Indiana, was the home of packaged prescription medicines under the direction of a young Civil War veteran named Eli Lilly . . . Cleveland, Ohio, offered premixed paints in a can . . . San Antonio, Texas, introduced barbed wire . . . Minneapolis, Minnesota, changed from stone mill wheels to steel rollers to multiply flour production in Charles Pillsbury's mills . . .

Young men were taking risks, trying new ways of doing things, developing new methods, new products, new attitudes. The future was infinite, with infinite promise, and it had already begun.

"Well I'll be danged, it's Mr. Lemon Wrapper himself. How're you doing, Nate?"

"Just fine, Buck. Good to see you."

Nate smiled at the tall redhead who stopped him near the counter in Angier's General Store. Looking up made his neck feel stiff, and Buck Duke unsettled him. They'd been running into each other for years. Buck sold his family's smoking tobacco to the same stores Nate supplied with his own. Early on Nate recognized Buck as a threatening competitor. Buck worked equally hard, he knew tobacco equally well, he was equally welcome as a down-home good old boy. And he was just as ambitious, Nate could sense it. He was pretty sure Buck sensed the same in him. They were two of a kind. He had to watch his step. Buck was smart, and he had a head start. No more farming for him. His father and brother and he were already operating a good-sized factory. It wasn't Blackwell's, but it was a handsome brick building on Main Street with machines and hired hands and an output that Nate gloomily estimated at about 1,000 pounds a day. Plus, Duke had started advertising—

There were twelve tobacco processing factories in Durham. Duke's wasn't the biggest, but it was the one that worried him. Because Buck worried him.

"How long do you figure to be in Durham, Nate? We could have a meal together—I don't suppose you've given up teetotal."

Good, I worry him, too, Nate thought. Then—not good, I

don't want him watching me too close. "I'm just getting some supplies, then I'm heading out. Maybe the word ain't out yet. I'm quitting tobacco. I reckon a man should quit when he's ahead, and the lemon wrapper is the best farming I was ever going to do. Besides, I got myself married and my wife doesn't like for me to be out on the road."

Duke guffawed. They both knew what temptations lay on the road.

"I'm building a gristmill on some land I bought," Nate said. "It's only about five miles out, so I'll be in Durham a good bit. My wife has a yen for city life. She comes from near Richmond."

Chances were Buck already knew about Chess. Tobacco was a small, talkative world of its own. Let Buck think he was henpecked. It would ease his mind. And his curiosity.

The two antagonists parted as cordially as they had met. Nate was pleased with his deception. Until he learned an hour later that Buck had started producing cigarettes.

"Yessiree, it's the biggest news since the fires took down half of Main Street," said the man with the mules. "About a hundred Jews from New York City. Specialists. Wait till you get a look at them. Pale as a fishbelly. You can tell they been in some factory all their lives. They'll never last, can't even talk English right. . . . Now this is a fine big animal here, could pull a wagon out of mud ten yards deep. . . ."

Nate could hear his own heart beating. He was running out of time. Buck Duke wouldn't stay with hand-rolling long. Not if the Bonsack machine worked and he could get his hands on it.

Nate paid more than he wanted to for the mule. Time mattered more than money now. He and Jim were on the road to the mill site within an hour.

"Goddamn it, Nate, you said we could stay the night in Durham. I want to hear that black devil of a bull sound off again with its hellfire holler."

"If the wind's blowing right, you'll be able to hear it at the mill. We've got work to do."

Chapter Fifteen

CHESS FOLDED NATE'S LETTER carefully, as if the bad news could be kept small. I should have been with him, she thought. She wanted to cry. He shouldn't have had to be alone, with no one to talk to. No, it was even worse; Jim was with him and he had to act like nothing had happened.

She wanted to get up on the mare and ride to Nathan, not back to the farm. But she couldn't. She had to go back.

Not that things were all that bad, really. As she'd told Nathan in her letter, the hullabaloo about his leaving had worn itself out in only a few days, and now everything was quite peaceful. She'd started reading a new book aloud in the evening. It was *The Three Musketeers*—without French pronunciation—and his mother seemed delighted to concentrate her outrage on Cardinal Rich-loo, the papist.

Daytime was for watching spring's advance. There were buds on all the trees and bushes, and the sun melted the night's frost before it was halfway up the sky.

No sign of green in the seedbed yet. She and Alva and Susan removed the canvas in the heat of the day, then covered the bed again before sunset and frost.

There were patches of green in the field, but Josh or Micah plowed it under right away. Chess thought it wonderfully funny that farmers called tobacco "weed." That meant they had to protect their weed from weeds.

She couldn't believe that Nathan had been worried about her taking Jim Monroe's place. The work hardly even qualified to be called "work." Certainly not her duty ride to Pleasant Grove every week to mail her report. She enjoyed seeing the woods coming to life, and the road was no problem because she could ride on the verge, avoid the mud. And in the little town she always saw someone she knew, often more than one. She enjoyed the sociability. She enjoyed Livvy Alderbrook, too. She walked over to see her nearly every day.

Life at the farm was happier for her than it had ever been. Even though Nathan wasn't there.

March defied tradition and came in like a lamb. Chess and Alva folded the canvas, filled buckets from the creek and hauled them to the seedbed, watered it, then replaced the canvas. There was no rain. Everyone helped, even the men. The seedbed period was the most dangerously delicate of the entire growing year.

When the fragile green haze appeared, Chess brought out her hoarded sugar and baked a cake, with frosting.

The next day it rained. A perfect spring rain, gentle and steady. The world smelled fresh and new.

She began to teach Susan how to write. Susan learned so quickly that Chess suspected she had started on her own, weeks before. "I'm going to teach you something else, too," she said. "It's a beautiful game, with kings and queens and knights."

"Like the *Idylls of the King,*" Susan gasped in wonder. When she saw the chess set, she washed her hands carefully before she touched the pieces. Then she looked at each one for a long time. "I've never seen anything so beautiful in my life," she said. "Is it named after you? It's just like you."

Chess hugged the girl tight. She had grown very fond of Susan. When it took Susan only an hour to learn the moves, Chess wasn't surprised; she already knew how intelligent Alva's daughter was.

But when Susan nearly beat her three days later, Chess was amazed. "It took me much, much longer to learn to play that well," she admitted. She looked forward to playing often. Her mind needed the exercise.

Her body got the exercise instead. In April the tobacco seedlings were six inches high. It was time to put the canvas away and transplant them to the field.

The horror was beginning.

Josh and Micah plowed the field again. And yet again, in the opposite direction, forming a grid pattern of furrows. Where the rows crossed, the loose, sandy earth formed a low mound they called a "hill."

While the second plowing was being done the women got water from the creek. Leaving the full buckets near the seed-bed, they brought wooden trays from the factory. These were curiously constructed, with tall spindles at each corner and a loose-fitting calico roof stretched over them. The seedlings had to be shaded from the sun when their roots were exposed.

"Chess, you start out easy," Alva said. She meant to be kind. "Take a bucket and pour a couple of ladles-ful into the center of as many hills as the water lasts."

Chess stifled her sigh. She already had a backache from hauling the heavy pail from the creek. Remember, she told herself, it'll get lighter as you go along. She set to work with a brisk step. The bucket was empty after twenty hills. She looked at the field. There were hundreds of hills, many hundreds.

And, she saw when she walked back to the seedbed, there were many hundreds of seedlings.

The transplanting process was thus: a section of bed was

sprinkled liberally with water. Then each seedling was lifted carefully from the soil. It was essential that their fragile white roots not break. Quickly the seedling was placed on the shaded tray. Full trays were carried to the field and seedlings were dropped by one woman—one at a time—on the edge of a dampened hill. A second person pressed a hole in the center of the hill with a short wooden dibble, then set the seedling inside. A third came behind, firming the soil around the seedling's roots and lower stem.

Before the end of the day Chess had learned all the steps. They were rotated among the women. Before the end of the week, she had become nearly as quick as Susan. Alva did everything with seemingly effortless precision and speed. She'd been doing it since she was younger than Susan.

Miss Mary returned to the house after the buckets were filled. Her back could no longer endure the constant bending. And someone had to cook. "Chase won't have time for that no more."

Chess lived in a blur of perpetual stiffness and pain. When she learned that not all the transplants "took," that sick or dead ones had to be pulled from the hills and replaced, she lost control. "But we haven't even finished putting them in for the first time," she wailed.

"It generally takes about six or seven weeks," Alva told her. "And if it don't rain, we've got to water them."

Chess bit her lip so hard it bled. Then she bent over to pull out the dead seedling. She could get through this. She had to; she'd promised Nathan.

The transplanting is going fine, she wrote to him. *It's lovely being outdoors in the spring air.* She was careful not to let tears fall on the paper. Seedlings were too delicate to be handled by gloved hands. She had dirt embedded in her reddened skin, and no amount of washing would get it out. It was mixed in with gummy tar from the leaves of the tiny plants.

She wondered if his letters were as full of lies as hers were. The stone foundation was completed, he'd said, and the frame walls were going up as fast as the sawmill in Durham could turn logs into planks.

Lies or not, the weekly letters were her lifeline. They gave her the strength to endure. Thank heaven she'd made friends with Mrs. Henderson, who ran the post office from her parlor. She allowed Chess to do her collecting and mailing on Sunday, when Miss Mary forbade work on the farm.

"Lordy that feels good," Alva said.

"Amen," agreed Chess. She took off her dusty straw hat and turned her sweaty face up toward the rain. Thank God there'd be no need to hand-water today. She bent to pat the hill in place around the transplant. Her back hardly bothered her now, the constant ache was so familiar she couldn't remember a time without it.

"That's the last of this bunch," said Alva as she set the plant in place. "Susan, you go and bring us some cool water to under the tree." The rain was heavier now. It would wash the new transplants out. Chess knew they'd have to replant the most recent ones; this had happened before. She accepted it with dull resignation, the way she had come to accept everything else about the unremitting toil the weed demanded.

The wide branches of the longleaf pine tree sheltered them from the rain, and it was cool in the shade. She drank thirstily. April was as hot as summer when you were working in the unprotected expanse of the field.

She looked over at it with a stir of emotion, despite her fatigue. The rows of green were as straight as arrows, the earliest transplants already twice their original size. She was proud.

"Momma, can I go in the house and read till the rain stops?" Susan asked. Alva nodded, and the girl scampered off.

Chess was proud of that, too, being Susan's teacher.

"She's a good girl," she said to Alva.

"Look at them legs," Alva sighed. "It hardly seems fair that the young ones never get tired. Mine are heavy as tree trunks." She removed her boots, pulled her skirt up to her knees, poured some water on her swollen ankles.

"What a good idea," said Chess. She did the same. "That feels wonderful." A fitful breeze danced within the rain, cooling the sweat that clogged the hair at her temples, and she was thankful.

Thankful, too, for the rest, and for Alva's companionship. They had become easy with one another. They talked some while they worked, and sometimes Alva told stories about Nate and his sister when they were children working at the same tasks. She never talked about Gideon. "Him!" she had snorted when Chess asked. "Mary took him out of the field the minute he got the rapture. All he did was read the Bible and study on it. Momma's boy. The rapscallions were left to me to raise."

Chess thought of Alva as her friend. Even though there was no intimacy between them they were united by the hours in the field and their dislike of Mary Richardson. Chess tried very hard to be sympathetic to Nathan's mother because of the tragedy she'd known. But she couldn't like her.

The steady downpour was like a curtain around the umbrella of the old tree's branches. Chess and Alva were isolated from the farm, the work, the others. It made Alva bold. "Can you keep a secret, Chess?"

Chess smiled inwardly; keeping secrets was what she was best at. "Of course," she said.

She was going to send Susan to school in Pleasant Grove, Alva confided. Sally, too, when she got old enough. She didn't care what Josh might have to say about it, this one time in her life she was going to stand up to him. Her girls were going to have an education. Susan was like a different girl now that she'd learned about books. She was happy all the time. It gladdened Alva's heart to near bursting.

Chess didn't know what to say. Alva was looking at her with tear-filled eyes. When Alva looked away, into the rain, she felt more comfortable. "I believe you'll be doing the right thing," she murmured. Was that what Alva wanted?

"It's a strange thing that you should be the one to bring me so much joyfulness," Alva said. "I wasn't one bit glad when you showed up last summer. I thought it meant the end of the only joy I had with Nate.

"He was only nine years old when I came to the farm and a real sweet boy; even when he was up to some devilment, there was never any meanness in it. And funny—sometimes he made me laugh so hard I got a stomachache. We were like two kids, even if I was six years older than him. His sister Mary acted more grown-up than me, for all that she was four years younger.

"When Josh was around I toed the line, of course. He is my husband, and I know my duty. There's no joking and laughing in Josh's neighborhood.

"Nate was a sight to see when the boy troubles started. It just makes Micah mean, his voice skittering up and down and his pecker standing up for no reason atall. Nate never had no meanness, not even about that. And when I showed him what to do about it, how it is between a man and a woman, well, he was as happy as if he'd put a shovel in the dirt and opened up a gold mine. After I taught him how to pleasure a woman when he's pleasuring himself I felt kind of like I'd struck gold myself. Sometimes we'd be out in the woods two or three hours, doing it over and over again. He's a sweet man, same as he was a sweet boy. He always called me 'Honey.'

"Natural enough, he started strutting like a rooster all over kingdom come. But he never stopped giving me my share. I called it my honey time, to myself. All these years I could look forward to when he came home. When he came home with a wife, I knew those days were done. There's only Josh doing the way husbands do, pumping away at me when he takes a mind to and then snoring in his sleep when he's done.

"Like I said, I minded you taking Nate from me, Chess, but what you gave Susan matters a lot more. A mother cares more about her child than about herself or she's no kind of mother at all—what's the matter?"

Chess was vomiting, but she had nothing in her stomach to expel. The sound she was making was horrible.

"Here, drink some water," Alva urged.

Chess knocked the dipper from her hand. She stumbled to her feet and ran into the woods. Away. Anywhere. Just away.

When her tired legs gave way, she fell. The thick accumulation of fallen pine needles were soft beneath her. She didn't know where she was; she'd been running, she thought, for a long time. But she had no strength left. The emotion she'd been fleeing captured her; she threw her arms wide and screamed until she was hoarse.

Chess had experienced most of the feelings that ruled mankind. She knew envy well, anger too often, despair, happiness, pride, shame. Even love had caught her and surprised her by its might. Nothing had prepared her for the gut-wrenching power of jealousy.

She was physically spent, but jealousy filled her with heat, and the illusion of strength. She felt like a titan, and she wanted to smash Alva, rip her arms from their sockets, destroy her face, force dirt into her mouth, throat, eyes, to stifle her voice and bury her knowledge.

She felt the power roaring in her blood and she had run from it. Otherwise she would have killed Alva.

Because Nathan loved her. "Pleasured" her. While with me, he acts like a husband. Like Josh does with her.

But not anymore, Nathan doesn't "pleasure" her anymore. Chess held the protective thought close. Since we married, he's had nothing to do with Alva. Nothing like that. He's true to his marriage vows.

"I want what he gave her!" she shouted the words at the rainy sky.

But I don't have it, she admitted silently. I must be content with what I do have. It's more than I ever expected.

Chess sat up slowly. She ached from head to toe.

She saw, astonished, that she was barefoot. She must look a mess. That wouldn't do. No matter what, no one must ever know that she was jealous. No one must ever suspect that her marriage was less than perfect. No one must ever, ever, ever feel pity for her. She would not tolerate pity.

She was a Standish, and Standishes held their heads high. They did not whine, they did not feel sorry for themselves.

As she plucked pine needles from her hair and brushed them from her frock, Chess thought about what she must do. She had made a spectacle of herself back there, vomiting like a sick dog. Suppose Alva made the connection, realized that her revelation was the cause of it?

I'll say it was Miss Mary's greasy breakfast. Alva doesn't know I didn't eat any. I'll say I ran off to be sick some more, and then just kept on to Livvy's cabin to get some of her herb remedy. Everyone knows I used to spend hours and hours at Livvy's. However long I've been in the woods, it won't seem peculiar at all. It will look all right.

Chess had been well trained in her childhood. The most vital thing in life was to keep up appearances.

"Good gracious, child, you look like a drowned rat. Come in and dry off." Livvy Alderbrook snatched the quilt off her bed and wrapped it around Chess. "It's not warm enough yet for you to get soaked like that and not take a chill from it. I'll get you some coffee, it won't take more than a minute to boil."

Chess sank gratefully into the comfort of Livvy's presence. Here, at least, she had a real friend. Not like Alva—no, she mustn't think about that. She must do what she had come to do, then get back to the farm. If the rain stopped, there might even be time enough to do the last batch of trays.

Suddenly it was very important to her to finish the transplanting.

"Drink this. You must be worn out. I know what a misery those seedlings can be. Are you nearly done? I haven't seen hide nor hair of you for months, and I missed your company. I'd have come to visit, but I know there's no time for sociability till the field's planted."

The old woman's affection was even more warming than

her strong sugared coffee. "I've missed you, too," Chess said fervently.

Then she laughed. She hoped it sounded natural. "But I came for doctoring, Livvy, not just for pleasure of seeing you. I think Miss Mary's fondness for fatback is getting stronger all the time. What I ate this morning made me sick to my stomach."

Livvy put her gnarled hand on Chess' forehead. "No fever," she said, "so she didn't poison you. Slide off that quilt and let me poke your stomach. Stand over here near the stove where it's warm."

Chess submitted patiently.

"You didn't yell, so it's not your appendix," said Livvy. "That's a blessing, I don't do knives. When was your last monthly bleeding?"

Chess was bewildered. No one had ever told her about menstruation, and she did not know it was supposed to occur every month. She had been malnourished for so many years that there was no regular cycle for her at all.

"I don't remember," she told Livvy.

"Thought so!" the old woman crowed. "You can't blame this on Mary Richardson. By my best guess, you're going to have a baby 'round about Hallowe'en." She winked at Chess. "You must have sent Nate off on his travels with a big smile on his face."

Chess put her hands on her flat stomach. She couldn't feel anything at all.

"Are you sure, Livvy?" It was too good to be true.

"Haven't I been a midwife since donkey's years before you were born? If there's one thing I know all about, it's babies."

Chess just stared at her, dazed. Livvy lectured her about her condition. She had to start eating right away, she was much too thin. And she must drink milk, lots of milk, a pailful every day, with an egg beat up in it at every meal.

"And start wearing your boots every day, too," Livvy ordered. "You don't want that baby born with ringworm, do you?"

Chess threw her arms around her friend and burst out crying. "I'm so happy," she sobbed into Livvy's bony shoulder. "I'm so happy."

"Don't tell anybody," Chess said as she was leaving. "I want Nathan to know before anybody else."

"You'll be showing pretty soon."

"Not for a while, though. Isn't that right? Till then it'll be our secret, Livvy. I like secrets."

Chapter Sixteen

When Miss Mary's even breathing signaled that she was asleep, Chess walked quietly to the cupboard where the milk and eggs were kept. She used a cookpot to mix up what she called in her mind the "baby brew." Then she carried it to the bench outside. The night was clear, stars and moon bright and high. Her old woolen wrapper was welcome in the cool air.

Tomorrow was Sunday. She'd already written to Nathan, but she hadn't told him about the baby. Livvy might be wrong this once. Chess didn't feel any different, and she could feel no difference in her stomach. She didn't believe that she was pregnant. Not the whole-hearted conviction kind of believing.

She drank the brew. It took a long time because she gagged repeatedly. Next time she'd put some sugar in it. She was going to drink it, she was going to do everything Livvy told her to do. Because maybe Livvy was right.

Chess looked up at the mysterious beauty of the distant sky overhead. "Thank you," she whispered.

She wondered if Nathan was still up, perhaps looking at the same sky. No, that was romantic foolishness, she wasn't going to waste this special time with such nonsense. It was enough to just sit here, maybe with his baby growing inside her, and love him with all her heart.

Tomorrow there'd be his letter, with a report on the progress of the mill. Even if it was only one plank farther along, it would be good news. Their time together was coming closer every day.

Her report was good news, too. The rain had stopped in midafternoon, the softened damp earth was easy to handle, the transplants were done.

Her time of working side by side with Alva was over.

"We'll be taking the wagon, Chase." Miss Mary's cheeks were red with excitement. "While you were off swapping pleasantries with Ol' Livvy Alderbrook, a fellow come by to tell the news. The circuit rider is there in Pleasant Grove. There'll be services today."

Chess felt excitement warm her face, too. That meant a whole day there, not simply the fastest possible ride there and back. There'd be lots of people ... music ... life ... celebration.

She wore her pearls and her best outfit.

The milk and egg went down easily with three spoonfuls of sugar in it. It was a tonic Livvy ordered, Chess told Nathan's mother. "She says I'm kind of peaked."

Mary Richardson sniffed. "She's mighty free with other people's cows and hens." But there was no venom in her comment. She was already humming her favorite hymn.

Going home that night the whole family sang hymns. Chess sang as loudly as anyone. She had to admit that the Methodists had much more singable hymns than the Episcopalians. To her surprise the church service wasn't all that different, either. Much of it was the same as the prayer book she'd used in the small old church near Harefields. She'd have no objection at all to having her child brought up as a Methodist.

If she had a child. She had prayed very hard that Livvy was right.

Micah's mouth organ was a jubilant accompaniment to their singing.

"Onward Christian soldiers . . . Stand up, stand up for Jesus, ye soldiers of the cross . . . Rock of ages, cleft for me . . . Amazing grace! how sweet the sound . . . Abide with me . . .

"O worship the king all-glorious above
And gratefully sing his wonderful love;
Our Shield and Defender, the Ancient of days
Pavilioned in splendor, and girded with praise."

The mill house was finished, Nathan's letter said. He and Jim were beginning to make the wheel.

Chess raised the thick leaf a few inches, then bent low to look at its underside. Thank God, it was all right. No worms.

She hated them. They were longer than her longest finger and thicker than her thumb. Their bodies were segmented, and sometimes they looked as if they were humped in the middle, if you found one when it was moving. Mostly they were still, hidden under the leaf they were eating, their bright green bodies the same bright green as the undersides of the leaves. They attached themselves with nasty little feet like hooks, four under each segment, and you had to hold the leaf steady and peel them, pull them off, while the hooks gripped tight and the sticky tar from the leaf held them, too. The ultimate awfulness was when you pulled one loose and it wrapped itself around your fingers or your hand as if you were a tobacco leaf and it was going to hold fast to you while it bit and ate. You could actually see its horns sticking up on its head then.

The tobacco worm was a monster from some green hell. Chess screamed the first time she saw one.

She stamped them to death after she pulled them off the leaves. Stamp, stamp, stamp in a fury of disgust and hate.

Sometimes she kept stamping after the crunching sounds became pulpy noises.

Susan stamped them, too. The others grabbed the worm in four fingers and slit its belly with the thumbnail. That was quicker, but Chess knew she would start screaming and never stop if she touched a hornworm with her bare hand. Her gloves were stained black by tar, but they were still a protection.

She lifted the next leaf. There it was. Her throat closed with repugnance, and she could hardly breathe. Her fingers grasped the worm and pulled.

Ahead of her Susan was doing the same thing. Each of them checked every leaf on every other plant. In the row next to them Micah was worming. He was already several yards farther along.

Josh and Alva were well in front with hoes, chopping and killing the weeds in the two rows.

All day every day, six days a week, the four of them were in the field. Some days Chess had a hoe. She preferred that, but so did everyone, so the chores were switched. Everyone wormed.

It would never end. By the time they finished the last rows, the weeds and the worms were back in the ones where they had begun so many days before. It would be like this until all the leaves were harvested, until August.

And it was only the end of May.

But—she was certain now that she was pregnant. Her stomach was still flat, but her breasts were rounded. She loved them. She'd been flat-chested all her life, with hardly any womanly shape at all. Her waist was thicker, too, and her hips curved. That might be a result of all the milk and eggs, but she preferred to believe it was because of the baby.

At night in bed she covered her stomach with her hands. Livvy said that she would feel kicking soon. But she fell asleep at once, no matter how hard she tried to stay awake and notice any movement. She was going to write Nathan and tell him about the baby as soon as that happened.

She would have been the happiest woman in the word if only God had not created tobacco worms.

Early in June Chess was wakened in the middle of the night by a rolling, moving churning under her palms.

At last, she thought triumphantly. She smiled into the dark room. "Hello, little baby," she said. The blissful activity went on for more than a half hour. Chess was ignorant. She did not recognize the contractions. She realized something was wrong only when the burning knives of pain attacked. Then she screamed.

Mary Richardson was kind to her after the miscarriage. "I know what it is to lose a child," she said. "You sleep now, Chess. While you're sleeping you can forget for a little while."

It was the only time Miss Mary demonstrated any kindred feeling for her daughter-in-law, the only time she put aside her hostility and her deliberate mistake about Chess' name.

If Chess had not been numbed by grief, she would have noticed, and responded. But she was unaware of everything, and uncaring. Despair was a wall between her and the rest of the world.

Chapter Seventeen

THE STILLBORN BABE WAS BURIED the next day. Livvy Alderbrook supported Chess on one side, Mary Richardson on the other. Josh read the burial service.

Chess could not watch. She looked down at her dusty boots. Thoughts zigzagged through her brain: I really must remember to buy some shoelaces . . . the pea-vine flowers smell so sweet—I think I'll put some in a jar of water for the house. . . . Grandfather must think I've lost all my manners, I haven't written him a letter in ages. . . . Look at the bluejay flapping his wings—what a showoff. . . . It's so hot—I'd sell my soul for some ice custard cream like we used to have for my birthdays when I was little. . . . There's no excuse for me letting these boots get so ratty looking. I'll have to steal some of the horses' saddle soap. . . . Which one of her herbs does Livvy put in her water to rinse her hair—she smells so fresh. . . . Why is everybody singing all of a sudden? I don't know that hymn at all . . .

> *"O God, our help in ages past*
> *Our hope for years to come . . ."*

Livvy jiggled Chess' arm. Chess raised her head. "Do you want to name your son, Chess? Josh will carve it on the grave marker."

"What? A name? Yes. I want to name him for my father. Francis Standish. No, make it Frank. Everyone called him Frank. Frank Standish. He's dead, too."

Livvy looked at Mary Richardson. They were both thinking the same thing. It wasn't healthy. Chess had not shed a tear.

"None of us knew she was expecting," Mary said later to Ol' Livvy. "She should have said. There'd have been some way to keep her out of the field in the hottest part of the day."

"She didn't tell Nate, neither. I'm going to write him a letter. He ought to be at his wife's side at a time like this. She'll be able to weep once her husband's got his arms around her."

"That's not a regular marriage, Livvy. It's more some kind of business deal."

"He got her with child, didn't he? I call that pretty regular."

No one wanted Chess to go back to work in the field so soon, but she insisted. "I need to be busy," she shouted, "can't you understand that?"

She was chopping weeds when the mule-drawn wagon turned into the gate, and she didn't bother to look up. She felt no curiosity. She felt nothing anymore. Nothing was infinitely better than hurt.

"Chess!" Nate shouted as he ran toward her. "Chess! Chess!" He lifted her in his arms. "Oh, Chess, you shouldn't be out here under the sun." His face was covered with tears. "Oh, Chess." He carried her to the house without acknowledging the greetings of his kin. "Go visit with Livvy, Ma," he said to Miss Mary when he saw her. "Take Sally with you."

Nate sat Chess in a chair, knelt beside it. His hands held her face between them and his eyes searched hers. "We should share the suffering," he said quietly. "He was son to both of us. Let me grieve with you, Chess, and you grieve with me."

Tears brimmed in his eyes. He was man enough to cry without shame.

"Nathan," Chess whispered. She shuddered, then began to weep. He folded his arms around her and held her close.

"What are you looking at, girl?" Miss Mary had returned. Livvy would come over later, she reported, to see Nate and take supper with them. Nate's mother was chopping greens and peeling potatoes. And looking at Chess, who stood like a statue in the open doorway, oblivious to Sally's tugging at her skirt.

"I'm wondering what they're all doing out there in the field," Chess replied. She could see Nathan, gesturing and talking with Josh and Micah and Alva. Susan was some distance from them, hoeing weeds.

Alva was laughing, probably at something Nathan had said, and Chess was racked with jealousy. Alva looked so much younger when she laughed; she was almost pretty. She had pushed her sunbonnet back, to hang down her back.

"Sally, stop pestering me. Leave me alone!" Chess shouted. The child began to wail.

"I can't stand being cooped up like this," Chess said. "I'm going out." She had to know what was going on.

Nathan walked to meet her when he saw her coming. "You should stay inside," he said.

She felt desperate. He'd rather be with Alva. She clasped her hands tight together to keep herself from grabbing at his arm. "It's not hot anymore," she said. She hated the pleading note in her voice.

"I don't want for you to have anymore doings with tobacco," Nate said. He sounded angry. "I hate tobacco, and so should you."

"Then why are you standing out in the middle of it?" Why couldn't she control herself, why was she starting an argument, why couldn't she leave it alone? Chess felt helpless, captive and victim of her emotions.

"Come on, Chess, be sensible. Go on back to the house. Josh and I are having a disagreement about topping."

"What is topping?" Chess demanded stubbornly. She wanted more, she wanted to know why Alva had been laughing, but she couldn't ask. All she could do was keep him with her, talking to her, not Alva, even if it made him mad.

"Great Godalmighty, woman." Nate was extremely irritated. He reached out and snapped off the top of a tobacco plant. The noise was sharp, like a distant rifle shot. He thrust the pale green plant tip in her hand. "That's the top, it's getting ready to flower, and it has to be broken off to stop the growing from leaving the leaves for the flowers. That's topping. I figure it can wait a week, Josh figures two."

"But you were laughing. What about?"

"How do I know? What's the matter with you?"

Chess crumpled the budding leaf in her hand. It was sticky. She had to stop this, she was making a fool of herself. "I'm sorry," she said to Nathan. "I was just curious. I'll go help your mother. Livvy Alderbrook is coming to supper."

Walking away, Chess was careful not to stumble. Her knees felt weak. You must never, never do that again, she told herself. You were driving him away before you even thanked him for coming. That's what counts. He came to comfort you.

Damn him. He didn't have to leave her the minute his mother got back, even though her crying was long since over.

"It's good to have you here, Livvy," said Nate with a grin. He lifted his cup in a salute to her. It was half full of the home brew she had brought with her. The other half was in his stomach, making him mellow. Miss Mary was frowning. She disapproved of alcoholic beverages.

Livvy returned his salute. "A toast to Richardson's Mill," she said. "When do you figure to start the wheel?" Nate had done considerable bragging.

"Soon," he said. He turned to Chess. "Can you get your packing done tomorrow? I'm going to take one of the horses and ride around some saying goodbye to folks. We could head out the next day."

All the family was at Miss Mary's supper table. Chess resisted the urge to look at Alva. "I'll be ready," she said.

Nathan rigged a canvas canopy above the seat of his wagon. He regretted having allowed Chess to work on the farm. He should have remembered that she was a lady, he told himself. She needed to be sheltered.

Chess was overjoyed to be on the way to their new home and their future. She wanted to leave the loneliness behind. And the backbreaking labor. And the tobacco tar that stained and stuck to everything.

Most of all she wanted to leave the corner of the room where there should be a cradle, and the sensation of fullness that she got sometimes when she forgot that there was no longer the precious life within her womb.

The baby was so real to her, as real as if she had carried him to term and given birth and held him in her arms. She ached for what had never been, and there were times when she was afraid that she could not continue for even five more minutes pretending that she had recovered from her loss.

Frank. She was sorry now that she had named her son after her father, because it brought back the terrible memories of his death and the desolation she still felt that he had abandoned her.

She would never hurt a child of hers. Chess drank Livvy's prescribed baby brew twice a day. She would be healthy and strong and able to give her next child the strength and health he needed to survive.

That was the future. She rushed to meet it.

But her long habit of responsibility bothered her. She had never before left a task uncompleted. What would happen to Josh and the others, she asked Nathan.

He laughed. Oh, Josh would go back to doing things the old way, he said. It would make him a lot happier. There'd be no more factory work, all the tobacco would go to auction instead. And the fly would get at least a quarter of the seedlings as soon as they came up.

He gestured with his thumb over his shoulder to Augustus Standish's model. It was swathed in thick folds of muslin. Josh would never use the fabric, so he had taken it.

She needn't fret, though. Josh was a good farmer, always had been. And auctions would give the family plenty of money to live on. He had signed over his share to Josh.

And only a crazy person would want to see out the rest of the season. Once the plants were topped, new growth appeared down below. Suckers—thick tendrils—grew at the place where each leaf joined the stalk. They had to be pinched out by hand. They grew back at once and had to be pinched out again . . . and again . . . and again.

"The worms get worse, too."

"I *hate* them."

Nate grinned. "You were a stomper, I suppose, not a slitter."

Chess admitted as much.

"When I was a boy, the thing to do was to pull them off and bite off their heads to kill them. It proved you were a man."

Chess groaned. She felt sick at the thought of it.

But not for long. There were better things to think about. The mill, the machine, and Durham, a real town filled with people and life. That was where their post office was, only five miles away by a good road. She had already written the overdue letter to Augustus Standish. She would mail it in Durham.

She could hardly wait.

It took four days to make the journey. Along the way they heard that President Garfield had been shot. He had just begun his first year in office.

That was all the way up in Washington, D.C., Nate said. It made no difference in their lives. The would-be assassin was a man who had expected a government job but had not gotten it. Nathan was of the opinion that a man who counted on handouts should be the one shot, not the one doing the shooting.

Chapter Eighteen

"NOW AIN'T YOU JUST A GODDAM SIGHT for sore eyes, Chess! Welcome to the Hellhole—that's my name for this damn big mill your devil of a husband worked me to death on." Jim Monroe helped Chess climb down from the wagon. He handled her like breakable china; he knew all about the miscarriage.

Chess kept hold of his hand. She was truly happy to see his familiar smiling face, and she wanted him to know it. "Thank you, Jim. It's real good to see you, we missed you— all except Miss Mary." She wanted to hug him, but it would be improper. Also, Jim was very shy.

When she saw his gift for her, she did hug him, making him blush bright red. While Nate was gone, Jim had patched the roof and walls of the old haunted house. He and Nate had been living in it the whole time, but they had ignored the need for repairs. The mill came first. Now the structure was sound and snug. And the mules were in the shed he made from the materials he salvaged from the collapsed end. They hadn't troubled him and Nate when they shared their room, but Jim didn't think it a proper arrangement for Chess.

Jim had cleaned the repaired half, too. The floor was washed and shined. Near the fireplace there was an armchair made of split logs. "Take a load off your feet, why don't you?" he said, gesturing.

"Jim! Everything's beautiful," Chess lied. The other furniture consisted of a makeshift table—boards across sawhorses—two three-legged stools with bark still clinging to the legs, and piles of straw with blankets on top for bedding. She had a lot of work to do.

But first she wanted to see the mill.

It was an impressive accomplishment, and Chess let Nathan know that she was impressed. He and Jim basked in her praise.

The foundation was made of heavy gray and brown stones. The mill building upon it was a tall rectangle of new wood, hewn from the tall pines that clustered behind the mill. Big square windows were framed by shutters, and the entrance door was fronted by a stone porch, with wide steps to the ground. Beside it, bottom in the creek, was the immense waterwheel. The rushing water made it revolve in majestic ponderous slow turns, spilling water trapped in trough-like vanes as it turned, making rainbows in the sunlight.

"Forty-eight and a half feet high," said Nathan, with no modesty at all, "and ready to be connected to the millstones as soon as I get them."

"Won't be long, neither," Jim added. "There ain't been no damned rain for more than three eternal long weeks. One more and there's a crick we know about that's going to be no more than a goddam wet spot by the damn road. Poor dumb son-a-bitch miller's going to lose his damned shirt. Nate'll get the goddam stones for next to no cash money at all.

"Going to have to build a goddam sledge to haul 'em over here, though. There's not a godcurst wheel or wagon in all creation strong enough to carry the damn things."

Chess shook her head in admiration of Jim's eloquence.

Of Nathan's business acumen. Of the wide heavy plank bridge they had built over the creek to carry wagons loaded with grain. Or a sledge with a gigantic granite millstone.

"You two deserve the best supper I can make. Which one of you is going to shoot some meat? The other one can draw a pail of water from the creek and get a fire going in the house."

The next day they went to Durham for supplies. Chess wrinkled her nose at the odor of tobacco that filled the town but she was delighted by the neat houses, each with its own lot surrounded by a whitewashed picket fence. The iron-fenced big houses impressed her not at all. Harefields would have dwarfed every one of them. The roar of the Bull at noon made her clap her hands over her ears. When it was over, she clapped her hands together in applause. She found Durham very much to her liking. It wasn't a city like Richmond; it wasn't a city at all, at least not yet. But the dusty unpaved streets were full of activity, and the plank sidewalks were crowded with people.

Best of all, the general merchandise store had a polite, helpful proprietor and everything she needed for the haunted house. She selected the absolute essentials and promised the storekeeper that she'd be back. She told him her name.

She placed her few parcels in the wagon carefully. They were as precious as rubies to her, because she was beginning a home of her very own.

Chess also introduced herself to the clerks at the post office when she mailed her letter to Augustus Standish. They promised to take extremely good care of all mail that arrived for Mr. or Mrs. Richardson.

"We're official residents now, Nathan," she said when they left the building. "All we need now is a cow and a few hens and a rooster. I'll plant the seeds we bought when we get home." She loved the sound of it. Home. "We'll have our own corn to grind in our own mill. And the best cornbread you ever put in your mouth."

"I'll be mighty hungry by then, Chess. I hope you bought a little bit of flour to tide us over."

They drove back to the mill without Jim. There was a
friendly girl who'd caught his eye, Nate explained with care.
He failed to mention that she worked as one of the "hostesses"
in a saloon—no, barroom.

Three days went by before Jim showed up. Chess poured
him a cup of coffee and added some of Livvy Alderbrook's
farewell gift home brew. While he drank it, she had her milk,
sugar, and egg mixture.

Day after day the sky was clear, with a blazing sun. Nate
walked over to the other mill at daybreak to spy out the water
level in its creek. "Down a lot since yesterday," he said when
he got back. His smile was predatory. After he checked their
own stream and found it racing deep and dark, he always
grinned.

Finally, in mid-July, he judged the time had come to make
his move. He walked over to the other mill in midmorning.
"Hitch the mules to the sledge, Jim!" he shouted when he
returned.

It took two trips and two more men, hired for the day, to
get the millstones moved. They were more than four feet in
diameter and fourteen inches thick. Dusk was beginning to
soften outlines when it was done. "Give these boys a taste of
Livvy's sweetener, Chess," Nate chortled. "It'll give them the
pep to walk home. I've got one more trip to make, with the
wagon. I bought all the barrels he had, too. We can sell them
when people forget to bring their own for the flour after it's
milled."

He came home in the last, fading light. With the barrels
there was a big, handsome pine table with sturdy turned legs.

Chess stretched her arms across its smooth top, then lowered her head and kissed it. "No more splinters in the soup.
What bliss."

The next morning she washed her hair, ironed the shirtwaist
she had washed the night before, and dressed herself with
care to go work in the mill.

"You'll get covered with flour, you know," Nate warned her.

"I don't care. I want to look nice for our first day in business. Run through it one more time, please, Nathan."

"All right. The farmer drives up with his grain in sacks. Jim helps him unload. I go up to the big window in the loft and drop the hook down on a rope. Jim ties up a sack, snags the hook around the tie, and then I haul it up with the pulley. When all the sacks are up, Jim goes inside the mill. He pulls the handle to engage the gears and the wheels turn while I feed the grain down the chute to them. When the milling's done, Jim disengages and you scoop the flour into the farmer's barrel or the one we're selling him."

"And then all we have to do is weigh the flour and take the farmer's money. Simple."

" 'Simple,' " Chess agreed. Her step was as light as dancing when she walked across the bridge to the mill. Her feet felt like lead when she walked home at the end of the day. No one had come with grain to be milled. She and Nate and Jim had stood around, waiting. Then they had tested the mechanism. Then they had cleaned the clean millstones and the clean floor. Then they had tested the mechanism again. Nathan made an infinitesimal adjustment, which, he said, should improve the way the cogwheels meshed. So they did another test run.

The day had been a hundred hours long, Chess thought to herself.

After supper Jim said he figured he'd walk over to Durham. It wouldn't be dark for hours yet, and he'd like to stretch his legs. He promised to walk back at sunrise, in plenty of time for work.

"Do you think he'll really be back in time?" Chess asked Nathan. "He was gone three days before."

Nate was sure he would. "Jim's a good man," he said. He carried the boxed model to the table and removed its wrappings.

Chess began washing the supper plates. It's not fair, she raged inside her mind, it's not fair. He's worked so hard, and it's going wrong through no fault of his. He must be halfway to desperate.

When the supper things were washed and put away she went to her valise. It served for the chest of drawers she didn't have. She removed the newspaper story about Nathan's lemon wrapper triumph. The cheap paper was beginning to yellow.

"Look what I came across when I was tidying my things," she said. She carried it across the room to Nate.

He looked up from the model. When he saw what she had in her hand he laughed. "Are you hinting that you want to go back to tobacco farming? The hornworms should be peaking just about now."

The expression on her face was her reply.

"I didn't think so. Don't fret about me, Chess. One day don't mean a thing, except that I can be a first-class fool sometimes. When Jim and me first got over here, I called in at every farmhouse, telling them about the mill and getting their promise that they'd use us. I don't know why on God's green earth I figured that would be enough. You have to remind people who you are and what you've got to offer. You've got to cram it down their gullets.

"First thing tomorrow, when Jim gets back, you and me are going to go paint signs on every rock and every wall along the road. If anybody by accident shows up for milling, Jim can handle it. In a pinch one man can do everything that needs doing.

"Throw that old paper in the trash, Chess. That's over with. I'm only concerned with what's to come." Nate touched the model with a careful finger. Its miniature gearshaft moved up and down. "This is a genius piece of work," he said. "When you write the old man, tell him I said so."

"I don't have to. Augustus Standish has never had a minute's doubt about his genius."

"Do you miss home a lot?"

"How could I, Nathan? This is my home, right here."

Nate looked around the room. "It's not what you were used to. Once in a while I think about that."

Chess made an impatient, rude noise. "Poof! Don't be imbecilic. You can build me a house just like Harefields when you're the cigarette king of North Carolina."

" 'North Carolina?' " Nate roared in mock anger. He was grinning. "You've got to think bigger than that, woman. America, at the very least." Then he touched the model again. "I'll do it, too." He was no longer joking.

"End of the week I'll give Jim his walking-away money," he said, "if he hasn't already quit."

"Nathan, how can you fire Jim? He's your friend."

He looked at her as if she'd spoken a foreign language. "What's friendship got to do with business?"

Nate resumed his scrutiny of the model. Chess watched him for a minute, then looked away. I don't really know him at all. I'm married to him. I love him. But he's a stranger, inside. I wonder if the day will ever come when he stops surprising me? I hope not.

"I've decided to move to town," Jim told them when he came in. Chess was relieved.

"I'll miss you," she said.

"You'll have to wait till tomorrow," said Nate. "We've got things to do today and I need you to mind the mill."

"Tomorrow will do just fine," said Jim agreeably. He smiled his shy smile. "I'll count on seeing you when you come to Durham, Chess. I've got a job at Mr. Angier's store."

And she had worried about Nathan firing him. Chess decided she had a lot to learn about business.

When a wagon turned onto the track toward the bridge they could hear it from the house, and they came out to accompany it to the mill. Each time Chess felt a giddying surge of relief. Nathan's savings were being spent at a frightening rate.

He, on the other hand, grew increasingly annoyed as the number of customers increased. He was totally engrossed in the work he was doing in the house.

He was making the cigarette machine, carving each piece with painstaking precision. Augustus Standish's invention was being reproduced at four times its size.

Chess enjoyed watching him, especially in the evening when the kerosene lamp made soft shadows in the hollows of his throat and face. His concentration was so intense that he never knew she was looking at him. Thin pale shavings curled from his knife blade and fell silently to the floor, like shooting stars. The smell of the wood was sweet and fresh. There was no sound, save the scraping of grasshoppers outside and the occasional muted call of an owl. She drank the intimacy like champagne.

In the morning she swept up the shavings and added them to the accumulation already in the sack she had made from the muslin used originally on the tobacco seedbed. By the time Nathan finished the machine, they would have a mattress instead of a heap of straw. She would tell him then that she wanted to make another baby.

Unlike Nathan, Chess ran out to the wagons eagerly. She enjoyed the mill, everything about it. Inside, the high ceiling and windows high in the wall made the big space airy and bright. The grinding fascinated her; the heavy stones' rumbling as they turned made the wooden floor vibrate beneath her feet, and the husks flying out from them made patterns that reminded her of ripples on the river at Harefields.

The flour felt like silk against her fingers. They left white marks on everything she touched. She loved the clean look of the powdered floor at the end of the day; it was almost a shame to sweep, then wash it. But she was proud of the pristine appearance the next day when she opened the door for the first customer, and she was sure that it was one of the reasons that each week was busier than the one before. She remembered the sour odor of the mill near Harefields. She had loathed going there.

Most of the farmers stayed outside with their wagons, but some wanted to watch the milling, suspicious that they might not get all the flour from their grain. Chess enjoyed making shouted conversation over the noise of the grinding. She urged them all to bring their wives next time they came. "I'm just starting to get acquainted," she yelled. "I want to make lots of friends."

One day in October she cursed herself silently for being so friendly. The farmer was a tall thin man with pale hair and a long nose that had an intriguing bend in the middle. Somebody won that fight, Chess thought when she saw it.

When the grindstones stopped he walked through the scattered husks to stand beside her as she scooped his flour into his barrel. "I beg your pardon, Mrs. Richardson, but I must ask you—are you from Virginia? Your accent seems to say so."

His voice and his words were educated, gentlemanly, very different from the speech of the North Carolina farmer. Chess looked at him, curious. "I'm from Tidewater," she said. Would he know what that meant?

He bowed from the waist. "May I take the liberty of introducing myself, ma'am? My name is Henry Horton. You might know my cousin Horton Barton?"

"Of course I do! I'm afraid I was the horrid little girl who pushed him in the river at his sixth birthday party. How is he? Is he well?" Chess was elated. Hearing about him was the next best thing to meeting an old friend.

Henry Horton had a laugh like a steam whistle: shrill, intense, and extremely startling. It stopped as abruptly as it started, and that was startling, too. "Do you know," he said, "he's terrified of water to this very day?" His eyes were merry. Chess suspected that Henry Horton did not especially like his cousin.

She held out a floury hand. "How do you do, Mr. Horton. I've been terribly rude. I should have given my name at once. Francesca Richardson. I was Francesca Standish."

"Your servant, Mrs. Richardson." Horton took her hand, bowed over it without quite kissing it. Everything was perfectly *comme il faut*.

"What a happy accident this is," he said. "I'm sure my wife will want to call on you, if that's all right. We have a plantation nearby. I hope we will have the pleasure of welcoming you and Mr. Richardson there in the very near future."

Chess smiled. "That sounds lovely, Mr. Horton. I'll look forward to it." Her heart was sinking as she spoke. She had no clothes to wear for visiting. Her best was what she had on, and daily laundering had almost worn it through. She wanted very much to make friends in the neighborhood, but not friends she couldn't live up to.

Nate came down from the loft. "Another wagon coming. I'll get the sacks unloaded and tied."

Chess took her broom to sweep the grindstone clean, ready for the next customer. I was a goose to worry, she thought. Nathan would never in a million years leave his work on the machine to go socializing. . . . oh, my Lord, I forgot to give Mr. Horton his flour.

"Of course we'll go if we're invited," Nate said when she told him about Henry Horton. "I've heard about him. He's got more than three thousand acres, and a lot of it is in wheat and corn. He could keep the mill going all by himself.

"Land means power, too. Horton most likely has a lot of friends in state government. We might need his help one of these days."

"But Nathan, I can't go. I don't have a suitable dress."

"We'll buy one in Durham. We'll buy two. Didn't you say his wife's coming here?" Nate's eyes traveled the room. "That's it, isn't it? You don't want them to see how we live. That makes sense. Write a note saying you're too busy. I'll deliver the flour, and the note with it."

Chess wanted to hit him. "You don't understand anything at all, Nathan Richardson. I don't give two figs about impressing the Hortons. If she calls, she takes me as I am, in my own home. But if we visit them, I have to be suitably attired for her house. Those are the rules."

"You'd invite her in here?"

"Certainly." Chess looked around her. "I'd better dust. Everything's white with flour."

Nathan shook his head in wonder. "Chess, you're a real lady," he said, "stuck-up as all get-out, but a lady through and through."

Edith Horton was a real lady, too. She gave no indication that there was anything unusual about living in one room and drinking coffee out of tin cups. She told Chess that she loved to show off her rose garden and asked if the Richardsons might come to a luncheon party she was giving on October 18. If the fine weather continued, she hoped to have the tables outdoors, in her garden.

Chess accepted graciously. "Edith Horton is a real lady," she told Nathan later. "She gave me nearly two weeks to find something to wear, and she made it a daytime party because if there's one thing I obviously do not need, it's a dinner gown."

Nathan laughed. "It's a good thing I only have to do business with men. Even the crookedest of them is straightforward compared to you ladies."

"Hush up. When do we go to Durham?"

Chapter Nineteen

THE WEATHER WAS PERFECT, a mellow Indian summer day with warmth, but no heat. There were second-bloom roses on many of the bushes, perfuming the gentle intermittent breeze. Chess wanted the party to stop, just as it was, and stay that way forever.

She was wearing the very first dress made just for her and not refashioned from one in her mother's wardrobe. She knew she looked good, how could she not? Jim Monroe knew the name of a dressmaker in Durham, a customer at Angier's store, who got her pattern books direct from Europe. Miss Mackenzie had educated Chess about fashion. Chess was wearing her first corset of her own, too, the latest thing, in the long, narrow line called the "cuirasse shape," after the military breastplates worn in olden days. It was ideal for a tall thin woman and made shorter, plumper ones look ridiculous. Chess reveled in the comparison between herself and most of the ladies at the luncheon.

Her gray-and-white-striped dress was dignified. It had the

princess seaming that not everyone could wear. The stripes emphasized it, so did the black velvet band that outlined the wide V-shaped neckline over its white pleated silk underbodice. White pleated lace trimmed the poofed Polonaise-type back of the skirt, with a wide black velvet bow below the poof and above the saucy rear ruffles of the white pleated underskirt.

Chess was wearing the latest thing in ladies' boots, too; they were thin black leather, with inch-high narrow heels and shiny black buttons all the way up the side.

She had changed the white buttons on her white kid gloves to black ones.

With her grandmother's paisley shawl and her heirloom pearls, she felt like a queen.

She was being treated like one, too. The South's passion for its history and its lost grandeur had transferred the Tidewater gentry into an aristocracy, the only one America could lay claim to. Chess was its incarnation, and she was all but worshiped.

She hoped Nathan noticed and was proud of his wife. She certainly was proud of him. He looked very nice in his Richmond wedding-gift suit, she thought, and the haircut he'd gotten in Durham two days ago was worlds better than his customary self-barbering with a hunting knife. He seemed to be having a good time. And so did the three men he was talking to; they were laughing their heads off. They looked pale and ordinary next to him.

Wouldn't it be nice if there was champagne with the dessert? It would be so appropriate for Nathan. Because—more than the weather, or the roses, or the social delights, there was something very, very special about this day. Nathan had finished carving the final piece of the cigarette machine an hour after midnight. He should have nothing less than champagne to mark the occasion.

There was, indeed, champagne. And an extraordinary luncheon of seven courses. Chess was very aware of her fashionable cuirasse before it was over.

She admitted as much to Nathan when they were on the way home. He chuckled for more than a mile. He was completely satisfied with the day. Not the fancy food—he didn't recognize half the things he'd put in his mouth. But he had met three members of the legislature, who liked hearing about his legal adventure in Hillsborough. And he'd collected a lot of news about what was going on behind the scenes in Durham's business world.

He told Chess about it after they got home and he paid off the two men he'd hired for the day. James Bonsack had finished rebuilding his cigarette machine and had repatented it, describing it as "improved." He had also set up a company to market it.

"He wouldn't do that if it didn't work, Chess. I feel him breathing down my neck. Allen and Ginter are testing it."

She interrupted him. "I'll write Grandfather tonight. He can find out everything from Uncle Lewis."

"Just what I was going to ask you to do. Now, let's say it does work. What does that mean to us? We'll need four months at least to get ours in operation, and then there's the problem of buying the tobacco we need for it, and the fixings, and the selling."

"Don't they have auctions in Durham? No, don't tell me. That was an idiot question. You'd be recognized. What about . . ."

They talked for hours, working out solutions, making schedules, figuring costs and probable income from the mill, identifying problems, and making notes about information that they needed before final decisions could be made.

Nate partitioned off a corner of the mill's single big room; he made the walls thick, the door thicker. An iron hasp with padlock held the door closed. He wore the key on a leather string around his neck, under his shirt.

The model went on a stand inside the door. Nate arranged the pieces he had carved on the floor.

Chess wrote letters inquiring about rolls of cigarette paper.

Now the machine had to be assembled. In secrecy. At night. While they ran the mill all day. When it was done, they would learn whether it worked. The model did. Without paper and without tobacco. The model was an idea, not a piece of machinery.

"Nathan, this won't do. You're driving yourself too hard." Chess' eyes were reddened, dark-ringed with fatigue. The kerosene lantern swayed in her grasp.

"Hold that light steady, can't you? How's a man supposed to see?" In spite of the night chill he was sweating from the effort to hold the machine piece in the proper position.

"He isn't," Chess said sharply. She set the light on the floor.

The heavy wood hopper fell from Nate's hand. "I might kill you!" he bellowed.

"Right now you'd be doing me a favor. Stop for tonight, Nathan. It'll be getting light soon, and we haven't had any sleep at all."

He sighed heavily; it was very near to a groan. "You're right, you're right. I've started making mistakes. Let's go to bed. But hold up the lamp for a minute first while I rest this hopper someplace safe. . . . Oof, it's heavier than I remembered. I might have to shave it down thinner."

"Put the miserable thing down, and come on."

The unrelenting work was affecting both of them. Too little sleep night after night was not the chief problem. It was the need for Nate to do further sanding or planing on virtually every major piece to achieve the perfect fit. Some had required more—starting from scratch. He'd been working like a man driven by demons for six weeks, and the cigarette machine was little more than a framework. It was December already, and his estimate of completion before spring was obviously impossible.

In the meantime, everywhere around them barns and rocks and signs on trees blared the virtues of the Duke factory's cigarettes, "Duke of Durham." The word in Durham was that Duke's imported hand-rollers had already produced more than

9 million cigarettes, and that every single one of them had been sold.

The only good news had come from Augustus Standish. Bonsack's machine broke down with such frequency that Lewis Ginter had rejected it. The girls at the tables were faster in the long run.

The old man added in some more news, with a stinging bit of humor:

> You doubtless heard about the unfortunate mis-hap that befell Jimmy Bonsack's first machine. In shipment to Lewis Ginter, it was left overnight in the Lynchburg, Va. freight yards. Somehow it seems to have caught on fire and burned to a cinder.
>
> My dearest Chess, you haven't been reading Hans Christian Andersen, have you? I would be saddened to imagine that my granddaughter would emulate a drudge like Cinderella instead of an interesting hero-ine like the Little Mermaid.

Nathan asked her what Augustus Standish meant by that.

"He's wondering if we burnt Bonsack's machine." Suddenly Chess looked at Nate. "You wouldn't—"

"If I'd known about it of course I would. But I ain't been anywhere near Lynchburg. And it didn't do no good, did it? Bonsack just built another one.

"Which is a lot more than I can do. I can't even put together the first one."

Standish immodestly added that his design had none of the frailties that afflicted Bonsack's.

"All the weaknesses come from me," said Nate bitterly. "But I'll beat them, if it kills me."

The mill had its busiest day ever on December 11. That might have been because it was a Sunday. Richardson's was the only mill open on the Sabbath, a practice that caused a lot of criticism but also generated a lot of trade.

Chess felt her smile growing ever more stiff as the day wore on. She was grateful that sunset came so early. The sky was red when she waved goodbye to the final wagon; her temples were throbbing with headache, there'd been no chance to stop and eat since sunrise. She dutifully drank her eggnog, but supper consisted only of dinner's leftovers warmed over. Nathan did not notice. He worked on his whittling and sanding for hours after Chess went to bed. When he finally joined her, he fell into deep sleep before his head was fully settled on its pillow.

A half hour later, Nathan sat up. The motion woke Chess, but in the darkness she couldn't see his face. What was wrong? His hand clamped down on her nose and mouth. "Don't make any sound," he whispered in her ear. Then he lifted his hand and she could breathe again.

She could tell by the quiet sounds he made that he was pulling on his Levi's and getting his revolver. She couldn't identify the other sound—a dull thumping from the direction of the mill. Chess put her feet on the cold floor.

Nathan's whisper made her jump. She hadn't heard his approach. "Here's the shotgun," he said, and she felt it pressed into her hands. The metal of the barrels was so cold it felt hot at first. "You scrooch down behind the mattress with it pointed at the door. If anybody comes through it, blast a hole in him, it doesn't matter where. If it's me, I'll holler your name. Don't shoot."

She discovered that she was holding her breath when fleeting dots of color danced in the darkness in front of her eyes. She was breathing in again when she heard the shots. Crack! Crack-crack! Crack! Crack!

Her hands were slippery. How could she be sweating like this in the freezing air? Her whole body ached with the strain of long listening to silence.

Then she heard footsteps on the bridge. They were very quiet. Chess wiped one palm, then the other, on her nightdress and raised the gun to her shoulder. I abominate shotguns, she thought, they hurt my shoulder when they go off. She felt a mad desire to giggle.

"Chess!"

She came dangerously close to firing when her body jerked at the sound.

Nate hurried inside, tossed some fatwood kindling on the gray coals in the fireplace. They caught in an instant. The popping sound seemed very loud. Sparks flew when he dropped a log on top.

"Next time I go after people in the middle of the night, will you kindly remind me to wear my boots?" He was smiling, but the firelight showed the unnaturalness of the smile.

"What happened? Are you all right?"

"Put down that gun. Too many guns—" Nate bent over, as if he were in unendurable pain.

"You're hurt!" She dropped the shotgun on the mattress and scurried to him.

He held up an arm to keep her away. "I'm not hurt. I didn't give them a chance. Oh, God—" His words were a cry of despair, a prayer for forgiveness. "There were two of them. One was holding a quilt against the door to the cigarette room while the other one hacked away at the lock with an ax.

"They never even saw me, Chess. I shot them in the back."

He looked up at her as if she were his accuser. His face was twisted with shame.

"What was I supposed to do? Challenge them to a duel? I plugged them, the same as if they were weasels or skunks, because that's what they were."

His eyes were dazed. "First time I ever had to shoot a man," he said. Huge ripping shudders shook his body. Chess put her arms around his shoulders. Her left hand held his head close to her breast.

She felt a strange still calm and an all-encompassing love for this man. She closed her eyes, willing her peacefulness into him.

When the storm passed, Nate wiped his face on her skirts. "Forgive me," he mumbled.

"For what, Nathan? I'm proud of you. For doing what had to be done and for hating it. What will we do with them?"

"I already dumped them into the creek. The current will carry them halfway to Raleigh. I'll wash the floor at daylight, when I can see."

"I'll help you."

There was no sleep for them now. Chess made coffee, and they talked. The mystery was, how did anyone know about the machine? That had to be what they were after. The cash box still had the day's receipts in it. She'd forgotten about it because she was so tired.

Second mystery: Who had sent them and why? To steal? To destroy?

Eventually Nate closed the speculation. They'd never know. But whoever had sent them for whatever purpose would never know what happened to them. What mattered was that someone knew about the machine and believed it was important enough for a raid in the dark of night.

"Remember Bonsack?" Chess said. "His was burned at Lynchburg."

"I remember. Could be it's the same person. Whatever, we need to be extra careful from now on. And I need to go to Durham so I can hear things."

The bloodstains were not noticeable at all after a thorough scrubbing and a sprinkling of flour. The killings were safely secret.

But Chess' nights were full of dreams, old dreams that she had put behind her, she'd believed. In them she was young, and it was spring, and there were flowers blooming at her feet and on branches overhead. The trees were dogwoods, their white white blossoms floated downward on a sweet-scented breeze. Down, down onto the mass of red wet pulpi-ness which stained them shiny crimson. There was a red-stained gray hat nearby and a wet red coat with gold dots beneath the red and an outflung hand with a gold ring on the smallest of the long elegant fingers.

It was the nightmare of her father's death all over again. Only now there were two blasted bodies and so much more blood, so much that it made a river of red that floated them slowly, slowly out of sight, leaving only the smell of death mixed with the smell of blood-spattered flour.

Mercifully, she did not remember the dream when she woke. She knew only that she was glad to be awake, even though she did not feel rested at all.

He was going to hire a man for work at the mill, Nate said. The biggest one he could find, with the meanest look about him. "I figure he can cover for me every Tuesday and Wednesday. That'll give me time to shape the machine pieces here in the house and go to Durham, too."

They could easily afford the wages. The mill was making money and they were saving it.

"Give me a look at him before you hire him," said Chess. "I'm the one who'll be working with him. And I want to add another day, when you work with him and I stay home. I need to do something different, I have to. I want to fancy up some. This place is turning into a pig sty. Also, I want to do some entertaining. I've met a lot of farmers' wives at the mill, and four of the ladies at Edith Horton's luncheon have left their calling cards when I wasn't home."

"Why didn't they just come over the bridge and see you at the mill?"

"Because it was a social call, Nathan."

"More of your ladies' rules, huh?"

"Don't worry your head about it. Just pick one afternoon a week to be over at the mill with the monster man and leave me the house all to myself.

"Oh, and bring me some nice letter paper from Durham. I have to let people know when I'm at home."

Chess used her Thursdays to visit the wives who lived closest. Only the fiercest cold could stop her, so hungry was she for friends. And for a normal life. Gradually the nightmare went away.

Nate went to Durham on Tuesdays. The weekly newspaper, *Tobacco Plant*, was distributed on Monday afternoon. He solved one mystery on his first trip into town. Jack Burlington, the postmaster, greeted him like an old friend: "Hey, there, Nate. You've been a stranger so long we was thinking you'd gone to California looking for gold."

Burlington's jowly face was red and he reeked of whiskey and chewing tobacco at ten in the morning. His pouched eyes were avid with curiosity.

Nate hid his disgust, joined the man's hearty laughter at his own joke. California gold had been played out for more than twenty years, and only the most credulous greenhorns believed otherwise. Traveling slicksters sold shares in fictitious gold mines to credulous tobacco farmers with auction money in their pockets. Nate registered the insult and filed it in his memory. The day's going to come, he silently promised Jack Burlington, when you'll call me "Mr. Richardson," and take off your hat when you do it.

"Any mail come while I was gone?" he asked when he'd laughed long enough.

A big pile, said Burlington. Christmas greetings always added to the post office's burdens. He put a bundle of letters on the counter in front of Nate. Topmost was a typewritten envelope from the Ellansee Paper Company. "You got relatives making cigarette fixings?" he inquired. "Blackwell's gets a lot of packets from Ellansee since they started rolling those funny tube things." He aimed a stream of juice at the cuspidor near his feet. Real men had nothing but contempt for the sissies who smoked cigarettes, said his action.

"My sister's husband," said Nate. Even if Burlington believed him—which was doubtful—Nate knew the lie was too late to stop speculation. The intruders at the mill had proved that.

At least he'd learned why they were there. And also that

Blackwell's—the Bull—believed in the future of ready-made cigarettes, too. Time was really running out.

He felt as if he'd been punched in the chest by an iron fist. Nothing showed in his manner when he wasted valuable time talking about the ins and outs of the milling business with the postmaster. Long-winded conversations were a required part of any kind of transaction. Hurry made people wonder, and talk.

Nate shoved the mail in his pocket unread. It could wait. A talk with Jim Monroe could not. Jim knew the things the paper didn't print. The general store where he worked was a good place for picking up news. The barroom where his Dorena worked was even better, and she told him everything when they were in bed.

Jim had heard that both Blackwell's and Buck Duke were dickering with the Bonsack people. He made no mention of any Durham men being mysteriously absent from town, which meant that Nate would probably never know who it was he'd killed.

He ate a big dinner of pork chops and turnip greens with Jim in the Dixie Barroom. Dorena brought the heaped platters to them, and Nate swapped pleasantries with her, agreeing that winter cold gave a man an appetite, and Christmas came so fast it always caught a person unprepared, and Jim sure had gotten to be a fancy dresser since he started working at the store.

"A fine woman," Nate commented when Dorena left.

"You said it!" Jim agreed. He leaned forward. "She's got a friend who'd be damned interested in meeting any friend of mine, Nate. Name's Julie. A goddamn nice girl, too, pretty as a baby duck and real clean."

"Thanks but no thanks, Jim. Funny thing is, when a man's working real hard, he forgets all about women."

"Goddammit to Hell, Nate, that's pretty near the saddest damn tale I ever heard in my whole goddamned life."

"I got me a wife, you know."

Jim blushed. Chess always did make Jim blush.

Nate hid his smile. Then he lost any thought of laughter. He wasn't being fair to Chess. He'd promised her a baby, and he hadn't done anything about it for nearly six months.

After dinner he bought her a present at Angier's store. It was a brightly painted cardboard Christmas greeting card— the newest thing to come down the goddam pike, according to Jim. "Put it inside that decorated tin box of candy," Nate said, "the one with the manger scene."

Later, that night, he pushed up her nightdress. Chess opened her legs to welcome him. "Just put your arms around my neck, honey, you remember," Nate murmured.

Chess pushed him away. "Do not call me 'honey,' " she cried. "Not ever again." She could hear Alva's dreamy, remembering voice in her head. "I hate that word, Nathan."

He didn't know what to make of her anger. Maybe she was afraid, after losing Frank. "Don't you want to make another baby, Chess?"

She could hear the concern in his voice, see it on his moonlit face. "Yes, I do. But I want you to say my name."

"Chess. Hold on around my neck, Chess. I won't hurt you, I promise."

She put her arms around him and closed her eyes, the better to feel the brief minutes of closeness and possession.

For Christmas she gave him the completed mattress of wood shavings. It smelled sweet and clean; it was theirs only, and Alva was gone.

Chapter Twenty

BOBBY FRED HAMILTON WAS THE NAME of the huge bear of a man who worked at the gristmill. Nate called him "Soldier." He had a thick grizzled beard that made him appear even bigger and more threatening. On the first day he was there he learned that Chess was the daughter of a man who'd been in Robert E. Lee's army, and he became her gallant servant.

Bobby Fred had soldiered under Nathan Bedford Forrest and got a frog in his throat when he talked about his General's death in '77. But his voice was clear as a trumpet when he refought the glorious days of cavalry raids against the damn Yankees—pardon me, ma'am—in the Tennessee hills. Chess sat beside him on the stone steps in the thin winter sunlight for hours, listening. There were very few wagons coming over the bridge. The holiday baking was past, the fields frozen, the road an icy danger to horses. Bobby Fred came to work on foot from his cousin's farm three miles away. His beard was rimmed with frost when he arrived.

Chess worried about him; he wasn't a young man and he'd been wounded in the chest at Vicksburg.

Bobby Fred worried about her. A fine lady whose daddy was one of Marse Robert's officers shouldn't have to scoop flour and scrub floors.

They quickly became devoted friends.

"I'd lay down my life for Mrs. Richardson, Nate," said the old soldier. He refused to call Chess by her first name, but Nate's daddy hadn't done anything remarkable at all in the War.

"I believe you would, Soldier. It's a comfort to me." Nate hated to pay good money when there was no work to be done, but Hamilton had a reputation as an eye-gouging fighter and a crack shot. He was worth his pay as a warning to anybody with designs on the property.

"Of course he'll probably scare off everybody with grain to mill when business picks up after the thaw," Chess laughed. "I can picture people whipping their horses' backs raw in the race to run away."

"It won't matter. We'll be making cigarettes by then." Nate's voice was rich with confidence.

Chess prayed that he was right. His work on the machine was increasingly obsessive. His whole heart and mind were fixed on it.

In mid-February it was time to test it.

There were problems. The gear connection to the water-wheel was similar to the one for the grindstone, and the motion it produced was much too slow.

But the shafts moved and the cogs meshed smoothly and sluggishly; the chute from the hopper opened and closed; the paper wheel turned, without paper; and the canvas belt moved slowly underneath the empty paste container's brush, to the knife that clanked on its block, slowly cutting empty space.

Chess and Nate stared at each other, dumbfounded. When a

dream becomes reality, disbelief is the only possible response. Only very small children truly believe that it's natural.

"Now what?" she whispered.

Nate drove the wagon all the way to Richmond for the "fittings"—special paste, rolls of cigarette paper and wrappers, and cartons. He bought cutter leaf in small amounts from four different warehouses. For each transaction he paid cash and used a different assumed name. He gave Allen and Ginter's factory a wide berth. It was unlikely that he'd be recognized, but he was more cautious than ever now that he was so close to the goal.

He slept in the wagon on the long hard journey back to the mill, his revolver under his hand. For the first time in nearly twenty years, he went unwashed for days.

Chess half-listened to Bobby Fred's war stories and watched the road.

Nate returned at night, so that Soldier wouldn't see the load in the wagon. Bobby Fred nearly shot him; he was hidden in the woods, protecting Chess. "Thank the good Lord for the moon," he told Nate. "I'll help you unload." He gave his word "as a Confederate soldier" not to reveal to anyone what he had seen.

Nate worried; Chess did not.

There was still a lot to do. The leaf tobacco had to be stemmed and shredded, the attachment to the waterwheel had to be adjusted, the company had to be named and registered at the Hillsborough Courthouse. "We'll call it 'The Standish Cigarette Company,' after your grandfather's machine," Nate declared. "But we'll do that last, after we've made the cigarettes and sold them. Once it's in the court records, we're out in the open and the buzzards will be flying overhead."

On April 1 Soldier helped load 500 cardboard cartons into the wagon. Each carton held a 100 packets of 10 cigarettes.

"It's the best possible day to play the fool," said Nate with a laugh. Chess recognized the look in his eyes. He was loving the risk and the challenge. "I'm going to head straight to Durham," he had decided. "That's where the Bull and Buck are the strongest. I'll hit them before they have a chance to hit me."

The first wagon of grain crossed the bridge just as he drove onto the road. The mill had more business each day, now that warm weather had come.

At least I'll be busy, Chess thought gratefully. It makes the waiting go faster.

She was scooping flour when she saw Nathan in the doorway. Her hand tilted and spilled. He hadn't been gone a full half day. What had gone wrong?

"All of them!" he shouted. "Chess, they're all sold, every single sweet stinking tube. We've got a lawyer filing the registration papers and an account at Morehead's Bank and a wagon full of cutter, already shredded. Hold on to your hat, the rocket's going up."

He noticed the customer for the first time. He was from a nearby farm. "Alec," Nate said loudly, "let me shake your hand. You are getting your milling done today on the house. I'm a Godalmighty lucky man, and I want you to have some luck, too."

"Why, thank you, Nate." When Alec got home he told his wife that that Richardson fellow had gone clean out of his mind.

The cause of the sell-out was simple. Standish cigarettes were dramatically less expensive. The hand-rolled brands, from Duke, the Bull, and Allen and Ginter, sold to the retailer for $5.00 a thousand. Nate's price was $3.75.

"I'd only just finished buying the danged government tax stamps, and I went to get Jim to help me stick them on the boxes. Your Uncle Lewis' drummer was in Angier's store, and bought the whole wagonload. He'll sell them as he travels. What he'll probably do is sell the stamps and cigarettes separate, but that's got nothing to do with me. I got my receipt from the revenue office, so I'm clean.

"Jim's mad as a hornet, 'cause he didn't get none for the store. I was hoping he'd take maybe a thousand or two. Since he couldn't get them, he wants five thousand."

Nate shouted up to Bobby Fred. "Come on down here, Soldier. You're about to be promoted."

He pounded the big man on the back when he reached the bottom of the ladder. It was a recognized masculine expression of regard. "Soldier, I'm fixing to go down the road and hire another hand. He'll be working for you. From this minute, you're the boss of this mill. Mrs. Richardson and me will be busy building a cigarette factory."

He dashed off before Chess had time to ask any questions. She looked at Bobby Fred. He shrugged. Then they both grinned. Riding Nate's whirlwind was fun.

The next day the cigarette machine ran whenever there was no customer for flour. Nate disengaged the grindstone mechanism and connected the power drive to the machine.

He berated the small output—only 5,000 cigarettes.

"That's enough to fill Jim's order, Nathan. And it took hardly any time at all, if you don't count the changeover time."

"But don't you see? If we made cigarettes full time, we could do more than fifty thousand a day. That's close to two hundred dollars' selling price. Take away the dollar seventy-five for the tax stamp and the cost of the fixings and tobacco, and you've still got a profit of fifty dollars a day. Every day, Chess. Before the week's done, we'll have more than what I got for the lemon wrapper."

"I don't like to bust your bubble, Nathan, but you don't know for sure that you can sell fifty thousand cigarettes a month, never mind every day. We do know that making flour turns a profit of almost twenty dollars a month. That's a lot of money."

"Did I say we're going to stop grinding flour? I said we're going to build a factory, exclusive for cigarettes. We've got more than four hundred dollars in the bank, lady. We could build a palace if we wanted to."

Chess' knees gave out. She sat on the floor with a bruising

crash. Four hundred dollars? That was all the money in the world. She shouldn't be so surprised; after all, she and Nate had done the arithmetic together, then set the price. But she'd been working with "per thousand" numbers. How could she have missed the meaning of 500,000 cigarettes in the back of the wagon? She came to her senses, her mind crackling with energy. "We should hire a crew to build the waterwheel for the factory," she said. "It took you and Jim almost two months. I think the factory should be brick, not wood, too. A fire could be disastrous."

At that moment, she looked very much like her husband. It was the expression in the eyes.

The Durham County Sheriff rode in with two rifle-carrying deputies three days later. While his man stood guard he served Nate with legal papers. He was charged with patent infringement; the Bonsack Company was suing him for $50,000 in damages.

The sheriff nailed shut the door of the gristmill and left a guard to watch it. "The premises are out-of-bounds until the lawsuit's over," he said. "That contraption you've got in there is evidence in the trial."

Soldier drawled in best Tennessee that he had a mind to hang around for a spell. "I never did cotton to the notion of setting a fox to watch the hen house. I'll keep an eye on this badge-wearing little boy."

"Now just you watch your mouth, Mister," the deputy sputtered. He looked defiantly at Bobby Fred. For a few seconds. Then he turned away, ostentatiously rattling the door handle to be sure the door was immobilized.

Nate ushered Chess to the house. "Dig out the patent," he said urgently, "we'll go see Pete Bingham, the lawyer in Durham I told you about. Come on, I don't trust that sheriff. He's got no business here at all. We're in Orange County, not Durham County. I told you the buzzards would be after us. Somebody—or a bunch of somebodies—in Durham is real riled."

"The legal papers say it's Bonsack."

"He got the idea from somebody in Durham. Roanoke's a long way off. Pete ought to settle this in no time. Your granddaddy's machine was first, and that's the end of it."

"I'm not sure. Wait just a minute and let me think this through. . . ."

Bonsack's machine kept breaking down—they knew that from Augustus Standish's letter. Whereas Augustus' design worked fine. So they must be different. Chances were they could make Bonsack fold up, by using the earlier patent. But wouldn't it be better to let the competition use Bonsack's machine with all its faults? If they went to court, the Standish machine would be evidence; the lawyers for the other side would have the right to examine it as closely and as often as they liked, see what made it better than Bonsack's.

"Wouldn't you send in some engineer passing himself off as a lawyer? I would. He could take measurements and make drawings to his heart's content.

"I think we should go straight to Bonsack and reach an accommodation. We'll leave him alone if he'll leave us alone. We'll leave all the lawyers out of it."

Nate pondered what she had said.

"You make a lot of sense, partner," he said after a while. "There's only one more thing. We've got to make sure the sheriff doesn't get hold of our machine, or bring in anybody to take a look. I've got an idea. . . ."

A little later Chess left the house carrying fresh coffee. The smell was tantalizing. "I felt so sorry for you two," she called out. When she handed a cup to Bobby Fred, she whispered, "Say no, and meet Nathan back by the wheel."

While she chatted and sipped coffee with the sheriff's deputy, Nate and Soldier rode the vanes on the huge wheel up to the platform outside a loft window. Bobby Fred wrapped the end of a rope around his waist. Nate fed the other end through the unconnected gear of the power drive, then slid down it, barefoot, with Soldier holding it fast.

Chess laughed and talked until her throat was raw. Then

she laughed and talked some more. While Nate dismantled everything but the framework of the Standish machine and sent the pieces up to Soldier in flour barrels tied to the rope.

After he shinnied up to the platform Nate rode the wheel down. Soldier lowered the barrels to him, freed himself from the rope, dropped it into Nate's arms, rode down to join him. They concealed the barrels under leaves deep in the woods.

"I ain't enjoyed myself this much since my scouting days in the Army," Bobby Fred rumbled, deep in his scarred chest.

"Mr. Bonsack, I believe you had some conversations with my grandfather. He is Mr. Augustus Standish, of Harefields Plantation."

Chess looked and felt quite elegant in her gray and white dress and cuirasse corset and a straw bonnet Jim Monroe had let her have on credit. The new account in the Morehead bank was frozen, as evidence in the lawsuit.

Bonsack's lawyer tried to speak for him, but Nate advised him to hold his tongue. "My wife is speaking, Mister. You wouldn't be so low class as to break in on a lady's speech, now would you? I might regard that as an insult."

"I can tell by your expression, Mr. Bonsack," Chess continued, "that you suspect what I am about to tell you. But you needn't be alarmed. . . ."

Agreement was reached in under an hour.

Nate accompanied the lawyer to the Western Union office. "I want to make sure you call off the dogs, and for good," he said. In fact he was primarily interested in the dogs' names.

"Like I figured," he told Chess later, "it was Buck and the Bull. Along with your Uncle Lewis."

She gasped. "But he knows you're married to me. And he's Grandfather's friend."

"I told you before, Chess, business doesn't have room in it for friends. It's butt horns in a charge, and devil take the hindmost."

When they arrived back at the mill, Nate and Soldier hired a dozen men for patrol and guard duty. Only then did he reassemble the machine. Only then and after he replaced the old padlock and added two new hasps and locks.

"Now we can get down to business," he said. His eyes were bright with anticipation. "Let's make those bastards shake in their boots. They tried to do it to us."

Chapter Twenty-One

CHESS WORRIED THAT NO ONE would bring grain to be milled because the sheriff's deputies had turned all the wagons away until the lawsuit was withdrawn.

On the contrary, there was a line of wagons every day from dawn to dusk. Everyone had to wait, and no one seemed to mind. There was a carnival atmosphere.

"Isn't it nice, Nathan? I'm tired to the bone, but I don't care. Everybody wants to show their support."

Nate laughed at her naiveté. "Everybody wants to see the criminals, Chess. Lots of them brought their whole families. They don't know what we did, but they figure we got away with it, and that makes us heroes. Country folk don't like sheriffs. The law meddles in a man's business without being asked in. Nobody likes that at all, especially not in the South."

He went into Durham every day. There was some business to do: he ordered bricks for the factory, although he said they were for the house he was going to build. And he delivered Jim Monroe's 5,000 cigarettes. He also left sample boxes of

100 with the other stores in town and the barrooms. "No charge for a taste," he said. "Smoke some yourself and try them out on your customers. At five cents for a bundle of ten, you make a penny and a quarter profit if you decide to place an order later."

Mostly he let people see him, especially tobacco people. Let them see him smiling, stronger than they'd suspected, the winner. He made a point of "apologizing" to Eugene Morehead, president of the bank, for "the inconvenience the mistake must have caused."

He accepted Morehead's apology for the embarrassment and inconvenience he'd suffered.

When he walked out of the bank, he felt ten feet tall. Nate Richardson from Alamance County walking in to a bank and being greeted by the president of it. It was what he'd dreamed of, and it was happening. And this was only the beginning.

"Hey, Nate! Is that you?"

Nate turned, and saw his brother Gideon. He was overjoyed. "Hey, Bro! You're looking good."

It was true. Gideon was lean and tanned and muscular. He was well dressed, in a city suit, complete with waistcoat and gold watch chain. He looked successful.

Like me, thought Nate. The Richardson boys are winners. He thumped Gideon on the back. Maybe they could have dinner together—or did preachers have to stay out of places like the Dixie Barroom? Before he could ask, Gideon gave him his answer.

"I'm just on my way to catch the train," Gideon said. "I wish I'd known you might be here, I'd have done things different. It's mighty fine to see you. Do you hear anything from Ma and the rest? I've been on a circuit for two months, so I'm out of touch."

Nate stammered that well, he'd been awful busy, and he'd never been much for writing letters.

"I'm nearly as bad. Lily's the good one. She writes to Ma regular every month."

Lily. Nate felt the blood draining from his heart. He'd actually been able to put her out of his mind. Work and planning and the cigarette machine had pushed her to one side. He saw her golden hair, the tobacco-heavy air suddenly seemed to have an overlay of the warm sweet smell of her skin. He had an erection; it was painful, constricted by his heavy denim Levi's. Nate was afraid his stance gave away his secret, afraid his brother would know that he lusted after his wife. He wanted to beat Gideon insensible because Lily was his.

"The train won't wait," Gideon said, "and I've got a connection to make in Raleigh, so I'd better get a move on. God bless you, Nate."

Nate watched his brother walk away. Then he took leaden steps to the Dixie.

"Nate! You're the big news in town, I guess you know that." Jim's Dorena was perfumed and painted and for sale. Nate was tormented by his mind-picture of Lily's fresh innocent beauty. And her rounded breasts, tiny waist, pouting, soft mouth.

"Where's your friend Julie, Dorena? I'd like to get to know her."

Chess was pouring coffee for Edith Horton. It was Thursday, and she was "at home" in her patched-up one-room house. She sat on one of the stools, her best dress' striped skirts spread around her. Edith had the chair.

"Cream and sugar?" Chess asked.

"No, thank you, just black. I hate it, but I've got to lose some weight. You're so fortunate, Chess. You're as slender as a girl."

Edith was becoming the friend Chess had always longed for, someone she could talk to about personal, female things. "You should have seen me a couple of years ago, Edith. I looked like a broomstick. I drink quarts and quarts of milk, or I'd still be too skinny to throw a shadow. I don't care much about eating. . . . Except lately, I seem to be hungry all the time. Do you know if that happens when you're going to have a baby?"

"Why, Chess, how exciting. When are you due?"

"I don't know. I'm not even sure I'm expecting. I've always been irregular with my bleeding."

"You have to see a doctor. I always went to Arthur Mason, in Raleigh. He's the best in North Carolina. I'll write to him— no, I'll get Henry to telegraph from Durham—no, that's too public, you don't want the world to know about it. My goodness, I'm in a positive dither. I'll write and ask if he's still practicing and his office hours and so forth. Jessie, my youngest, is nearly twelve, you know. I rather lost touch with Dr. Mason. Now, tell me, how is your stomach in the morning?"

The afternoon passed rapidly and happily in talk about babies, Edith's children, Dr. Mason, possible names for girls and boys. Chess had never in her life enjoyed herself so thoroughly.

Except when she was with Nathan. But that was a totally different thing. He sent out sparks of energy and risk and adventure. He made her feel more alive, almost dangerously so.

With Edith, everything was placid, cozy, easy.

I'm a lucky, lucky woman, Chess decided. I can have both.

Working at the cigarette machine was noisy, but simple. Nate filled the hopper, adjusted the tension on the long ribbon of paper, then turned it on. With a racket of moving, clanking, churning, chattering, turning, chopping, the machine spewed cigarettes into a box below the guillotine. Chess straightened them to form even layers, replaced the box when it was full, again and again.

After Nate turned off the machine, they inspected the cigarettes and culled any that were damaged. Then they arranged groups of ten on cardboard squares in the center of larger squares of paper, folded the paper around them, and placed the bundles in a cardboard box.

While they were wrapping the bundles Thursday night, Chess told Nate she might be pregnant.

"Great Godalmighty, Chess, you shouldn't be wrapping cigarettes, you should be sitting down. Come on over to the house and rest. I can finish this. I'll walk you over and come back."

She was pleased and amused, like women throughout the centuries. "Don't be silly," she said. "I'll let you know if I get tired." She laughed at him, and Nathan knew that everything was all right. Her laughter always made him feel that way.

Augusta Mary Richardson was born on October 10, 1882. In a real featherbed, in a proper bedroom, on the second floor of a neatly built brick house with the latest modern conveniences and a white picket fence surrounding its front and back yard. Dr. Arthur Mason, Jr. came from Raleigh to be in attendance. Nothing was too good for Mrs. Nathaniel Richardson.

Her husband was a very successful man.

To the rear of the house, near the creek, there was a brick building. Large windows made a broad glass ribbon near the roof on three walls. They were protected by exterior iron bars. The fourth wall was a background for an immense wooden waterwheel, larger than the one on the mill across the creek.

RICHARDSON'S MILL was painted over the door. The brick building was adorned with tall black letters that blared THE STANDISH CIGARETTE COMPANY. Smaller letters read N. RICHARDSON, PROP.

A windowless brick structure not far from the factory was almost completed. Its roofline was the same height as a mammoth pile of coal nearby. Once done, the building would house the equipment for burning the coal and releasing the gas hidden in it. The house and the factory would have gaslight. Pipes were already in place to the copper boiler in the house's magnificent bathing room. It was marble-clad, exactly like the one in Danville's Hotel.

Chess had worked with Nate at the cigarette machine until two weeks before the baby came. Dr. Mason, Jr. had very advanced ideas. He also encouraged her to take walks and forbid her to wear corsets.

She felt and looked better than ever before in her life.

She was still plain. Her lot in life was to be plain. She was pale in a time when rosy coloring was regarded as pretty. She had pale hair, too, that flowed back from a high forehead, when curly bangs were desirable. Her aristocratic thin nose was too long and too sharp for beauty. And her gray heavy-lidded eyes were hardly visible in her pale face because of the silvery gold brows and lashes above and around them. High cheekbones made her cheeks hollow, and her wide mouth had rather thin lips. But her skin was luminescent, her silver-gold hair and gray eyes shone with health. There was a firm layer of flesh on her thin frame, which was very becoming. Happiness was a transforming natural cosmetic.

Standish cigarettes were handsomer, too. The paper that wrapped them was now printed with the brand designation CASTLE and a drawing of the chess piece known as the rook. Beneath it was the company name, in tiny letters, with tiny crowns over the S of Standish and the C of Company, and the address, Durham, North Carolina. The same designs were printed on the business stationery, order forms, invoice forms, and checks.

Messrs. M. E. McDowell & Co. in Philadelphia were the tobacco-products wholesalers who distributed Standish cigarettes. They bought all they could get, and begged for more.

A great deal had happened in the past six months.

A great deal more was planned for the next half year. Nate fairly crackled with energy and ideas. Chess would have liked to pause for a while, enjoy the plateau they'd reached so rapidly, but that went against Nathan's nature, so she didn't bother to mention it. After more than two years as his wife, she believed she knew him.

"Do go on to the State Fair, Nathan," Chess said near the end of the month. "You missed the last two, and there's no

need at all to miss this one, too. I'll be just fine, you know I
will, and so will Augusta. Bobby Fred and Bonnie will look
out for us."

Soldier now lived in the one-room house that had been
theirs. And Bonnie, the farmer's wife hired to help with the
housekeeping, was sleeping in a spare room until Dr. Mason,
Jr. pronounced Chess ready to resume normal activities.

She had had a difficult time with the birth, including more
than nineteen hours in start-and-stop labor. She considered
the torment nothing, once the baby was in her arms. She knew
in her head that Augusta was quite an ugly baby; her soft
skull had not yet recovered from the impress of the big forceps
used to aid delivery. But her heart saw only perfection, and
she was awestruck at the miracle granted to her. She was
again grateful for Dr. Mason Junior's advanced ideas. His
father had required a wet nurse for Edith Horton's children.
Chess had the exquisite pleasure of holding Augusta to her
breast.

Raleigh was draped in bunting from one end to the other.
The streets surrounding the State Capitol were thronged with
people staring up at its massive copper-covered dome, or
exclaiming at the goods in shop windows. Nate pushed his
way through to the edge of the street. He wanted a front-row
view of the parade. He was sure that if he lived to be 100,
he'd never stop being stirred by the music of a parade. His
feet twitched when the marching bands approached, and he
cheered loudly when they passed. There were seven of them,
two more than on his last visit to the fair.

The floats were good, too, but nothing to touch the bands.
Blackwell's had a dandy, with a big statue of the Bull standing
next to a papier-mâché pyramid and palm trees made from
dried tobacco leaves. People said that Blackwell's salesmen
had painted an advertisement for Bull Durham on one of those
triangles in Egypt. Nate was prepared to believe it. He was
proud of Bull Durham, all North Carolinians were. Just so
long as Blackwell's kept their minds and their advertising

fixed on their smoking tobacco and let their cigarette business stay a small sideline.

Maybe one day he'd decide to put a float in the parade himself. Chess would have some good ideas for it, he was sure. She had thought up the Castle brand in no time flat. Maybe she'd want a big castle, with a girl sticking her head out the top, like the carving old Augustus had done in her set of chess pieces.

He felt good that she had the baby she'd wanted so much. It made her happy, and that pleased him. She'd been fine about not complaining when things were tough. Now he was going to see to it that she got everything she wanted.

There'd likely be some things in the exhibition tents, new things, modern inventions like the crank mangle he'd bought her for laundry day and the automatic potato peeler and knife washer. It was a perpetual wonder to him, the things men thought up. Next to the parade, the exhibition tents were the best thing about the Fair.

Nate joined the crowd that followed the parade all the way to the fairgrounds. Almost everyone was marching to the beat of the music up ahead. When the band started "Dixie," rebel yells filled the air.

Nate recoiled from the piercing noise next to his left ear. He scowled at the source, then saw that it was a girl. "I swear, I never thought a little thing like you could make such a big noise," he said with a smile. She was very pretty.

She tucked her hand in the crook of his arm. Her dark eyes looked up through her auburn ringletted bangs. "That's 'cause I'm a redhead," she said. "We're just naturally more rambunctious than most people."

"Then I'll call you 'Red,' " Nate said.

She lifted her skirts for him later, behind the stand where you could win a hand-painted vase if you could toss three hoops around its neck. Red's husband ran the game.

Afterwards Nate spent hours in the exhibit titled "Electricity and the Home." There were pressing irons, a rotating fan, lamps, chandeliers, a two-sided bread toaster, and a copper kettle to heat water to boiling. He had heard people talk about electricity, read about it in the newspaper, but nothing had prepared him for the fact of it. He talked to the crew manning the big generator until long after dark.

"You should see the light it makes, Chess! Brighter than day. I tell you, it's the wonder of the world." Nate could talk about nothing else. New York City already had whole buildings lit with it, and London, England, had whole streets.

"Maybe you should take the train up to New York City and see it."

"I don't want to see it, I mean to have it. And I will, one of these days. The factory could be running night and day. Electricity could run the machines, a dozen of them, a hundred if the market would bear it. What do you think, Chess, about expanding?"

She smiled. "I'm not surprised."

She got out of bed the next morning after the baby's 6 A.M. feeding. Bonnie argued with her; the doctor had said to wait six or seven weeks, and it had only been three since the baby came.

"I'll go stark, staring mad if I don't start doing things, and that'll be a fine kind of mother for Augusta to have won't it?" Chess put her shabby old plaid wrapper on. She wanted to talk to Nathan before he went to the factory, or Durham, or wherever.

They talked for more than an hour, with intensity, laughter, finishing each other's sentences, sharing one another's enthusiasms. They decided to invest every penny they had in expanding the business and their lives in the community of Durham.

Nate and Soldier would make plaster models of the pieces of the Standish machine, take them to different and distant blacksmiths and casting foundries, and put together five cigarette machines of indestructible iron.

While the replicas were being made, housing for future

machine operators had to be built, plus a general store for them to shop in. "The store first," Nathan insisted. "All the farmers waiting for their flour to be ready at the mill will find it real handy for a length of rope or a keg of nails or a bag of fertilizer."

"Or a bundle of Castles," Chess added. "We'll need more wagons, too, to haul that many cigarettes to the railroad, but that can come last. In the meantime we'll have to enlarge the stables and be on the lookout for drivers and loaders and stable boys. Men, really, who can be all three.

"Right now I want a buggy. We can't drive a big farm wagon into town for church on Sunday." For Augusta's sake and for Nathan's position as a respected businessman, it was imperative to join the center of social and political power—the congregation of Trinity Methodist Church.

"I'll feel better, too. I went to church with Grandfather every Sunday and it doesn't seem natural not going. . . . I'll have to get some clothes, of course, but I'd planned on that anyhow. Nothing fits me now. And I'll make the arrangements for Augusta's christening. Edith has already said she'd be honored to be godmother. What about godfather? Would you like to write your brother and ask him?"

"No!" Nate's reply was instant and explosive. He recovered quickly and explained calmly that Gideon was too distant, his whereabouts always at the mercy of the bishops. He'd rather ask Soldier.

"Grand!" said Chess. "Go and tell him now, Nathan. We've got to do everything just as fast as we can. It's nearly November, and winter will stop things dead."

"When Chess gets the bit between her teeth, the rest of the world better get out of the way," Nate commented to Soldier. "I'm going to ride into town and find a fancy buggy. You'd better go up to the house soon as you can and get your orders, too."

"And see my godbaby," Bobby Fred said with a grin. His eyes were suspiciously bright for a toughened veteran of Forrest's cavalry.

Nate's mind was busy while he rode into Durham. There was so much to do—talk to builders, find out about foundries, talk to Jim Monroe about running the store. Plus pay a visit to the bank and then to the cottage where he had set Julie up as his mistress. He'd give her an envelope full of money and a train ticket out of town. It was a pity, the arrangement was real convenient for when he came to town. But Julie liked her whiskey too much; he couldn't trust her not to show up at church and make a scene in front of people.

Oh, well, there were plenty like Red around.

He drove back home in a shiny black Victoria, a carriage, not a buggy. It could seat four, and its leather roof would fold down in good weather.

He lit the shiny brass-fitted oil lamps before he pulled up in front of the house. They were the latest thing in convenience; and it was nearly nighttime.

On Sunday, November 19, the rearmost pew of Trinity Methodist Church was occupied by Edith and Henry Horton, Bobby Fred Hamilton, Nathaniel and Francesca Richardson, and Miss Augusta Mary Richardson, aged five weeks and four days. The Sunday service was long, with many hymns that were sung with great verve and volume by the large assembly. Miss Richardson slept like an angel through the whole hour and forty minutes.

After the service, the Reverend Sanders invited the congregation to remain and welcome a new family into the fellowship of Trinity Methodist Church.

Many of them did, including the entire Duke family and a partner in Blackwell's, a distinguished silver-haired gentleman named Jule Carr.

Nathan told Chess later that he could feel their eyes on him like knives in the back.

After the christening, Mr. Sanders escorted Augusta and her adults down the aisle and outside. His wife rushed from the vestibule to coo over the baby. Augusta stirred. Her feet thrashed inside the long silk skirt of her christening gown.

"Oh, my," chirped Mrs. Sanders. "What beautiful needle-work, Mrs. Richardson." She fingered the gown. "Did you do it?"

"No," said Chess pleasantly. "I never did learn to make my satin stitch smooth." She felt like hitting Mrs. Sanders. Augusta was squirming and her face was contorted, in preparation for a scream.

Edith Horton saved the day. "Mrs. Sanders, please excuse me for interrupting, but I wanted to ask you about the altar flowers. Where did the magnificent chrysanthemums come from?" She took the minister's wife by the arm and eased her away. Augusta waved tiny fists, blew a bubble and settled down.

Chess smiled and made polite noises at an avalanche of well-wishers. Nathan and Bobby Fred were going through the same well-meant ordeal. She could hear Henry Horton's steam-whistle laughter somewhere off to her right.

It was a beautiful day, sunny and crisp. The pervasive smell of tobacco was sweet and somehow autumnal. She felt very happy. They were going to belong here, with these kind, welcoming people. She was going to have everything she'd always wanted, give Augusta the best, busiest, happiest life any little girl could ever have.

Edith and Henry hosted dinner at a boardinghouse known for its cook, and Chess used the room reserved for her to feed and change Augusta. Then they all went to the rented studio of a traveling photographer who was in Durham for a week.

He took a family portrait: Chess seated with baby in arms, husband behind her.

Then an identical one—minus baby—of Edith and Henry.

After that Chess insisted on one of Bobby Fred holding Augusta.

Then she and Edith each had her own individual portrait done, while the other held Augusta. These were for the *cartes de visite* they were going to have made. The portrait calling cards were the very latest fashion in Durham, according to Miss Mackenzie, dressmaker and oracle.

Also the latest fashion were the big, elaborately draped bustles on their dresses. "Bustles are back!" Miss Mackenzie shrieked happily at all her clients. "And they're bigger than ever." Chess was still having considerable difficulty managing the iron-strapped support that was tied around her waist. It was heavy, and precariously balanced, and wanted to pull her whole body over backwards. She could not stop looking over her shoulder from time to time to make sure that it was in place and that the complicated braid-trimmed folds of brown velvet had not slid off to one side.

Her tightly fitted braid-trimmed jacket was no problem; she could pull down the points at the bottom of it so they were centered over the swagged front folds of velvet. And she loved the lavish jabot of cream-colored lace at the neck of it. Nathan had bought her a crescent pin of filigreed gold that gave just the right amount of shininess for the sedate costume.

She loved the luxury of new clothes, the frivolity of fashion, the brand-new pleasures of wealth. Tight corsets and iron cabooses were a small price to pay, she thought.

Chapter Twenty-Two

WINTER CAME LATE. Frost whitened the ground through November and December, but days were sunny and as warm as autumn. Chess made the most of the halcyon interlude.

Augusta's feeding schedule kept her close to home but she didn't mind. She was getting acquainted with leisure, a new experience for her. She watched the store and cottages go up, made lists of items she personally wanted Jim Monroe to order for the store, wrote long letters about Augusta and sent them, with copies of the family portrait, to Miss Mary and her grandfather. She played with her baby, bathed her, dressed her, brushed her thin golden hair with a soft silver-backed brush.

And she read, the greatest luxury of all. She ordered books, magazines, newspapers, and wallowed in words. The parlor of the neat little house became crowded so quickly that she had one of the carpenters make shelves on every wall of the spare room to hold her treasures. Bonnie still came in every morning to dust and sweep and scrub, but she no longer slept there.

In the evening, after supper, the gaslights made it easy to read until late. Sometimes Nathan pored over *Scientific American* and the half dozen journals devoted to the tobacco business while Chess laughed to herself at the wit of Mark Twain. The only sound in the room was the rustle of pages being turned, the slow bubbling of the lights, and the soft shifting whisper of ashes in the grate. She would put her finger in the book to hold her place, close her eyes, and savor the peaceful happiness.

Soldier minded the baby on Sunday morning while Nathan and Chess went to town for church. That was another kind of happiness. Chess loved the music, the singing, the conviviality outside after the service. She was learning names, identifying men and women she had read about in the *Tobacco Plant,* making up her mind about who she wanted to make friends with, who might be helpful to Nathan. Or dangerous.

On the drive home, they compared impressions. Often they sang. Always, they talked about their future. Nate was anxious for it to arrive.

When the new machines are ready . . . when the houses are done . . . when the store is open . . .

He had hired a boy to do Chess' old job of catching cigarettes, and he was shipping 200,000 a week, for a profit of nearly $200. An average man would be satisfied. Nate was not average. He was spending $250. Expanding.

Chess knew all about it. She kept the business records and did the bookkeeping. Their bank account was melting away like butter in a skillet.

Buck Duke showed up on the Wednesday after Christmas. Chess was plucking a chicken to fix for supper and singing a nonsense song to Augusta, who was in a basket on a kitchen chair. He opened the kitchen door and said hello; Chess was so startled she dropped the hen.

"Hello, yourself." She was angry.

"I did knock. I guess you didn't hear me 'cause you were singing. Can I come in?"

Now she was angrier. She'd been deficient in basic manners. She forced herself to smile. "Of course."

Duke bent his head when he walked through the door. He was very tall. And very charming. He picked up the hen, sat down, and began to pull feathers. "I'm Buck Duke." His smile was curiously intimate.

"Yes, I know. I've seen you at church. You can hand me that hen now, Mr. Duke."

"I'd rather pluck it while you go fetch your husband. I'd go, but I figure he won't want me busting in on him at his factory." His eyes crinkled, sharing the humor with her.

Of course he was right. Chess gave a quick nod. "I'll get him."

"Do you mind if I sing to the baby? I don't carry a tune real good."

"She's not very discriminating. Go ahead."

Buck stopped singing and stood up when Nate and Chess walked in. "Nice family, Nate," he said affably. The hen was clean down to the pinfeathers. "I come to talk business some. Where will we go?"

"We'll stay right here, Buck. My wife's my business partner. Take a chair."

Duke's eyebrows rose. His look at Chess was both appraising and admiring. He sat. So did Nate. And Chess.

"Here's the gist of it," said Buck. "There's talk that you got kind of overextended. I'm here to buy that machine of yours or go partners with you, whichever one suits you best." His voice was slow and quiet. Beneath the words, power was only half submerged. The unspoken threat quivered in the air.

Nate lounged in his chair, grinning. "That's right sporting of you, Buck. You shouldn't listen to talk, though. People get things all mixed up. Why, some fool even told me that those rollers you hauled down from New York are real homesick and are fixing to walk out on you."

It was like lances clashing. Chess looked from Nathan to

Buck and back to Nathan. They were two of a kind. Behind the smiles lay the will to win, with no holds barred.

"I can make the figures real sweet, Nate. I'd sooner not have to wait till you get sold up to pay your debts."

"You'd have to wait till Hell freezes over."

Duke shrugged. "The cold's overdue," he drawled. "Should be along any day now." He stood, smiled at Chess. "A pleasure to see you again, Mrs. Richardson. S'long, Nate." He walked out.

They heard his horse's hooves on the road. When the sound diminished to silence Nate put his head between his hands. "I might have cut things too thin," he said. "I'm worried, Chess."

Her breathing stopped. Then began again. When she spoke, conviction was strong in her voice. "Don't be silly, Nathan. I know you'll win."

"Buck sold nine million hand-rolled this year."

"Next year we'll sell twenty million."

Nathan looked up. He laughed softly. "You sound mighty convincing, partner." He stood and stretched. Then he pumped water into the sink and washed his hands. "One of these days I'll get away from tar," he muttered, "can't come too soon to suit me." He began to laugh, a lazy, rumbling kind of laughter. "The sorry part is that maybe I missed my chance to put a real scare into ol' Buck. My stomach started reminding me it was hungry as soon as my feet hit the kitchen floor. The whole time we were having our standoff, I was worried that it was going to let out a growl."

"February 18, 1883," Chess wrote in the record book. "Two iron Standishes begin operating. Four Negro families in cottages. Store open. Jim Monroe and wife Dorena in charge. Cigarette production today 100,000. Corner has been turned."

The record book was nearly filled, only one page left. She decided to be spendthrifty and buy new ones, several of them, one each for the mill, the Standish factory, the store, and rents from the cottages. But this one would probably always be her favorite. Chess turned back to the first page.

July 17, 1881	open gristmill
No business	

July 18	
paint rocks	

July 19	
Earnings 14 cents	

July 20	
Earnings 22 cents	

She smiled. It certainly seemed like a very long time since then. Her smile broadened as she turned pages and read notations of hiring Bobby Fred, testing the Standish, choosing names for company and cigarette, building the house, Augusta Mary's birth and christening. Yes, definitely, this would always be her favorite record book. She'd find a very safe place to keep it, and give it to Augusta when she was grown.

Chess made no note in the record book of another turning point: Augusta was weaned, and Chess could leave home for the whole day, if she wished. Bonnie was delighted to have the additional paid hours of work.

The *cartes de visite* came out from their box, and Chess watched the weather with special interest. On warm days she drove the Victoria to the half dozen plantation houses in the region to pay calls. Edith's was nearest; she always began

there, and often Edith went with her for the rest of the calls.
There was a close bond among these women. They were all
in their thirties or forties, they all remembered the days before
the Civil War, and they all worked hard to maintain a semblance of the old graciousness in the crumbling great houses
of their husbands' family homes.

Too many times conversation degenerated into plaintive
stories about "the old days" compared to today's world, where
upstarts were taking over everything with their vulgar new
money. That cut too close to the bone. Nathan was one of
those upstarts. Chess became very Tidewater when that happened. Who had ever heard of North Carolina anyhow in
elegant Virginia?

Nevertheless, she was comfortable with Darcy Andrews
and Louella Simms and Harriet Truelove and Beth Fielding.
Edith Horton, of course, was her best and oldest friend.

The plantation mentality caused the first big fight between
Chess and Nate.

It was triggered by Jim Monroe. "Dorena's got that place
upstairs decorated to a goddamn fare-thee-well," he boasted
to Nate when he stopped in at the new store. "You never saw
so many damn miles of fringe in your whole goddamned life.
Why don't you and Chess bring the baby over for supper
tonight and take a look?"

"I'm not going to go there," Chess said to Nathan. "How
could you even think of accepting? I don't care if Jim did
help you build the mill. I don't care if he did fix the old house
for me. I don't care if he'll cry his eyes out for the rest of
his life if we don't go. That Dorena person is trash. She wears
paint on her face, and she reeks with strong perfume.

"If we go there, we'll have to invite them here, and I will
not have that low creature in my house." Chess was shaking
with rage.

Nate responded in kind. He knew he'd made a mistake the
minute he'd told Jim yes, he'd spoken without thinking, but
the deed was done now, and one supper wouldn't make all

that big a difference. Chess did not have to invite them back. He'd explain to Jim.

"And apologize for my manners, I suppose."

"I didn't figure to, but now that you mention it, maybe I will. Not because of Dorena. You're right, she's not fit company for a lady. But you're carrying your plantation lady stuff too far, Chess. I got a lot of apologizing to do on your account."

"*You?* Apologize for *me?* And to whom, may I ask?"

" 'To whom,' " he said in a mocking falsetto. Then he shouted. "To the tenants, that's 'whom'! The way you sashay around asking their business and patting them on the head makes me ashamed on your account."

"How dare you? I was watching out for black tenants when you were walking barefoot behind a mule in a tobacco field. Who do you think you are to be ashamed of me?"

"Don't put on your high and mighty accent with me, Chess, and don't you ever look down your nose at me that way, like I was dirt beneath your feet. Your kind have had their day. It's over, it's been over for twenty years, and nothing you or Edith Horton or any of your other friends ever do will bring it back."

The truth of what he said hit Chess like a blow. Her eyes filled with tears, and she was furious at herself, but they spilled over and she began to cry.

"Great Godalmighty!" Nate bellowed. "I'm going to Jim's. I can't stomach any more."

Chess continued to weep. The shouting—hers as well as his—terrified her.

Nate tromped off into the woods, not to Jim's. Her tears disturbed him deeply. Except when baby Frank died, he couldn't remember her ever crying; tears made her a stranger.

About Dorena, Nate knew that he was wrong. About the tenants, he was sure that he was right.

Chess believed that she was right, too.

Both of them were right, and both of them were wrong

regarding the black families in the new cottages. The tenants were former slaves, or the children of former slaves, on Fairlawn, the biggest plantation in the North Carolina Piedmont.

To Chess, reared in paternalistic plantation thinking, they were a responsibility, they were like children.

Nate, product of rural farm life, remembered freed black farmers, who fought the same enemies of weather, the fly, and the hornworm. Some made it, some didn't, like white farmers. Black or white, the losers lost and the winners won. He respected the winners and gave no thought to the losers, and he didn't owe any of them anything. The workers he'd hired were tenants in houses he owned. The men would work hard, or be fired, and pay rent, or be thrown out.

Chess wanted them to be happy. She never thought of their pride.

Nate respected a hard worker's self-respect. He had no interest in his other emotions.

As for the tenants, they were a unit, because they shared experience and blood. Generations of slaves at Fairlawn had married, borne children, seen them marry. A few of them missed the security of being taken care of, and they welcomed Chess' attitude. Others valued freedom more than ease, and resented her solicitude. All of them knew that whites had enslaved them, other whites had promised them freedom, still other whites had translated that freedom as a condition of servitude in low-paying jobs, another form of slavery.

They would use the skills developed in the slave years. They would give the white man and white woman the responses they expected. And they would reveal themselves only to their own kind, their own kin, keeping their secrets from the whites. Whites couldn't be trusted.

Nate and Chess had fought bitterly about people they knew nothing about.

"I'm sorry," said Chess when Nathan came home, "I shouldn't have said all those terrible things."

"I'm sorry, too. I know Dorena's out of bounds."

Neither of them referred to the tenants again. Chess visited the houses less often, but she didn't stop altogether.

Nate bought bricks for building from no one but a black businessman named Richard Fitzgerald, because they were the best bricks. When he talked to Soldier or Jim, he called the black workers "niggers."

When Augusta was six months old, Chess decided to take her to Harefields. "Grandfather's handwriting has been getting awfully spidery the past few months, Nathan. He denies it, but I'm afraid he might be declining. You know, he's very old. I think it would mean a lot to him to see his namesake great-grandchild."

Chess looked bleak. "And if he's nearing the end, I have to make some arrangements about my mother, and about managing the plantation. I don't know who or how, but it's got to be done. Mr. Perry can give me some advice, maybe. He's been Caesar's lawyer for years and years . . . unless he's dead, or retired." She sighed. "I'd rather stay home."

Nate said she was right to do it now and get it over with. "We'll take the train up and take Bonnie Wilson along to help you with the baby. I'll be glad to see the old man. Lord knows I owe him a thank-you. I'd like to hear what else he's been dreaming up, too.

"How would you like to spend a few days in Richmond? I'm thinking of changing over to a wholesaler there, but I want to talk to them before I make up my mind."

"I'd absolutely love it! Richmond's a real city, not a mud pile like Durham. It has sidewalks and brick streets and wonderful shopping. I used to see things in the windows but I never could afford to buy anything."

"Things are a little different now."

"A little! We're filthy rich, Nathan, and you know it."

"Not 'filthy,' Chess, you'll make my skin start to itch."

"It is tobacco money, Nathan."

"Merciless, you have no mercy. I'm going to order up some hornworms and put them down the back of your neck."

Chess pretended to cower. "I give up, I take it back. We're clean as a whistle, spanking-fresh new rich. *Nouveau riche.* And I like it very, very much.

"Richmond is going to be wonderful."

Chapter Twenty-Three

"SEE, AUGUSTA, that's where Mother and Daddy were married, in that pretty little church." Chess propped the baby up to look out of the window of the carriage. Nathan had gone all out, hiring an elegant dark green brougham driven by a dignified elderly black man in an elegant dark green coachman's coat and tall black beaver hat.

"And look, darling, look at the big stone rabbits. We're home. This is Harefields."

She hadn't expected to feel this way. Home was her neat brick house in Orange County, North Carolina. But ever since she had smelled the river when the train neared Richmond, she'd felt Harefields calling to her heart. She was flooded with memories of her childhood, when the world was beautiful and ordered and safe. Of a swing hanging from a live oak draped in wisteria. Of tea parties at her special low table set on the broad lawn, with her French dolls, each in its own chair, dressed in laces and silks. Of picture books, with wonderful stories, read in the wicker rocker on the wide veranda.

Of music floating down from the ballroom and the jeweled ladies escorted up the stairs by handsome men, past the crack in the door through which she peeked, although she should have been asleep.

The wisteria should be blooming now, and the tide must be high because the salt smell was strong. Her heart was beating "hurry, hurry, hurry home."

The carriage passed through the gates, and suddenly there were dozens of people ahead, running out to the drive. Harefields' tenant farmers. Men, women, children. From the fields, from the houses, running and shouting her name, welcoming her home. Chess couldn't ride past them. She was too happy to see them. "Stop!" She cried. "Stop the carriage." She put the baby in Bonnie's lap and fumbled with the unfamiliar door handle.

"I'm home," she called out, and stepped down onto the weed-grown drive. "Scylla!" She recognized the cook. "It's me, Miss Chess, and I still haven't learned to make a decent gravy—what is it? What's wrong?"

The running people were wailing and Scylla's face was streaming with tears. She put her arms around Chess. "Pore chile," she sobbed, "pore orphan child. They'se gone. Ol' Mr. 'Gustus, and your momma, too. The preacher didn't know how to find you, they done buried, Miss Chess, three days now."

Chess held tight to the big woman's strong body. "No!" she cried. The sound was lost in the high wailing keen of the women, the basso moans of the men, the gasping sobs of the children. Inside the brougham, Augusta began to scream.

Firm hands clasped her shoulders. "Tell me," Nathan said to Scylla. "What happened here? I'm Miss Chess' husband." He pulled Chess away, into his arms.

Scylla rocked back and forth. "Fire," she moaned, "the house. In the nighttime. The sky was lit up like noonday." She threw her apron up to hide her face, wept into it.

Chess pushed Nate away. "I need to see." Her voice was hollow, without life. "I have to see." She put her foot on the carriage step. "Damn you," she screamed at the driver. "Whip up those horses and take me home. I have to see."

Nate grabbed her above the elbow and thrust her onto the seat. The bustle of her dress skewed wildly, like a grotesque deformity of nature. He mounted onto the driver's box and grabbed the reins. "Coming through," he shouted. "Get out of the way." The crack of slapping leather was like a pistol shot.

He had no idea how big the house was. The charred ruins stretched for a quarter acre. Six blackened brick chimneys still stood, like giant markers of mourning. Gouts and feathers of gray ash eddied overhead in the wind. They seemed to be playing some ghastly game, a dance of death.

Chess was still and silent as the chimneys. Her fingers were intertwined, her face as pale as her white gloves. She stared at the remains of her past, unconscious of the swirling ash, of her child's crying, of her husband's presence.

At last she turned. Her eyes met Nathan's. "I have seen it," she said slowly, "and I must believe it. I'll never forgive myself for waiting so long to come.

"Please take me to Richmond, Nathan. I have to see Mr. Perry."

Chapter Twenty-Four

THE GINTERS WANTED THEM to stay at their house. Mrs. Ginter pled with Nate to influence Chess, but he told her that he could not.

As next best thing, Lewis Ginter provided a floor in a hotel he owned, instructing the staff to keep all unoccupied rooms empty and to provide special service to the suite of rooms housing the Richardsons.

And his wife sent her dressmaker to measure Chess for mourning clothes. Boxes were delivered, containing black veils, gloves, stockings, shawl, dressing gown, pelisse, bonnet, handkerchiefs.

While her black garments were accumulating, Chess wore the pale blue silk dress she'd had made for the trip and went over legal papers and questions with Mr. Perry. Nate sat quietly by her side while she learned the details of Harefields' death.

Augustus Standish had deeded their farms to the tenants

in return for regular deliveries of food and—in Scylla's case—service as cook until his death.

He had left instructions in his will for his daughter-in-law to be turned over to the Confederate Home for Widows and Orphans in Richmond.

And he had left Harefields' house, plus the remaining ten acres surrounding it, to his granddaughter, Francesca Standish Richardson.

The property taxes had not been paid in 1881 or 1882.

"Let the state have it," said Chess. Nathan was about to remind her that the amount of money was insignificant. He would pay it gladly. But she spoke first. "Nothing is left there for me."

Chess looked at photographs of grave markers and chose simple granite slabs with lettering in Roman style. "I do not know the birthdates for Marcus or Diana," she said. "Their deaths will have to suffice. I want their graves moved. They should rest with the family."

"Your mother's rubies might have come through the fire," Nate mentioned. "They could be reset."

Chess shook her head. "Paste," she said. "The real ones were sold back in the sixties. She never knew."

Then she gave the lawyer a strange instruction. "I want trees planted around the graveyard. Chestnuts. Not our chinquapins, Mr. Perry. You'll have to find the genuine *chasteine*. It's true, is it not, that the graveyard must remain untouched, no matter who owns the property?"

"That is true. But, these trees—"

"There will be no discussion, Mr. Perry. Increase your fee to reflect the difficulty of the task."

Nate learned the reason late the following night. Augusta woke up from a dream and called her MaMa. Chess went to her. Nate followed, in case of need.

He waited, unnoticed, in the shadows of the room while Chess sat with the baby in her arms, in the moonlight that came through the tall window.

She soothed the fretful child by stroking her hair, talking softly all the while. "Shhh, shhh, little dear, there's nothing to be afraid of. Your MaMa's right here.

"So lovely you are, my angel, your hair is like the moonlight, all silvery shine. Your grandmother's hair was the same. Sometimes she let me brush it with her ivory brushes. It flowed down her back to the seat of the bench where she sat. It was like silvery gold silk, I would stroke it, like this, to feel the soft smooth silkiness.

"She loved having her hair brushed. I loved brushing it. She would close her eyes and tell me beautiful stories about when she was young and my father was young and they took the great ships to Europe. They danced on the quais in Paris when the chestnuts bloomed and in the palace of the King in London when the roses filled the air with sweet musk and in the ruins of Rome when magnolia blossoms were like moons on the dark branches.

"She left me when I needed her, Augusta. She went to live in her stories and left me all alone. But I will never leave you, never, never. I will love you and keep you safe forever and ever. You'll never be lonely or afraid.

"I loved her so much, and now she's gone. So sad, so sad . . ."

Until now, Chess had been unable to weep for Harefields. But as she talked to her little girl, tears flowed down her cheeks. Her colorless face shone silver in the pale light of the moon.

Nate walked silently away and left her to her private grief.

"I'm up the creek without a paddle, Chess. Will you help?"

She forced a pretense of interest. As Nathan described his problem to her, genuine interest sparked and caught fire.

Nate had spent most of the day in meetings with Jos. Barker & Sons, the wholesale distributor for tobacco products. Barker wanted Castle cigarettes, but only if Nate inaugurated an aggressive program of promotion and advertising for his cigarettes.

"That's what's going to make the difference," he said "between being big and getting lost. Lower prices are a big selling point, but that's not enough anymore. The man who's going to smoke them has to want your cigarettes and not somebody else's. The competition knows that."

Nate handed Chess the pile of papers Barker had given him. "The Bull is bellowing louder than ever since Blackwell sold the company to Jule Carr. They're putting a pack of cigarette papers with every nickel bag of tobacco, so a man can roll his own or smoke a pipe out of the bag. And they're blowing their own horn from one end of the earth to the other."

Chess skimmed quickly through the newspaper reports from all over America; the gigantic 150-foot-tall billboards of the Bull were news in New Orleans and Mexico, Seattle and San Francisco, Boston and Quebec. The Bull reared or leered from half-page advertisements in magazines and big city papers.

"He must be spending a fortune," she said in wonder.

"A couple of them. And sales are making twice what he's spending. We're going to have to get on the bandwagon, Chess. The other fellows are stepping on each other's necks to get aboard. Look at this bunch—Liggett & Myers has got practically a whole page in this Chicago paper. Major Ginter's Richmond Gems brand is in the *Saturday Evening Post* magazine.

"We've got to get going; will you do it? You thought up the Castle name and the picture and all. This is right up your alley."

Chess' mind was spinning. "I'll need help, I don't know what towns have newspapers, and there must be a hundred magazines—five hundred, for all I know. How exciting! Of course I'll do it. At least I'll try."

"Can't say fairer than that. I'll tell Barker that we're going to play, and ask him about finding somebody that knows the ropes."

Chess began to read the pile of clippings again. Slowly. She had a touch of color in her cheeks. The tragedy at Harefields no longer dominated her mind.

"Good morning, Mrs. Richardson, I'm Doctor Fitzgerald." Chess looked up at the very tall, very thin young man in puzzlement.

"I think you must be on the wrong floor, Doctor. We are all in excellent health, thank goodness."

He laughed with delight. "There you are, Mrs. Richardson, the power of word associations at work. I am, in fact, the advertising director you need, not a medical man at all. 'Doctor' is my given name, sanctified at baptism; you naturally assumed it was a professional title. Some people show me where their lumbago's bothering them immediately. May I come in? We have a great deal of work to do."

Chess stepped back out of his way, swept on the tide of his rapid speech and overwhelming self-assurance. She had no time for any other reaction.

She had just been introduced to the secret of successful product promotion. Doctor Fitzgerald was both promoter and product, in this instance.

"I told the desk to send up coffee and biscuits," he said. "While we eat, I will tell you all about myself and you will tell me all about your Standish Cigarette Company. Where shall we sit? In this charming sitting room would be pleasant. Please . . ." He indicated a chair. "Make yourself comfortable."

"I sat down," Chess reported to Nathan, "there didn't seem anything else to do. I was spellbound. When the coffee and biscuits came, I didn't say a word about the eggs and ham and grits and sausage that were on the tray, too.

"Nathan, you won't believe your eyes when you see that man eat. I would swear that he never chews at all, nor swallows, either. The food just goes in his mouth and disappears while he keeps on talking.

"He's from Highland County, Virginia, way up in the mountains. And he's the seventh son of a seventh son, that's why they named him Doctor. It's assumed that a twice times seventh son will have special powers, like second sight. Well, he's got special powers, all right. He could talk the walls of Jericho into dust, he wouldn't need a trumpet at all.

"I did get a few words in sideways. I asked him about his qualifications and experience and education. That uncorked a hymn of praise to himself with a couple of hundred verses.

"Eventually it turned out that he studied classics at the University of Virginia, and I had a qualm or two. But when he said—cool as ice—that he'd been caught dealing off the bottom of the deck and expelled, I knew for sure that he was just what we needed for advice on advertising."

Chess laughed. The secret happy purr within her effervescent laughter told Nate that all was well. He'd hire this Doctor person for that, if nothing else. He had made Chess laugh again.

"I told him to come back in the morning to meet with you," she said, giggling. "Get a good long sleep tonight. You'll need your strength tomorrow."

"Whoosh," said Bobby Fred. "That Doctor is almost more than a man can take."

Chess laughed. "That's why I sent him over to live with you. He was headed upstairs to the spare room, and I came to my senses in a flash. Don't worry, it won't be long. He's headed out tomorrow to visit all the big cigarette dealers, and by the time he gets back, his own house will be ready."

The sounds of wagons, saws, hammering, axes, and shouting were constant from sunup to sundown. Nate was expanding in three directions at one time.

The Standish Cigarette factory #2 was going up downstream; the Richardson sawmill was half-built upstream; and ten men were felling trees in the woods behind the gristmill to clear room for the road that would proceed from the end of the bridge.

Again, the money was pouring out at half again the rate at

which it came in. "It's your daddy's style, darling," Chess told Augusta. "Sooner than you think, everything will settle down . . . for a little while."

She was grateful that they were leaving the plank bridge as it was. For a while she had worried that Nathan might have grandiose plans, because he had sputtered with excitement about the engineering on a recently completed bridge at a place in New York called Brooklyn.

He had actually taken the train up to see it a week ago. Chess didn't know when to expect him home. She could only hope the State Fair would entice him back. She was looking forward to going. Probably it would seem downright tranquil compared to Doctor Fitzgerald.

They were really lucky, she thought, that the people at Jos. Barker had gotten rid of him by sending him over to the hotel. He'd already assembled shelves full of magazines and newspapers, with their advertising rates and schedules attached. They took up half the space in the dining room, until the new factory building was finished. Doctor would have an office there.

So would Nathan, although the chances were slim that he'd spend much time in it. He liked to be out and about, checking progress on the expansion.

And dreaming up more. When she'd asked him why he wanted a sawmill, he'd answered her as if she were a simpleton.

"To make lumber, why else? The ten workers' houses cost over five hundred dollars each, and nearly a half of that was for lumber. If I have my own, I can build twice as many houses."

Chess decided not to ask what the future houses were for. Doctor needed a place to live, but who else?

She found out when Christmas came. Nate drove her and Augusta out the new road to a shiny white house that looked like an elaborate decorated cake she'd seen in the window of a Richmond bakery.

It was three stories tall, plus a big round turret that rose yet another level and a high mansarded attic with dormer windows topped by pointed arches. Every bit of it was decorated with lacelike jigsaw designs in wood, even the wide swing on the deep porch and the flower boxes beneath all the windows.

"Nathan, it's huge! And beautiful. Why didn't you tell me? We could have had Christmas here. Those doors will look wonderful with holly wreaths on them, and I'll bet there's room for a huge tree inside. Come on, let's go in."

"Not yet. I mean, yes, I want to hear what you think of it. But the stained-glass windows haven't come yet, so it's cold and windy inside. . . ."

Chess raised her eyebrows. "There's something else, isn't there?"

"Now that you mention it—I planned on electric lighting, but we can't build the power plant until next summer. The dynamo has to be constructed in New York and brought down here on the train."

"I see." She began to laugh. "Please promise me they're not sending down the Brooklyn Bridge, too. I wouldn't put it past you."

Nate smiled. "I've heard that sharpsters do sell it to rubes, but I got away untouched. This time."

The unfinished house was the most popular entertainment at the holiday party Chess and Nathan hosted. They had Open House in the small brick one. The dining room and parlor were crowded with people all afternoon. They came and went—the plantation families, the farm families who traded at the gristmill and store, even Dorena with Jim, and the workers who lived in the rented cottages. One of the factory wagons was especially fitted with benches for the occasion. Bobby Fred and Doctor took turns ferrying guests up the new road to see the new house. It had wreaths on its doors and icicles inside, hanging from the elaborate woodworked lace trim on the broad staircase.

Everyone congratulated Chess and thanked her as they left. Nate was deeply involved with Augusta and some taffy; he could only wave goodbye from the dining room.

Dorena grabbed Chess' arm and pulled her through the door onto the porch. She'd been drinking the punch designated for the men, Chess realized. She tried to extricate herself.

Jim caught hold of Dorena. "Goddammit, Dory, stand up straight," he said between his clenched teeth. "Sorry, Chess."

Dorena shook Chess' arm. "Jim here told me to thank you for inviting us. But I told him I don't like being classed with niggers."

Chess recoiled at the ugly word. "I'm sorry you feel that way, Mrs. Monroe. My family has always offered holiday hospitality to their tenants." It was no one's business to know how pitiful the hospitality had been at Harefields, and how few friends there were besides the tenants.

"Hoity-toity," Dorena sneered. " 'Hospitality,' is it? That's what you have to offer. No wonder your husband set up housekeeping with Julie."

"Goddammit, woman, shut your mouth," Jim said. He slapped her face. "She's drunk, Chess, she don't mean what she's saying."

Dorena thrust her head forward. Her thick lipstick was smeared by Jim's hand. "The hell I don't," she snarled. "This bitch made Nate ship that sweet little girl out of town. And now Julie's dying of consumption. She could have stayed at the Dixie, she would have been all right."

"Let go of my arm, or I'll kill you," Chess said. Her voice was quiet, and cold with venom. Dorena backed away, stumbling. Jim hustled her down the steps and along the road.

Chess put her arm around a porch pillar for support. I can't breathe, she thought, my corset's laced too tight, I feel sick. Her mind refused to accept what she'd heard. Her body reacted. Sour, hot vomit spewed from her nose and mouth. She bent over the railing just in time to avoid soiling herself.

She took a handkerchief from her pocket, wiped her mouth,

went back to the house. She still had guests inside. She made herself smile.

"MaMa," Augusta caroled. Chess couldn't look at her child's happy face. Not when she was in her father's lap.

I have guests, Chess said to herself, I must smile and chat, even if it kills me. Even if I wish it would.

Chapter Twenty-Five

CHESS HAD FORGOTTEN THE PAIN, the size and strength of it. Now that it was tearing her apart again, she remembered. Remembered Alva's caressing voice and her cruel, casual words, "he pleasured me," and the torment they created. Chess' hands clutched her throat, trying to reach the cramping constriction that strangled her breathing, that was stretching down, clamping her heart, then her stomach, and then her bowels. Her whole body was a knot of agonizing pain. Jealousy's iron claws were squeezing, squeezing, ripping her with pain.

This time it was worse, worse than before, worse than mind could imagine or dread. Chess thought of this Julie, this whore; oh, yes, she was a whore. Chess knew what kind of place the Dixie Barroom was. Dorena was proof of it.

To be subjected to that creature's criticism! The indignity of it. A woman like that shouldn't dare to speak to her at all, not at all, not even "good morning."

How could Nathan have touched such a low creature like

that? Did he "pleasure" her, too? Oh, dear God, what's wrong with me that makes him go to a whore? Isn't it enough that we try every night to start a new baby? I hate her. I hope she does have consumption, I hope to God she chokes on her own blood the way I am choking on my breath and my pain. My betrayal. Nathan betrayed me.

An arrow of fire tore through her heart.

Chess had made a shaky peace with what she knew about Nate and Alva. It happened before the wedding, before he was her husband. This was a thousand times worse, a million times, an infinity of betrayal.

She looked around the room at the guests. Oh, why couldn't they go home? Didn't they sense something, feel it in the air, know that she was in Hell, was suffering the torments of the damned?

No, better that they didn't. At least she still had her pride. It would have to sustain her.

Chess smiled, talked, refilled punch cups, smiled . . . and smiled. . . .

She managed, until all the guests were gone. And then until Augusta was fed, and bathed, and put to bed, and "Now I lay me" said, and a story read, and good-night kisses bestowed.

She walked slowly downstairs, holding tight to the banister rail for support. The pain was unbearable and yet she had to bear it.

"A fine party, Chess," said Nate. "Everybody's eyes bugged when they saw the new house, did you see?"

"Oh, yes, I saw." She was suddenly calm and cold. Death must feel like this, she thought. "Did you build a house for Julie, Nathan, or did you simply buy it?"

His smile wavered, then stretched bigger. "What the blue blazes are you talking about?"

Anger destroyed both calm and cold. "For God's sweet sake, Nathan, don't lie, too. You're an adulterer, that's enough. Don't be a liar on top of it."

Nate shrugged. He was no longer smiling. "Dorena, I suppose. We won't invite her and Jim again, you were right about that. I'm sorry."

"You're *sorry*? That's all you're going to say? Is that supposed to make everything all right?

"Nathan, 'I'm sorry' will do for breaking a plate or being late for supper. It's not enough for what you've done."

"Godalmighty, Chess, what are you making such a fuss about? You're not a child, you know men have needs, physical needs, I mean, that ladies just don't know about. All men are that way, not just me. You told me yourself about your daddy and his slave women. I can't figure why you're so upset." He was annoyed, but not yet angry. He was, he supposed, facing the illogical, incomprehensible nature of woman. The only thing for a man to do was be patient and wait for the nonsense to blow over. He regretted the fact that Dorena had embarrassed Chess. For that matter, he regretted the fact that Jim had married Dorena; it had caused trouble from the beginning. But that wasn't his—Nate's—fault. He refused to feel guilty because he was a man.

Chess felt a terrible sorrow. It was heavy, oh, so heavy, and she was overcome with fatigue. At least the twisting, cramping pain was gone. Sorrow had taken its place. What could she say? That her father had been wrong, too; that her mother must have suffered as she was suffering; that she had been blind and heartless not to realize it—none of that would make any difference now. Nathan didn't care—not about her parents, not about her.

She tried to make him understand. "You're not my father, Nathan, you're my husband, and you have hurt me."

Now he was angry. "I've never, ever done anything to hurt you, Chess. How can you say a thing like that? What I do with that kind of woman has nothing at all to do with you. You're my wife. I honor you, the way a man should honor his wife. And on top of that, I respect you and admire you, which is more than most men do. You and I are full partners, not just married.

"I've had enough of this carrying on. I'm going to go over to the factory and see how supplies stand. When I come home, I hope you'll have come to your senses."

Chess sank down onto an ottoman. Honor . . . respect . . . admire . . . but not love. Well, she'd always known that, why should it hurt so much now? She'd let herself stray into a fool's paradise, thinking that because they were so happy together it must mean that he loved her. They were happy, weren't they? Nathan, too, not just her?

She remembered all the laughter, the teasing, the planning, the shared adventure of their life together, the quiet evenings in the parlor, reading. There was no question: Nathan was happy. He just didn't love her, that's all.

He never had loved her, and yet she'd been happy. She would have to put Alva and Julie out of her mind and get on with her life. She could be happy again. She would make it be so.

That night she dreamed: her father was unbuttoning his uniform jacket, and his breeches. A naked woman was stretched on a couch, reaching out to him with her arms. She smiled, open-mouthed and loving. And then she screamed when he bent to embrace her. His hat rested on the bloody faceless pulp of his head.

Chess woke, a scream trapped in her throat. The cramping pain consumed her, and she jerked her knees up to her chest to relieve the pressure.

It half-woke Nathan. "What?" he mumbled.

"Cramp," she said. Speaking hurt, and her voice was choked.

He sat up in the bed. "The quilt slid down, you're chilled." He straightened the coverlet and tucked it around her shoulders. "Go back to sleep."

He fell asleep again at once. Chess rested her hand on his back and made herself breathe in unison with his slow, even, deep respirations until, like him, she was asleep.

Chess felt stiff and unrested the next morning. She did not

remember her dream. She did remember her vow: she was going to be happy.

It's up to me, she thought. I've been worse than foolish, I've been weak. Only a spineless ninny would measure her life and her own self by how often somebody smiles at her, what that person says to her, whether that person is pleased with her. I've worried so much about Nathan respecting me. Why should he? Or anybody else, for that matter? If I don't respect myself. And I don't, when I'm no better than a mongrel dog, begging for attention like crumbs from the table.

I've got so much. Everything I wanted, and more. I longed for a husband and a baby and a home of my own, and I have them. On top of that, we're rich, something that never even occurred to me to wish for. Ever since I was fourteen, I've done without. Now I can have anything I want. For my baby, for myself, for my house.

Romance is something in a book, not in real life. I wasted too much time believing in it, wishing for the moon. What I have is a lot better than a lot of green cheese.

Nathan and I are partners, working together to build a business and a good life. That's much more than most women ever have; what's normal is to be obedient, do what your husband tells you to do, and make sure his meal is on the table when he wants it.

What on earth have I been feeling sorry for myself about? I'm ashamed of myself. It's going to stop. Right now. I've got better things to do with my time.

Edith Horton was delighted to go with Chess to Raleigh for ten days. She even provided the carriage and driver. Chess provided the entertainment. She furnished the new house, ordering from samples and pattern books available in the capital city's most luxurious establishments.

She bought all the embellished vases, bowls, compotes, and other ornaments she could find. She selected layers of curtains and fringed draperies for each window in the big house; patterned carpets; carved furniture with velvet upholstery; gold-framed mirrors; genuine oil paintings of craggy landscapes, and vases of flowers and piles of fruit with a dead bird arranged artistically at the base of the fruit.

With Edith's advice and encouragement, she ordered complete sets of china in four different patterns. And heavy sterling silverware with twenty-four twelve-piece place settings, plus serving pieces for pickles, olives, sardines, cheeses, sauces, soups, punch, pie, cake, sandwiches, pastries, puddings, salads, fish, chops, roasts, hams, terrines, bacon, sausage, game, ices, and terrapin. Then ten dozen linen sheets, pillowslips, tablecloths, napkins, hand and face towels.

"Won't Nathan be furiously mad?" Edith asked.

"Not a bit," Chess answered. "He's so wrapped up in getting the electric plant operating that he won't notice a thing. I plan to have the house all furnished by the time the electricity's hooked up. Then we can simply move in."

Edith grimaced. "Henry notices if there are new candles in the candlesticks. He always wants to know exactly how much I spend. You're a very lucky lady, Chess."

"I know. I'm grateful for it." And I'm happy, Chess reminded herself silently. Being rich is very, very nice.

Five Standish machines were producing a quarter of a million cigarettes a day, six days a week. The gristmill was busy from sunup to sundown, six days a week and, for certain customers, Sunday as well. The store was so busy that Jim had had to hire a boy to help, and it remained open until eight o'clock at night.

The dollars were pouring in as fast as they could be spent.

It was a wonderful time to be alive, in America, in business. Because business drove the country, and drove it at top speed. Railroads were stretching out in every direction, in every state, crossing the whole continent. Inventions were jamming the patent office and new products appeared every week to make life easier, more elegant, more entertaining. Factories were rising, creating towns where once there was only a country crossroads. Fortunes were being made by young men everywhere. Nate Richardson was only one of thousands.

Money fueled progress. Money was everywhere. It needed only determination and hard work to get a share of it, in a very short time. From all over the world, people were coming to America, where the streets were paved with gold.

The country was growing in every way. In population, in wealth, in opportunity. All because of business. The businessman was the new aristocrat, the Vanderbilts the new royalty. Only a generation ago, a Vanderbilt was growing vegetables on an island near New York City. Last year his son and daughter-in-law gave a party that cost $250,000.

America in 1884 was an exciting place to be.

Chapter Twenty-Six

ON APRIL 30, Buck Duke installed a Bonsack cigarette machine in his factory on Pratt Street in Durham. For the next six years, Duke was the most important factor in Chess and Nate's world.

Life didn't stop while they battled Duke. It was busy and exciting and full of change. Nate's power plant was completed shortly after the Bonsack arrived five miles away, and all summer people came from miles around to see the lights blazing from windows in the factory and mill and store. It was like a carnival, with thrown-together stands selling barbecue and ham biscuits and corn on the cob and pie and cake and fruits and vegetables and eggs and every kind of homemade craft. Sellers of cure-all elixirs brought brightly painted wagons and magical promises. Fiddlers and jugglers performed, then passed the hat for coins.

Chess and Nate became the most sought-after couple for all major social events in Durham. There were weekly parties in the brilliantly lit new house. Nathan was invited to join the Commonwealth Club, where Durham's powerful businessmen congregated. Chess became a member of the Durham Literary Society. They had their own box in the clubhouse/grandstand at the racetrack in Blackwell Park.

In their little village, a dry-goods and hardware store opened, and a smithy, with a livery stable. Other businessmen talked to Nate about renting or buying buildings with electric service. He enlarged the sawmill.

And later Nate built a cotton mill. Two years after that, he opened a bank, which offered services that included mortgages and business loans to the growing community. Streets were cut through the woods behind the gristmill. Nate named the widest one Richardson Avenue.

But when the population neared 1,000, and a post office was installed, the town was named Standish, North Carolina. By then, there was a Standish Cigarette Company Factory #2, and a building with offices for the managers of both factories and mills. Plus warehouses, storehouses, stables, and sheds for horses and wagons. And a larger power plant.

Chess marked time by Augusta's growth. The town's growth could take care of itself. When Augusta was four, she discovered the thrill of riding in front of Bobby Fred on a horse and screaming the rebel yell as he made a cavalry charge at Yankees disguised as tall weeds. He called her "Gussie," and the little girl adopted that as her chosen name. Nathan said it suited her. Eventually Chess had to give in.

Gussie had the normal allotment of childhood diseases, bumps, bruises, skinned elbows and knees. Chess was overjoyed when a doctor settled in Standish.

Nathan moved his family from Alamance County to Standish, too, which gave Gussie a grandmother and two girl cousins, one of them only four years older than she.

And when she started school at the Female Seminary in Durham, Sally was there, in the fifth grade, to settle her in, and Susan was assistant teacher of reading and penmanship. Chess was very happy to have Susan nearby. She had missed the sweet young girl she'd left on the farm, and she was proud of the quiet young lady Susan had become.

Chess had dreamed of a doll-like daughter in ringlets and smocked silk dresses. She adored the reckless, stubborn, sun-freckled tomboy with thick, untidy silver-gilt braids who was Gussie. So did Nate. He got her a goat and cart and taught her to drive it when she was five, bought bicycles for both her and himself when they appeared two years later and learned as she was learning, by trial and crashing error, how to ride.

To all who knew them, the Nathaniel Richardsons were a family blessed with everything a benevolent Providence could bestow.

In reality, behind the closed doors of the library in their fashionable, luxurious house, they were battling for survival in a cutthroat world.

"The Bonsack don't work," Nate crowed when Buck Duke installed one. "Allen and Ginter tried it, and it was a bust. Ol' Buck's bought the Brooklyn Bridge. Do you know the deal Bonsack made? He rents his machine, and the mechanic that operates it. Buck's paying rent, and a salary besides, for a pile of junk."

Doctor Fitzgerald grimaced. "That doesn't change what I've been saying. Duke is making and selling over two hundred thousand hand-rolled cigarettes a day. Selling. That's the point. The salesman of his is named Small. Small's his name, and big's his game. The man's a genius, and I speak as one who knows, being one myself."

Small had just moved cigarette-brand promotion off the sides of barns on rural roads into the realm of gossip and the libido. Stopping in Atlanta on a selling trip, he saw that the city was in a ferment of scandal over a naughty French farce at a downtown theater and its star, Madame Rhea, in deep décolleté. Small persuaded her to let him use the poster of her outside the theater. He reproduced it with an addition— a pack of "Duke of Durham" cigarettes in her hand. Every tobacco store in Atlanta sported the poster in its window, and a half-page ad appeared in the newspaper. Decent people were scandalized; customers began asking for "Duke of Durham" by name.

"There must be other actresses," Nate said. "How do we find out, Doctor?"

"No," Chess said quickly. "If we start copying everything Duke does, we'll be run ragged, and we'll always be second best. We've got to be different. Better."

"For instance . . . what?" demanded Doctor.

"I don't know," Chess admitted.

The three of them debated the problem for nearly a week. It was Nathan who came up with the answer. "Class!" he trumpeted, "that's it. The men who smoke ready-mades instead of roll-your-own are most of the time town folk. And most of the people in towns came there from the farm. Just like me. Just like Buck. They like to think they're pretty classy, but they always wonder if they've still got straw sticking in their hair. We'll tell them that if they smoke Standish cigarettes, people will mistake them for a real gent."

Doctor was afire with ideas.

Nathan grinned. "Run things by Chess, Doctor. She's the real article. She's a lady."

Chess made them both gasp. "But it'll have to have some sex in it, too," she mused aloud. Nate and Doctor were shocked. A lady wasn't supposed to know that word, much less speak it.

The first poster for Castle cigarettes was a drawing of a rough-hewn man wearing elegant evening clothes, but no top hat on his thick unpomaded hair. He was standing on the steps of the Vanderbilt château-mansion, a building known from newspapers and magazines to all Americans. The well-endowed bare-shouldered woman on his arm was looking up adoringly into his face. In her outstretched hand, clad in a long white glove, she held a pack of Castles.

"Don't forget these, Standish," read the caption underneath. "I love a man who has Castles."

The poster was two inches longer and wider than the ones Duke was putting up all over the country. Other cigarette manufacturers were already tearing down Duke's, or Kinney's, or Allen and Ginter's posters to put up their own. Nate was not the only owner who was fighting back. Standish posters were simply pasted on top of what was already there.

"Standish" later appeared on his yacht, at the races, driving a fancy gig—always accompanied by a delectable female companion. In time, the name came to epitomize the American dream of manhood. Boy babies were baptized "Standish," romantic novels had heroes named "Standish," girls referred to attractive bachelors as "Standishes."

But the posters were only one small part of Duke's armament.

Six months after the Bonsack was installed in Durham, Buck Duke moved to New York.

"We've got him on the run," Chess exulted.

"Don't fool yourself," said Nathan. "Buck's no quitter. He's gone where the money is. All the big players are on Wall Street. He's thinking big."

The following week the news swept the Commonwealth Club. The Bonsack was producing 100,000 cigarettes a day. Whatever the problems had been, they had been corrected.

And Duke had opened an office and a factory in New York to handle northern and western markets. Additional Bonsack machines were on order for Durham and New York.

The Bonsack-made cigarettes were named "Cross Cuts." A colored picture of Lillian Russell, the famous, voluptuous actress, was on the pasteboard card in the cigarette pack.

"We need our own sales force," said Doctor. "The wholesaler can't do what needs doing, and we can't just send me to a town to pick up some poster hangers for a day like we've been doing."

"Then we need more money," said Nate. "Salesmen have to be paid."

"We'll start a new brand, at five cents a pack, like everybody else. Castles will stay at four cents."

"More machines," they all agreed.

"Knight" cigarettes were packaged in a sliding cardboard box instead of a paper wrap. The chess piece appeared under the name. The Venus de Milo was printed on the inside of the sliding drawer, where her nudity was hidden from the easily shocked.

Nate fired the clerk who was caught copying sales figures and customer names in the middle of the night.

Chess fired the maid whom Gussie saw listening at the keyhole of the library door. Then she lectured Gussie about the naughtiness of being a tattletale.

Doctor reluctantly stopped visiting a too-curious young woman whose companionship had been a pleasure whenever he was in St. Louis on a sales trip.

None of them was surprised. The tobacco business had always been fertile ground for double-dealing, spies and informers, price manipulations, rigged weighing devices—all the dirty tricks the human mind could invent. Nate had two men inside Buck Duke's factories, a woman at Allen and Ginter, others at the offices of Kinney Company, Goodwin's, and W. S. Kimball, the "big four." Reports came on a regular schedule. They were paid for within twenty-four hours. It was all a normal part of doing business.

Week after week and month after month and year after year the war went on. A new factory was built to house more Standish machines. Nate opened his own printing plant to make posters and cards faster and in greater quantities.

Duke added more and more Bonsacks to the ones already in production.

Nate built more Standishes.

More Bonsacks ... More Standishes ... more ... more ...

Duke introduced his "Cameo" brand, in a sliding box. Advantage: Standish.

He began paying under-the-counter rebates to major dealers. Standish orders fell off.

Doctor paid rebates, too. In gold. Orders soared.

Cigarette sales in the United States grew at a staggering pace. The smallest manufacturers began to go out of business.

Duke inaugurated a bonus program. Retailers ordering 1,000 packs of "Cross Cuts" were given a wooden folding chair.

"The filthy object pinched me in a place I dare not mention in the presence of a lady," Doctor moaned.

Standish chairs had padded seats.

Duke began including coupons in cigarette packs. Stores gave customers free books to paste the coupons in. Completed books could be accumulated and exchanged for premiums: the perennial folding chair, or a mantel clock, or a pocket watch, or—for 500 books—a grandfather's clock.

Standish matched Duke and added china tea sets, crystal epergnes, and painted washbowls and pitchers. "Let the wives and mothers start encouraging their men to smoke," Chess giggled. "They send the poor devils outside to do it now, no matter how bad the weather is."

She enjoyed the battle of wits they were engaged in. Even though her record books had been taken over by trained double-entry bookkeepers when the business grew so big, she still liked to go over the figures every so often, admiring the full extent of what she and Nathan had accomplished. The cost of the battle with Buck was horrifying, but she still enjoyed being a strategist. More and more it was left to her and Doctor, because Nathan was occupied with a new plan. He wanted to build a railroad from Standish to Durham to facilitate shipping.

"And to play with," Chess teased him.

He admitted that was so, with the grin that made him look like a boy and turned Chess' heart over. Once in a while she wondered why he could still have that effect on her. She decided that there was no accounting for love. Nathan treated her more like a man, a friend, than a woman. Except in bed— and why, oh why, hadn't she conceived yet? He didn't love her, he liked her. He never kissed her, never had, not once. So why did she still love him? It made no sense, it was just a fact.

No one expected the cigarette cards to do what they did. They became almost the tail wagging the dog. People began buying a given brand of cigarettes because they wanted the card that was in it.

Standish began using decorated cards as soon as Buck Duke did. To counter his Lillian Russell, Chess insisted on Sarah Bernhardt. As Camille, she added, explaining that the character was a famous prostitute who coughed herself to death because her gowns were cut so low in the front.

Allen and Ginter soon jumped on the bandwagon with a Floradora girl.

But then "Castles" changed to Eleanora Duse when Chess saw a portrait of the young actress in *Harper's Bazaar*.

And the race had begun. Duke added Lillie Langtry and Madame Rhea and seven other actresses, to make a set of ten. Collecting the full set became the public's new fad.

Doctor was disconsolate. He should have thought of it first, he moaned pitiably.

"Stop that," Chess said crossly. "I can't think with all that noise. There aren't enough famous actresses, and I won't have just any half-dressed woman with no talent. Let's try something else. If it's collecting that matters, it should work for anything that there's at least ten different ones of. More would be even better. And we can give an album to everyone who gets the whole set. The stores can hand them out."

A blizzard of cards soon covered the country. The presidents of the United States. The Kings and Queens of England. Great composers. Great writers. Famous rivers. Varieties of carriages, or horses, or dogs, or birds. All the cigarette companies were desperately trying to keep pace.

Doctor was supremely confident that he had topped them all when Jack the Ripper was in all the newspapers and Castle Cigarettes proudly introduced its "Great Murderers of History" series with Brutus and Julius Caesar.

Soon after that Buck Duke came to see Nate again.

He appeared at the house, not at Nathan's office. Exactly as he had done before. And he complimented Chess on her lovely daughter, exactly as he had done when Augusta was a baby in a basket.

Everything else was different. Duke was wearing a superbly tailored suit that fairly screamed "big city," and the latent power Chess had sensed before was no longer in hiding.

"I sent a man to fetch Nate," he said. "I've got something to tell him that he'd be smart to heed."

"Go find Soldier, Augusta," said Chess. "He'll take you to ride on your pony. Come in to the library, Mr. Duke. My husband and I have all our business talks there."

She did not offer Buck Duke any coffee.

Duke stood until Nathan arrived. Then he stepped forward, arm extended to shake hands.

Just like he owned the place, Chess thought indignantly. As she watched the men shake hands, it struck her what an interesting thing civilization really was. It would have been so much more natural if they had instantly started hitting each other. Maybe outlawing duels wasn't the advance everyone said it was.

"Would you like to sit down, Buck?" It was an assertion of ownership, and a warning that Duke was an invader, not an invited guest. Nate took his favorite chair. Chess sat in one beside him and a little to the rear. Buck was left with only the slick, hard, horsehair-covered settee. He ignored the discomfort. He was infuriatingly relaxed.

"I got to congratulate you on those 'Great Murderers' cigarette cards, Nate," he said. "Your Castles were outselling my

Cross Cuts nearly two to one for a couple of weeks. Your friend Doctor has kept my boys hopping all along."

Nate waited, saying nothing.

"That kind of thing has seen its day, I figure," Duke drawled. "It's cost all of us too much money, money that could be put better places."

And who started it, you hypocrite? Chess thought.

"I started it," said Buck, "to get people to pay attention to my brands and to weed out the little fellows. Now there are only six of us left who count. You and me, we're the upstarts. While they were laughing at us, we've caught up with Kinney and Goodwin and Kimball. Two Southern boys showed the New Yorkers why we almost won that war our daddies fought. We've even showed the cream of the crop."

Nate interrupted smoothly. "I don't want you to dislocate something, patting yourself on the back like that, Buck. Why don't you get to the point?"

Duke smiled. "You kind of zinged me there, Nate. Yep, I was softening you up for the pitch. Forgot you used to sell on the road, too."

Watch out, Nathan, Chess warned silently. He's being charming.

Buck shifted his weight a trifle, leaned forward a fraction, stopped smiling. "I'm getting everybody together. Not a takeover, just an association so we can quit spending so much cutting each other's throats. With the six of us combined, we'll have the cigarette business locked up. We can set prices where we want them, selling cigarettes and buying tobacco both. And we can slow down gradually on the premiums and such, weaning the smokers back to where they belong, just buying cigarettes and smoking them."

"That sounds like a smart move," said Nate. He nodded appreciation. Then he asked, "Who's going to be top man in the association, Buck?"

"There'll be shares for everybody, divided by what percent each one puts in, his assets and sales figures."

Nate grinned. "Very smart," he said. "I admire you, Buck,

I really do. What's the other end of the stick? What are you threatening, if people don't go along with you?"

"I don't need to threaten. They know. They'll go under. Already Kinney's had to close their Baltimore plant because they're not selling enough cigarettes to pay their help for making them. They've only got their New York plant now. Five years ago, they were the biggest in the country."

Nate stood. "Waaal, Buck." He stretched out the drawl in an exaggerated backwoods manner. "I don't aim to join, and I don't aim to go under neither. I'm betting it's not worth your while to put my demise at the top of your list. Not when you got all them bones to pick—your 'associates,' I mean. That ought to keep you kind of busy for a while.

"I was really busy with something my own self when your boy come running like his pants was on fire and told me to hustle over here for something important. Now I'm going to get back to what I was doing, so I'll bid you good day."

Nate held out his hand. Buck Duke stood, shook it, nodded to Chess, turned halfway toward the door. "If a man draws a line in the dirt and dares me to cross it, Nate, I feel obliged to oblige him," he said. Their eyes met and held.

"I'm exactly the same as you, Buck. Only my costs per thousand are nearly half what yours are. I got a lot of room to operate in."

"Watch your back." Duke walked out.

All was quiet in the room until the outside door closed behind him.

Then, "Can he do it?" Chess asked.

"Put me under?" Nathan shrugged. "I'm pretty sure he could. But he doesn't know that. And it would take a long time to do it, win or lose. One thing Buck don't seem to have is a lot of time. He likes to hit hard and win fast. Like I told him, I'm betting it's not worth his while. We've got ourselves a stand-off situation, not a shoot-out." His eyes were dancing.

"You're having a good time, Nathaniel Richardson!"

"You bet your life I am. With all this fancy fiddling at a

distance, I'd almost forgotten what fun a face-to-face show-down can be. It adds a zing to the day."

The American Tobacco Company came into being officially on January 31, 1890. It was incorporated under the friendly laws of the state of New Jersey, with James Buchanan Duke as president.

The Standish Cigarette Company immediately released its new brand, a premier packaging job that included a box of matches with the cigarettes in the larger sliding box. The cover was printed in black and white squares. The brand name was overprinted in bright red. "Check." Customers were told that if they collected ten empty boxes, they would be entitled to a free chess set and a book of instructions on how to play.

Chapter Twenty-Seven

CHESS HELD THE SCISSORS ready until the band concluded the number with a clash of cymbals. Then she cut the broad red ribbon, the cymbals crashed again, and the Standish station of the S & D Railroad was officially open.

The little building was extremely charming, a sort of closed octagonal gazebo with a deep, decorated overhang extending from its pagoda roof. Flower boxes full of bright pelargoniums decorated its corners, and lacy iron benches sat near the entrance door. Chess had helped design it, and she was pleased with the way it looked, but it saddened her strangely to see it there, so sparkling fresh and modern on the site where the haunted house had been.

So much had happened since she and Nathan made their home in that single drafty room. That seemed to have been a thousand years ago, when it was, in fact, not even ten. Doctor was gone. A new kind of business called "advertising agency" had wooed him and won. Jim Monroe was gone, too, and Bobby Fred was showing his age. So was the gristmill; it would have to be replaced soon.

I wonder, Chess thought suddenly, just when I stopped having friends among the farmers' wives. They used to come to the haunted house for coffee while their grain was being ground. To the brick house too, I think, but I'm not sure.

She smiled. Come to think of it, I can't remember the last time I had coffee in my kitchen myself. Chess directed the smile at the photographer. The Durham newspaper was doing a big story on Nathan's railroad and the private car that he had had made for himself.

Nathan's toys! Well, he has his railroad, and the brass band he always wanted, and the Western Union office opened in the post office last week. He'll get the telephones next, I'm sure. When he sets his mind on something, anybody in his way might as well give in at once.

The photographer emerged from the black cloth he'd been under. "Thank you, Mrs. Richardson."

"Thank you. I hope you'll join us at the picnic grounds."

"Thank you very much, ma'am."

Chess was free now to join the celebration. She turned, smile still in place, and allowed people to come up and greet her.

Somehow, as Standish grew, she had become a sort of grande dame of the town. Everyone was very respectful, and slightly awestruck by the wife of the owner of the industries that gave the town its life. It made Chess feel very old.

But she liked it, too, in some unexamined part of her heart. She'd been taught as a child that she was someone special, an aristocrat, better by birth than all other people, except those exactly like her—great landowners for many generations. The admiration and envy of the less privileged seemed natural, and she responded as she'd been trained to do, with graciousness at a slight remove.

She accepted the assistance of the bank manager to step up into the green-painted surrey with S & D in gold on its side. The gold fringe on its green top swayed frivolously as she drove to the picnic grounds in Richardson Park to join Nathan and the family. Behind her the band played a noisy march while it led the crowd from the station to the much bigger crowd at the picnic. There would be a band concert later in the afternoon, just the same as there was every Sunday afternoon and every Thursday evening from April through October. Standish was a very pleasant place to live. Richardson Avenue, its wide main street beyond the bridge, was cobbled, with brick sidewalks shaded in the summer by awnings projecting from the stores on both sides of its three blocks. The elementary school had a large grassy playground. Baptist churches for a white congregation and a larger black congregation were almost completed, and ground had been broken for a Methodist church only weeks before.

Chess privately wished that the Methodist church would never get built. Now that they had the train, going to Durham on Sundays would be easy, and all of their friends in Durham went to Trinity. But she supposed that they would have to change over to the Standish congregation. Gussie wouldn't mind. She had a best friend in Standish, Ellie Wilson, who would be in Sunday school with her. . . . What on earth was Nathan thinking of? He was letting Gussie baste the pigs in the barbecue pit! She might fall in the coals.

Chess handed the reins to the nearest reaching hands and jumped down to run to her child's rescue.

"Of course she was furious, Edith," Chess told her best friend. "Gussie can't abide protection from killing herself, you know how she is."

"Well, she's not dead, Chess, so maybe there's something to be said for her point of view."

"I do hate it when you're reasonable. You're supposed to agree with me."

"Then we'd have very dull conversations, wouldn't we?"

"Would you rather talk about the bloodlines of horses?"

"Unkind! Chess, how can you hurt a poor defenseless creature like me that way?" Edith's husband Henry had been breeding and training racehorses for four years, ever since he sold the majority of his plantation acreage to Nate. He was totally and blissfully absorbed in his work. It made him a great bore, except to other horsemen, and Edith complained constantly to Chess.

She riposted with whatever was Nathan's current passion. The railroad period had been particularly trying. Nate knew the names, mileage, and major stops on every one of the several hundred railway lines in America, Chess believed. And gave Gussie a model locomotive for each one of them. The two of them spent raucous hours on the porch pushing the toys along at top speed and making engine sounds.

She looked over at father and daughter handing plates of spicy meat and coleslaw to the line of hungry, laughing picnickers. They were having a good time. For some reason almost no one regarded Nate as awesome.

"Can we ride in the private car when we go to the races?" Edith asked. "I'm dying to loll about on the bed."

Chess laughed. "It's only a fifteen-minute ride, Edith. Five miles of track isn't exactly the Northern Pacific."

"Still, it's the nearest I'll ever come to the *Orient Express*. When are you and Nathan going to hook on to whatever train is going someplace grand? Florida? California? Saratoga? Henry is talking an awful lot about Saratoga these days."

"That would be fun. I vaguely remember my parents talking about Saratoga. I'll mention it to Nathan and see what happens."

"But no private car to Durham, huh?"

"Maybe. Does Henry have a horse running?"

"Who knows? I'm afraid to ask. He'll tell me all the dams and sires back to the pair that Adam and Eve drove when they fled the Garden."

As it turned out, the Hortons and the Richardsons did go in the private car to Durham, but not until the end of the summer, for the last races of the season at Blackwell Park. Although Edith didn't loll on the big bed in the room at the rear of the car, she enjoyed herself tremendously spinning around in one of the velvet-covered swiveling armchairs in the parlor area.

All of them had a good time at the races; they always did. The clubhouse/grandstand was always crowded and always festive.

But, just before the final race, an announcement was made. The race coming up was special; it would be the last race for all time. The park and racetrack had been donated to that most deserving institution, Trinity College, by that well-known and well-loved patron of progress and the arts, Mr. Julian Shakespeare Carr. Now they would all be privileged to hear a few remarks from Mr. Carr. . . .

"Ol' Jule can talk the hind leg off a mule," Nate muttered. "I'm going to take a little stroll." He got up and walked away.

Chess and the Hortons were not even aware of his departure. The racetrack closing! It would destroy Henry's training and breeding program.

They'll move to Saratoga, Chess thought, and what will I do without Edith? She's been my one truly close friend ever since I got here. I'll never find anyone else like her.

"Henry," said Edith, "didn't you tell me that there was a dark horse in the last race? Put a bet on it for me, and one for Chess, too." Her tone of voice was calm, slightly giddy as befits a lady playing at wickedness. She did not sound at all like a woman whose whole world had just collapsed. Ladies did not break down in public places.

Chess put her hand on Edith's arm and squeezed it gently, a tribute to her courage and control.

After the races, the two couples strolled in the park beside the track area, as was the custom on race days. Edith and Chess held their ribbon-trimmed parasols in firm grip, nodded and greeted people they knew, smiled and chatted, agreed with everyone that having a college move to Durham would raise the intellectual opportunities in the city quite markedly.

Nate took Henry to a quiet corner behind the clubhouse

for a drink from the flask he had bought and filled when he took his walk.

Riding back to Standish in the private car, it was no longer necessary to keep up appearances. Edith put her head on Chess' shoulder and wept. Henry was concentrating all his attention on getting drunk.

"Will you look at that," Nate said after five minutes of gloom-filled travel. "My wife and my neighbor don't even have the kindness to congratulate me on my good luck. I've been wracking my brain for a way to make the S & D pay, and it's fallen into my lap. I'm going to buy another passenger coach. The two I've got won't be enough to hold all the people who'll be riding out from Durham to go to the races at the track I'm going to build."

Henry's calliope laughter all but deafened the other three.

Chess stole a suspicious glance at Nathan. His reasoning was as full of holes as Gussie's stockings after a day climbing trees. His expression was innocently bland.

Later, in the evening when they were alone, she told him how grateful she was for his generosity to Henry and Edith.

"No such thing," he protested. "I'm a businessman, not a do-gooder. You get Durham people out here, show them what a short, easy ride it is, and they'll move to some decent clean air faster than you can shake a stick. They won't have Jule Carr's Bull bellowing at them three times a day, either. I'll be selling lots and mortgages and lumber all day and all night."

It made sense. But still Chess wondered.

Nathan wound his watch, snapped the case closed, and slid it into the watch pocket of his vest. Then he put on his jacket, shrugging his shoulders to adjust the fit just right.

"You look very elegant," Chess said. "Where are you going, all dressed up in your new suit?"

"I might go back to this new tailor in Raleigh. I like the way he cuts jackets. Where I'm going right now is to see Ma.

When she hears about the horseracing, she's going to hit the roof. I'd just as soon get it over with right now."

"Good luck."

"There's not that much good luck in all the world."

Chess chuckled. Poor Nathan. Miss Mary had not sweetened any when her son provided her with a nice house, and a housekeeper, and a horse and buggy and driver. She was just as cantankerous as she'd been when she was drudging in the dark, cramped, dilapidated farmhouse in Alamance County.

She didn't bother Chess much. Other than criticizing the way Chess let Gussie "run wild," Miss Mary didn't have much to say to her. She saved all her considerable energies for Nathan's iniquities, primarily his extravagances.

Like her house and servants, Chess longed to say. But she couldn't, not even to Nathan. He was still so much the deferential, respectful, honor-thy-mother son that sometimes Chess wanted to kick him.

But, she admitted to herself, she had very little cause for complaint about her in-laws. On Sundays, the whole family went in to Durham for church and then had dinner together afterwards at Mrs. Mattie Brown's boardinghouse, where the food was country-style and to the liking of Miss Mary. Other than that, she seldom saw any one of them. Alva had found friends quickly, Susan and Sally the same. Josh and Micah were busy supervising the farmers on the land Nathan had bought to grow his own tobacco for cigarettes.

They made no difference in her life. Her jealousy of Alva now seemed like the foolish overreaction of a green girl. She could hardly remember it. Her own position as Nathan's wife was unassailable. Chess was quite certain that there must be a woman, or women, in Nathan's life. Maybe in Raleigh, he went there often to lean on politicians about one thing or another.

She refused to think about it. It had nothing to do with her.

Instead she thought about what she called her "little secret." It made her incredibly happy. She had been sort of down in the dumps after the stirring tensions of the Duke wars were over. She had too little to do. But those days were over.

No more melancholy. No more sense of uselessness. Everything was fine now. Better than fine, everything was wonderful.

Chess rode the train into Durham, and then the train from Durham to Raleigh. She was alone, something quite improper for a lady, but she didn't care. She was on a special mission, too precious to share with anyone. Even Nathan, not yet.

She was going to see Dr. Arthur Mason, Jr. After all these years of disappointment she was at last going to have another baby.

Chess smiled at her reflection in the sooty window, then looked quickly away. Oh, dear, she was embarrassingly old to be a new mother. Gussie would be mortified. That was her new word, and Chess wished to high heaven she'd never learned it. Everything had "mortified" her for weeks now.

The day was perfect. High, wispy white clouds in a blue, blue sky, the air warm and fresh with just enough breeze. Chess decided to walk to Dr. Mason, Jr.'s office. She hadn't written for an appointment because the return address on his reply would start the news spreading the minute it reached the post office. He'd be in his office, though, she was confident. Nothing could go wrong on a perfect day like this.

It was two months to the day since she had missed her first period. That meant, if her calculations were right, that Gussie would have a baby brother or sister for Easter next year.

"You're not having a baby, Mrs. Richardson. I'm sorry." Dr. Mason, Jr., was sympathetic. "There is no way to tell bad news except to be quick and then find a way to make it less painful, if possible."

"I don't believe you. I've missed my monthly bleeding for two months. For years and years I didn't bleed every month, but that was long ago. Ever since Augusta was born, I've been as regular as the calendar."

"Have you experienced any nausea ... cramps ... headaches ... insomnia. ..." He questioned her for twenty minutes.

"No, Doctor, no. I tell you there's nothing wrong with me. I'm pregnant, that's all there is to it. You must have made a mistake. Maybe, if I come back next month—"

In the end, Dr. Mason told her that by all indications she was undergoing menopause.

"Impossible! I was forty last July. No one has change of life at barely forty."

He told her that some few did, and she was one of them. Chess didn't want to believe him, but he was very convincing. His sympathy was the most convincing thing of all.

"I'll leave you alone here in my office for a while, Mrs. Richardson. The old wives' remedies are still sometimes the best, better than all our modern science. Have a good cry." He laid a freshly laundered large handkerchief on the desk near her hand.

She couldn't cry. With news this bad, weeping was a frivolity. Her life as a woman was over, only ten years after it had begun. Thank God no one need know.

She had planned to go home with gifts for Nathan and Gussie, celebratory accompaniments to the good news she had for them. There was no good news, but she could still buy the gifts. And something for herself, as well. She needed cheering up.

Chapter Twenty-Eight

SHE BLAMED NATHAN. If he hadn't been away so much ... if he hadn't worked such long hours that he was exhausted and his seed weakened ... if he hadn't bedded all those other women and spent his seed in them. From the profound depths of ignorance Chess invented reasons for the disastrous words the doctor had spoken. She would never have another baby.

She was too old.

When she arrived at home, Nathan and Gussie were riding bicycles on the lawn. Now it would have packed brown lines of dead grass next spring instead of a new birth of green freshness. It was Nathan's fault. Everything that was wrong was Nathan's fault.

She raced upstairs to their bedroom and began to empty the drawers of her bureau onto the bed. Dresses followed, then shoes. I will not cry, she promised herself over and over again.

"Great Godalmighty, Chess, what are you doing? Spring cleaning in September?" Nate stood in the doorway, blue eyes wide open, a smile twitching his lips. He was in his shirtsleeves, coat and vest slung over his shoulder, suspended from an index finger. He looked like a boy. It wasn't fair.

"I'm moving my things to the corner room in the back," she said. Her voice was matter-of-fact. Chess was proud of that. "I had a checkup at the doctor's today, and he says I can't have any more children. There's no reason for us to share a room any longer."

Nate's eyes clouded, his smile vanished. "I don't understand."

"That was our agreement, wasn't it? You'd marry me and give me children in exchange for the patent? You've done that. There's Gussie. But there can't be any more, so there's no reason for us to share a bed any longer."

Nate thought of the warm comfortable closeness of sleeping and waking side by side. It was so familiar now, it felt like home ought to feel. He'd never wondered how Chess felt about it. Now, he saw. She must have put up with it all these years, to have children. He'd been a fool to forget that she was a lady.

"Why don't you get the maids to do that?" he said. "There's a lot of stuff."

There was a lot of stuff, an awful lot. And, Chess decided, almost every scrap of it was out of fashion. According to the latest magazines, the bustle was virtually gone. No one in North Carolina seemed to have noticed, she thought, but what could you expect in a backwater like this, where Durham was considered up to date because it had streetlamps and plank sidewalks. You still had to teeter across the mud- and dust-covered streets on stepping-stones to keep from ruining both boots and skirt hems.

She went to Richmond, where the streets were paved and fashion more up to date, and embarked on an undisciplined orgy of shopping from which she emerged exhausted and depressed and with more stuff than ever.

"What are you all ruffled up like that for?" Gussie asked curiously.

"This is called a tea gown," Chess told her. "All the fashionable ladies wear them in the afternoon for drinking tea."

Gussie collapsed into fits of raucous laughter. "A special dress for a cup of tea? That's the silliest thing I ever heard." She had the deplorably uncompromising logic of an eight-year-old.

Chess glared at her daughter. Then, against her will, she began to giggle. In a few minutes she was laughing as hard as Gussie.

"Come here and give me a hug, you wretched child," she said.

"Poof," Gussie snorted from the suffocation of cascades of lace.

Tea gowns were a failure, Chess conceded. Nevertheless she continued to devote her all-too-ample free time to self-improvement. She added tall vases holding clumps of peacock feathers to the corners of the front parlor, mammoth wax-flower arrangements under glass bells to the rear parlor, a three-foot-tall epergne filled with fruit made of marble to the center of the dining room table. She replaced the furniture in her new bedroom with a suite of matching pieces in rosewood decorated with carved and gilded twining ivy vines. The big dressing table held a new set of brushes and combs and covered jars and nail-grooming implements, all with handles or covers of gold, engraved with ivy leaves.

In the New Year, she persuaded James Dike to move his bookstore from Durham to Standish. The town was growing like Jack's beanstalk, just as Nathan had foreseen, and it could well support a bookstore now. Chess admired James Dike; his genuine scholarship intimidated her, though; she wasn't sure whether she felt comfortable enough with him to like him. He had moved to Durham years before, because the harsh winters in Boston were dangerous to his fragile health. He was pale and somewhat languid. Chess liked vigorous men. Like Nathan. She was miserable about the distance between them. She couldn't put her finger on any specific change, but she knew it was there, and she didn't know what to do about it. He was busy all the time, and so was she.

Dike had been the untitled leader of the Literary Society in Durham. It was natural for Chess to organize a similar group in Standish. Soon ten, then fourteen, then twenty women were holding weekly meetings in her front parlor to discuss the book they were all reading. The series of Trollope's novels about English politics and society promised to keep them fascinated and occupied for years.

That summer Nathan's racetrack opened. Edith Horton was the ribbon-cutter this time, because Henry had designed it and was president of the Green and Gold Club; members had boxes in the clubhouse.

Standish was a nightmare of noise for months. Richardson Avenue was extended, new streets cut through the woods, roomy Victorian houses built on both sides of them, new stores built on the Avenue to cater to the needs of their inhabitants.

By Thanksgiving Standish had an elected city government, a jail, and a Dramatic Society that presented shortened and expurgated versions of Shakespeare's plays, with Chess' double parlor opened up to make a theater.

The tickets were sold to the public. Some of the public. Standish had become a real town with the advent of the railroad. Its track ran between the road and the creek, beside the gristmill to the Standish station, then continued on spurs to the loading docks of the factories and other mills. Tenant houses, the original store, and buildings from the earliest expansion had become the wrong side of the tracks.

The right side of the tracks was very busy, and Chess was its queen bee, working ceaselessly, entertaining frequently, laughing and talking constantly. Proving to herself that she wasn't old and useless.

The Richardsons' Christmas party of 1891 was the biggest, most elaborate social event that any of the guests had ever seen. Gussie and her best friend Ellie were greenish for days

afterwards from eating too many sweets and drinking pur-
loined champagne.

Nate gave Chess a magnificent parure of pearl and cameo
jewelry: necklace, two bracelets, brooch, ear bobs, and hair
ornament. She made a huge fuss of delight, as if she and
Edith had not chosen it together. Her delight was unfeigned
when she found time to enjoy her gift from James Dike. It
was a subscription to *The Strand Magazine*, an English
monthly. The featured story was about a character named
Sherlock Holmes.

"There will be one every issue," James promised her.
"Holmes has become all the rage in England, according to a
friend of mine."

"I can see why," Chess said. "The story is so ingenious, I
believe my husband might even enjoy it, and usually he only
likes to read about business or inventions."

James Dike smiled. "I'll order some books for you. Have
you ever heard of Jules Verne?"

Chess decided that she did, in fact, like James Dike very
much. He wasn't too intellectual at all. She looked forward
to a winter of reading.

"Chess, I need to talk to you," said Nate. She tensed. Was
he going to complain about the cost of all the parties, or the
multitude of people who always seemed to be in the house?
Well, let him. It was her house, too, wasn't it?

"Buck Duke has rolled out the big guns," was what he told
her.

Chess hurried to close the library doors.

Two years had passed since the formation of the American
Tobacco Company. During that time informants had reported
disagreements and struggles among the participants, with
Duke consistently the winner. Employees had undergone a
drastic jobs massacre, and now there was one sales force, one
financial department, one administrative staff. Plus, as Nate
and Chess had seen, the premiums and rebates had dwindled
and disappeared.

"Now the squeeze is really starting," said Nate soberly. "Buck's planning to make an ultimatum to wholesalers and dealers. If they sell any cigarettes that are cheaper than the price of American's brands, they'll be blacklisted. American won't ship to them."

"That means Castles. Our biggest seller."

"Right. We've got to figure out what to do."

Chess knew she should be upset, distraught even. Everything they had worked for was in danger. But she could think only that they were together again, together. Nathan needed her. The partnership wasn't dissolved.

They talked late into the night.

And the next day. And late into that night, too. A new brand—no. Castles was their best seller. Raise the price on Castles—no. People would be outraged, and rightly so.

So many hours had elapsed and so many ideas discussed that when the answer came, neither could be sure who had originated it. The Check brand already used an oversized box. They would make Castles oversized, too. Longer. Call them Castles still. Advertise them as "King" sized. The King is in the Castle. Raise the price to five cents, like the American brands.

The alterations on the Standish machines would be minimal. Except for the paper. They'd have to find a new manufacturer, one unknown to tobacco people, or their response to Duke's threat would be known before the first King was past the guillotine.

"Did you hear that, Nathan?" Chess giggled. "The King and the gullotine." She began to hum *La Marseillaise*.

Nate frowned for an instant, got the joke, began to laugh.

At last. They hadn't laughed together for such a long time. Chess felt unseen tears mingle with her laughter. Nate was very happy to hear her gurgly laugh again.

Eventually they decided the only thing to do was to make their own paper. There was no time to build a paper plant. Nate set out to find one with the necessary machinery, capable of adjustment to their needs. And unassociated in any way with the tobacco business. "I won't haggle," he said. "I'll buy it."

His face brightened. "Say, what do you think, Chess? Maybe a pulp mill. Standish could use a newspaper."

She loved him so much she thought she might burst.

As usual, when Nate went after something the action was fast and furious, the outcome a certainty. On May 1, 1892, posters and newspapers in every city across America trumpeted the news. Literally. The announcements were designed with tall liveried pages blowing long horns from which a banner was suspended. The message, with a picture of the new Castle pack, was on the banner. In major cities, musicians in bright-colored costume blew genuine brass horns with banners on street corners, and young women in enticing milkmaid costume gave away free sample packs.

Doctor sent a telegram of congratulation:

> INCREDIBLE SUCCESS STOP EVEN WITH-
> OUT ME STOP WELL DONE STOP BRAVO STOP
> MISSING YOU STOP DOCTOR

Chess wrote him a long, affectionate letter. With it she sent a copy of the first-day edition of the Standish *Courier*. "Only four pages, and only a weekly, but you know Nathan," she scrawled above the masthead. "Come home and be our James Gordon Bennett—only better, of course."

FATTEN CALF STOP ARRIVE JUNE 2 STOP DOCTOR

The first edition of the *Courier* under Doctor's direction carried the headline ONE STRIKE AND YOU'RE OUT! The front page printed the entire text of a speech Nate made to the assembled workers of all his Standish enterprises. They were sitting in the racetrack grandstand. He leaned against the fence that edged the track, his elbows on the top rail.

"About five or six years ago a fellow named Gompers got

the idea that if enough men got together in a mob, they could make everybody else give them anything they wanted. His name should have been Stompers, because that's what he wanted to do. Stomp the bosses. Not with his boots—oh, no, that would be the kind of fight every one of us has been in one time or another. Mr. Stompers does his fighting with a thing he dreamed up called a 'union.' The way it works is this. Some fellows with no jobs except doing Mr. Stompers' dirty work go around and talk real slick to men who do have jobs. All you men get together, he says, and refuse to do your work, and your boss will get so scared that his factory won't be able to fill orders that he'll give you Saturdays off as well as Sundays and twice the wages you're getting now and any other little thing you think you might like to have. That's called a strike, men.

"Now, Mr. Stompers don't have a job, and his organizers don't have a job. You know how they earn a living? I'll tell you. Everybody in one of their unions pays dues out of his own pocket for the privilege of belonging to the union and doing whatever Mr. Stompers tells him to do. Guess where that money goes.

"I'm not going to ask you to reach in your pocket and give me any of your hard-earned cash. I'd a sight rather have you bet it on a slow horse the next time you come to the races. That way I'll get even more of it, and I like as much as I can get.

"So far Mr. Stompers' boys haven't come around here. They've been in Kansas and Illinois and New York and just a little while ago in Pennsylvania. One of the strikers shot Mr. Frick, the boss out there. Didn't kill him, but Frick ain't real happy.

"I don't want anybody to shoot me, and I don't want any strikes. So I'm talking to you before any of Stompers' boys start whispering sweet words to you.

"A union would be a real bad idea. You'd have to pay dues instead of enjoying the Saturday night races, for one thing. For another thing, the law says that Stompers has to give the boss of the factory the names of all the men in the union. The day one of them lists comes to me is the same day every man on that list gets fired. Simple as that. There's a lot of boys on farms just down the road who'd be real happy to leave the seven-day week and the get-paid-at-the-end-of-the-season-if-you're-lucky job they've got and take the one you've got, with a pay envelope every Saturday whether there's drought or early frost or a plague of beetles or not.

"I don't figure it'll ever come to that. You men are too smart. But I don't believe in putting things off, so I figured I'd lay my cards on the table before any kind of misunderstanding could get started.

"That's all I got to say. Anybody that's got any problems with this can see me later."

"Nate, you're getting as long-winded as Jule Carr," Doctor complained. "I was going to do a big story on the front page about the brilliant new editor at the *Courier*, and you used up all the room."

"Come on, Doctor. One measly front page wouldn't satisfy you, and you know it," Nate said.

"It's good to have you back," Chess added, "but I've got bad news for you. Gussie has decided to be a newspaperwoman."

"Say it isn't so. I thought she was going to be a locomotive engineer."

"You're out of date, Doctor. You missed the jockey stage, too. Now it's Nellie Bly. Gussie wants to beat her record, though. She plans to go around the world in only fifty days. Or be president of the United States, depending on which mood she's in."

"You scare me to death. Where is she now, the fearless Miss Richardson?"

"Visiting her friend Ellie. The Wilsons have a summer house up in the mountains."

"Maybe she'll meet George Vanderbilt and terrorize him into marrying her."

Everyone knew about the latest and greatest Vanderbilt

extravagance. George, a thirty-year-old bachelor, had bought thousands of acres in western North Carolina and was building a house there that some people said was going to be the biggest house the world had ever seen.

"Heaven help poor George," said Nathan. But privately he was quite certain that even a Vanderbilt wasn't good enough for Gussie.

When she came home for the races and band concert and fireworks on the Fourth of July, almost the first words out of her mouth were about George Vanderbilt.

Her mother and father looked quickly at each other and then bewildered her by bursting out laughing.

She stormed up the stairs to her room, outraged.

"I'll go make peace," Chess said. Before she left the parlor she saw the look on Nathan's face and smiled to herself. Gussie had been talking about the huge machines at Vanderbilt's building site that were erecting an entire town almost overnight to house the workers for the real construction project.

I suppose Nathan will be over in Asheville by day after tomorrow, Chess bet herself.

She was wrong by twenty-four hours. Nate left for Asheville the next morning.

That afternoon Chess sat in a rocking chair on the porch arguing with Doctor, who was pacing back and forth in front of her being difficult about doing yet another newspaper story on the Shakespearean Dramatic Troupe.

"MaMa—" Gussie was at the bottom of the steps to the yard. Her face was livid, with a sheen of perspiration.

Chess leapt to her feet. "Darling—"

Gussie gave a cry of pain and fell to her knees. Then she vomited with such force that bits of undigested food and a foul yellow-green fluid fell on the ground three feet away.

Chess was running, shouting to Doctor, "Go get Dr. Campbell. Quick!"

Chapter Twenty-Nine

CHESS CARRIED HER LITTLE GIRL upstairs to her bed. It was almost impossible to hold on to her. Gussie was nearly ten, and heavy, plus she was jerking spasmodically, retching and vomiting. "Sor-ry," she gasped, then the terrifying, choking heaving began again.

"Hush, baby, hush, that's all right. Hush, now, darling, MaMa will make it better. Hush, hush, baby, my angel, sweet baby . . ."

Chess lay Gussie on her bed. She put her hand on her child's forehead, feeling for fever. But Gussie's skin was cold. Cold as death.

"MaMa—" Chess thrust terror aside.

"Yes, my angel, MaMa's right here. Dr. Campbell will be here in a minute and you'll have some medicine."

Gussie cried out, clutched her stomach and vomited again, a thin dark fluid. Chess bit her lips. She had to be calm. Strong, to give Gussie strength and take away her fear. Oh, God, what should I do? Bathe her? She's chilled, it might be the worst thing for her. Hold her to warm her? Chess put her arms around Gussie, but she whimpered and pushed feebly at Chess, so Chess released her.

She hurried to the washstand and wrung out a towel in water. Gussie's mouth was caked with filth. It had to be all right to clean it; the smell must be making her even sicker.

Gussie made little animal sounds when Chess washed her face. Her eyes were terrified, yet pitifully grateful. "Everything will be all right, baby," Chess told her. "Soon. You feel terrible now, I know, but soon it will be better." Please, God, Chess prayed silently.

Archy Campbell took the stairs three at a time. He was young and fit and scared to death of what he might find at the top of them.

Doctor stayed downstairs in the hall just long enough to tell the servants to clean up the porch and stair carpet and then to get on with their work. Then he ran up to Gussie's room. The stench of sickness stopped him in the doorway. He saw Chess, her frock stained and stinking, her face ashen with horror, but with a convincing loving smile. Dr. Campbell was bending over the child on the bed.

"Does it hurt here, Gussie? . . . here? . . . here? . . . here?" She retched again, a raw painful sound, then vomited weakly, the fluid dribbling down her chin. Dr. Campbell looked closely at it. "Are you thirsty, Gussie?"

She rasped an unintelligible word.

"Water, in a spoon," the young doctor said sharply to Chess.

Her hand was shaking so badly she had to steady it with the other one before she could get the spoon to Gussie's lips. The little girl sucked greedily, then a second spoonful, then a third. And suddenly she vomited again.

"Mrs. Richardson," said Dr. Campbell, "I'd like for you to have some warm water brought up. I want to bathe Gussie."

"I'll do it. Let me." Chess looked up, saw Doctor in the doorway. "Tell the servants."

Heaven forgive me, Doctor thought, I'm glad to get away. He had seen Gussie's face. Her skin looked blue.

Downstairs there was no one in sight. Where were the servants? What should he do? Doctor stood, paralyzed by panic. Then he heard a rumbling voice from the back of the house and the thunder of heavy boots, hurrying.

Soldier shoved him aside and climbed the stairs. Doctor saw that—absurdly—the old man was trying to tiptoe in his thick, worn old work boots. For some unaccountable reason, the sight freed Doctor from his panic. He walked rapidly to the back of the house, to the kitchen, to relay the doctor's order.

Young Dr. Campbell was trying to comfort Chess, but his uncertainty leaked out. "She has all the symptoms we learned about," he said. "I'm almost certain it's cholera. It has this sudden onset, but the course of the disease is seldom prolonged. Forty-eight hours is almost always the maximum—" He stopped himself too abruptly. Chess knew what he wasn't saying. Two days until death.

"Let old Soldier in to see his baby." The tall, lanky figure moved Chess firmly to one side and sank onto one knee beside the low bed. "Hey, there, trooper," he said quietly to Gussie. He took one small hand in his. "Hear tell the bellyache's got you. Ol' Nathan Bedford always used to say he'd sooner go through a ton of grape shot than have a bellyache."

He turned his head toward Chess. His eyes dismissed the young doctor at once. "This young'un has got the kol-ree, Mrs. Richardson. Any time now, she's going to get the shits. Haul out a bunch of sheets and towels. I seen plenty of kolree in my day. You and me is going to pull her through."

"Ah, yes, diarrhea is the secondary symptom of the—" Dr. Campbell was babbling.

Soldier glared him into silence. "You brung any opium with you?" Campbell reached for his leather satchel. "Give Mrs. Richardson a handful of pills and a bunch of powder packets," Soldier commanded him. "Then skedaddle." His voice was gentle when he gave Chess her orders. "You go put on a clean frock, Mrs. Richardson. Something in a pretty color for Gussie to look at." Then he devoted his attention totally to the little girl. He lifted her head and shoulders with a crooked arm and dipped spoons of water for her flaccid mouth with his other steady hand.

Chess was back in under five minutes, wearing a pink silk dressing gown that Gussie had frequently admired. Beneath it she was wearing only a camisole and petticoat. Her corset was abandoned. She needed freedom of movement.

"I've put everything in my bedroom, Bobby Fred. The bedstead's higher, we'll be able to reach better."

Soldier nodded approval. Chess was calm and collected, ready for battle.

Gussie cried out, her body contracted in spasm, and her bowels emptied a torrent of foul-smelling black fluid and clumped soft matter.

"Help me get her clothes off," said Soldier, "then we'll move her."

She had never noticed that Bobby Fred's hands were so big. The thought was random, distracted, a godsend to keep her from fixing on the terror of what she was seeing—her child's death-like discolored face and body, the grimace of fear and pain that marked her small face.

"You always did hate this frock, Gussie, isn't it lucky you weren't in the overalls you love so much?" Her voice was warm, even a touch amused. It was so much easier to comfort now. Now that the old soldier was there to steady her.

Chess had laid a dozen sheets on her bed, folded in half for easier removal when they became soiled. For an hour Gussie continued to cramp and to evacuate dark stinking fluid. Ten of the sheets were piled in the hall outside the bedroom door before the child's body was empty. Soldier's tender embrace had held Gussie up time and again while Chess bathed and dried her. Wet towels and stained cloths made a larger pile.

The child's appearance was worse than death. She looked

almost decomposed. Her eyes were sunken, and surrounded by bruised purplish skin. All her bones looked sharp and prominent, covered only by her cold skin. Her flesh had shrunk, dehydrated. Her pulse could not be found. Only a rough, shallow, irregular, rasping breathing told that she was alive.

Gussie was too weak to swallow any more. Chess had to put the remaining opium aside and watch the resurgence of unblunted pain assail her beloved little girl.

Give me the pain, Chess begged God. I could bear that. I cannot bear this.

"Rip up one of them towels," Bobby Fred told her. "I'll make a water tit out of it, like the sugar tits for babies." He placed the twisted, dampened end of the towel inside Gussie's mouth with gentle callused fingers, then dripped water through the twist, drop by drop.

Gussie's eyes drooped with momentary relief.

Why did she have to be conscious? Why couldn't the drug have put her to sleep, given her some respite? Chess clenched futile fists, longing to howl her protest. Then she opened her hands and stroked Gussie's forehead. "Soon, baby," she crooned softly, "soon it will be so much better. You're a brave Gussie, braver than Nellie Bly or anybody else, ever."

Bobby Fred said, "Now, just you wait a little minute there, ma'am. Not even Trooper here can be braver than General Nathan Bedford Forrest."

Gussie tried to smile. Chess felt her heart break.

"Things are quieting down," said Soldier quietly. "A mustard plaster'll give her some warm."

"I'll be right back, darling," Chess told Gussie. She leaned close, kissed Gussie's forehead, and whispered close to her ear. "You are ten times braver than any old general."

When Chess spread the yellow-daubed linen across Gussie's stomach, the child's wince made her catch her breath. No more pain, she entreated the heavens. Surely she's suffered enough.

For a while all was quiet except for the hideous weak

straining breath. Then Gussie's eyes opened wide and she moaned. Her left leg began to twitch, then jerk.

"Cramp," Soldier said. "Rub it."

Soon the other leg was afflicted as well, and he had to abandon the water drip in order to massage the cramped muscle. Gussie's leg looked very small in his big hands. They were gnarled and scarred and thick with calluses from decades of hard work. But they kneaded the knotted muscle with a firm gentleness that looked to Chess like an angel's touch must be. She did her best to match it.

Gussie's moans were like the mewling of a tiny animal. Hours later they stopped.

She's dead. Chess heard the words in her soul. Gussie's leg was limp and cold in her hands, but she continued to rub it, willing warmth and life back into it.

Bobby Fred put a heavy hand on her shoulder. "You can stop that now," he said.

"No! No, I won't."

Soldier circled her wrists with his fingers and pulled her hands away. "No need for that. She's sleeping. She's made it through. Where is there a quilt to cover her up with?"

Chess didn't believe him. She snatched her hands away, touched Gussie's cold face and cold limp hands and feet. Then she saw the child's sunken chest rise and fall, in slow, even breaths.

Chess turned to Soldier. "Oh, Bobby Fred," she whispered. She put her arms around his waist, rested her head on his chest, and poured out her relief and the weight of fright-filled hours in tears and shuddering sobs. He held her safe.

When her emotions were spent, she looked up at him through washed, shining eyes. "Thank you, old friend."

Soldier smiled. He looked worn but victorious. "Cover that baby up, child, and then go wash your face. You're taking over the water drip while I go find me some whiskey."

Nathan came home, loaded with statistics about the engineering wonders near Asheville. When he heard what had happened, he was stricken. "I'll never leave Gussie again, not even for an hour," he declared. He was shaken when he saw his daughter's weakness.

Chess laughed at him. "You're forgetting what Gussie's like when she's healthy. She'd wear you out before the day was half over." Chess could laugh now. Gussie was improving dramatically, almost by the hour.

But she was still very feeble. She slept often and easily, and she had to be fed the soft puddings and milky drinks that Chess prepared for her. In her listlessness, she wanted to be read to, rather than to read for herself, and it was obviously tiring for her when her friends and family came to see her. It was almost as if weakness stole years from her. What she liked best of all was for Chess to tell her again the stories that had been her favorites when she was very young. Stories of Harefields, again and again.

"MaMa, tell about when you were a little girl."

Chess settled herself in the low chair by Gussie's bed. "When I was a little girl . . ." she began. Gussie settled herself in her nest of pillows, with a sigh of pleasure. ". . . I lived in a big white house beside a beautiful wide river.

"There was a swing with wisteria hanging over it . . ."

"Just like mine," said Gussie.

"Just like yours. And I used to swing in it, in the shade of the big tree for hours and hours. Then I'd go out on the lawn for a tea party with my dolls—"

"Dolls, ugh!" Gussie was quite decidedly still herself, even though she was weak.

Chess smiled. "There would be tiny little sandwiches and cakes. The birds would fly down and peck at them. Then I'd pretend that the dolls had taken bites."

"You were very silly."

"I was very silly. And very happy. I used to go all the way upstairs to the ballroom and stretch my arms out and spin around and around, all over the shiny waxed floor, sliding and laughing. Then—if no one was near—I'd slide down the banister, round and round, all the way to the bottom."

"Tell me about the stairs."

"They were called 'flying stairs.' They were attached to the curved wall on one side only, and the other side, where the banister was, looked like it was suspended in mid-air, going up and up in swooping wide circles that made you dizzy to look at.

"Way up, so very, very high, there was a window in the roof, shaped like a great big egg. The panes were beveled, and the sun made rainbows when it shone through them."

Gussie's voice was getting sleepy. "Like our stained-glass flowers window?"

"No, darling, it was different. It didn't have flowers like our window. Do you have a favorite flower in our window?"

Gussie always said "iris," and then Chess told her that Iris was the goddess of the rainbow. But not now. Gussie was asleep.

Chess smoothed the lank heavy hair from her child's pale forehead. Then she kissed the relaxed, blessedly warm, small hand near her. For a long while, she gazed on the greatest treasure in her life, her little girl. Then she left the room with careful, quiet steps. A soft rain was falling outside, and a cool breeze fluttered the lace curtains at the windows. Everything was peaceful.

Chess walked slowly down the elaborately decorated massive staircase of the house into the front parlor. Things, she said to herself angrily, all these things. There's barely room to turn around in here, no wonder it's so hot and airless. She pushed aside the layers of draperies and curtains and shades and pushed up the heavy leaded-glass window. One of the thick silk tassels that decorated the draperies hit her on the shoulder, and she had a sudden memory of the arguments she'd had with the shopkeeper about making these in the particular shade of green that she wanted, not the shade that he had in the shop. All the time she'd spent chasing things. Why had she thought that things—and more things—and still more things—were so important?

Nate came in. "How is she?"

"She's fine. Sleeping again. It's the best medicine for her. She ate almost all her custard."

"I think I'll go up and sit with her for a while. Just in case she might wake up and want something."

"I know," said Chess. Both of them still needed the reassurance of being with Gussie many times every day.

Nate sat watching Gussie sleep, and deep inside he quaked with fear. It was the first time in his life that he was conscious of his own vulnerability. He was not an introspective man. To view the unknown capacity for emotion inside himself was deeply disturbing, and he tried to close his mind to it. But he wasn't strong enough. His arms quivered from the control he was exercising. He wanted to grab Gussie and hold her to him where he could keep her protected, where his body would stand between her and the dangers that he now knew were everywhere.

Nate's family had never touched. He had known no embraces, no kisses, no demonstrated affection until his uncle brought Alva to the farm. He was confused by his need to hold his daughter. Her childish hugs and kisses had always delighted him, but he had never thought of them as very different from a puppy's onslaught of ecstatic face-licking. Now he dimly understood that he'd been given gifts by his little girl that he valued above all his riches.

His mind did not form the word "love." That was an ordinary word. People "loved" peaches, or a song, or flowers. What he felt had no name, or if it did, he did not know it. He was not a word-minded person. All he knew was that he felt weak and helpless against the forces that had nearly taken his child from him, and that he would willingly give his own life for hers if those forces returned. She was the holder of his heart.

His hand reached out, against his will, and his finger touched her palm. Without waking, Gussie curled her fingers tight around his, as she had done when she was a tiny baby. She smiled in her sleep.

Nate's breath caught in his throat. Slow heavy tears slid down his cheeks.

Chapter Thirty

WITH THE FRIGHTENING RESILIENCE of youth, Gussie was a blur of energy and noise again after only two more weeks. Chess and Nate had no choice but to let her be.

And the merciful amnesia that protects humans from their own memories gradually blurred the fear that held each of them in its talons.

But Chess thought again and again of the stories Gussie had wanted to hear, and her own happiness as a child at Harefields. The house was more real to her now, almost, than it had been when she lived there.

Late on an autumn day, when the evocative smell of burning leaves filled the streets of Standish, she went in search of Nathan. He had just come home; he was in a rocker on the porch, reading Doctor's editorial about the need to pave all of Standish's streets.

"Did you see the *Courier?*" he asked Chess. He was chuckling. "That crazy fool says that the proof of civilization is shiny boots and so we're living in the wilderness."

Chess smiled. She had never quite forgiven Doctor for running away when Gussie collapsed. He had apologized, confessed his shame at his own weakness, punished himself verbally with bitter eloquence. But she could not feel the fondness she once had.

"I have something I want to do, Nathan." He closed the *Courier*. "I want to build Harefields again. Here, for us to live in. I've always regretted that Gussie never got to see it."

Nate didn't fully understand why Chess wanted it, but it was enough that she did. The next day they walked through the gold and red fallen leaves in the still-quiet woods beyond the town and chose a site on top of a low hill. Gussie went with them, dashing ahead, then returning to urge them to hurry. She was eager to get on with the project. She wanted to slide down the banister of the stairs.

Nate's mother had something she wanted to do, also. She announced it at the dinner table on Sunday. The family were all members of the Bethel Methodist Church in Standish now. The weekly trip to Durham and Mrs. Brown's Boardinghouse dinner was a thing of the past the instant Bethel Methodist opened its doors.

Miss Mary's house was the place for Sunday dinner, even though Nate's dining room was much roomier and he had a full-time cook. "She's an old woman," Nate said when Chess protested the arrangement. "She likes to have things her way, and it gives her something to do."

Chess understood; she liked to be busy and useful herself. So she forced herself to eat Miss Mary's tasteless, overcooked food and bribed Gussie to do the same. "It's only an hour or so, and you owe your grandmother the respect due to her. You can have ice cream afterwards at home if you behave yourself."

Miss Mary made her announcement as soon as Josh finished blessing the food. "I'm going to ask you something, Nate, 'cause I'm sick and tired of waiting for you to do what you ought to do on your own."

"What's that, Ma?"

"I want you to make the church the gift of a steeple. It ain't right not to have a church pointing up to heaven."

"Mary, Nate already gave the church that organ," said Alva.

Mary Richardson waved the remark away. "You're a rich man, Nate, and a sinful one, with your horse-racing and whiskey-selling saloon down by the railroad track. You should be on your knees begging God's mercy. I'd be fearful you could burn in Hell for all eternity except that you got your brother praying for mercy on your soul.

"I want you to give that steeple, with bells in it to call the people to church, and I want you to do whatever needs doing to bring Gideon here to preach from the pulpit."

Nate had been doing what he had done all his life, letting his mother's bitter words flow smoothly in and out of his ears with little pause. But now he had to pay attention.

Gideon. And Lily. Everything in him was shouting "No."

"I'll see what I can manage, Ma," he temporized. "Have you got any more of those good sweet potatoes?"

He wasn't prepared for Chess to plead his mother's case. After they went home, she talked about Gussie's cousins coming to live nearby until he felt like shouting at her. Gideon and Lily had two girls, Mary and Martha. Their photograph was displayed in a place of honor on Miss Mary's parlor table, right next to the Bible.

"Good gracious, Nathan, aren't you at all curious to see your own brother again? How long has it been?"

"I don't remember. I saw him in Durham one day, four or five years ago, I suppose." It had been seventeen years since he'd seen Lily.

The arithmetic brought Nate up short. He'd never counted the years.

Chess asked him what he was laughing about.

"The steeple," he replied. "I hope you can keep Gussie from climbing it." His lie didn't bother him; he was too lighthearted. Why had he been afraid of seeing a sixteen-year-old girl all these years? She was a middle-aged woman by now.

Chess shivered. A goose walked over her grave when Nathan combined the steeple and Gussie.

Edith Horton was not in favor of Chess' desire to rebuild Harefields. "Why on earth build big drafty old rooms when you've got a new house full of nice cozy ones?" But the Horton plantation house was an invaluable aid. Like Harefields, the Hortons' house had remained unchanged since the time before the Civil War. There had never been any money for modern improvements, or anything new. For thirty years paint had peeled, silks and velvets had become thinner and more faded, leaks in the roof had stained walls and rotted floors in the upper stories. So many things were like Harefields; Chess recognized furniture woods and styles that she had taken for granted in Virginia. Edith knew what they were. Chess learned about Sheraton and Chippendale, Hepplewhite and the Adam brothers.

James Dike's bookstore provided her with reference volumes on the eighteenth century and Palladio. Dike also knew of an architect in Boston who specialized in "antique" houses.

Chess was writing a letter to him when Nate came over from his office with a visitor. "This is Dick Reynolds, Chess, and I want you to be in on our talk. We should go in the library."

She was fascinated. She'd heard of Reynolds from Nate. She'd heard even more interesting gossip from women in Durham whose husbands were involved in tobacco. Richard Joshua Reynolds was, like Nate and like Buck Duke, a risk-taker who had made a fortune in tobacco manufacturing. He specialized in chewing tobacco, not cigarettes.

He built a one-room factory when he was twenty-four, lived in a room above it and worked with a driving ambition that, inside of eight years, propelled him to a pinnacle of accomplishment.

His success transformed the village of Winston into a small

city with a new railroad. Its centerpiece, in 1891, was Reynolds' block-long six-story factory.

Now, in 1892, he was under attack by Buck Duke's American Tobacco Company. "You beat him some way, Nate. I want you to tell me how you did it."

Chess had trouble taking her eyes off him. Dick Reynolds had a strange, narrow, wispy long beard that moved whenever he spoke. And the stories about him! He was unmarried, but had fathered untold numbers of children. His womanizing was flagrant; he even named brands of his tobacco after his mistresses. And it was said that he gambled at poker for such high stakes that men came all the way from New Orleans to try their skills at his table. They usually lost.

"I figured you cigarette fellows was crazy to throw away your money on all that advertising and them crazy folding chairs and such. Word of chewer's mouth was my motto. I'm in it now up to my neck, though. Started last year; I just hope I'm not too late. Buck's out to get me, Nate. Back in February he bought a big Louisville plug outfit, then two more from Baltimore in April. Now he's cut prices to what it costs to make the plug and he's telling wholesalers they won't get any cigarettes from him unless they favor his 'Battle Ax' brand of chewing tobacco over everybody else's."

Nate opened a bottle of whiskey. "You stay here tonight, Dick. We got a lot of talking to do. And I hear you're a man who can really hold his liquor. Get started, you're going to need it."

"I'll send someone to fetch Doctor," said Chess.

The next day, Doctor left with Reynolds to begin a new war against Buck Duke.

"Do you think they'll win?" Chess asked Nate.

"I don't know. Dick's got the sand for the fight, and Doctor dearly loves a punch-and-gouge dust-up. But Buck is Buck. I'm just glad he's turned his eye on the plug makers for a while. I can quit looking over my shoulder every minute of the day."

Chess nodded. "I guess that means we'll have telephones pretty soon."

Nate laughed. "You know me inside out, don't you? The Bell patent runs out on March the third next year. I figure if I stir my stumps we'll be all ready to hook up our wires at twelve-oh-one A.M. March fourth."

On March 1, Gussie dug the first shovelful of earth for the new Harefields, with her parents looking on, puffed with pride.

On the fourth, she talked on the telephone to her friend Ellie Wilson.

On the seventh, she met her aunt and uncle and cousins for the first time. She was too excited to observe that her father looked as pale as a ghost.

When the S & D pulled in to the station, the hissing cloud of steam billowed up the sides of Nate's private car. He looked through it, a smile of welcome on his face for his brother's family.

Lily was standing in the open doorway, dressed all in white. In a split second, Nate became an awkward, awestruck boy of eighteen again.

"Hello, Nathaniel," said Lily. She held out her hand. "Aren't you going to help me down?"

Chapter Thirty-One

"SHE'S SO BORING," Gussie wailed. "Do I have to go over there?"

"Yes, you do, darling. Martha's your first cousin, and she's new in town so she hasn't made any friends yet. Give her a chance. Maybe she's shy."

"But I was going to play mumblety-peg with Soldier. I promised him."

"You mean he promised you, after you pestered him into submission. I was there, remember? Maybe you can teach Martha to play mumblety-peg."

"Ha! She'd squeal and run away the minute she saw a knife. All she likes to do is sit still like a goody-goody and play Chinese Checkers or something. She's boring."

Privately Chess sympathized. She was finding her in-laws pretty boring herself. Gideon was interested only in getting new members for Bethel's congregation, and Lily was so sweet that it set her teeth on edge. Boring was exactly the word for the whole bunch. Except for fifteen-year-old Mary.

To say Mary was boring would be a compliment. She was so quiet that she faded into the woodwork; she wasn't there at all.

Still, Miss Mary was in seventh heaven to have her favorite son at her beck and call. At least *she* was happy. As for Nathan, he didn't pay any attention at all. You'd think he didn't even know that his brother was in town.

Nate was at the parsonage, suffering the torments of the damned. Lily was sitting beside him on the stiff, velvet-covered settee in the parlor. Her gentian eyes were wide, luminous with unshed tears. "I'm afraid you must think I'm terrible, sending you that note," she said. Her voice trembled.

"No. Not at all. What was it you wanted to talk to me about?" He felt as if his tongue was thick in his dry mouth. He couldn't look Lily in the eye. She was so beautiful. Her golden hair was tucked up under a white lace cap, but tendrils strayed in soft curls on her temples and her neck. She smelled like roses.

"I'm so distressed that you're avoiding us, Nathaniel. Chess and Gussie are in and out all the time, but you never come here. Have I done something to offend you?"

He had to look at her then. He saw his heart's desire, just like all those years ago. He was blind to the tiny marks of the years. His palms were sweating from the need to touch her milky white skin. He hated himself for the urge he felt to defile her purity. He couldn't force any sound from his throat.

Lily put her hand on his. An electric shock raced up his arm. "Promise you don't dislike me, Nathaniel. That would make me even more unhappy than I am." One single tear fell from her right eye. Nate lusted to taste its salt on his tongue.

"I like you," he managed to say. "I don't want you to be unhappy."

Lily made a small, suffocated sobbing sound. The lace ruffle over her full breasts quivered. "It's not your fault, Nathaniel, it's mine. You tried to tell me, but I wouldn't listen.

I should never have married Gideon. I should have waited for you. You were my favorite, do you remember when I told you that?"

She was turned toward him, her eyes searching his. "Do you remember how it was with us? I've never forgotten." Her fingers were on his wrist; they moved up, inside the cuff of his shirt, until they rested on his pounding pulse.

"I think of you all the time," she whispered, and her body swayed toward him. Her lips were soft, rose-colored, slightly parted, so near to his hungry mouth.

Nate lost control. His arm circled her, pulled her to him, and his lips crushed hers in a grinding despairing kiss that sucked her tongue into his mouth. It touched his teeth, his tongue, slid and darted and exploded passion throughout his entire body. Then his mouth moved hungrily to her throat. Her blood beat strongly in her neck, the pulse moving against his lips. Her arms closed around his shoulders, and her fingers raked the back of his neck, grabbed hold of his hair.

"I wanted," she breathed. "I never knew what I wanted, but it was this, it was you. I always . . . always . . . every day . . . yes, oh, yes, Nathaniel, this is what I want."

His hand found her breast; it filled his hand with softness. Her nipple was hard, straining against her gown.

Lily moaned, deep in her throat, and then her fingers released his hair, moved like lightning over her bodice, undoing tiny buttons. "Kiss me, Nathaniel. Here." She spread her bodice apart and cupped her white breasts in her hands, offering them to him. His mouth closed on one tall red nipple.

Her mouth was beside his ear. "Never, I've never known . . . never felt . . . never done this before. Oh, it's wonderful, I'm on fire. I want you to devour me. Lick my breasts, my beloved, suckle me, hurt me, bite my flesh and mark me yours. Because I am, I always have been." Her breath was hot, tiny explosions in his ear.

His hands found her waist, circled it, moved up her body to push aside her hands, to stroke the soft globes that had haunted his dreams for so many years.

Then she grabbed his head, forced it away from her breast, forced him to look at her. "Do you want me?" Her voice was hoarse.

"Yes, great Godalmighty, I want you."

She kissed him then, still holding his head; her tongue teased his. His hands squeezed, moved, circled on her breasts.

Lily's tiny teeth caught his lower lip, tugged it, let it get away. "We'll have to meet somewhere, Nathaniel. This is madness. Anyone could come in any minute. I'd be ruined."

Her hands moved, covered his, pressed them harder against her. "I don't care," she whispered. "I don't care if I'm ruined. I've never felt like this before. I can't give it up."

Her words penetrated the red haze inside Nate's brain; he drew back, horrified. He must protect Lily, in spite of the clamor, the drive of his desire. His fingers fumbled, clumsy, trying to close the buttons of her frock. She was breathing heavily, the edges of the bodice kept slipping away from him.

Nate looked at her in supplication. Lily's eyes were half-closed, her lips swollen, open, revealing her pink tongue. It moved, ran over her lips. They gleamed wetly. He was dizzied with lust.

He lurched to his feet, tore his eyes away. "I must go." It was the most difficult demand he had ever placed upon himself. He had to do it. For her.

Lily nimbly closed her bodice, stood, stepped toward him. "Is there any place? I'll die if I don't see you again."

Nate clutched his head, trying to clear it, trying to think. "The Clubhouse," he said at last. "It's closed except on race days."

"I'll meet you at the park. At the bandstand."

"Yes, yes, that's good. I can be showing you the town."

"Tomorrow?"

"Yes." He was torn into pieces—needing to leave, hating to leave, feeling her close to him like a burning brand, afraid to look at her or he would lose the fragile rein on his need to possess her. Now.

Lily put her hands on his shoulders. "You can't go out like

this, you're all mussed up." She smoothed the lapels of his coat, his cravat, the disorder of his vest. Her side brushed against the aching bulge of his penis, and hot release spurted inside his trousers then down the inner part of his legs.

The architect for the new Harefields was named Lancelot O'Brien. When James Dike first told her about him, Chess declared that she could not do business with anybody who had a name like Lancelot. She'd laugh in the poor man's face.

But when she saw photographs of other classical-influence buildings he had done, she changed her tune. They met almost daily, either in Durham where he had set up a studio in a suite at the new Carrolina Hotel, or in the guest room at the house. Chess had converted it to a special Harefields workroom, with shelves full of her reference books, two big library tables and a drafting table for O'Brien.

She was engrossed in the work. Day after day she went over drawings O'Brien made from her descriptions of Harefields. At night she dreamed, woke, made notes of details in her dreams.

Weeks went by before she became aware of the change in Nathan. He looked haggard, and she had a sudden terrifying memory of Gussie when she collapsed with cholera.

"There's nothing wrong with me," Nate insisted.

In fact, he was in Hell. Every time Gussie gave him one of her hasty hugs, or Chess repeated how happy she was about the new house, guilt and shame gripped his heart like a crab.

Nate had never concerned himself about fidelity; he would have considered it ridiculous, if he had considered it at all. He kept a mistress in Raleigh, another one in Georgetown, South Carolina, where his paper mill was located. In addition, he often accepted the invitations of women he met casually when he was traveling. But they were not near his home, their existence did not intrude on his life in Standish. Whereas his affair with Lily, if discovered, would be embarrassing, even humiliating, for his entire family. He owed them better than that. He was a disgrace.

The tobacco world enjoyed the latest development in Buck Duke's life that spring. Buck had fallen completely under the spell of a sophisticated New York divorcée, a certain Mrs. Lillian Fletcher McCredy. Insiders reported that he would even leave vital business meetings when L.M. telephoned. Buck the predator had become Buck the leash-led. It was an endless source for ribald joking at the Commonwealth Club.

Nate knew that he was no better off. Lily controlled his life, dominated his thoughts, filled his dreams. He lived for their clandestine meetings. He was obsessed.

He made her want things, she told him, shocking things. She was ashamed to admit that her mind could even imagine such things. But when she was with him, she went crazy, her mind went crazy, too, because she wanted him so much, wanted to belong to him, totally, completely, in every part of her body. And so, at her direction, he inserted his penis, his finger, his tongue, into each and every fold, crevice, opening of her pale tender flesh.

He had had sex with many women. Gentle sex, playful sex, exciting pounding sex. Giving pleasure was pleasurable to him. Never had he used a woman the way Lily begged to be used. Never had he experienced the heightened thrill of causing pain or degradation. Never had he unleashed the animal in the deep darkness of his spirit.

He loathed himself. And he wanted more.

PANIC.

Headlines screamed it in giant type on every newspaper. On June 27, the Stock Market plummeted, wiping out the on-paper fortunes of thousands.

"What does this mean, Nathan?" Chess asked. "The New York paper says that banks are in peril, and railroads, and factories. Are we in trouble?"

Nate shook his head. "The folks who believed in paper are in trouble. I put my money into bricks and machinery. We'll do just fine. There'll probably be a run on the bank—people want to hold their money in their hand when they're scared of losing it—but I already told the boys over there to pay out with a smile on their faces. It'll settle down quick enough and then everybody'll deposit their cash again."

"Should I call off the work on Harefields?"

"Go ahead and build your house, Chess. Make it bigger if you want to. Prices for materials will start going down pretty soon, is my guess."

"Are you sure we're all right?" Chess thought that money worries might be the cause of Nathan's sick look.

He grinned, and for a moment he looked like the old Nathan. "When people get panicked, they smoke more than ever. We'll just get richer and richer."

All Nate's predictions came true. There was a brief run on the Standish Bank. It was all over in less than two weeks. In the country as a whole, more than 600 banks closed, leaving depositors without any hope of recovering their savings. Seventy-four railroads went into receivership, including the giant Union Pacific, the Reading, and the Santa Fe.

Before the end of that year, 15,000 businesses would declare bankruptcy.

Every week, big city newspapers reported at least one suicide by a prominent citizen.

Chess watched Nathan grow thinner and more worried-looking all the time. She went to the office building one Sunday afternoon and pored over the ledgers, looking for the cause, but she couldn't find it. The double-entry system was difficult, and the interlocking nature of all the businesses was like a maze.

She became increasingly anxious. Edith Horton told her not to be such a goose. The time to start fretting would be when Nathan stopped looking worried. "Like Henry," she said. "He doesn't have sense enough to worry. If he buys one more colt to train for racing, I'm going to kill him. He hasn't bothered to wonder if the people with enough money to buy racehorses still have any money."

Bobby Fred, whose wise old eyes saw more than most people's, also told Chess not to be upset. He figured he might as well do the worrying for both of them, and what she didn't know might possibly blow over before it hurt her.

"Nathaniel, I don't have anybody to turn to but you. Will you help me? I try to save a little every week out of my housekeeping money, but Gideon just doesn't understand how much it costs, with growing children. Martha has her heart set on taking piano lessons, and I don't know how I can manage. The parsonage doesn't even have a piano."

Nate gave Lily an envelope the next day. It had a $1,000 in it.

She took it to the locked drawer in her delicate writing table. A parishioner had already promised to give a piano to the preacher's daughters, and the music teacher was honored to give free lessons. Lily's pretty mouth formed an angry snarl when she looked in the drawer. The account book from the Savannah bank was worthless now. Her $9,127.40 was lost. The bank was closed. All those men, in all those different churches over the years, all those furtive little "gifts," all of them wasted now.

It didn't really matter. The money had never been important in itself. What could she have done with it? A minister's wife was watched like prey by the hawk-eyed ladies of the congregation. Any hint of extravagance or self-indulgence would have been noticed at once. The money was only another kind of power over the fools who gave it to her, a proof that they would do anything she asked.

Nathaniel, perhaps, was a different matter. He had such a great deal of money, much, much more than any of the others. And he was still trying to hold back, fighting her control. What a triumph it would be to make him openly betray his wife and his own brother. And how much it would hurt them.

Lily took the envelope back out of the drawer. She had decided to return it to him and tell him she had just learned about the gift piano and lessons. He mustn't think he could satisfy her with a few dollars. That was too easy for him.

Chess made her voice cheerful. "Mr. O'Brien told me the most extraordinary thing today, Nathan. He says that Mr. Vanderbilt is putting some kind of machinery in that house in Asheville that will heat it in the winter and cool it in the summer. You didn't see that when you were there last time, did you? Is there any way to find out about it? It would make Harefields better than perfect."

She looked down at the canvas-work embroidery that she was making such a mess of. She couldn't look at Nathan. Chess was not devious by nature, and she knew it would show on her face that she was trying to stir up a new interest in him. Never, not for as much as a week, had Nathan not had some consuming fascination for a new project. Never, until these last months.

"I can't imagine any machine like that," said Nate.

There was curiosity in his voice. Chess risked a glance at him.

He was frowning slightly, and his eyes had a faraway look.

Childishly, Chess crossed her fingers for luck.

"If I'm going, I'd better go tomorrow," Nate muttered. "There'll be snow in the mountains soon, if it's not on the ground already." He hoped there was snow. There was something so clean about snow. The air in the mountains was cleansing too. It cut through the flesh, stinging a man into life. And the distances—miles and miles of openness, only mountains and forests and broad, broad skies as far as a man could see. There was freedom in the cold, clear, clean mountain air.

Chess led Gussie from room to room at Harefields. They weren't rooms yet, only the wooden framing for the walls that would be there. ". . . and this is the morning room, because it's on the east side, and the sun streams in. We'll have our breakfast on a table down at that end. A small table, just big enough for us, not like the big table in the dining room, with lots of chairs for company . . . and look, come through here, Gussie, this is the conservatory. My mother had orange trees and lemon trees so we had lemonade and orange juice whenever we wanted it. Flowers, too, all winter long. Just wait until you smell jasmine blooming when everything's frozen outside . . . and through this door—"

"When will the stairs go in? I'm getting too old for baby things like sliding down banisters."

Chess raised her eyebrows. "Do you mean that a person gets too old for that? I'm going to whoosh down the minute they're in place."

"MaMa, are you serious?"

"Cross my heart and hope to die."

Gussie flung her arms around her mother's waist and squeezed the breath out of her. "I love you, MaMa."

"I love you, Gussie," Chess gasped. She hoped she wouldn't break her neck on the stairs. What had possessed her to say a thing like that? It must be because she was so happy. Nathan had been away for more than a week. Mr. Vanderbilt's machinery must have really captured his attention.

Lily nibbled the rough edge of a fingernail. She didn't like what was happening at all. More than once she had found excuses not to see a man for long enough to drive him half crazy and bring him to heel. No one had ever done it to her. Nathaniel was more of a challenge than she'd expected. It would be exciting to make him crawl.

Nate's face was ruddy from windburn. It made his smile look especially bright.

"You had a good time," said Chess.

"Splendid—that's what George Vanderbilt says all the time. 'Splendid.' He's a strange bird, but all right underneath it all. He knows a lot about engineering. The water system he's putting in there . . ."

Chess heard all about a number of things. Harefields was

going to be even more elaborate than Lancelot O'Brien imagined. And he had a very active imagination.

Nathan took a deep breath. "I did some thinking up there in the hills," he said.

Chess recognized the mischief in his voice. He was clearly pleased with himself. She saw it in his eyes, too. She reminded herself to seem enthusiastic, no matter what it might be. It was so good to have him back, his old self again.

"I figure," Nate drawled, prolonging the suspense, "that you and me and Gussie ought to take a little trip next summer. How would you like to go to London?"

"London?" Chess was thunderstruck. "*London*. Nathan Richardson, I'd sell my soul to go to London, and throw yours into the bargain as loose change!"

Chapter Thirty-Two

WHAT NATE HAD IN MIND was daring in conception but simple in its logic. He reasoned thus: English cigarette companies imported the majority of their tobacco from North Carolina and Virginia, then manufactured the cigarettes in England, and shipped the greatest part of them to overseas markets. They could eliminate two costly steps by combining their operations with his. He grew his own tobacco, whereas their representatives had to compete at auction. And operating factories close to the source of the raw material made packing and shipping to the distant factory unnecessary. The finished product would still have to travel great distances, but the cross-country railroads in America made the Pacific easily accessible; from there, it was a direct route to England's enormous markets in the Orient.

The same was true for England's cotton mills, and he planned to talk to them, also. But tobacco was the most important.

"I've been staving off Buck Duke practically from the day

I got started. That's no way to make a man feel good. Not getting beat ain't enough. I want to win. With the English and me together, the American Tobacco Company's going to look like a midget."

"Do you think you can do it, Nate? Chances are, nobody in London even knows where North Carolina is."

"Then I'll just have to tell them. They're so used to being all crammed together in that island that they'll fall all over themselves when they hear how much room we've got around here."

There was a lot to do. He had to buy more land, a lot more land—tobacco-growing land and cotton-growing land—and he had to put together the numbers. What the English costs were for their tobacco and cotton manufacturing enterprises, and what the costs would be under his plan. The legal aspects had to be investigated, too, and the trade agreements between countries . . . Nathan was electric with excitement.

Chess was in a daze. London. All her reading, her memories of her mother's stories, her own family heritage. All of them were English. She felt in a way that London was already familiar to her. But to see it! The streets where Shakespeare walked—and Sherlock Holmes. It was almost too thrilling to take in.

Harefields would be finished by summer, too. She would be able to do what those earlier Standishes had done; all Harefields' furnishings had been imported from England when the house was built in 1780.

There was a lot for her to do, too. A lot of studying, a lot of remembering, a lot of daydreaming. She forgot the cold bleakness beyond the heavily draped windows. Inside her mind she was in the big, high-ceilinged drawing room at Harefields, with water-scented spring breezes making dancers of the thin curtains at the tall windows to the veranda. The light and shadows were gentle, and the walls soft blue, like dappled birds' eggs in a down-lined nest. It would be that way again. A gentle life, with quiet grace notes of beauty. It would be her gift to Gussie—a perfect life for a little girl.

*   *   *

As always, the holiday season was festive and happily exhausting. Parties in Durham, parties in Standish, parties at home. Caroling, and baskets of food for the poor. A Christmas pageant at the church. Stockings. Presents under the tree. Gifts to wrap and deliver. Food, food and more food. The Watch service Christmas Eve and the Celebration of Christ's Birth Christmas Day. Music, singing, choirs, the Brass Band playing on Richardson Avenue.

Two important events stood out from the rest. Susan blushingly told the family about her engagement to a youthful teacher at the new Trinity College. And Gussie ruthlessly replaced Ellie Wilson with a new best friend. Barbara Beaufort was a redheaded imp, eleven years old, like Gussie. Her father Walter had recently moved to Standish to open an insurance agency. He and Frances, his wife, were both from distinguished families in Wilmington, the old North Carolina city near the Atlantic that had once been an important seaport. Walter's grandfather was famous throughout the South for his exploits as the most successful blockade runner of the Civil War.

By Twelfth Night, Nathan was begging Chess to do something to cool down the friendship. "The telephone line is busy every time I try to call you from the office," he complained. "And when I'm not at the office, it seems that Barbara's always here. I never knew what an irritating sound giggles could be."

"Frances says that Walter has the same problem, Nathan. Gussie's over there just as much as Barbara's over here."

"Then why do they talk on the telephone all the time?"

"I don't think they do. From what I overhear, it seems they just giggle."

Nate raised his eyes to heaven. "Give me patience, oh Lord."

Chess giggled. "Our little girl is growing up, Nathan. Didn't you meet the other member of the Beaufort family at the

Church Social? Their son was there, in full uniformed glory. He's a student at a military academy near Wilmington."

"That toy soldier with the brass buttons?"

"The very same. He's called 'Beau.' And he's an older man. Thirteen years old."

Nate was furious. Chess had to be lying. "Not Gussie!" he insisted.

Chess simply smiled.

Nate was away a great deal after the first of the year, accumulating the information and the acreage liens he needed for his English venture.

Lily was not pleased. Two weeks after he returned from the mountains she had met him, as if by accident, on the train to Durham. In town they met by design in a room at the hotel near the railroad station. Nate was ensnared again. But his absorption in business was stronger than her hold over him. It displeased her a great deal.

One afternoon she tapped on the door of Gideon's study, then entered. "Dearest, I have such happy tidings that I could not wait until you completed your work. The doctor says that I no longer face any danger if I have another child.

"Oh, my dear, will you be my husband again?"

Gideon left his desk, hurried to embrace her. They went to their bedroom at once. He had been starving for her body for years.

Lily did not introduce Gideon to any of the practices that held Nate in her thrall. But she knew how to make him happier than he felt he deserved to be.

That same day she stopped taking the bitter mixture she had learned from a woman in New Orleans. And she summoned Nate to the Clubhouse nearly every afternoon.

When she heard about Chess and Nate's plan to go to England, she was so angry that she tore out a handful of her own hair. The ripping pain satisfied her for the moment.

* * *

The bookstore was empty when Chess went in. James Dike hurried forward to greet her. "I have just finished reading a shocking book that I hesitate to recommend. But it's so good that I hate to keep it a secret."

Chess was glad to see her friend so lively. He'd been gloomy for months, even wearing a black mourning band on his sleeve because Sherlock Holmes had been killed in the December issue of *The Strand Magazine*.

The power of literature was the driving force in James' bookish existence. Chess was curious to read his new, renewing favorite.

The novel was *The Picture of Dorian Gray*. She read it, then read it again, then concealed it on a high shelf in her wardrobe. Gussie was growing up, but she wasn't old enough yet for the horrible, fascinating story by Oscar Wilde.

She gave Gussie the Baedeker guidebook to London that James had ordered for her. Chess kept her own copy beside her at all times. It bristled with the ends of ribbon bookmarks. She wanted to see everything.

"Chess, my dear, you are becoming the most boring woman in Orange County," Edith said one day. "You know I love you dearly, and I am sincerely happy for you, but if the word 'London' issues from your lips one more time, I will stuff your Baedeker down your throat.

"Now tell me something interesting for a change. Exactly how many flush toilets are going to be in the new house? I fully intend to ride Henry's fastest horse over there every time I have a call of nature."

Chess made a face. "Four. And I'm going to lock all the doors. You're a terrible person.

"And I'll miss you," she added.

They settled happily into yet another delighted series of speculations about the scandal that dominated every newspaper every day. Mrs. Vanderbilt had sued Mr. Vanderbilt for divorce.

Divorce was unthinkable. Unheard of. The only one they

had ever read about before was Henry the Eighth's, and that was in schoolbooks it was so long ago. Decent people simply did not do things like get divorces.

"Of course Buck Duke's lady friend is divorced," said Chess. "Everybody knows that."

"But is she decent?" Edith leered. Like all conventional women, she and Chess loved to speculate about "women like that."

In the case of the Vanderbilt divorce they enjoyed even more the speculations about what Mrs. Vanderbilt was like. Was she the one who had given the $250,000 ball? Or the one who had the yacht with seventy servants on board? Or the one who had the solid gold dinner service for 200 and a dining room big enough to use it all?

"It's such a shame Nathan's a man," Edith sighed. "He spent all that time talking to the Vanderbilt over in Asheville and came home with no gossip at all."

Lancelot O'Brien also thought it a shame that Nate had spent all that time with George Vanderbilt. The changes Nate demanded at Harefields had meant a great deal of additional work.

The last fittings for Chess and Gussie's London wardrobe were on April 4. Everything else was ready. The tickets for the suite on the Cunard steamer were in the safe at the bank. The letters of credit were there, too. And all arrangements were confirmed for Chess to have a stewardess on the ship as her personal maid and an experienced lady's maid from the staff at the Savoy assigned to her for the eight weeks of her stay.

"I've never had a maid just for myself before, and I'm certainly not going to hire one to take to London. She'd be underfoot all the time," Chess declared firmly. She preferred to do her own packing, too. That way she'd know where things were.

"Most of the steamer trunks go in the bottom of the ship," she explained to Gussie for the tenth time. "So you have to be very, very sure that you put your favorite frocks in the trunk that goes to the cabin. Isn't it exciting? We'll get all dressed up every night, just like Cinderella going to the ball."

Gussie tried to smile, but her mouth crumpled and she started crying uncontrollably.

Chess was terrified. "What's the matter, darling? Do you feel sick?"

Gussie put her head in her mother's lap. "I don't want to go to London," she sobbed. "I want to stay home. Bonnie can watch out for me."

Chess was incredulous. "Not want to go to London? Gussie, why?" She felt her child's forehead for fever.

With many hiccups, and rivers of tears, Gussie poured out her woeful heart. She didn't care about pictures and churches and parks with walls around them. She knew she'd be miserable doing all the things the guidebook said to do.

She didn't want to leave school a whole month early and miss being Puck in the school play of *A Midsummer Night's Dream*.

She wanted to be the other bridesmaid, with Sally, in Susan's wedding in June.

She wanted to go with Barbara and her mother to Wilmington. They were going to stay with Barbara's grandmother in her house on a real beach by the ocean and go swimming in the waves every day.

Chess said, "I suppose Beau will be there, too." She was suspicious of Gussie's overemotional outburst.

"I don't know. There's the ocean, and crabs try to bite your toes, but you catch them and put them in boiling water instead."

She's not that grown-up yet after all, Chess thought fondly. "I'll talk to your daddy and see what he says, Gussie."

She knew what Nathan would say already. He had backed off with horror, too, when she mentioned the monuments and museums of London. But she did not want Gussie to get the idea that impassioned tears would always let her get her own way.

Gussie hugged Chess fiercely. "Oh, thank you, MaMa. Thank you so much."

She knows what her father's going to say, too, Chess thought. I'll play out the hand all the same.

She waited until supper was over before she talked to Nathan. On evenings when they weren't going out or having guests, Gussie was at table with them. Chess was sure that if she had to live through another emotional crisis, she'd fall apart, so she ignored her daughter's heavily meaningful looks across the table and ate slowly, with a pretense of tranquillity.

"Run on up to your room, Gussie," she said when dessert was done. "I want to have a private talk with Daddy."

She led the way to the library. After Nate followed her, she closed and locked the door.

Nathan grinned. "What is this? Have you hatched a good plot against Buck Duke?"

"I just don't want Gussie crashing in. Sit down. I have to tell you what happened this afternoon."

As Chess expected, Nathan's sympathies were with their daughter. "I always wanted to go to the ocean myself," he said. "Maybe we should plan a trip there next year."

"That wasn't all that happened this afternoon, Nathan. Lily called on me, and she advised me to divorce you. She says you're desperately in love with her. Isn't that silly?"

Chess had planned and practiced exactly what she'd say, even the half-laughing way in which she'd say it. Nathan would laugh. Silly was the word for it all right, he would say.

"I'll wring her neck!" he said instead. His face was ashen.

Chess mentally examined the inside of her body. Curious, there was no broken heart there. There was nothing at all. Only a hollow, filled with darkness.

"Do you want a divorce?" That was her voice. She recognized it. Strange, it had no connection to her.

"Godalmighty, no, Chess! A million times no. I deserve to have you divorce me, I deserve whatever is the worst thing that can be done to a man. But I don't want to lose you and Gussie. You two are my life."

His eyes were staring, as if he were seeing some apparition, some monster. "I can't explain it. I can't understand it." He stumbled to his feet, to his knees, in front of where Chess was sitting. His eyes searched her face for pity and found none.

"She's got a hold over me, and I can't break it. I can't keep away from her. I've tried, God knows I've tried. But she whispers in my ear—God help me, Chess, the things she says—and I'm lost. It's hell. I've been burning in hellfire, but I still can't stop."

He put his hands on her knees, his head in her lap. His grip was painful, and his shudders shook Chess' whole body.

Like daughter, like father, she thought, crying their eyes out with their heads in my lap. But this time I will not give in.

She could see Lily's sneer, hear her laughter. And the words: "I'd think a fine lady like you would have too much pride to hang on to a man who didn't want her."

Three weeks later their private railroad car delivered Mr. and Mrs. Nathaniel Richardson and their twenty-three pieces of luggage to the Cunard pier on the Hudson River in New York City.

"If I could just get away from her," Nate had said. "I'd be able to come back to my senses, I know it. When I went to the mountains, I was all right. Help me, Chess. I need you to help me."

I will try, Chess told him.

She would have London first, and then she would decide what she should do. Those other times—Alva . . . and Julie— she had been so jealous that she hated the women. Now she was afraid that the one she hated was Nathan.

Chapter Thirty-Three

THE *CAMPANIA* WAS THE ULTIMATE in modern luxury, with mahogany paneling, silk damask draperies and upholstery, marble columns, crystal chandeliers, Aubusson carpets, and gargantuan gold-framed mirrors to reflect the magnificence of its passengers.

Nate and Chess had a suite of cabins that included a sitting room, a smaller silk-walled dining room, two bedrooms, and three servants' cubicles. Nate took over the empty bedroom that was to have been Gussie's for his trunkful of business papers. He kept the door locked at all times.

Chess was giddy from the thrill of the salt air; it was so much stronger than the saltiness that reached up the James River on high tide. The opulent fittings of the ship were impressive; however, what dazzled her were the people. On the very first evening in the main dining saloon, she was unable to eat her meal, so busy was she looking from side to side at the elegantly gowned and jeweled women and their formally dressed escorts. This was what her mother had told her about, so many years before. Everyone she saw looked beautiful, handsome, happy, confident.

She suspected that she appeared uncultivated and dowdy, even though her ice-blue gown was an authorized copy of a Worth design that she had ordered from Lord and Taylor, a New York store. It had the stunning balloon sleeves that were the latest thing in fashion, and the lace butterfly trim was lavishly embroidered with pearls and crystals. She was wearing a diamond and sapphire necklace, too, a surprise gift from Nathan. A frock-coated gentleman from Tiffany & Co. had delivered it to the ship before it sailed. Nevertheless, she knew that she was lacking the polish of the women she saw on all sides of her. Their gowns somehow fit them better. It didn't matter. She was content to look at them.

Nathan was Nathan. He did not even observe how different the other men were, how much better their tailcoats sat on their shoulders, the indefinable something that seemed to make their hair fit their heads better, too. As always he was himself, inside his own skin, and pleased to be exactly that. The only thing that bothered him was the estrangement between the two of them, and his guilty shame.

"It's going to be different now, Chess," he said earnestly. "I've escaped, I'll be all right again. I'll make it up to you."

Chess didn't want to think about Lily, or about Standish, or about anything back there behind the wake of the ship. She wanted to enjoy the magic of the moment. "We've left all that, Nathan," she said. "Let's forget it, pretend it never happened. I won't let anything spoil this trip."

Nate sighed with relief. It was more than he had expected; and God knows more than he deserved, he thought. And yet, somehow he wasn't greatly surprised. He was convinced that sex meant nothing to Chess. Therefore, he reasoned, his obsession for Lily would not matter all that much. He should have kept his mouth shut, not told Chess about it. Then, he reckoned, everything would have been fine. As it was, he was happy to follow Chess' lead, to pretend nothing had happened. He turned to the fascination of all the new things there were to learn about sea travel. He concentrated briefly on the nearly imperceptible movement of the ship and vibration of the huge engines far below. He'd go find the engineer tomorrow, he declared, and have a look at everything.

Wine tastes good, he decided. If they had dinner in the evening as they did on shipboard, instead of the middle of the day, then they could have wine, too, back home.

"I wonder what kind of grapes you have to have."

"Not one vine. We can buy it in bottles, from the wine-merchant in Richmond." Chess thought of the cool dampish cellars at the original Harefields. When she was a child she used to go down there in the summer if she got too hot. How could she have forgotten? She'd write Lancelot O'Brien tomorrow with instructions to add one to the new Harefields. She could mail the letter when they reached Liverpool.

Unfortunately the *Campania* reached squally weather first, and the letter did not get written. Chess woke before dawn, thinking that she must have somehow been poisoned.

She was seasick for the remainder of the Atlantic crossing. The stewardess assigned to care for her assured Nate that Chess was not going to die and that she knew how to make victims of the illness as comfortable as possible.

Nate investigated every mechanical wonder the *Campania* had to offer, became friends with the stokers, the engineers, the Captain, and most of the other male passengers who were not in the toils of mal de mer.

Chess was very pale, and unsteady on her feet when she left the *Campania*. It felt to her as if even the longed-for dry land beneath her boots was rising and falling. She revived on the train journey to London, but only partially. The rocking train carriage was all too much like her cabin on the ship.

So was the cabriolet from the train station to their hotel. Not until she woke very early the next morning did she regain her appetite for food and for travel. London! She was here at last.

The Savoy Hotel was located on the bank of the River Thames. When Chess drew open the curtains and opened the window, she saw the wide waters reflecting the pink and gold sky of dawn, smelled the harbor smell of oil and coal and fish and smoke and spices, heard the sound of shouting from the dozens of small and big boats and then—near and far— church bells in peals of sweet echoing notes.

She threw open her arms to embrace it all; then she ran to get dressed.

The Savoy's reputation for unsurpassable service proved to be justified. When Chess emerged from the bathroom, her maid was there, dressing gown in her hands, ready for Chess to put on. "My name is Ellis," she said, and she bobbed a curtsey. "Would madam care to have breakfast sent up? The dining room will open at seven."

The bronze clock on the mantel said that it was ten minutes to six.

"Yes, please. Thank you, Ellis."

"If Madam would care to observe . . ." Ellis went to a trumpet-looking object on the wall. "This is a speaking tube. Anything Madam wishes, at any hour, she has only to speak into the mouthpiece."

"Don't do it yet, Ellis. My husband will want to see this. He's in the sitting room. Use the tube there."

The breakfast was strange and delicious. There were three different kinds of fish, each in an aromatic, creamy sauce. And meat that looked like ham but was—the waiter said— bacon. The scrambled eggs were flavored with something unidentifiable and served in a buttery pastry shell shaped like an open flower; and there were also soft-boiled eggs surrounded by a shimmering aspic that held petals of real flowers just below the surface. Some kind of hashed meat nestled in a ring of puréed vegetable that was so wondrously seasoned only its green color identified it as a vegetable. And tiny roasted birds sat on top of toast that was coated with something rather like mushrooms turned into whipped cream. Chess was famished, but even so she could eat very little.

She was too excited. London was there—just beyond the walls of the hotel—and she wanted to see it.

Everything was arranged. An experienced guide had been engaged, by mail, from the International Lady Couriers, recommended in the Baedeker Guide. But she wasn't supposed to arrive until nine, and it was not yet eight o'clock. Chess walked impatiently from the windows in their sitting room to the ones in the bedroom and then back again. The sun was shining, the Thames sparkling.

"Let's go for a walk along the river, Nathan. I can see a nice, wide, paved sidewalk."

"You go on, if you want to. I need to get my papers arranged in the desk."

Chess swallowed her angry reply. Nathan knew full well that ladies don't go walking unescorted in a city. This wasn't Standish, North Carolina, for heaven's sake.

The temptation was too much. After all, who would see her? She didn't know anyone in London, and it was so early; no one would be about. She promised herself that she would behave properly all the rest of the time. But just this once . . . She couldn't wait.

She took her elegant and expensive hat out of its leather travel case and arranged it on her head. The wide brim was piled with egret feathers and silk roses; it required a very long hatpin to stabilize it. Chess stabbed it into place with unnecessary ferocity. How could Nathan start directly in on business when London was waiting to be explored?

Her temper improved when she smoothed on the ivory kid gloves that matched her walking costume. Even after all this time it was still a pleasure to have all the gloves she wanted. And more. Her hands were still very nice. In spite of her age. You'd never know that she had picked worms off tobacco leaves, or scrubbed the floor of a flour mill. Her mother would have been pleased with her. She had always made a big thing of "you can tell a lady by her hands."

Her father, too, in his own way. He had refused to throw

her up in the sidesaddle if she didn't have on heavy gloves for riding.

Chess shook her head, fluttering her egret feathers. She could remember her parents later, when she visited the places they had talked about. This was her time, her London.

She looked down at her lapel watch. Almost eight, she'd better hurry. The "ascending room" was too slow; she'd take the stairs.

The smells and sounds of the river surrounded her the instant she stepped through the door of the hotel. Chess walked toward them quickly, her speed increasing with every step. This was what she'd come for. This was London. The Thames. Good Queen Bess, Shakespeare, Dick Whittington, Richard the Lion-Hearted—any one of them might have trod exactly where she was walking now. All of them had certainly passed by, on the river, in boats or barges, and had felt the same fresh, fishy breeze that she felt now, fluttering the feathers on her hat. Chess lifted her face to it, smiling a greeting.

Her eyes traced the graceful arches of Waterloo Bridge, marveled at the noisy thick traffic that clogged its broad pavements. And just ahead, too, at the base of the path she was on. She watched the rapid streams of drays and hackneys and carts in the roadway of the Embankment until she saw a gap. Then she grabbed up her skirts and ran to the walkway on the other side.

To her right she could see Cleopatra's Needle. She knew all about it, had seen etchings, read descriptions. But she was unprepared for the actuality. It was so very high, so delicate looking, and so astonishingly pink. She tilted her head back, following the elegant narrowing contour of the obelisk to its pointed tip. "Oh, my," she said aloud. To think that a person—any person—could just walk up and put a hand on it, a monument more ancient than anyone could reckon, a stone that had seen the pharaohs of Egypt, the pyramids and the Sphinx. And it was here. Right in front of her.

Again Chess gathered her skirts and ran. The granite was

warm against her palms. She pulled off her gloves, traced the incised mysterious symbols with her fingers, unable to believe that she—Francesca Standish Richardson—was really here, actually touching a message from distant centuries in the past. She must surely be the luckiest woman in the world.

Suddenly the warm pink stone beneath her fingers lost its color. Chess looked up at the clouds that had covered the sun. The refreshing breeze became chill. All the tales she'd read about English weather must be true. She hoped she could get back to the hotel before it rained. Her gloves had fallen to the ground. No matter, she had plenty more, she'd leave them.

Her pace was brisk walking back to the Savoy.

Near the entrance, she slowed. She must look a mess, all windblown. What would the formally dressed head porter think? The English looked down on Americans anyhow; that was common knowledge. She didn't want to add to the hotel staff's low opinion.

For heaven's sake—what was she thinking of? They could think what they liked. She wasn't an ordinary American. She was Miss Standish of Harefields. She held her head high and walked regally into the imposing marble and gold reception hall.

"Standish!" said a man's voice.

Chess turned her head quickly. Who knew her? Why was she being addressed by her maiden name? And in such a strange way. She searched the faces in the shifting crowd around her, trying to identify the speaker. It had to be someone she knew, but who?

Suddenly she drew in her breath with a gasp. She'd seen a ghost, the ghost of her father.

Then sense prevailed. She didn't believe in ghosts. And no one called a lady by her last name alone, with no "Miss" or "Mrs." before it. The man she'd seen must be a distant relative, one of the British Standishes. She knew they existed; her parents had visited the original Harefields when they were in England.

She had to meet him. A cousin. Family. What incredible

luck. Chess jostled the man in front of her and, without a word of apology, pushed past him in pursuit of the stranger.

She was breathless with excitement when she reached him. The beard was more closely trimmed, the mustache a bit fuller, but the face was her father's. He was talking and laughing with another man, bending his head to hear what his shorter friend was saying. He was moving toward a doorway, away from Chess. She caught hold of his arm to stop him. He turned.

His gloved fingers touched the brim of his hat in courteous recognition of her presence. "Do you wish to speak to me, madam?"

Chess was horribly conscious of her bare hand on his sleeve. She snatched it away. What was she doing? Accosting a total stranger like this. But still ... the name ... and there was the same thin nose ... she had to know. She'd already made a spectacle of herself, so she might as well finish it.

"Are you Mr. Standish?"

His dark thick eyebrows rose. "I am," he said; he waited for an explanation of her intrusion.

"Standish of Harefields?" Chess continued desperately. She felt as if everyone were staring at her.

The man shook his head. "I do not have that honor."

She felt hot shame wash over her from head to toe. When she spoke, she stammered. "I'm so sorry. Please forgive me." She ran in desperation to the nearby staircase and up, stumbling in her haste to get away.

"What in God's name was all that about?" said the tall man's friend.

"I haven't the faintest idea," said Standish.

"My dear fellow, I'll dine out on this story for weeks. Standish has definitely lost his touch, I'll say. Middle-aged Americans are importuning him now instead of delectable young actresses. That was American, wasn't it, that deplorable accent?"

Standish chuckled. "Yes, it was. But that's not at all the most bizarre aspect. Didn't you observe, Wembley? That woman blushed like a schoolgirl. I haven't seen anything to equal it for decades."

"You mean the delectables don't blush?"

"They make me blush, Wembley. That's what makes them so delectable."

"I was mortified," Chess moaned. "How could I have done such a thing, Nathan? I must have taken leave of my senses. I've never felt so humiliated in all my life."

He patted her shoulder, glad that her head was bent low and that she couldn't see his face. It was impossible to keep from smiling just a little. Chess, of all people. Lady-of-the-manor Chess. Miss Tidewater Aristocracy herself. He wished he could have been a fly on the wall.

"Put it out of your mind, Chess. This is a very big city. Biggest in the world, didn't you tell me? You'll never see this fellow again. And if you think anybody saw what happened, all you have to do is get rid of that terrible hat and nobody will connect you with the lady they saw. No way they could have seen your face through all those feathers."

Chess looked up at him, forced a smile. "I didn't know you didn't like my hat."

"It looks like a fox got in the chicken coop."

She began to laugh, in spite of her embarrassment. "Oh, Nathan, you do make me feel so much better. Thank you."

"Hush, now. You do the same for me. . . . What time's your little old lady due?"

"Good heavens. What time is it? I've got to wash my face and get ready." She leapt to her feet and dashed toward the bathroom. On the way there, she threw her Paris chapeau into the wastebasket.

Nate smiled. Great Godalmighty, Chess was laughing again! It had been too long since he'd heard that strange cat-like happy bubbling sound. Everything was going to be all right again. Better than all right. He felt as if a mountain of stone had just slid off his shoulders.

Chapter Thirty-Four

MISS LOUISA FERNCLIFF WAS ROUND. Her face was a circle, with round pink cheeks on flawlessly creamy skin. Above them, she had round eyes of china-blue and a "fringe," or short bangs, made up of small, round gray curls. Her bonnet was in a long-outdated style, with a rounded bowl shape, and her equally dated bustle was a rounded protuberance behind her, topped with a bow. She was firmly corseted, but chubby nonetheless. And she was short, not even as high as Chess' shoulder.

A darling little butterball, Chess thought to herself when Miss Ferncliff introduced herself. I do hope she doesn't prattle. If she does, I'll have to remind her that she is employed by me to do what I want—and without constant chatter.

"I've been studying my guidebook," Chess said, "and I think we should begin at the beginning, with Saint Paul's Cathedral. It's close enough to be a pleasant walk."

"Indeed it is, Mrs. Richardson, and that is precisely why we will save it for a later date." Miss Ferncliff's pretty blue

eyes looked up at Chess, and they were the eyes of a person
accustomed to being obeyed.

Chess took a deep breath. She'd have to establish at once
just who was in charge.

"Our London cabbies," said Miss Ferncliff serenely, "are
threatening a strike. It's quite the talk of the town. If they
follow through on their warning, it will become extremely
difficult to travel any lengthy distances. We will therefore
design our own routes. I recommend the Tower as commence-
ment. This is also a logic to beginning there; it is much the
oldest and most historic of the city's sights. Young Queen
Elizabeth, you recall, was held prisoner there before she
achieved the throne. And, of course, the beheadings are always
of interest. You will, no doubt, also enjoy the display of the
Royal jewels."

Well! thought Chess, she does chatter, but I wouldn't call
it prattle. "You are absolutely right, Miss Ferncliff," she said.
"Let's start with the Tower. I'm longing to see it. We don't
have much in America that's very old."

Miss Ferncliff had a delightful smile. It made her cheeks
look like apples.

When they were settled comfortably in a hansom, Miss
Ferncliff sat quietly. Chess looked frantically from her window
to the opposite one, fascinated and excited by everything she
saw. The street was full of vehicles of all kinds, the sidewalks
crowded with people of every sort, the shopwindows colorful
with enticements. By the time the cab stopped, she felt as if
her brain were overloaded, suffering from a kind of mental
indigestion.

Miss Ferncliff handed some coins up through the opening
in the roof to pay the driver. "There's a teashop next to the
admission gate," she said. "Perhaps we should take a little
refreshment and become acquainted with one another before
we tour the Tower."

Chess nodded. "You're very thoughtful, Miss Ferncliff. And
very experienced, I can tell. That's a fine idea."

She was surprised to realize that she was hungry. Breakfast had been a long time ago. While she ate buttery crumpets, Miss Ferncliff sipped her tea and recounted her history.

She understood, she said, that Americans weren't afflicted with the formality that kept Englishmen separated from one another. Her American clients were more comfortable if they knew all about the person they were spending their days with.

Her life had been interesting always, she said, smiling. She was the daughter of an army officer, a colonel in the Fourth Dragoon Guards. He was killed at Balaclava. "Lord Tennyson's poem made the Light Brigade famous," said Miss Ferncliff with a restrained sniff of disdain. "My father was one of the officers in the Heavy Brigade. No one remembers them. But they drove the Russians back. The Light could only go foolishly to their own slaughter."

One of the young lieutenants in her father's command was to have been Miss Ferncliff's husband. The wedding date was set, and the trousseau completed. He, too, lost his life in the Crimea. No one else, said Miss Ferncliff in matter-of-fact tones, had ever lived up to her memory of the lieutenant, so she had never married. She received a small pension from her father's regiment, so there was no need.

She studied under Miss Florence Nightingale in her school at Saint Thomas' Hospital and nursed there for many years. One day she decided she was too old to keep up the pace. She still occasionally took on the care of private ladies or gentlemen who were convalescent, but she enjoyed being a companion-guide much more. Sickrooms were essentially all the same, while visiting the attractions of London was always different.

Miss Ferncliff counted out the coins to pay their bill. Chess was glad that she didn't have to cope with the bewildering currency. The inclusive charges for Miss Ferncliff's companionship would be paid by Coutt's Bank out of Nathan's account. She followed meekly, content to let the remarkable older lady take the lead. Imagine—Florence Nightingale!

* * *

"So then we went to a very frilly tearoom for lunch, and after that I walked about three hundred miles in the British Museum, scampering to keep up with that sweet-faced, gray-haired, little old lady. I haven't been this tired since the summer I was a field hand growing tobacco."

Nate laughed. "Do you think you can limp as far as the band concert?"

"I'll crawl if I have to. I love London, and I don't want to miss a single thing."

Nathan smiled behind his napkin. Chess was like a greedy child. For the first time in all their years together, he felt older than she.

He could understand her excitement, but not about museums and the stories of a bunch of dead kings and queens. London, now that was a different matter altogether. He'd never known anything like the perpetual buzz of the place, and the mammoth scale of the wonders of it. A railway just for the city, packed with people going from one place to another faster than a racehorse could run. And much of it below ground, in tunnels as tall as a high building. Everything was like the future come to pass.

The engineers in the hotel were the smartest men he'd ever met. They told him about marvels of progress in the works all over the place, even while they were casually showing him the wonders that lay below the ground floor. To hear them talk, you'd think there was nothing special about that generator as big as a barn, or the machinery that operated the mammoth elevators, or the equipment that made—not kept, mind you, made—hundreds of pounds of ice every day. It was like magic to Nathan, but these men just shrugged it off. Old stuff to them. What they were talking about was the day, soon to come, when the telephone would reach right across the ocean and men would figure out how to fly.

Great Godalmighty, it was good to be alive in times like these.

* * *

Nathan had been told by a friend made on the ship that business acumen took second place to good tailoring when dealing with English company presidents. Therefore, on Wednesday, May 2, he set off for a recommended tailoring establishment.

Chess went shopping, too, but with a very different attitude. She could hardly wait to taste the temptations of a truly great city. Miss Ferncliff was delighted to oblige. "Regent Street, Piccadilly end," she told the hansom cab driver.

Chess was overwhelmed. She bought gifts for everyone at home, that was easy, but when she saw the array of fabrics and fittings for Harefields, she was staggered by the abundance of options. "I can't make up my mind," she sighed. "I haven't seen anything old. That's where I meant to begin, with the furniture. But everything is new."

"My dear Mrs. Richardson, we live in an age of progress. Soon we shall enter the twentieth century. No one wants inconvenient, outmoded accoutrements for the home."

"I want Hepplewhite," said Chess stubbornly, "and Chippendale. They made their furniture in London. There must be some of it here somewhere."

Miss Ferncliff tried to look agreeable, but her pursed mouth gave her away. She was a modern woman with modern attitudes.

Chess took pity on her. "Tomorrow I'd like to go to the art gallery," she said.

It was a lucky decision. Thursday was rainy, and the low skies held down the smoke from the thousands of chimneys that emitted it even in summer. The wet air was acrid, thick; it was a good day to be indoors.

Chess bought a guidebook at the entrance to the massive building and took a deep breath. The British Museum seemed small in comparison.

She walked in and stopped dead. Never—she'd never dreamed there could be anything so huge, so richly decorated, so beautiful. Marble walls and marble columns in green, rose, yellow. Stairs as wide as a house and as tall as the tallest tree. She was awestruck. "That's a Gainsborough," Miss Ferncliff chirped professionally, "and over there a Raeburn . . . Lawrence . . . Reynolds . . ."

Chess had never seen a great painting. Harefields had been hung with family portraits, landscapes, etchings of Roman ruins and mythological stories. All were pleasing, none was great. The guidebook drooped, forgotten in her hand, as she followed Miss Ferncliff from room to room, ignoring her guide's commentary and looking, looking to her heart's content.

Italian masterpieces wrenched her heart with tender madonnas, piqued her curiosity with fascinating faces, made her smile with bulbous pink and blue horses.

"Now this is the Flemish collection," said Miss Ferncliff, "accepted by authorities to be the major richness of the entire gallery."

Chess gaped at the wall ahead of her. Then, as if pulled by magnetic force, she walked closer and closer to a painting of a man and a woman in a room so full of light that she looked up to see where it was coming from. But it was in the painting alone. Light in the gallery room was gray; rain was pouring down the windows.

Miss Ferncliff called out. Chess turned to see what she wanted. But the pink-cheeked, smiling little woman wasn't calling her. "Lord Randall," she called again. "Good morning."

There was a man studying a painting not far from Chess. He removed his top hat and turned to answer Miss Ferncliff.

Chess shook her head. No, this couldn't be happening. No, it was too horrible. It was the man she had forced herself upon in the Savoy reception room.

"It's such a pleasure to see you, Lord Randall," Miss Ferncliff burbled. "How is dear Lady Hermione? You will recall, I attended her during her recovery from the influenza."

Lord Randall smiled, and his saturnine face looked less

forbidding. But not to Chess. She began to edge away slowly. There was a doorway at the end of the big room.

"Miss . . . Ferncliff; is that correct? How very well you look. I'm happy to say my sister-in-law is well, also. Your nursing has excellent lasting effect. I shall tell her we met. I am certain she would wish me to thank you again on her behalf."

"She was an excellent patient," Miss Ferncliff pronounced. "I spoke to you because I believe I am in the company of a connection of your family. Mrs Richardson has told me that her maiden name was Standish and her people's place named Harefields."

"Indeed?" Lord Randall looked toward Chess. Her back was turned to him. "Miss Ferncliff?" he prompted.

There was no escape. Chess steeled herself for the touch on her arm or the voice calling her name. If God was merciful, she thought, the floor would open and let her fall through it.

Louisa Ferncliff tapped her on the elbow. "Allow me to present Lord Randall Standish."

Chess looked at the man's face for mockery. But it was perfectly composed, with exactly the right mixture of polite curiosity and uninterested politeness that such a meeting called for. Maybe he really didn't remember.

He bowed when she was introduced, murmured "Mrs. Richardson" in acknowledgment. He did look very much like her father. His eyes were hazel; they seemed almost bronze in the dull light. And his dark hair had the same tendency to curl in damp weather that she remembered her mother teasing her father about. She couldn't tell if the mouth was the same. Lord Randall's mustache covered the top line of his lips. If his jawline was square, his clipped beard hid the resemblance.

She was staring. Chess looked away quickly, embarrassed.

My God, the woman's blushing again, Standish thought. She must have a disease of the circulatory system. Nonetheless he was obligated to certain minimum courtesies.

"I would be honored if you would allow me to call on you

and Mr. Richardson," he said. "Where are you staying in London?"

Was it possible? Did he really not remember? Chess held out her hand. "We'd like that very much," she said. "We're at the Savoy."

Standish took her hand, bowed over it. "Until later, then." He nodded to Miss Ferncliff and walked away.

"Such elegance," said the former Nightingale. "His brother doesn't approach Lord Randall in that. But of course he'll inherit the title, so he doesn't need to be elegant, too."

With urging from Chess, she prattled on about the Standish family, Randall's brother David, his wife Hermione, their children. . . . The complexities of the English peerage were so confusing to Chess that she doubted she would ever understand. Lord Randall was the second son of Edgar Standish, the Marquess of Harefield, who was addressed as Lord Harefield, or—by friends—as Harefield. Randall's brother, David Standish, was the Viscount Willbrook, called Lord Willbrook, or, by friends, simply Willbrook. Until he inherited. Then he would be Harefield, and his eldest son, Willbrook. For the Marquess' younger son, Lord Randall Standish was the "title of courtesy." He was called Lord Randall by inferiors and strangers, Standish by equals and friends.

"Does anyone call him Randall?" Chess asked in desperation. It seemed that baptizing a child was a waste of time in this world.

Miss Ferncliff smiled as one who knows a family's innermost secrets. "His family call him that, and his mistresses. He has not married." Her voice dropped to a whisper. "They say that his very closest friends call him Mephisto because of his resemblance to the devil. I do hope they refer only to his dark hair and pointed beard."

Chess tried to explain all the names to Nathan, but she became hideously tangled. She did remember that "Lord Randall" was the name they should use when her cousin came to call.

Nathan laughed. "I'd rather call him 'Devil' and be done with it. . . . Don't fret, I won't. Too bad we don't have some of Ol' Livvy's 'sweetener' to offer him. Ma always called it 'devil's brew.' Alva told me that Livvy's funeral celebration was the longest, loudest party anyone ever saw. She'd left a whole kegful marked for the occasion."

Lord Randall Standish dutifully called on the Richardsons the following afternoon. He had learned long before that it was easiest to dispose of obligations at once; then they could be forgotten.

He gracefully declined Chess' offer of tea, and Nate's suggestion of a drink. The rules of London society specified that a call need not exceed fifteen minutes, but if refreshment was taken, the caller was required to stay for three quarters of an hour.

Nate intrigued Standish. The Englishman had a number of American friends and acquaintances but none of them was in business. Nate was a new species.

However Standish was there because of family duty, so he addressed himself to Chess. He had remembered, since their meeting at the Gallery, he said, what excitement was caused by her parents' visit to Harefield. "My father—who is known as the Standish of Harefield—told me about it later."

Chess felt her face redden. So he *did* remember the scene she had made. She wanted to run into another room and lock the door. But her cousin was smiling at her as if they shared a delightful secret. The lid of his right eye quivered in a wink. He clearly thought nothing disgraceful had happened. Perhaps he was right. She certainly hoped so. It was so exciting having him here, a genuine English cousin. Talking about the family, her family, her parents.

"I was away at University, so I missed meeting them," Lord Randall was saying. "Both my brother and my father fell helplessly in love with your mother, I'm told."

Chess laughed. She was enjoying herself too much to worry about the early mistake. "That sounds like Mother," she said.

"When the Yankees came to loot Harefields, she charmed them into leaving us alone."

Standish was entranced by Chess' purring, gurgling laughter. It was unlike anything he had ever heard, and novelty was a rarity in his life. He was a product and a captive of privilege, and—although he had wider interests and activities than most members of his class—he was, like them, constantly battling boredom.

"Mr. Richardson, I've changed my mind about that drink, if the offer still stands."

"Splendid." Nate walked to the speaking tube. "I always enjoy using this thing. One of the engineers is getting me the directions for putting them into our new house. What'll you have?"

"Whiskey and soda, if you please." Standish smiled at Chess. He wanted to hear her laugh again. "The story in the family is that when your first Standish went to the colonies, he named his lands Harefields instead of Harefield because his property was twice the size of his father's. Is that true, do you know, Mrs. Richardson?"

Chess only smiled as she shook her head. It was a delightful story, she said. She'd never heard it.

Had he ever visited America, she asked.

No, said Lord Randall, although he looked forward to doing so one day.

A room waiter came with the drinks tray. Standish resigned himself to the additional half hour. He thought now that he had made a mistake. The Virginia branch of the family must have become quite widespread, he said casually, the name had even gotten attached to a kind of cigarettes.

"But that's us!" Chess exclaimed. "Don't tell me we got all the way over here. Did you know that, Nathan?"

Lord Randall was thoroughly surprised. He began to laugh. "So you are the cause of all my troubles. Friends in America send copies of those advertisements about the man named Standish to everyone in London. People made sport of me for months on end. H.R.H. kept asking me why I was too stingy to give him some of my castles, if I had them in such quantity."

Chess looked at Standish's perfectly groomed Englishness and remembered the well-dressed farmer type in the ads. She laughed. "You poor thing," she said, and laughed again. She couldn't help it, even though she knew she was being rude.

She didn't know that she was delighting Lord Randall Standish. He wished she would never stop laughing.

"I'll have a few cases of Castles sent to you, Lord Randall," said Nathan cheerfully. He was already thinking of the good luck that had fallen into his lap. Chess' fancy-dancy cousin might just set a style with Standish cigarettes. It would be a good card in his hand when he started talking to English cigarette manufacturers. If he got a letter in the mail tonight, it would get to the factory in a week. The cigarettes could be in London only a week after that.

The post office took outgoing mail until seven-thirty at night. If he could just get rid of this cousin and write the letter now. . . .

"Why don't you come back and have supper—dinner—with us tonight, Lord Randall? I know Chess wants to ask you a million questions about the rest of her cousins."

Before Standish could refuse, Chess did it for him. "I am sorry, that won't be possible. We're going to the theater this evening." She felt like throwing something at Nathan. Things had just been getting relaxed. She made herself smile. Covering up for her husband's faux pas, she wondered angrily why Nathan had done such a thing.

Standish was asking politely what play they were going to see.

"*Camille*," she answered Lord Randall. "I'm looking forward to it. I've always loved Dumas."

"You're very fortunate. Duse is magnificent, according to all reports. There are no tickets to be had." Standish glanced quickly at the clock. He put his half-finished whiskey on a table beside him. Nothing was more uncomfortable than being in the company of a couple about to quarrel. He'd take his leave.

But he was no match for Nate. Without knowing quite how it happened, Standish found himself committed to taking his cousin to the theater in her husband's place. He was to call for her at seven.

After Nate had escorted Standish to the elevator, he returned to the room and an irate wife. "You can tell me all about my faults later," he said agreeably. "Right now I've got to write a letter." He told Chess what he had in mind about Standish and Castles.

She had some ideas herself. For the moment Chess shelved her anger. "What you don't realize, Nathan, is who Standish's friend really is. 'H.R.H.' stands for His Royal Highness, the Prince of Wales, the next king of England. This is what we've got to do. . . ."

The letter did get to the post office in time to leave that night for loading on the next steamer to New York. It gave instructions for shipment of two cases plus an extra two cases, holding special boxes of Castle cigarettes. "Made Expressly For H.R.H. The Prince of Wales" the box would say at the top, above the figures of the lion and the unicorn. Below the royal animals a line would read, "As A Gift From His Friend Standish."

The English were besotted with the Royal Family. If the cigarettes got only as far as the front door, Nate would be welcomed with open arms by the people he wanted to do business with.

Chess thanked Lord Randall for escorting her to *Camille*. She didn't apologize for her husband's bullying; that would have made an already awkward situation even more embarrassing. In Standish's carriage they talked about Dumas, father and son, for the brief time it took to drive to the theater.

When they arrived, the hum of excited anticipation captured Chess in its magic. When the curtain rose and the play began, she forgot everything else. She had never seen a professional performance, only Gussie's school plays and the carnival entertainers at the State Fair. She was swept away.

Standish watched her face rather than the stage. There was something entrancing about Chess' rapt, responsive involvement in the play. It was spontaneous, unfeigned, wholehearted, and innocent. The opposite of everything in his life.

When the curtain fell, Chess turned her tear-drenched face to him and smiled a radiant, tremulous, watery smile. "How wonderful," she sighed.

How was it that this rather plain woman had become beautiful? How many more surprises was she capable of? Standish was enjoying himself enormously.

Chess wiped her eyes with a handkerchief and rose from her chair. While Lord Randall placed her cape over her shoulders, he noticed two women in the box opposite. They were studying him and Chess through opera glasses. He inclined his head in salute, and they lowered the glasses quickly.

"Would you like to meet a duchess?" he asked Chess. He was certain the duchess would like to meet her. In the small world of London society, gossip was the major form of entertainment. It would be a coup to be first to know whose was the new face seen with Standish at the theater.

"Is she nice?" asked Chess. "I'm enjoying myself too much to let an unpleasant person cast a shadow."

Another surprise. It was an article of faith that all Americans worshiped titles.

"You are a remarkable lady, Mrs. Richardson," he said.

"We are, after all, cousins, Lord Randall. Do call me 'Chess.' "

"Remarkable name. Do you play?"

"It's from 'Francesca,' and I do, but poorly."

"And will you call me 'Randall'? I'd be happy to challenge you to a game."

Standish assumed that Chess was expertly reading and responding to the double meanings of the subtle flirtation. Season-long love affairs were commonplace in his circle.

He broke out laughing when, after inviting him to the suite

for a late supper, Chess went to her bedroom and returned—not in a negligée, but with a box that contained an extraordinary chess set.

"What's funny?" she asked him.

"I believe the world has gone mad," he replied obscurely. "Is your husband joining us for supper?"

"Certainly not. He's fast asleep. He's likely eaten four times while we were out. He loves to use the speaking tube. I hate it, it's like talking to a ghost in the middle of a whistling windstorm. Will you place the order, please?"

"What would you like to have?"

"Anything will do. The food is very good here—now what are you laughing about?"

"The Savoy chef is Escoffier; he's the most famous artist of cuisine in the world. If he knew that anyone called his creations 'very good food,' he'd cut his own throat with one of his knives."

Chess laughed. It had not been his imagination. Her unforced throaty purr was unique in all the world. Seducing her would be a delicious enterprise. Perhaps she would laugh while making love.

They ate omelettes, prepared in a silver pan over a spirit lamp by an impassive, carefully unobservant waiter. And they drank champagne.

She was sorry, but she couldn't have luncheon with him tomorrow, Chess said. Miss Ferncliff would be collecting her as usual at nine for a day of sightseeing.

Standish was surprised by his feeling of disappointment. Pleased, as well. Conquests that were too easy were the least amusing. He suggested a drive to Hampstead on Sunday, when all the museums were closed, and Chess accepted, with thanks. On behalf of Nathan as well.

After supper they played a game of chess, and she checkmated him again. Lord Randall Standish was not at all pleased. If Sunday was not more to his liking, he would abandon this provincial cousin and concentrate on a woman of his own class who played courtship games by the rules he understood.

Chapter Thirty-Five

CHESS SAT IN THE SITTING ROOM for a very long time after Standish left. She was, in almost every way, even more innocent than she seemed. Her life, in spite of her voracious reading, had in fact exposed her to few of life's complexities.

But she was not stupid. As soon as Standish expressed a wish to see her again, her antennae quivered. He had called out of politeness; that she understood. Nathan had bullied or tricked him into escorting her to the play. Again, understood.

Why, though, invite her to luncheon? Courtesy did not demand that, even for a relation closer than a cousin many times removed. Even more so when it came to a second invitation after she declined the first.

Was he flirting with her? That was absurd, Chess told herself. She was forty-three years old. Not only that—no man had ever flirted with her. She was not the sort of woman who attracted men, and she never had been.

Then, why? Did he enjoy laughing at her country-come-to-town lack of sophistication? But he had not made her feel foolish and ignorant.

On the contrary—he had made her feel comfortable. Except at the end of the evening, and then he made her uneasy in a strange and different and exciting way. She had felt as if he admired her.

No, be honest, Chess. You felt as if he wanted you. That's what was exciting.

But a man like that—what would he want with me?

Round and round her mind went, recapturing moments, conversations, expressions. Chess became more and more confused.

More and more tempted to play with fire. Randall Standish was the most worldly man she had ever known. He was certainly the handsomest. How could he have such a lean body and yet give such an impression of muscularity. He was no youth. There were touches of gray at his temples, and definite lines radiating from the corners of his eyes.

Those tiger-like topaz eyes.

Chess stifled the dangerous tingling languor that was creeping through her veins.

Mephisto, his friends called him. That should be warning enough to stay far away from him.

But suppose—just suppose, even though it made no sense at all—that he did find her attractive.

What harm would it do to enjoy being admired and wanted? She had never had that. Yes, she wanted it, was that a crime? Just once, for a little while, to believe that she was desirable.

I know it's not so, but if I could just feel that it was, even knowing it wasn't.

Oh, yes, I would like that very much. After all, nothing would actually happen.

On Saturday Miss Ferncliff led Chess at a steady pace through the Houses of Parliament, followed by a ladylike luncheon and then Westminster Abbey. Chess felt like lying down on the tomb of Geoffrey Chaucer and begging for mercy. She'd had very little sleep the night before.

She was dragging her feet when she got back to the Savoy. A groan was her reply to Nathan's "welcome home." For the first time in her adult life, she had a nap for an hour in the afternoon.

It was over dinner that Nate told her about his successful day talking to his banker. "I'm going to Manchester tomorrow. It's all arranged for me to meet four of the big cotton-mill owners next week."

Chess dropped her wineglass. While three waiters whisked away all traces of the accident, Nathan assured her that there was nothing for her to worry about. She still had a lot of museums to visit with Miss Ferncliff, and he had gone to see her cousin that afternoon. Standish said he'd love to watch out for her until Nate returned. "So you'll still get to go to the opera and those plays you want to see. You won't even know I'm gone. It will only be a few weeks."

Standish was driving the carriage himself on Sunday. It was a Stanhope, a small sporting rig with bright green paint and a red leather seat just wide enough for the two of them. Chess had to rest her feet on the big wicker hamper he'd brought along.

"It's a rarely beautiful and sunny day," said Standish. "We'll picnic on the Heath."

When he opened the hamper, Chess laughed. "You've got enough food for an army, Randall—what's wrong?"

"Nothing whatsoever."

The air was bracingly fresh, and scented with resinous sweetness. "I have decided to eat like a pig," said Chess. "What do you recommend most from this banquet?"

Randall smiled. "Taste everything. That's the best approach to life."

She took his advice. Most of the things in the hamper were new to her. Tiny eggs that Standish identified as coming from a bird called plover, even tinier black eggs from a fish called sturgeon, cold pheasant and lobster claws, mixtures of meats and herbs baked in crusted pies . . .

"You have a crumb in the corner of your mouth," Standish murmured, "I'll get it for you." Before Chess could move, his lips brushed hers.

They were soft, his lips, and warm. His mustache was soft, too. It surprised her. The clipped hairs should have been bristly.

Perhaps she'd imagined the whole thing. It had happened so fast, the kiss had been so gentle.

But her lips felt as if they had been touched with fire. They pulsated with heat. She put her fingers to them.

"Have you never been kissed before by a man with a mustache?" Standish's voice was lightly teasing.

Chess looked at him. She felt a little dizzy. The sunlight seemed to be shimmering on the leaves of the trees, forming a halo around Standish's head. "I've never been kissed by any man," she said, "until now."

Lord Randall was going to laugh, but the expression on her face closed his throat. It could not be true, what she had said. But he knew it was.

"My dear Chess," he whispered hoarsely. For perhaps the first time in his life, he did not know what to say.

Then she laughed. Softly. Happily. "Much, much better late than never," she said. "Will you please kiss me again, Randall? I liked it a lot."

He knelt beside Chess, cradled her face in his two hands, and bent his head to kiss her. Carefully, with closed unde-manding lips. He had anticipated delightful novelty in an affair with this surprising American woman. But what was happening was not simply novel, it was completely unknown. He wondered if it were possible that he was afraid.

"Thank you," said Chess.

Standish ran his index fingers over her cheekbones, down the sides of her face, along her jawline, up to and around her lips. His golden eyes watched her reaction. Her breath came faster, her gray eyes grew misty, and the lids half-closed. Her mouth waited for his kiss.

He removed his hands, sat back on his heels. He could have her; he knew very well how to make that happen. What he did not know was the effect it would have on Chess. Or on him.

"You do know where this path will lead, Chess."

Her dreamy eyes open, became thoughtful. After a time she said, "I don't think so, Randall. I've never found sex very pleasurable. I don't want to go to bed with you."

Standish threw his head back and yelped with laughter. Would this woman never cease surprising him? "You are in every way the most remarkable and delightful woman I have ever known," he told her. And I will change your views on the pleasures of the bedroom, he promised silently.

"Then tell me what you do want," he said to Chess.

"I want many more kisses. And I want to see London, not simply the Baedeker view of it. You're a Londoner, will you show me?"

Standish promised to give her everything she asked for.

To begin, he drove to Hyde Park, where they joined the procession of carriages on the wide unpaved road on the south side. "This is called 'Rotten Row,' " said Standish. "The socialists make much of the name, as you can imagine." He lifted his hat and bowed to a lady in the open phaeton that was passing them. She smiled and twirled her parasol. To the opposite side, another bow, then another and another for the length of the crowded long road. While he drove and bowed, he talked. "Early in the morning, the Row is used by horsemen—and a few ladies. Then, at noon, ladies drive themselves, with a groom behind. Five o'clock—now—the scene changes to larger carriages and more elaborate clothing, and the ladies are driven by their coachmen. There are chairs—see there, beneath that tree—painted green things that can be hired from a park attendant, for people who want to watch the show rather than be in it."

But why, Chess asked, go to so much trouble. For exercise,

there were places like Hampstead Heath with wonderful air and plenty of room.

"To see and be seen. To remind Society of your existence. To snub, to flirt, to display new horses or a new costume. To have something to gossip about. We will be the subject of a hundred conversations tonight, because you are not being driven by a coachman, and no one knows who you are.

"These are your London friends-to-be, Chess. They will ask me to identify you, and then the calls and invitations will begin."

Afterwards Chess asked to ride the omnibus. "I got a very sniffy turndown when I mentioned it to Miss Ferncliff," she said. "I've been wanting to sit up there and look down on all the traffic since the first day I saw it." The horse-drawn omnibuses were red, or brown, or yellow, with snail-spiral stairs that led to an open upper deck that had wooden benches along its elbow-high sides and down the middle. They were conveyances for the working classes, and Lord Randall had never entered one. However, he had promised to satisfy Chess' curiosities. The horse and rig were left in the care of a porter at the Savoy, and Standish escorted Chess along the Strand to a loading stop.

The bus was nearly full, but people slid over on the bench to enable them to sit side by side on the right side of the top. A bell rang, and the bus moved into traffic.

"Isn't this fun?" Chess said. "Look how far you can see. I think all the traffic and rush is thrilling."

Even on Sunday the Strand was jammed from sidewalk to sidewalk with drays, hansoms, carriages, risk-taking pedestrians, other buses, a herd of goats being driven who knew where, and riders on horseback finding openings in the wall of traffic and racing dangerously on a zigzag stop-and-spur course. It was like a great stage, with dozens of dramas being acted simultaneously.

Standish had never regarded traffic as other than a hindrance. But then, he had never before been in it and above it at the same time. He was soon fascinated. Was this, he wondered, the same thing as "having fun"? He wasn't familiar with the phrase.

There was a holiday spirit among the other top of the bus travelers. There was a warm sun and a blue sky and no need to work until tomorrow. A boy in a plaid cap took a harmonica out of his pocket and began to play popular songs from the music halls. His friends, girls and boys both, sang lustily, until a conductor mounted the stairs and told them to stop.

"How disappointing," Chess complained. "They weren't doing any harm, and I was enjoying it."

"Do you know, Chess, I believe you may have the heart of a bohemian."

"What is a bohemian?"

"I will show you tomorrow."

Standish had accepted an invitation to a dinner party that evening, so he returned Chess to her rooms at the Savoy after their bus ride. "I'll call for you at four," he said. "We will take tea with some friends of mine, and perhaps dinner as well. They are extremely relaxed about such things." When she offered her hand, he bowed and kissed it. Then he turned it over and kissed the palm. It sent a thin hot streak of lightning up her arm, and she caught her breath.

"Tomorrow," said Lord Randall.

"Tomorrow," Chess whispered in echo.

"Standish, what were you doing driving the Row today? I was alarmed. Thought you might appear in a dress tonight and mess up Agatha's table seating." His host slapped Lord Randall on the back with a force that would have sent him reeling had he not expected it. The Earl of Lepworth, otherwise known as "Binks," always punctuated his greetings to his friends.

"Mephisto, who *was* your astonishing companion?" The Countess made only the smallest effort to hide her malice. She was a legendary snob.

"An American cousin, Agatha."

"Oh . . . American. What can you expect? Such perfection of frumpiness did rather take my breath away."

Standish moved smoothly into the large group of London's titled elite, stopping, speaking, moving, stopping, speaking until dinner was announced. His assigned partner was one of the Season's debutantes. It was no surprise. A handsome fifty-year-old bachelor with a decent income was still a catch for any girl not beautiful enough or rich enough to hope for a titled husband.

Randall was kind to the overweight, tongue-tied young girl. He even grazed her knee once with his, by accident or deliberately, she could choose to believe whichever pleased her most. It was simple to guess that she liked horses and hunting. Her shoulders and arms were strongly muscled. So he chatted knowledgeably about terrain and hounds at the country houses of people who were friends of his, and of her parents. She recovered from her shyness by the third course. Standish had done the job he'd been invited to do.

The Countess "turned" the table then, and he was free to talk to the lady on his other side. She was an old friend. Only two Seasons earlier they had relished each other's wit and each other's body, and they shared fond memories. Standish smiled with real pleasure. "Clarissa, you are looking positively radiant. Who is the fortunate man?"

"My darling Mephisto, surely you're not suggesting that anyone could adequately take your place?"

It was a standard dinner party, better than some, less entertaining than some others.

Predictable.

The street looked very different from any that Chess had ever seen. Houses had doors painted bright blue, red, even purple. There were even entire houses with bright yellow or pale green walls.

"It's enchanting," she exclaimed. "So different."

"That's the essence of bohemia," said Standish. "Different

equates to superior for the artist. In some instances, it is even true. Are you nervous?"

"Should I be?"

Randall tipped up her chin and kissed her, his quick, brushing kiss. "You are quite different yourself, my dear. Everyone will love you."

The cab stopped before Chess could answer. Standish stepped down, then steadied her descent. He kept her hand in his as they walked to the open black door of a house painted a brilliant white.

A tall bulky man turned toward them when they entered. He was wearing a loose gray linen jacket with turquoise piped trim. His fleshy face looked sad, Chess thought. But when he saw Standish, a smile erased all the sorrow. "Mephisto, you are exactly what this appallingly sunny day calls for. We have all been painfully dispirited by the lack of menacing clouds. . . . And who have we here? An apprentice devil, I desperately hope."

Standish pulled Chess forward. "Mrs. Richardson, may I present Oscar Wilde."

Oscar Wilde. The terrifying, brilliant author of *The Picture of Dorian Gray*. Chess was overwhelmed. Without thinking, she sank in a curtsey.

"I am a great admirer of your writing, Mr. Wilde," she said when she rose.

Wilde grasped her shoulders in his large, well-kept hands. "Did Fisto put you up to that? No I can see by your candid, open expression that he did not. I do so adore Americans. But rarely have I met one of such exquisite literary discernment. My dear lady, do come inside another step and meet my disappointingly inferior friends."

Wilde put an arm around her shoulder and swept her into the most fantastic experience of her life.

The room was an extravagance of color. Shiny red woodwork vibrated against daffodil yellow walls, bright blurry paintings hung against the yellow from blue silk ropes that reached the ceiling. It was dark gray with a moorish design painted in gilt.

At least a dozen people were in the room. The names were uncatchable, so quickly did Wilde include them in paragraphs of outrageous biography and commentary. The men were all dressed less extravagantly than Wilde, but less conventionally than Randall, in his frock coat and narrow gray trousers. Two of the women wore loose flowing garments of patterned yellowish-green silk, with flowing hair loose on their shoulders. One beautiful auburn-haired girl had a single long braid down her back.

All of them talked incessantly, though none as much as Wilde. They traded insults with enormous affection and attacked names that Chess did not know with eloquent vituperation. They were extremely quick, and brilliantly funny. Chess laughed until her sides ached.

Wilde drew Standish to one side. "You are, of course, aware that your cousin's laughter should be captured in a jeweled coffer of purest lapis lazuli and venerated as a priceless treasure."

"Oscar, I could not have expressed it better myself." Randall's voice was bland.

"Devil." They smiled at one another. "In all seriousness, Randall, you are criminal to permit her to dress so deplorably. Peach ruffles. It sickens one."

"You recommend yellowy-green? She's not one of your aesthetic hangers-on, Oscar."

"Unfair, Fisto. I recognize uniqueness. She is like a Piero della Francesca. But she is following the dictates of some horrible arbiter of fashion, like that ghastly woman who fawns on the rich in her newspaper column. Take her to my friend Luther Witsell. He tried to be a painter and failed, so he is crafting with fabric and color. He will transform her. She would like to be beautiful, you know. All women desire that."

Standish was pensive. "I believe that I would rather she

not become beautiful," he said. "She is already a danger to my peace of mind."

Oscar's lips twitched. "What a pitiful devil it is," he said wickedly. "I shall recommend Luther to her myself."

Before Standish could react, Wilde strode off to greet a man who had just come in. "George! How fearless of you to show your face. Haven't they told you? Jimmy Whistler is over from Paris for a week."

Chess wasn't able to make sense of the rowdy, laughing exchanges that followed. Standish explained to her after they left. George du Maurier had been an art student in Paris years before, sharing a studio with several other students, including an American named Whistler. After years as a successful cartoonist for a humor magazine called *Punch*, George decided to become a novelist and illustrate his own book.

"I'll let you have my set of proofs, you might enjoy the book. It's a fantastical story, but it does give an excellent picture of youth and Paris and the art world there thirty some years ago. Unfortunately, George cut too close to the bone to suit Whistler, especially in a very nasty little illustration. He has delayed publication for more than a year by suing poor George for libel. Jimmy is a cantankerous fellow. But he is a genius. I did not know he was in London. I want you to meet him."

"Is that why we left? You said we might stay for dinner."

Standish considered. Was he honestly worried about Oscar's dressmaker friend? Reprehensible. What was happening to him?

"I generally prefer bohemia in small doses," he said. "We will eat in my rooms."

"Leftover picnic?"

"You might say that."

Standish's mind was made up. He had to possess Chess, explore her body and her mind; only then would he be able to understand and control the unsettling effect she was having on him.

But Chess said no, she was tired and wanted to return to the Savoy.

And Standish realized that he was tired, too. Sharing Chess' enthusiasms wore a man out.

Chapter Thirty-Six

CHESS WASN'T TIRED AT ALL. She was frightened. Bohemia had stirred her and relaxed her in a puzzling way. It was too vivid and too easy all at the same time. She had absorbed the atmosphere of contempt for all the grayness of society's confining dos and don'ts, the celebration of freedom, the message that whatever you want to do you should do. As long as you do it with style.

She'd never dreamed that Randall was that kind of person. He was so formal in his dress and in his manners.

Except when he kissed her.

She wasn't certain any longer that it was safe to play with fire. It frightened her that the bright heat of it was so appealing.

Chess had a light dinner sent up to the suite, and then she read her Baedeker. Miss Ferncliff was taking her to the South Kensington museums tomorrow, and she wanted to be prepared.

Her mind kept sliding back to the day Miss Ferncliff had taken her to the National Gallery. And introduced her to Randall.

He was going to escort her to the theater tomorrow night, to a comedy. He'd said he liked to hear her laugh.

Chess concentrated on her book. ". . . choir stalls, in carved oak, from the Cathedral of Ulm, by Jörg Syrlin (about 1468) . . ."

Tomorrow night seemed to be a hundred years away. So long to wait.

As Lord Randall had predicted, there had been calling cards left for Chess while she was out being bohemian. One from the Countess of Lepworth, two from the Earl.

Miss Ferncliff was impressed. "The Countess entertains constantly. You'll meet everyone there." And she was a well-informed guide. The single card from the Countess represented a call by her for Chess. The Earl's two cards represented a call on Chess and a call on her husband. Miss Ferncliff was appalled when she saw Chess' photographic *cartes de visite*. "It doesn't matter if they are all the rage in America. In London, you must have plain white or ivory with your name in italic letters. Nothing else will do. We'll go at once to Southwoods. All the best people use them."

Chess agreed with alacrity. "And while we are shopping, I want to go to Theobald's Road. A friend recommended a dressmaker there." Oscar Wilde's note had arrived before breakfast. It was locked in her jewel case, with her diamond necklace.

Luther Witsell was a short, wiry, agitated young man with curly hair in an unconvincing shade of orange. He horrified Miss Ferncliff and entranced Chess.

His studio was a big attic, up five flights of stairs. It looked like something out of the *Arabian Nights*. Piles and bolts and swathes of fabric in every color covered long tables, all the chairs, a large part of the floor.

"Oscar told me about you," he said joyfully. "Inevitably, he was perfectly, sublimely accurate. Yes, yes, magnificence, drama, line, always line, richness. I see you in plum, in deepest midnight black, in garnet—nothing so ordinary as ruby—"

Chess enjoyed every minute of the three hours Luther spent measuring, sketching, draping folds and drifts of color on her. When she left, she had no idea exactly what it was that he was going to make for her, but she was quite sure it would be different from anything she owned.

Miss Ferncliff did not stop radiating indignant disapproval until they reached the South Kensington Museum. The green and gold lunchroom was dark and soothing, as was the steak and kidney pie.

Chess searched her brain. "I'm especially interested in seeing the Ulm choir stalls," she said. Miss Ferncliff was happy.

After the adventure of Luther Witsell's atelier, Chess' pale blue evening gown looked pallid. But it was the most becoming one she had. Her bare shoulders looked like alabaster, and her necklace glittered quite as brightly as the ones she'd seen when she went to *Camille*.

The maid Ellis did her hair in fashionable heavy waves drawn back and up to a curled topknot. The curling iron was like an instrument of torture, but Chess wanted to look her best. When Ellis tucked red roses into the knot, the effect was, Chess thought, quite perfect. She kept her head absolutely still until a Savoy page came to inform her that Lord Randall Standish was waiting downstairs.

Ellis twitched the ruffled silk evening cape into place on Chess' shoulders. "Madam looks beautiful," she said.

"Thank you, Ellis. I'll be very late getting back from the theater, so have your dinner and a rest while I'm gone. I'll send for you when I'm ready to be undressed."

Chess thought she had done that rather well. Positively English, Rotten Row grand fanciness. At home, she undressed herself.

"Wasn't the play wonderful, Randall? I nearly laughed my head off."

"I know. I enjoyed it." The atmosphere in the cab thickened with unspoken thoughts. Standish took Chess' hand in his and slowly unbuttoned her glove, exposing her wrist. He took her pulse with his lips. "I'm hungry," he said, "for another of Escoffier's post-theater omelettes."

Chess' heart felt like a bird fluttering wildly, trying to escape its cage.

"I . . . I don't know."

Standish closed her glove. "Yes, you do." He was very near in the seat of the shadowed hansom. Chess could smell sandalwood and starched linen.

Then the bright canopy lights of the Savoy filled the cab, and she could see his face. He looked like Mephistopheles, saturnine, certain, dangerous, mesmerizing. Chess shivered.

"Are you cold?" Randall asked in a gentle voice. "Let me—" He adjusted her cape more closely around her throat. His fingers brushed her neck and the lobes of her ears.

When the door of the suite closed behind them, Randall dropped his hat on a table with his gloves. He stood behind Chess and put his arms around her shoulders to untie her cape. As it slid back, Standish kissed her on the side of her throat. His mouth moved down, across her left shoulder and then her right. His hands were warm on her waist.

"Turn around, my darling," he whispered in her ear. His breath was warm, moist. "I want to kiss your lips."

She turned, inside his arms, and lifted her mouth to his. His arms were very strong.

A dozen kisses later Randall's hands held her head, and his fingers caressed her scalp as they removed and dropped hair combs and pins. She felt the heavy tresses slide and drop onto her shoulders and back.

"So lovely," Standish murmured, "a curtain of golden silk. Do not let an iron touch it ever again." He kissed her.

She heard the rustle of her skirts when he lifted her in his arms, when he laid her on the bed.

"No," she wanted to say, but the sound came out as a tiny whimper of entreaty. His hands pushed down her sleeves and bodice and found her breasts. Chess cried out when the sensation raced through her body. Her back arched to press herself more deeply into his hands.

"My dearest," said Randall with a laugh, "I believe you are a true voluptuary. I promise to make you very happy."

Chess was drowning, she was flying, her skin was a living thing, separate from her, burning and shivering and screaming and demanding more of his hands, his lips, his burning skin. Her body stretched, turned, offering itself to his touch. She could not breathe; her gasping was harsh in her ears.

Randall teased her, thrilled her, enticed her, dominated her, delivered her into an ecstasy beyond thought or understanding.

And then, slowly and gently, he began again, with the merest brush of his lips across hers.

"I can't," Chess gasped.

"You will," said Standish. "My magnificent libertine darling, you will climb to the stars a hundred times, a thousand."

She cared not for numbers, only the whirling rising passionate soaring into crimson madness of screaming shattering burning desire satisfied.

Randall brought her cool water, lifted her head, held the glass to her bitten lips. His body was slick and shining with sweat, his black hair a tangle of curls.

"I never knew," she said weakly.

"Drink, beloved. Then sleep. And then we will make love again."

Before she could answer him, sweet darkness claimed her and she was asleep.

Then began the giddy time. Chess felt as if she had found the secret of life, the reason she had been put on this earth. It was to be held, touched, kissed, loved. She was breathtakingly alive. Every color, every scent, every breeze, every ray of sunlight, every drop of rain was a little miracle to be savored for its perfection. All her senses were turned to supernormal acuteness. And all waiting, all the time, to be explored in

Randall's embrace. She would have spent twenty-four hours of every day making love, if she could. But it was impossible, and so the hours away from him became sweeter because they served to heighten the anticipation of what was waiting until they were together again and alone.

When they were together but not alone, the passion that linked them was like a brilliant blue electric current, so strong that she could barely believe it invisible.

They went to the zoo, and she thought the animals turned toward them because they felt the current. Such animals! Chess was enchanted. The strangeness of the pelicans and camels made her laugh. The fierce beauty of the leopards and jaguars made her cry. Standish kissed the tears away in a secluded corner, then they left the rest of the animals unseen to go to his rooms and to bed.

He lived at the Albert Mansions, a new construction of red brick with flats as big as most houses. His rooms were scholarly and serene, with low cases of books on every wall, antique paintings and archaeological fragments in the spaces above them.

The exception was the bedroom. It was painted dark blue with gold and silver stars scattered over walls and ceiling. The bed was enormous; each of its four posts was the size of a tree and carved with figures of Greek and Roman deities. Their sandals were strips of gold.

She met Randall's brother, also her cousin, and his wife, and heard—because she was family—about the torment of waiting for years and years until the title and the lands were passed down.

She met James Whistler, too, and—because she was American—heard about the pains of expatriate life and anti-American prejudice.

Oscar Wilde called on her at the Savoy in a green morning coat and made her famous.

His protégé Luther dressed her so cleverly that every woman she met begged her to divulge his name.

She mastered the protocol of cards and calls and was busy

almost every afternoon entertaining or being entertained. She was on first-name terms with Honourables and Most Honourables, Countesses and Ladies.

It was the life her mother had lived, the life that should have been hers, would have been hers, had there been no Civil War. Chess gloried in it.

In the evenings, there were *Carmen* at Covent Garden, Mr. and Mrs. Beerbohm Tree and Mrs. Patrick Campbell at the theater, dinner parties at the Asquiths' and the Rothschilds'.

And always, always, there was Randall's embrace. After the day, or in the quiet middle of the day, or when the day was just begun and he was still sweaty from the hour of fencing with which he began every morning.

Her time was her own, to devote to the discovery of passion. The cab strike had begun the day after Randall first possessed her, and she had discharged Miss Ferncliff. Now, two weeks later, she wondered why she had ever planned to visit every starred attraction in Baedeker. London was for love and the pleasures of the Season. She could see that everyone felt the same. Now that she knew the joy of catching Randall's eye at a party and feeling the tie between them, she could recognize the same tie between other couples in the room. Love made the world go round, at least in London, in May.

She was late. Randall was waiting downstairs. But she had had to change. Her new friends would be scandalized if she failed to change from the costume she wore in the morning to another, different, one for afternoon. And another for receiving calls, if she decided to be at home. Then later, an evening gown.

Or nothing but bare skin. Her breath came faster. Perhaps after the flower show there'd be time for love before they went to tea at Daisy Merton's. They had no dinner engagement tonight. That meant hours and hours in each other's arms.

The Temple Gardens were wonderfully beautiful by themselves. Now, with the displays of the Royal Horticultural

Society on tables in front of the bloom-laden rosebushes, the color and perfume and beauty were overpowering.

The Duchess of Fife was the Royal Patroness of the show. " 'Your Highness' and curtsey," muttered Randall in Chess' ear. The Duchess was approaching them, flanked by two ladies. "Lord Randall," she said. "I am surprised to see you here. I salute your ingenuity. How do you raise flowers in the stone courtyards of the Albert Mansions?" She was a small, plump woman in her twenties, with a cheerful disposition that made up for her lack of beauty.

Standish's bow was courtly. "I tell the florist to deposit the delivery in front of the steps, Your Highness, and I carry the flowers upstairs all alone."

She smiled broadly. "I knew you would say something witty. I told my friends so." The two ladies with her were looking at him with wistful eyes. They were exceptionally unattractive.

"Your Highness, may I present my cousin from America," said Standish.

Chess acquitted herself well, as if she met highnesses every day of her life.

Princess Louise was the daughter of the Prince of Wales, Randall explained later. He'd known her since she was in nappies. Everyone said Fife was a good man. He hoped so. Louise had always been a sweet girl.

"Are you showing off for me, Randall?"

"Somewhat. Are you impressed?"

"Somewhat." The current between them crackled with urgency. "Let's walk back to the hotel. It's very close."

"No, we'll go to my rooms. The Savoy will be full of people connected with the Flower Show."

On the way to Randall's, they became trapped in motionless traffic. He was extremely annoyed. "Blast! I forgot there was a Drawing Room today."

"Let's get out and walk some, Randall. The carriage will be sitting right here when we come back. I want to gape at the jewelry."

Debutantes were presented to the Queen at Drawing Rooms, afternoon receptions for which all the ladies wore evening dress and the full panoply of necklace, brooch, bracelets, ear bobs, and tiaras or crowns. The elaborate coaches that transported the nervous young debutantes were always stuck in a line outside the Palace for hours, putting the unfortunate girl on display for the crowds of commoners that gathered for the show.

"This is unspeakably vulgar, Chess. You do realize that, don't you?"

"Yes, but I don't care. Look, Randall. Could those really be emeralds in that necklace? They're as big as chicken eggs."

"Incorrigible. What am I going to do with you?"

Chess looked into his eyes, then laughed. "Do you want me to answer you in public?"

Later, when they were relaxed after making love, Randall asked her if she'd like to be presented at Court. "It's not really limited to debutantes, you know. I could escort you to the State Ball if you were on the Palace list. I'm sure Hermione would sponsor your presentation."

"Let me think about it. Gaping is much more fun than being gaped at."

"Make up your mind soon. Hermione isn't very fast out of the gate."

"Unlike me." Chess rolled over on top of him. "Let's see if you can catch up." She nipped his earlobe with her teeth.

"Insatiable wanton."

Chess laughed.

She was laughing again when Randall couldn't get the key to her suite into the lock. Suddenly the door swung open. "Hello," said Nate. "Come on in."

Chapter Thirty-Seven

CHESS HAD VIRTUALLY FORGOTTEN that Nathan existed. Caught up in the Cinderella world of the Season, obsessed with the discovery of carnal pleasures, she had been living outside time and reality ever since he left almost three weeks earlier. For an instant, she did not know who it was standing in her doorway.

She descended from the heights of fantasy with a crash. This grinning, freckle-faced barbarian was her husband. She wanted to cry. The dream was over.

She felt telltale color stain her cheeks. Could he tell? Did he suspect? Her hands started to go to her hair, to check that it was smooth. Oh, God, she must be reeking of Randall's sandalwood soap. She always bathed before she dressed. Nathan was too smart to be fooled. What would he do? What should she say?

Standish managed the moment easily. "Welcome back, Nate. You should have been with us tonight; we saw a superlative play. How was your trip? Successful? Chess said it was some kind of business." He took Chess' arm to escort her into the sitting room. His tight grip was steadying.

"I didn't get what I went after," Nate said, "but I wouldn't have missed the trip for all the world. They've built a ship canal up there that's like nothing else in history. Do you know . . ." He was overflowing with excitement about the triumphs of engineering he had seen.

Chess listened, and she looked at his vibrant face, and she hated him with a power that made her bones ache. How could he have ruined her life this way? Why had he come back? Why couldn't he have stayed in Manchester with his precious canal and let her remain in heaven a little longer?

Why had he made her wait until so late to learn the truth about sexual bliss?

She wished he was dead. It was the punishment he deserved.

Standish watched Chess carefully. And cleverly; he did not appear to be looking at her any more than politeness required.

He was anxious. She was not practiced in deception. And he knew how extravagantly and spontaneously she reacted to events. That was one of her great charms, but it would be disastrous in these circumstances.

Luckily Nate said, after a half hour, that he'd had a long day traveling. "Manchester didn't pay much attention to this cab strike, so it surprised me. I had to haul my bags over from the train station on foot. The buses were jam-packed." He figured he'd take a bath and go on to bed, if nobody objected.

"See you in the morning, Chess. I want to tell you all about the cotton mills up there. They're really something."

"Good night, then, Nate," said Standish. He looked at Chess, willing her to behave.

"Good night, Nathan," she said. Her voice was flat.

The door had barely closed behind Nate when she flew to Randall. "What are we going to do?" she cried, throwing her arms around him.

"Shhh, it's all right." His tone was soothing, but his hands firmly moved her arms and placed them by her sides. "Nothing has changed, my love, we will simply have to be careful. Nothing could be more reasonable than that your cousin would see to it that you enjoyed your stay in London. We will continue to go places together. We will find time to be alone. Believe me, it is not so difficult.

"The only thing that can go wrong is if you make some silly blunder. Confession is not good for the soul, or anything else. You must control yourself, do you understand?"

She was weeping as if her heart were broken. "Kiss me, Randall. I can't live without your kisses."

"Stop it." He was cold. "You are a grown woman, not a child."

Chess was shocked into silence. He had never spoken harshly to her before. She looked up into his stern face, and her eyes spoke her hurt, and her fear of angering him.

"That's better," he said. "I don't want to lose you this soon, Chess. Can you do what must be done so that we can continue?"

She nodded.

"Are you quite certain?"

"Yes."

"Excellent. I will call for you at one tomorrow. We will go to the Royal Academy to see this year's exhibit of new paintings. Invite your husband to go with us. We will begin as we mean to go on—a happy family group. When we know what his schedule is, we can decide about ours.

"Chess, it is essential that he notice no change in relations between the two of you. Absolutely essential."

"I understand."

"Good girl. I will be downstairs at one." Standish smiled devilishly. "With a larger carriage." He picked up his hat and gloves, preparing to leave.

"Randall!"

His eyebrows rose, questioning, warning.

Chess lowered her voice. "Randall, don't you want to kiss me goodnight?"

He put down his things. "More than anything on earth," he said softly. He took her in his arms and his mouth devoured hers, drawing her into a whirlpool of passion.

"Remember, my darling," he said into her ear when he put her from him, "we do not have to lose anything if we are but discreet."

She was still swaying dizzily when he left.

Chess slept heavily, escaping from reality, but not from her dreams. She woke slowly, dreading the moment when she would have to face her changed world. And Nathan.

He was reading the newspaper and drinking coffee. " 'Morning, sleepyhead. I had breakfast an hour ago. What do you want? I'll do the tube telephone."

Chess was ashamed of herself. When a lady's entire life is in smithereens, she shouldn't have any appetite. But she was hungry. Last night she and Randall had drunk champagne and eaten strawberries. Nothing more.

"I'll have shirred eggs—and some poached salmon—and some toast, but tell them to butter it in the kitchen."

What luck. It wasn't at all hard to talk to Nathan as if nothing had changed, because he hadn't changed at all. He was still incredibly crisp and clean—she'd forgotten how scrubbed his skin and hair always looked. And he still boiled with energy, and plans.

No, he said, he couldn't go look at pictures. He figured his new suits must be ready by now, so he was going to go to the tailor and then get all the other English togs he needed. "I want to be all duded up and ready to start in on the tobacco companies on Monday. I'll have all day tomorrow to get my papers and numbers together. Striking out with the cotton mills wasn't all bad; it gave me a pretty good idea of how the English do business. Or don't do business, to my mind. Any route, I'll know what to watch out for where it counts—with the cigarette boys.

"Like I said, Manchester was a good idea, even if it didn't pan out. That canal! Can you credit it, they've got an eight-foot-deep canal in an open box, like. It goes up and over some railway tracks and a couple of roads. *Over* them, Chess. Eight feet of water. If I hadn't have seen it with my own eyes, I'd never have believed it."

He laughed. " 'Here goes Nate, off on one of his schemes,' I can hear you thinking it. Don't worry, I'm not planning to viaduct the creek over the S & D. It sure was something to see, though.

"How about you, Chess? Have you had a good time while I was gone?"

Her heart stopped. It gave a huge thump when it started again. Chess was surprised that the cups didn't rattle in their saucers; inside her head the sound of her pulse was deafeningly strong.

"I had lots of fun. Before the strike started, Miss Ferncliff took me to Westminster Abbey and a bunch of museums. One of them is all machines, you might want to go to it. It has early locomotives and the first James Watt steam engine—" She knew she was babbling. She drank some coffee to stop herself.

"Sounds interesting maybe," said Nathan agreeably, though without great conviction. Outdated machinery was out of date. "That's a pretty frock. I like purple."

Chess smiled. "It's called 'plum,' Nathan. I have a new dressmaker who is so strange that it's like a sideshow to go to his place. Oscar Wilde told me about him."

Nate looked pleasantly attentive.

"Oscar Wilde, Nathan! He's a world-famous writer. Randall took me to his house for tea. I met artists and other writers, too. I even have a copy of a book that hasn't been published yet. I get to read it before most of the people in the world know anything about it."

Now Nate was genuinely interested and impressed. His reading tastes concentrated on reporting about inventions or business, but he had profound respect for writers. They were creators, like inventors, though not as practical. "Can I see the book?" he asked. "That's a special item. What's he like?"

Chess gave him an account of George du Maurier's appearance, manner, and legal problems. The more she talked, the more she delighted in recapturing the memory of that fantastic afternoon. Soon she was giggling about the bohemian way of talking, dressing, and living. Nathan's enjoyment of the stories increased her own.

"I hope you're not planning to paint our chimneypieces red," he said with a grin. "Have you had any luck finding what you were looking for? Furniture and all, I mean."

Chess was at a loss for words. She could only shake her head "no." She had forgotten all about Harefields.

"There doesn't seem to be any old stuff anywhere," she said when she could talk. "I should ask Randall; I just didn't think of it."

"Nice fellow. Has be been taking care of you?"

"Oh, yes." She knew she was blushing. Surely Nathan would notice.

He did notice. Nate was observant of everything. He attributed her reddened cheeks to dismay about her failure with the furniture. Chess had always been so efficient in her shopping. It never occurred to him to suspect an affair. She had not ever evidenced any interest in sex, except in advertising campaigns. Also, she was a lady. In Nate's mind that meant sex was distasteful to her, maybe even disgusting.

His calm certainty somehow communicated itself to Chess, and the blushing stopped.

Standish had an elegant dark blue Victoria, with driver and footman in dark blue and burgundy-red uniforms. It was, he told Chess, the Standish livery. The Victoria belonged to David, his brother.

The presence of the servants was intimidating. Randall had to strain to hear Chess' voice. "We don't have to go to the exhibition, we can go straight to your flat."

"We will go to the RA first." He made no effort to speak quietly. Servants were trained in discretion. "You must be able to talk about the paintings, therefore you must see them."

"I saw reproductions of them in the *Illustrated News.* They're terrible."

Standish smiled. "You're right, my dear. You have a good eye for art. But everyone goes to the exhibition, and everyone talks about it with great knowledgeability—gleaned from the catalogue—and therefore it must be done." He squeezed her hand. "Stop sulking. We have all afternoon."

The limited time available added an urgency to their love-making that was a new dimension in excitement. Chess asked Standish if he felt it too.

"Of course," he said. He traced her ribs with his fingertips. "It's one of the reasons affairs are so satisfying. The danger of discovery is another spice. Are you managing well?"

"Yes. I'm sure Nathan doesn't suspect anything."

"Keep it that way." He kissed her shoulder. "I bought some soap for you from Floris. For here and for the hotel . . . Incidentally, I would like for you and Nate to invite me to dine with you tomorrow night. There will be a theatrical gala at the Savoy that we should not miss."

The great prima donnas were now all in one place, he said. Patti and Melba, of the operatic stage, Bernhardt and Réjane and Duse of the theater. They were all staying at the Savoy.

"Their entrances into the dining room will make Covent Garden seem tame in comparison. Each considers herself the greatest star and will be determined to demonstrate it. Even better for entertainment will be the sight of poor César Ritz juggling the demands for special treatment."

Chess giggled. "You and Nathan will have to tell me every detail."

"What do you mean? You will see everything. Don't tell me you are worried about respectability. A lady may not dine in a public restaurant, but when she is resident at an hotel, that becomes her home. Of course you may go to the restaurant in the Savoy." He amended his statement. "With your husband. I shall be his guest."

* * *

When Lord Randall escorted Chess to her door, they found Nate in a welter of boxes. Most of them were his "togs." The four largest ones were cases of cigarettes.

Standish was staggered. "How speedily you Americans do things, to be sure." The custom design for the Prince of Wales made him roar with laughter.

"I must go at once and arrange for the presentation," he said. "Hold tomorrow open. Bertie is always bored on Sundays. These will be the perfect antidote; if he isn't out of town. I'll send word about what will happen."

The following afternoon, a Sunday, the Standish Victoria carried Lord Randall, Nate, Chess, and a mahogany chest humidor filled with royal gift cigarettes to Marlborough House, the London home of His Royal Highness Albert Edward, Prince of Wales.

Nate and Standish were both flawlessly attired in the new fashionably shorter frock coat and striped trousers and blindingly white linen. Randall had seen the names on the boxes in the suite before he arranged the afternoon. Nate looked like Nate, all the same. He refused to pomade his hair. It was too much like tobacco tar, he said. Chess was in one of her new costumes: an afternoon "carriage dress" with leg o' mutton sleeves and a short train. It, too, sported white linen in a wide collar and tight wide cuffs. The color was garnet, the fabric an Indian chintz, both of them departures from the normal pastel organdies seen everywhere in Society. Her gloves and small straw hat were white and unadorned, another startling difference. She looked elegant and demure and different.

"My dear Mrs. Richardson, you must be kind enough to tell me who created that charming costume," said Princess Alexandra. She held her ear trumpet at the ready.

"His name is Luther Witsell, Ma'am. Everyone asks me, but you are the first person I have told."

Alexandra put a finger to her lips, "I shall not tell one soul.

Write the address for me, please. My lady-in-waiting will bring paper and a pen."

The afternoon had become very relaxed after the cigarettes were presented. The Prince insisted on shaking Nate's hand and slapping him on the back. "So you're the fellow who made Standish a laughing stock for two years. My compliments, Mr. Richardson. The fellow needed taking down a few pegs."

H.R.H. winked at Standish. "I like your friend, Mephisto. Present him Tuesday so we can see more of him. Ponsonby will arrange it." He turned his attention back to Nate. "Do you shoot, Richardson?"

"Only game and enemies, Sir."

"I like that. I wish I could say the same, but enemies are out of season all year. Tell me, are there many pheasant in your part of the world?"

"Not many. Mostly we get bobwhite. What the English call partridge, I hear."

"Excellent eating. I have a partiality." The Prince's eyes wandered to a nearby young woman. "A pleasure to have you here, Richardson."

Nate recognized dismissal. He stepped back "and cleared the track for him to do some hunting," as he described the scene later to Chess and Standish.

"What did you think of our future king?"

"Real just-a-regular-fellow. But I wouldn't want to test it."

"You're very acute, Nate."

Standish knew, as Nate and Chess could not, that their hour at Marlborough House had been a remarkably intimate view of the Prince's inner circle of family and friends. No more than two dozen people, all three of the Prince's daughters, Princess Alexandra with her needlework bag in her lap, and two puppies begging for scraps from the tea tray.

"I'll be able to brag about it for the rest of my life," said Chess, "but I'm glad it's over. I've decided to pass up the Drawing Room, Randall."

"What drawing room?" Nate asked. Chess explained. He

laughed heartily. "God bless America," he said. "You're right to pass."

Lord Randall cleared his throat. "I fear you don't have that choice, Nate. You are to be presented on Tuesday."

"What?" Chess was incredulous. "Nathan in silk knee britches? He never will." She whooped with laughter.

The laugh was on her. "Why not?" said Nate. "I've bought every other kind of monkey suit. The tobacco men might be impressed." He looked at Standish. "You're family, Randall, and I'm green as grass in this world. Manchester showed me that. I'd be glad for some advice from you about what's worth doing and what ain't. Do you know anything about the cigarette business over here?"

"I'm willing to learn. But first I must tell you that Tuesday's Levée is not optional. H.R.H. said he wanted you to be presented. His wish is our command."

Nate stiffened. "I don't cotton to being told what to do."

"No one does. Sometimes, however, one must accept the unpalatable."

Nate grinned. "I think I got the gist of that. Where do I get the fancy pants?"

"I'll take you there tomorrow. I always rent court dress myself. It isn't used all that often. If it's any consolation, I am obliged to accompany you, and I despise the damned Levées."

What a cozy pair! Chess thought it was wrong, somehow. Her husband and her lover should not be friends.

The promised drama at dinnertime was all that Standish had predicted. Each of the stars had her own sizable entourage and her own larger-than-life personality.

Sarah Bernhardt was wearing a gown so studded with colored gemstones that it could have stood up with no one inside it.

Eleanora Duse wore hot-house white camellias where Bernhardt wore jewels. The skirt of her white chiffon gown was covered with flowers, and a camellia was attached to her tall "dog collar" necklace of diamonds. She was flaunting her success as "The Lady of the Camellias," in Dumas' play.

Nellie Melba, who was to sing *La Traviata* the following week, had taken up the challenge. Her role in the opera was the same as Duse's in the play. Melba wore white silk gauze also. Her gown had a train four feet long, embroidered in pearls to create white flowers. Two pages in white satin were trainbearers. Her jewels were pearls. Eight strands surrounded her neck and hung in graduated sizes to her waist, which was circled with a belt woven of pearls. She carried an enormous white ostrich fan. Somehow, one of the airy feathers separated from it when she was led by the Savoy's manager past the table where Duse was already seated. The feather floated erratically in the air, capturing all eyes as it hovered over Duse's head. The actress was unaware of it. When it finally eddied to the floor behind her chair, the room itself seemed to breathe a sigh of relief.

Adelina Patti's long cape of peacock feathers seemed almost an anticlimax after Melba's errant ostrich. But Patti was not simply an opera prima donna. She was an Italian opera star, with all the extravagance and bravura of her heritage. When she threw her cape back into the waiting arms of an astonishingly handsome Italian youth, she revealed that the gown beneath it was also made of peacock feathers. Except that these feathers were not real. They were copies of the sinuous shape and jeweled colors, made of tiny turquoise, lapis lazuli, emerald, ruby, and topaz beads. The first course served for her dinner had been ordered well in advance. It was roast peacock, reassembled and with real feathers in place.

The French actress Réjane did not walk into the dining room. She ran, laughing and chattering in French, peeping over her shoulder from time to time as if she were fleeing pursuers. Her entire gown was made of blue ostrich plumes, their central quills studded with sapphires and diamonds. Bracelets of the same jewels reached from her wrists to her elbows.

Lord Randall had arranged to have their table strategically

placed behind a row of potted palms so that they could see without being seen. It was good planning, because Nathan's eyes were wet with the tears of too much laughter.

"Dear heavens," said Standish. "Ritz's cup runneth over. That's Lillie Langtry at the entrance."

Chess craned her neck. "Isn't she . . . ?"

"She was H.R.H.'s mistress for longer than any of the others," Randall said. "When her reign was over, he arranged for her to become an actress."

Mrs. Langtry was, like the other stars, an exceptionally beautiful woman. Unlike them, she was not flamboyantly gowned. However, her red-gold hair was dramatic color enough, and her black lace gown was cut in a décolleté that displayed her legendary attributes to a perilous degree.

"Do you think they'll fall out?" Chess whispered.

Nathan and Standish frowned at her. They had both, of course, been asking themselves the same question, as had everyone else in the room. It was precisely what Mrs. Langtry intended.

Virtually no one who dined at the Savoy that night could remember what it was that he or she had eaten. The occasion took its place in the folklore of the hotel, the theater, the opera, and London's dozen newspapers. Escoffier's special dishes, created and named for each of the stars, were copied for years by chefs all over the world. Peaches Melba even showed up on menus in the frontier town in Texas called Lillie Langtry.

Chapter Thirty-Eight

CHESS KNEW IT WAS FOOLISH of her to be angry at Nathan. It was none of his doing that the Prince of Wales wanted him to go to the wretched levée. But she was angry nonetheless. Nathan would be with Randall for two days, two days that Randall could have been with her. Monday reflected her mood. It rained. Not the light, passing showers she'd become used to in London, but a steady, gray, heavy downpour.

She wished Nathan good luck when the boy came to tell him Lord Randall was downstairs and then she wrote long letters to Gussie and to Edith. She threw the pen down afterwards. There were other letters that she knew she should write, but they would have to wait. She was too restless to sit still any longer.

She wanted to be with Randall. Yesterday was the first time they had not made love since the affair began, and her hunger for him was maddening.

And today? And tomorrow? And for all the days to follow? When would they be together again? It was unbearable.

She prowled the suite like a caged lion until a message was delivered that said the carriage Mr. Richardson had requested was now ready. It would be at their disposal for the remainder of their stay.

"Tell the driver to wait," Chess told the messenger. "I'll be down shortly." Rain or no rain, she had to get out.

She consulted the concierge about her search for old furniture; he provided her with a list of eight antiquarians, shops where she might find what she was looking for. She felt better at once.

In the early afternoon she returned with a headache and a feeling of near desperation. All the antiques were French, most of them gilded, and every shop owner had told her the same thing: there were no buyers for English furniture of the previous century, therefore no one offered them for sale. It was unlikely that she would ever find any.

Nathan was back. He was, she thought, excessively amused by his experiences at the for-rent tailor.

"You need something to eat," said Nate. "When your headache's gone, we can decide what to do about these." He gestured to a basket filled with large, square, white envelopes.

The news of their invitation to Marlborough House had spread like wildfire. There were eighteen invitations to receptions, teas, dinners.

"Good heavens," Chess said. "I'd better eat fast and then change. I have an idea a lot of ladies will be calling on me this afternoon."

There were thirty-seven of them. Luckily, the rules for paying calls were very precise. Exactly fifteen minutes was the outside limit. Ladies came and went, and the sitting room's supply of chairs was not overtaxed.

Between answering questions about who else was at the Waleses' and what was the Princess wearing, Chess managed to insert a question of her own, about old English furniture. One lady said she thought she had heard something about Daisy Pollinger's aunt—or was it great-aunt, she wasn't sure—at any rate, Daisy had inherited a mass of old-fashioned things she had to get rid of. No, Daisy was not in town, she absolutely never came to London. Such a sweet creature, but quite mad, you know.

The hour for formal calls was exactly that. One hour, from three to four. By a quarter to four, Chess' headache had returned. And she had made a grievous error. She had mentioned that Nathan was going to be presented formally at the next day's Levée.

The ceaseless chattering had, at least, produced three names of shops where she might find some Chippendale chairs. "A pretty poor harvest," she told Nathan, "but it's something. I'll go out in the morning. In the afternoon, while you're capering around the Palace, I'll pay calls instead of receiving them. It takes longer, but it's easier on the nerves."

She would go to Hermione Standish's, she'd already decided. She needed to speak Randall's name, to feel the word on her lips, and she was afraid to talk about him with Nathan. She had already asked him if Randall was going to dine with them. She hoped her despair hadn't been apparent when the answer was no.

"Why don't we go down to the dining room again tonight?" said Chess. She no longer cared whether it was proper or not. Maybe she'd be able to sit in the chair Randall had been in last night. She had to feel some contact with him somehow or she would go crazy.

"Good idea," Nate said. "There's bound to be some kind of sideshow."

There were no Chippendale chairs. Chess was drooping, and headachy again, when she got back to the Savoy.

Randall was there, and she was cured. "Nate's almost dressed," he warned. Then he kissed her quickly, while his fingers stroked her breasts. He was on the other side of the sitting room, and Chess was on the settee when Nate entered, resplendent in green brocaded silk, white stockings and velvet pumps with sparkling paste buckles.

"I feel like a jackass with bows tied on his ears and tail," he said. Randall handed him a long cape. Another one covered Randall's splendor. Chess didn't even notice that she was not seeing his elaborate Musketeer costume, his d'Artagnan. She had to hold herself back from running across the room to his arms. Being near him and unable to touch him was even worse than being away from him.

To add to the day's disasters, Hermione was not at home. Chess told the coachman to drive anywhere until it was after four o'clock and then to take her home. She huddled in a corner of the landau and cried.

"What's wrong with your eyes, they're red?" Nathan asked her.

She said that cinders had blown into them. "Did you have a good time?"

"No, I sure didn't. Looking like a jackanapes fool wasn't bad enough, His Royal All-Powerful Highness had to pile on more trouble. He 'wishes' me to join him at his club tonight to play cards."

Chess felt as if her feet were rising from the ground. Randall would come to her, she was sure of it, as soon as Nate left. Bless the Prince of Wales.

They made love on the narrow bed in one of the small servants' bedrooms that were part of the suite. "You don't know how I've missed you," Randall said when they were done.

"I've missed you ten times as much," Chess whispered into his mouth. She pressed her body against his, demanding more.

But he got to his feet instead. "We have to take chances, my darling, but we mustn't be reckless. Come to me tomorrow. Say that you're shopping. I must leave now, and you must bathe. You smell like love."

"I love smelling like love, like you," Chess argued, but she knew he was right. And soon it would be tomorrow.

* * *

In the days that followed, Chess learned the truth of Randall's words. Deception and the danger of discovery did add an extra thrill to their meetings.

Along with everyone else in London, she and Nathan went to the Derby, the most important horse race of the year. The course at Epsom Downs was a solid mass of spectators. Dukes rubbed elbows with street sweepers, countesses with barmaids, and everyone had a superlative time, even though it rained intermittently all day.

Nate found a wooden box for Chess to stand on, and his solid bulk protected her from the press of waving, shouting people around her. She cheered loudly when Lord Rosebery's colt won. Thousands cheered with her. The handsome new Prime Minister hadn't yet done anything to offend the people, and they liked having a sporting man at the head of the government.

Later in the afternoon Standish made his way through the crowd to say hello. When Chess saw him coming, she felt like the luckiest and most attractive woman on earth because he couldn't keep away from her. His bow and perfunctory almost-kiss on the back of her hand were all that society's rules called for, and no more. But through her glove she could feel the infinitesimally excessive pressure of his fingers. When he was laughing and talking with Nathan she enjoyed the game of schooling her expression to seem interested only in what he was saying to her husband, rather than the touch of his shoulder against hers when they were all jostled by the crowd.

Standish brought unhappy tidings for Nate. H.R.H. would be pleased if Nate would join him at the Marlborough Club again tonight. Eleven o'clock, for baccarat.

The game the previous night had pleased the Prince a great deal. For more than a week, Nate went to the club almost every night. Always at a late hour and staying until nearly dawn. Randall came to Chess then. In the mornings she went to him. She became more and more accomplished at lies about nonexistent shops that had none of the things she was looking for.

She also became more tired, because in the afternoon she received or paid calls, and practically every evening she and Nathan went to a dinner party. After the Levée, the invitations had multiplied.

Nate was near exhaustion, because he was spending the days talking business with the big tobacco manufacturers, trying to convince them to take part in the company he had organized. "I'd be glad to kill your cousin for getting me into this Marlborough Club life," he said, "if it didn't happen that two of the biggest tobacco men in England show up there. Then I make sure I lose money to them, too, along with Bertie." He chuckled, but the sound of it was tired. "It ain't bad when a boy from a tobacco farm in Alamance County can call the next King of England Bertie."

Chess felt sorry for him, and she hated having to lie to him. She was sure he had never lied to her. But she was in the grip of emotion stronger than anything she had ever known, and its focus was Randall, his hands, his mouth, his body. She was driven and drawn by passion.

Suddenly, on June 11, the cab strike was over. The streets had seemed to Chess to have too much traffic before. Now, the ride to Randall's flat took twice as long and made her twice as frantic to arrive there. Then, on the twelfth, he told her that he would be going away for the weekend.

"I don't want to be away from you, either, my love, but H.R.H. has commanded me to be on his yacht for the Royal Thames Regatta. You know I cannot decline. It's only two days, Chess, don't exaggerate."

"Why can't Nathan go instead of you? He's the one who can be depended on to lose at cards."

Standish laughed. "He told H.R.H. that he gets miserably seasick."

"He does no such thing."

"He's a smart man, your husband."

Chess thought she detected an emphasis on the final two words. Was he angry? Was he getting tired of her? She remembered the sugary viciousness of some lady at some party. "You are terribly fortunate to be the one who has won Mephisto's favors this Season, my dear. He is quite perfect as a lover until he gets bored." Chess voiced no more complaints and made herself act lighthearted when they were together for the two days before the weekend came.

That Saturday and Sunday were restful. Chess hadn't realized how much she needed some rest until it felt so very good to have it. She and Nathan walked slowly through the gardens beside the river, ate some ices, went to the band concert. And they talked. It had been weeks since there had been time for leisurely conversation.

He was close to getting one of the tobacco men into the company, he believed. Others would follow once the initial move was made.

Had he told her this before? Had he been telling her all along, after his meetings with these men? She couldn't remember.

For the first time, Chess felt guilty about having an affair. Nathan had never loved her. He had never made love to her. But he had given her full partnership in the part of his life that was most important to him, the birth and growth of his business. He had even given it her name, Standish.

She knew from talking to other women that their husbands shared nothing with them, except their names and—on occasion—their beds. She was infinitely more lucky than they were. Because of Nathan. She should never, ever, not for a minute, have shortchanged him the way she had. No matter how crazy she was about Randall, she should have been interested in what Nathan was doing, concerned about his success.

"Did you see this?" Nathan handed her that Saturday's issue of the *Illustrated News*, a fashionable weekly paper. He had circled an advertisement. "Full Dress" cigarettes were extolled in large print. Smaller print informed the public that they were available at all tobacconists. Even smaller letters identified the manufacturer: Kinney Bros., N.Y.

"That's one of the ones Buck Duke gobbled up," Chess said. "What are they doing in London? Do you think he knows what you're up to, Nathan?"

"Probably so, but I can't be sure. These Englishmen are so close-mouthed they hate to answer to their names when you speak to them. Like it's a secret that they're who they are, much less that they've got anything to do with business. I can see them chopping out the tongue of any clerk that tells anything to Buck's boys or anybody else."

"Do you think American Tobacco Company's going to start a price war over here? That's a specialty of Duke's, isn't it?"

"That's what he's up to now at home. Only it's still plug, not cigarettes, and he's got a real fight on his hands. Dick Reynolds doesn't have big money in the bank, but Liggett & Myers can cut prices right along with Buck and not feel the pinch for a long time.

"Our timing's just right. Buck's busy in his own back yard. I was glad to see this Kinney ad. I can use it to scare the people I'm dickering with."

Chess looked at him accusingly. "Nathan Richardson, did you put this thing in the paper yourself?"

"Would I do a low-down, dirty-pool thing like that?" His eyes were merry; Chess thought he looked less tired, more like himself. She made a solemn, silent promise that she would be a better partner from now on.

But then Randall came to call on Monday. He had good news: the H.R.H. cigarettes had made a big hit on the Royal Yacht. Bertie was going to use them as the official cigarette of the Marlborough Club.

"Everybody smokes cigars there," Nate mentioned dryly, "it won't cost him much."

"But you will order some more, won't you?" Standish insisted.

"I already did. Ten cases should be here before the end of the month. That's only twelve days from now."

Chess gasped aloud. She made a hasty apology, mentioning indigestion. In fact, she couldn't believe that time had slipped away so fast. She couldn't bear it; they had reservations to sail for New York on July 2. She couldn't leave Randall. She wouldn't.

She looked at him with wild eyes. His eyes cautioned her.

"You can start encouraging the switch from cigars at the club tonight, Nate," he said with a sympathetic grimace. "H.R.H. asked me to extend the invitation."

Chess looked down at her knees to hide the blaze of exultation on her face. She would be with Randall tonight.

July was still nearly two weeks away. Anything could happen in two weeks. Nathan's negotiations could be extended, the Prince could take him to the Continent to gamble, a million things were possible.

For now she would live for the moment when Randall's body was next to hers. Nothing else mattered.

Chapter Thirty-Nine

THE ASCOT RACES WERE THAT WEEK. London did not empty the way it had for the Derby; Ascot was for the gentry, not the world at large. Rotten Row was deserted, but not the Strand. Chess looked at the teeming traffic with irritation.

Everything in her life was an irritant. Nathan had said he didn't want to go to Ascot; Epsom Downs had given him sufficient view of racing in England. Their own race oval at home would provide enough racing for the rest of the year as far as he was concerned.

Randall couldn't escort her. He was going to be at a country house party near Windsor and would be attending the races with the other members of that group.

"Everyone goes to the country," he'd said. "I assumed that you and Nate would be invited by someone, too. You're invited everywhere else."

"Well, we weren't. And now I won't see you for three whole days."

He touched her mouth. "Think how things will be when I

come back, with three nights of hunger for you in my heart. . . . It will be much better, even, than this." And his fingers moved to her loosened hair to grasp a handful and draw her face toward his kisses.

But that had been two days ago. Also, she had done what she'd sworn not to do; she had been sulky and demanding instead of loving and amusing. Now she tortured herself with all the tales she had heard about country house parties. They were, it seemed, nothing more than carefully orchestrated adultery games, including charts of the bedrooms and who was occupying which one so that lovers would not enter the wrong room by mistake.

Who was with Randall, in the place that should be hers?

"Can't you go any faster?" she called out to the coachman, even though she knew he was doing the best he could. She wished that the miserable hansoms had never settled their horrible strike. A person would be able to get around.

Luther Witsell was violently happy to see her. He bounced on his toes, flung lengths of silk from a chair, and seated her with a flourish. "Only whisper your desire and it is yours," he declaimed. "A skirt of butterfly wings? A shawl of moonbeams?"

Chess laughed reluctantly. She did not want to give up her grouchiness, but Luther's high spirits were irresistible.

"The Duchess of Devonshire's ball," she said. Luther threw his hands in the air and fell recklessly on his knees.

"The event of the Season," he said, "I must outdo my muses." He tore at his unruly orange hair with his long fingers.

Chess could see the narrow cot and little table with a gas ring on it that was meant to be invisible behind a screen in the corner of the room. What a selfish pig I am, she thought. If I'd told everyone who asked where I got my clothes, poor Luther would be a raging success by now. I suppose the Princess was only asking to be polite. Luther's too avant garde for someone in her position. She's stuck with being the next queen; she can't afford to be different.

"I see your exquisite alabaster skin as the light of the moon in the darkness of a hidden garden," Luther pronounced.

Chess gave him her full attention. The invitation to the ball was testimonial to social success. She had heard a dozen stories about ladies—and gentlemen, too—angling desperately to get one. Never mind that hers was most likely due to Nathan's friendship with the Prince. She was invited, too. It made up for all her pique about the country house parties in which they hadn't been included.

"It mustn't be too heavy, Mr. Witsell," Chess warned. "It will be hot in the middle of July." She refused to believe that she wouldn't still be in England.

"And a thousand candles lighting the ballroom," Luther signed blissfully. "It will be like Hell itself."

When Chess went down the many stairs from Luther's studio, she exited into a gray wall of mist. It was frightening at first. She couldn't see her carriage, and she heard muffled footsteps but could see no people. It was the first thick fog she had experienced.

As soon as she understood what it was, she was thrilled. This was what she had read about. That shadowy figure she could barely see might well be a character from a Sherlock Holmes story.

"Hello," she shouted. "Is the Richardson carriage here?" The footman who perched in back found his way to her and led her slowly to the landau.

"Take me to Baker Street," Chess told the driver.

"Where, Madam?"

"Baker Street," Chess repeated. "Number 221B."

The coachman chose his words carefully. Mr. Holmes, he explained, was not a real person.

Chess laughed. "I know. And he's dead, besides. But I still want to go to Baker Street."

She looked out the window as the carriage crawled along the foggy streets. From the nothingness a face, or a horse, or a post box, or a lamp pole would suddenly appear and then vanish with the same suddenness. Sounds were distorted and dampened. Once Chess heard someone singing, another time the sound of sobs.

It was all very strange and strangely beautiful.

She walked the four sides of the block where Holmes had had his fictional home. She didn't see the entrance because it did not exist. But she couldn't see any markings on any buildings. One of them might have held the room with the great detective's scientific apparatus. Anything might be imagined in this world of swirling gray.

She had to keep her fingertips on the solid walls or she would get completely lost, just as her driver had anxiously predicted. Her progress was slower than a snail's. Where a staircase projected, she had to feel her way around the three sides to get back to the solidity of the walls.

It was a glorious adventure.

"I was worried you might be lost," Nathan said when she got back to the hotel.

"I was, for about an hour," Chess replied, "but it was on purpose." She told him all about the invisible buildings on Baker Street.

"I nearly walked into the river," Nate said with a laugh. "I thought I was on the Strand, but I was on some street at a right angle to it. If some little ruffian hadn't tried to pick my pocket, I'd be food for the fishes. When he knocked me down, I could see under the fog. It kind of floats up and down."

"I wish I'd known that, I'd have stooped down to see where I was."

"Want to try?"

"Oh, yes!"

They stumbled, hand in hand, through the hotel's gardens toward the Embankment.

"It's breaking up," Chess said mournfully. "Look, there are patches of sky overhead."

"Then lie down quick before it goes. They say this hardly ever happens in the summer."

She knelt then stretched prone on the gravel path. Her nose was almost touching some dianthus flowers. Their spicy scent was strong and sweet.

After a minute she felt Nathan's hand under her arm. "Better get up, or somebody'll see you and send an ambulance. The fog's going out fast."

Chess complied with reluctance. She hadn't had such outrageous fun in years and years, and she had never before seen how intricately beautiful a small pink flower could be.

They had dinner in the suite that night. Nathan said he didn't want to get all starched up, and Chess agreed with him. It would be very pleasant indeed to wear a tea gown and relaxed corset for a change.

After dinner they read. Nathan had a sheaf of reports from the factories. Chess took out the page proofs of George du Maurier's novel that Randall had given her. She remembered the way his fingertips had touched hers when he put them in her hands, and she felt a delightful brief tingling sensation. He would be back soon.

The novel was very bohemian. Chess was soon engrossed. The heroine was a young artists' model in Paris named Trilby. She was shocking; she posed nude, she swore, she slept with several men without feeling any guilt, and she smoked cigarettes.

Chess stopped reading long enough to report Trilby's tobacco habit to Nathan. "Maybe all loose women smoke. You should send somebody to the part of town where they are to find out. You could sell a lot of cigarettes there if it's true."

Nathan made a noncommittal noise and turned a page. He already knew that some prostitutes smoked. He had visited a recommended house several times, but he specified nonsmoking whores. He hated the smell of tobacco.

Chess stayed up late after Nathan went to bed. She was under the spell of a mad music teacher and seducer named Svengali who had hypnotized poor Trilby and made her his slave.

He also made her the greatest singing star in Europe. Under Svengali's spell she had a voice of such pure clarity that audiences worshiped at her feet, which were always bare.

Chess read the long pages of cheap paper, dropping each completed one on the floor. There was a large untidy pile when Svengali had a heart attack and died backstage at a London concert hall. Trilby, on stage, lost her voice at the instant of his death. Chess shivered deliciously and began the next page.

She wept happily throughout Trilby's downward path to destruction and her transformation through remorse to salvation. The all-stops-out death scene where Trilby found her voice again and died as she sang made Chess blubber.

What a lovely, wicked book, she thought. She stacked the pages neatly. She'd take them home and give them to James Dike. He certainly would never have a book like this in his store. She didn't think she should pass it around the Literary Circle, either. She giggled at the idea and went to bed. She felt rather bohemian herself. She had actually met the man who wrote *Trilby*. And he didn't look bohemian at all.

The Monday newspapers had big black headlines. PRESIDENT OF FRANCE ASSASSINATED and, equally big, ROYAL PRINCE BORN. Bertie was a grandfather, and the guards at Buckingham Palace were reinforced.

Chess loved the pageantry of the Changing of the Guard. Sometimes she timed her departure from Randall's flat so that she could watch it on her way back to the Savoy, but on that Monday she had not been to him. He had not yet returned from Windsor.

He had, at least, sent a note telling her that he wouldn't be back until the afternoon. The other news in the note was exciting enough to offset her disappointment.

One of the other house party guests was Daisy Pollinger, the lady who—rumor had it—desired to dispose of a lot of old-fashioned furniture. Standish had included the name and address of Miss Pollinger's trustee. Mr. Adderly had keys to

the house where the furniture was stored and would be available to show it to Chess at her convenience.

She watched the Guards until the last ranks disappeared
on the march back to their barracks and then was driven to
Mr. Adderly's offices on Bond Street.

He was a fragile, elderly gentleman with a whispery voice
and a courtly manner. He reminded her of her grandfather,
even though Augustus Standish had preferred shouting to quiet
murmurs. Her instant affection was very acceptable to the
old gentleman. "I trust that a gentlelady like yourself, Mrs.
Richardson, will find a home for Lady Elizabeth's treasures.
She would have been dismayed indeed had she seen the want
of appreciation Miss Pollinger demonstrates for her great-
aunt's legacy."

Chess hoped the things weren't too awful. She would buy
them even if they were, rather than join Miss Pollinger in Mr.
Adderly's disfavor.

Lady Elizabeth's house was on Russell Square, a neighborhood that had been out of fashion for decades. The house was
a simple square Georgian brick house set in a square garden
that had long since been taken over by weeds. The brick walk
from sidewalk to house was broken and tilted topsy-turvy by
vegetation.

The great front door was divided into two tall sections,
each paneled into four squares. A large, graceful fanlight
topped the double doors.

Chess tried not to hope for too much. The entrance reminded
her of Harefields.

She had to help Mr. Adderly turn the huge iron key to open
the doors. They squeaked a protest, but they swung wide.

And she saw home ahead of her. The wide hallway was
thick with dust, but a beautiful spiral of stair rose from the
shadows at one side. And high overhead a skylight scattered
rainbows through the air.

Chess began to cry quietly. "Mr. Adderly," she said, "I was
once a little girl in a house exactly like this one. Would you

mind very much if I went and sat on the bottom step and remembered?"

He was touched by her tears and her sentiment. He, too, had been a child in a house very much like this one.

"You may keep the key as long as you like, dear child. Return it whenever you are done." And he tottered away over the broken bricks.

Chess stayed in the old house until the sunlight began to shift to twilight. She forgot Randall, Nate, London. She was surrounded by the ghosts in her mind and in her heart. She was with her family and the child who had grown into the woman she had become.

The house was smaller than Harefields and more formal. But the tall shadowy rooms gave the same feeling of space and balanced restraint. Chess wondered how everyone, herself included, could have become so concentrated on the acquisition of things that they had given up the possession of beauty and tranquillity. She wondered how she, product of Harefields, had ended up in the situation that now dominated her life, where the illicit pleasures of the body meant more to her than honor or decency or her marriage vows.

Had her two handsome older brothers been like Randall— experienced and compelling lovers of women married to other men? Had her mother ever given herself to any of the men who adored her? Why had it been accepted, even expected, that her father and grandfather would beget bastard children with helpless slave women?

Did carnality really rule the whole world? And if it did, was the gracious order of the space around her only a sham of rationality where none could exist?

You are what I want, she told the silent dust-sheeted house. Serenity and beauty . . . And yet I know that when Randall touches me, I will be his creature for as long as he wants me, and there is no serenity for me in his arms, only wild wanting and wilder fulfillment.

She felt more confused than ever when she locked the big

doors behind her. But she knew that she had found an ideal
worth striving for, even if it was beyond her reach.

"Thank you for allowing me to stay in the house," she told
the elderly trustee. "Yes, I would like very much to have
whatever Miss Pollinger will permit me to buy."

"Nathan, I have found the furnishings for Harefields at
last," Chess announced triumphantly.

"That's real fine; I want to hear all about it. But we're
supposed to go to this dratted dinner you accepted, and it's
getting late. Your maid's been fidgeting for an hour about
what dress to get ready."

"I forgot all about it. I'll hurry."

Nate waited until they were in the landau and on their way
before he made his announcement. "Upchurch signed on the
dotted line today, Chess. I'll have the others before the end
of the week." He took a deep, lung-filling breath. "It's done.
I beat Buck Duke," he said after he exhaled slowly and luxuriously.

"Nathan, that's wonderful. What shall we do to celebrate?
There should be Roman candles."

"To show how I feel, they'd have to be volcanoes. Since
they ain't available, we'll have a secret toast to ourselves in
the host's champagne tonight. I've built up a considerable
fondness for champagne."

It was the twenty-fourth of June, 1894. Chess decided to
have the date engraved on cuff links, hairbrushes, a gold
watch, and a silver champagne cooler—no, four silver champagne coolers. They'd have a big party in Standish, complete
with Roman candles, and she'd give Nathan the presents.
Maybe at Christmastime.

It was a large party, about forty for dinner, Chess estimated.
She stifled a sigh. Service took so much longer at big parties.

Then she saw Oscar Wilde in a group not too far away,
and she felt lucky to be there. If only he was seated close

enough for her to hear what he said, the dinner could be the longest in the world, and she'd be delighted.

He saw her, too. "The Confederate beauty," he said loudly, "let me kneel in surrender. Or is my worshipful adoration a Lost Cause?"

"How lovely to see you, Oscar. Have you been reading American military history?"

He kissed her hand. "Not voluntarily, as you may well imagine. I was recently buttonholed by an historian of cataract eloquence. I am now an expert. If the South will but give me an army, a horse, and a magnificent uniform, I will right all its wrongs."

He looked her up and down. "Dear Luther has almost succeeded, though it's not sufficiently regal. You look beautiful."

Oscar was pleased for her, also a bit saddened. The ways of the heart were a territory he knew well, and he recognized the real source of Chess' beauty. She was loved. It made her feel beautiful, and so she had become beautiful. Her clothing was only an ornament to her happiness. If only love could last, he thought, how beautiful the whole world might be. As Chess was, tonight.

She looked different from the other women, but not too much so. Her gown had the fashionable hourglass nipped waist, and the stiff flared skirt with deep back pleats making a short train. It was low in the neck, too, as was required, and the elbow-length sleeves were huge, as expected.

However, instead of being made of silk, or organza, or lace, it was Luther's inspiration to create a patchwork of all three. Deep green silk, deep blue organza, and deep lilac lace squares had been sewn together, and then the pattern pieces were cut. The varied colors and surfaces attracted the light in the room, and all eyes.

Chess gave him full credit.

"Dear Luther has made me a fashion leader. He's a miracle worker. Tell me everything; how have you been; how are you?"

"My dear Chess, you must learn restraint. Never ask a man how he is. He might tell you, and you would have no one to blame but yourself for being stupefied by ennui."

"Never. Not with you. But if you won't talk, I will. I've had the most exciting time lately. I visited Sherlock Holmes, and—"

"You visited whom?" Oscar smiled gleefully. "I never suspected you of lunacy. How delicious."

Chess described her fog adventures. Oscar vowed to do the same thing on the next foggy day. "Such a madly diverting story," he said. "I shall, of course, improve it."

Chess felt a brushing touch on her neck, turned, saw Randall, and felt her knees turn to water.

"Oscar, my friend, you have become *de trop*," said Standish. "I waited for you all afternoon," he said quietly to Chess. "When I heard you laughing with Oscar, I wanted to kill him, then you, then myself. Why didn't you come?"

"I forgot."

"Now I will kill you. Damn! They're assigning escorts in to dinner. We cannot talk any longer. Come tomorrow. Early. Swear it."

"I swear it."

Lord Randall Standish was annoyed. Another unsuccessful debutante was on his right. He saluted her with his wineglass, made his eyes admiring above the rim. He did his duty.

Far down the table Chess was laughing. The sound filtered through the subdued clatter of silver against porcelain and well-bred conversation. Was it that remarkable laughter that had led him to make a fool of himself? There had to be a better reason than that. Because he was a fool. He had begged her to come to him tomorrow. Not that the hyperbolic language was unusual—it was part of the game lovers play. What was inexplicable was that he had meant it.

Everything had been prepared, planned for. She would come to him in the afternoon, when he returned from the country. He would make love to her, and then he would end the affair. She had become too demanding, too needy, it was time to get out. He knew the warning signals; many times in the past he had found it necessary to exit gracefully.

Why, then, had he been bothered when she didn't come? He was too worldly to feel the need to be the initiator of the finish. If the lady were clever enough to read the signs and exit first, so much the better. It was easier for both of them.

What was different about this affair, this woman? Why did he suddenly want her so much that he was counting the hours until morning?

If she kept her word.

No, he needn't worry about that. It was one of the unique things about her. She gave excessive weight to outmoded ideas like the sanctity of a promise.

"Unique." That had to be the answer. He supposed he would even remember her. The others were all very much a blur in his mind. He'd have to replace her with another unusual type. The little countess at the house party had definite possibilities.

Chess was seated at Oscar's end of the table. Everyone within earshot was being vastly amused by his comments on the menu card. Almost everyone. Some people realized that he was ridiculing them when he poked fun at the excess of food. Two soups and two fish dishes was sensible enough. A choice was a straightforward luxury. But why was it necessary to be offered venison, and chicken in cream, and lamb chops, and sweetbreads, and ortolans, and foie gras, and partridge? All of them before the main course was served, and then followed by ices and cakes, before dessert.

Excess was the cri de coeur, the standard raised for everyone to follow. Chess looked at the six gold epergnes on the table, each spilling a bounteous arrangement of sugar-coated fruits that glistened in the candlelight from the five monumental gold candelabra. She had to crane her neck to see Nathan, opposite and five chairs along. She would raise her glass to him when the champagne was served.

Nate was listening intently to the over-jeweled lady on his

right. How patient he was. Or how interested—with Nathan, one never knew. The lady might be a notorious bore, but he was interested in some very strange things. Chess decided she would ask him later. Perhaps it would interest her, too.

"What on earth was your dinner partner going on about, Nathan? She must have talked your ear off."

"It was very interesting. I'd been wondering ever since we got here, so I asked her. 'What do these people do?' "

"And?"

"She said they work very hard all the time at finding ways to keep from being bored."

"That's all she said?"

"She didn't put it quite that way. She told me about the parties and the races and the house parties and the grouse or rabbit or pheasant shooting and the tennis, the golf, the archery, the billiards, the croquet. They really do wear themselves out, doing, and going someplace else to do, and then going back to where they came from in the first place, to do the same thing again."

"Nathan, you sound like a socialist or something. What's wrong with having fun?"

"Nothing. But they don't have fun. They just run around in a fit, terrified that if they stop, they might be bored. . . . It's pitiful."

Chess stretched like a cat, moaning softly with pleasure, while Randall's hands moved slowly down her spine, teasing her with the anticipation of their touch on the rest of her body. Her own fingers and palms were on fire from the need to touch him, but she made herself wait, concentrating on the moment and closing out all thoughts of the future.

She had tortured herself enough with wondering; what would she do if he asked her to stay; what would she do if he did not. Later, later. Think and feel only the now.

And then—too soon—the now was the end.

"You have given me great happiness, my love; I will never forget you," he said.

"I will remember for the rest of my life, Randall. Now kiss me one last time, for I must go." She did not cry. She hurt too much to cry. She had never had to decide whether to stay or not. Randall had not mentioned it.

On the day after their parting, Chess went with Nathan to the gala celebration of the opening of Tower Bridge. All London was there, it seemed. The Thames was crowded with boats bedecked in pennants, both banks were thronged with people in holiday spirits.

The bridge was an engineering and architectural wonder. Its huge center span could be raised to allow ship passage, and the mechanism was concealed beneath two tall square towers with roofline decorations that were iron reminders of the ancient flag-topped turrets of the Tower of London nearby on the shore. The bridge structure was painted a bright sky-blue, the towers were dressed granite with gilded heraldic plaques, flags snapped in the sharp wet breeze.

The invited guests were shown to a striped canvas pavilion near the north end of the bridge. Blue chairs were arranged on stepped platforms that faced a dais draped with flags centered by the Royal Insignia.

Chess greeted the other guests and took a seat. It gave her a nasty satisfaction that almost all the others were scandalized that a barbaric American like Nathan could have become so close to the Prince of Wales that two of the coveted tickets were wasted on foreigners. It was even better, because Nathan wasn't even in his seat. He had, of course, made friends with the bridge engineers, and he was in the machinery room to witness the action from there.

Shortly before noon companies of soldiers and sailors marched onto the bridge and took positions lining both sides of the roadway. Each man held a small, brightly polished brass bugle.

A procession of open carriages appeared on Tower Hill.

Each was surrounded by colorfully uniformed horse guards, in perfectly matched step. As the crowds cheered, the bugles were raised. The Prince and Princess of Wales were in the first carriage. The shiny horns saluted them as their four-in-hand crossed the span to the poorer neighborhoods on the south side of the river.

Many of the laborers who had built the bridge lived there. The Prince and Princess were scheduled to drive through the decorated streets as a gesture of thanks to the workmen.

The brasses saluted again when the carriage returned after a half hour. Chess watched the bright bugles with admiration. How did those young men manage to be so precisely synchronized? It looked like one hand and one horn was reflected in a hundred mirrors.

Then the Royals were at the pavilion. Chess rose and curtsied along with the other ladies. When she sat down again, she could see the Prince's party opposite. Among the courtiers and officials was Lord Randall Standish. He was being attentive to the youngest royal daughter.

Chess didn't hear any of the many speeches, including H.R.H.'s. She was looking, not hearing, storing up memories of faces and smiles. Gussie would want to know what the princesses looked like. Her own heart needed to record every expression that passed over Randall's face. When there was applause, she applauded. When all the boats on the river began blowing their whistles, she saw that the central roadway was splitting, rising into the air. Then a cannon fired nearby, everyone applauded, and the ceremony was over.

London is over for me, she thought. She watched the Royal party proceed down to a special dock and gangway, board a flag-decorated steamship, and depart.

She watched it move slowly up the Thames, out of her life. Randall had not met her eyes once.

Nathan pushed through the crowds to find her. He wanted her to see the machinery. She would have the privilege of pushing the lever that closed the open bascules.

Chess felt separated from everything and everybody, espe-

cially herself. She was a spectator at a distance, observing
Nathan in his morning coat and top hat, conversing easily
and respectfully with the engineers. She saw herself, smiling,
talking, running her gloved hand admiringly over the gigantic
green-painted, red-trimmed engines. She watched and
admired herself as she supervised the packing, wrote notes
regretting the necessity to withdraw from parties previously
accepted, carefully lettered *P.P.C.* on dozens of calling cards,
hers and Nathan's.

Pour prendre congé, the polite, French announcement that
the Richardsons were leaving London. The coachman would
drive to all the houses on the list she gave him, the footman
would deliver the cards to the doors. The recipients would
throw them away. London would forget them, as if they had
never been there at all.

She found one of her old, improper *cartes de visite*. "P.P.C."
she printed on her photograph. This one would be left at
Randall's flat.

The *Campania* was familiar, their suite and servants the
same. It was almost as if they had never left it, never landed
at Liverpool, never gone to London. Except that nothing in
her life could ever be the same again.

When the storm clouds boiled up on the horizon, Chess
looked at them with dull satisfaction. Seasickness would be
so much easier than what she was suffering.

Chapter Forty

THERE WAS SO MUCH TO DO when they got home that there was
no time to think, and Chess was grateful. She organized the
celebration party and fireworks for Nathan first thing, inviting
all their friends, including Doctor and even Dick Reynolds. The
occasion was a huge success. In North Carolina, you didn't have
to worry about rain in July, so Chess used the park, and the
band played, and everyone in Standish was there.

Afterwards there was champagne at the house. Gussie was
home and was allowed a half-glass to share in the toasting.

"I like this better than I did before," she said. "I was too
little then." She would be twelve soon and considered herself
very grown-up. But her knees were still knobby and skinned.
Chess decided she needn't worry yet about her little girl
becoming a woman. She'd have to talk to Gussie one day
soon about men and women and babies and love. She didn't
know how to explain love, not the kind of love that obsessed
and possessed you.

She could see Nathan's struggles. Lily was pregnant, and

he thought the baby was his. Lily's hold over him was as powerful as ever; it was only a matter of time until he would be back in her bed.

Chess understood now. She had known the same help-lessness. It saddened her that she couldn't tell Nathan that she did not blame him anymore. But of course she couldn't because how could she know? She wouldn't tell that, it would hurt both of them too much.

The English partners were coming in August for vital meet-ings about the new company, and Chess was determined to have Harefields ready in time to celebrate the alliance there. She opened all the crates that had traveled with them in the hold of the *Campania* and experimented for days with the placement of the contents of the Russell Square house. She got dusty and tired and sometimes frustrated, but the serenity she'd known on Russell Square had crossed the ocean with its furnishings, and Harefields became her oasis of peace, in spite of painters and carpenters and seamstresses.

There were surprises, not all of them good.

Edith Horton embraced her, admired her clothes, Hare-fields' furniture, her amusing stories about Nathan and the Prince of Wales. Then she said, "Was he worth it, Chess?"

"What are you talking about, Edith?"

"My dear, you are not the woman who left here with Baede-ker in hand. You've had a love affair. Don't worry, it doesn't show, except to a woman who has been through it herself."

"Edith!"

"Oh, yes. Henry never knew, that's a blessing. And I got over him, although it took ten years. Now I know that he was worth it, even the ten years. I hope you can say the same."

"Ask me again in a few years."

Bobby Fred was dying. "It'll take a while yet, Chess, so don't carry on like that. I'm an old man, it's natural for me to go when my time comes."

"You called me 'Chess,' Soldier. It took you long enough, but I'm glad you finally got around to it."

"And you called me 'Soldier.' I'm grateful for that. 'Bobby Fred' ain't no kind of name for a grown-up man."

James Dike was thrilled to get *Trilby*. He had been reading the installments in *Harper's Monthly* magazine and was "going crazy trying to guess what happened."

"I can't believe *Harper's* would publish such a story."

"Dear Chess, it is taking America by storm, and I do mean 'storm.' Everybody is talking about it."

Chess was skeptical, but James was right. The very next Sunday, Gideon preached a hell-and-damnation sermon denouncing the immorality of Trilby the character and *Trilby* the book. He was one of thousands of preachers doing the same thing.

Chess kept her mouth shut, but she felt deliciously bohemian.

The three English partners arrived on August third. Nathan had sent his railroad car to New York for them. When they stepped down from it at the little Standish station, they could not conceal the fact that they were surprised by a degree of elegance in America that they had never experienced in England.

Nathan laughed about it with Chess later.

"What did they expect from a chum of His Royal Highness?" she said. "You can do anything you want with them."

"I think I'll go easy on them at first. They're still afraid there's a Geronimo behind every tree." He grinned like a boy. "I'll scalp 'em when they quit expecting it."

The meetings went on, day and night, for weeks. Armies of lawyers, clerks, embassy aides, surveyors, builders, and tobacco men filled Durham's hotel and Nate's offices.

Finally, on September first, three notaries put their seals on the signed articles of incorporation and subsidiary agreements.

Ground-breaking for the new complex of factories and support buildings would take place the following April.

There was a big champagne-soaked farewell, and the Englishmen boarded Nate's private car for their journey to New York.

As soon as the rear observation platform was out of sight, he took off his morning coat, top hat, and gloves, and rolled up his sleeves.

"What are you doing?" Chess asked.

"I'm getting on a horse and going to Raleigh. It's a lot faster than that plush-seated toy. Do you know what happened while I was sipping tea with my new partners? The infernal politicians in Washington passed a law putting a two percent tax on every penny I earn over four thousand dollars a year. I'm not going to stand for it, and I'm going to tell my 'elected representatives' so in terms they can understand."

"Nathan—don't hit anybody."

"I'm going to do worse than that. I'm going to quit lining some pockets."

Chess smiled. She was thankful for the politicians. Nathan had been holding himself in check for weeks while the necessary nit-picking was done on the business agreements. He wasn't used to talking about getting things done. He had always gone ahead and done them.

Now he could blow off steam at some senators and congressmen. It was their job to listen.

She went out onto the cool breeze-swept back veranda of Harefields and sat quietly in one of the tall-backed rockers. It squeaked gently when she rocked. It was like a lullaby. The house was quiet; Gussie was out somewhere. Sunlight shimmered on the wings of dragonflies—"darning needles" her grandfather used to call them—and a turquoise and green hummingbird fed briefly from the throat of a geranium in a clay pot on the step. It was summer in the South, a drowsy tranquillity. Chess cherished it. The Englishmen had been polite, undemanding guests, but their accents had made her think of things that were better forgotten. She closed her eyes and tilted her head back on the back of the chair and rocked with the lullaby squeaking until she was at peace.

Gussie shattered it when she came home; Chess blinked and woke with a start.

"MaMa?"

"Out back, Gussie."

"Oh, there you are. I brought the mail from the post office. May I have those funny stamps? Julia Bennet sticks them in a book."

"Not until your father finishes with the mail. The letters from England are business for him."

"There's a bunch on this big one for you, see?"

Chess recognized the handwriting immediately, even though she had seen it only once, in a brief note.

"MaMa, are you sick?"

"It's just the heat, darling, I'm fine. Would you please go ask Cook to fix us some lemonade?" She needed to be alone. Her hands were gripping the rocker's arms so tightly that her arms were shaking. What could Randall have to say? What did he want? She tore the thick wrapping on the parcel and dropped the paper on the floor.

A newspaper clipping lay on top of an inner wrapping. Chess could make no sense of it. Someone's art collection was going to be auctioned.

She looked at the date again. Had been auctioned, on June 30.

She unwrapped the inner package with careful fingers. Her breath caught in her throat when she saw the letter.

> *My dear Chess. This made me think of you. I was*
> *doing homework for this auction when we met*
> *at the Gallery. I hope you may find room on a*
> *wall for this small token of affection from your*
> *English cousin,*
>
> > *Randall Standish*

"Here's the lemonade, MaMa."

"Thank you, darling. Put it on the table, please."

"Oh, goody, lots of stamps. What was in it?"

Chess couldn't answer. She removed Randall's letter and opened the pressboard portfolio beneath it.

A graphite sketch, just a few lines, a preliminary drawing. But it brought back the painting. The man and woman with their hands joined standing in the golden-lit room, facing outward to anyone looking in, their faces serene with the peace that Chess longed for, that Randall's gift had shattered. She felt as if her legs were scalded by the words he had written on the paper that was in her lap. She wanted to hold the ink to her lips, to her breast. Instead, she offered letter and drawing to Gussie.

"Make sure your hands are clean, sweetheart. This is very old and very precious. The note is from our English cousin that I told you about."

She had to get away, to be alone. "I'm going to have a little nap, Gussie. The goodbyes to the Englishmen tired me out."

With shutters half-drawn and the door to her room locked, Chess could cry. Salt tears spilled into her contorted mouth as it silently called "Randall . . . Randall . . . Randall . . ." Her hands stroked her body in memory and imitation of his.

Nate was away for only three days, but it was enough time for Chess to recover from the shock of hearing from Randall. She was able to show him the letter and the drawing and talk about them as if they were no more than a delightful surprise.

"That's real nice," Nate said. "The other parcel that Miss Greedy Fingers got the stamps from before I had a chance to sit down—well, that was a little souvenir for you, too." He put the opened package in her lap.

"Oh, Nathan, how thoughtful, thank you so much." Chess handled the gift carefully; it was music—wax cylinders for

the Edison gramophone, one of arias sung by Nellie Melba,
the other by Adelina Patti.

"That show in the dining room that night was the most
comical thing I ever saw in my life," Nate said. He began to
laugh in recollection.

Then he brought out a new gramophone, with a larger, all-
brass morning-glory sound transmitter. Edison had improved
his original model, said Nate. This was newer and better.

Chess laughed, then. "Oh, Nathan, you never change." She
was genuinely moved by his thoughtful gift, but his boyish
affection for "toys" moved her even more—her laughter was
underlaid by tears. What a lovely thing it was to be able to
depend on someone to stay the same.

"Say, do you remember the one with the feather fan? You
know, she aimed that feather at the other one's soup plate."
He laughed again.

"How about the peacock feathers? Should we decorate a
turkey next time we eat one?"

They egged each other on with reminders. The shared laughter was almost like old times—before Lily and Randall.

Throughout the autumn months life settled into a kind of
equilibrium. Chess welcomed it. She couldn't forget London,
but, bit by bit, she incorporated it into her life in a useful
way.

Harefields was the best example. The house became theirs,
not a repetition of her parents' home, nor a re-creation of
the magical deserted house on Russell Square, but a living,
changing setting for the lives of the Richardsons, Nathan and
Gussie and Chess.

The tall reception rooms were bare and empty by the standards of the times. Pale colors covered walls and windows
and furniture and floors. Much of the faded tapestry upholstery
was left as it was, and the curtains were unornamented cascades of silk. The only ornaments were crystal chandeliers
and sconces and silver or porcelain bowls filled with fresh
flowers or fruits. The drawing room, dining room, morning
room might have been lifted intact from one of the earlier

houses. But Chess added elements that were all her own. Logs and kindling were kept in big, locally made, woven baskets on the hearths. Wildflowers and grasses found their way into the bouquets in the bowls. A crayon valentine made by Gussie when she was four was framed in gold leaf and hung on the same narrow wall space with the sketch by Van Dyck. A stereoscope and slides occupied half of a Chippendale console table. Chess' paisley shawl hung over the back of a Sheraton sofa, to cover shoulders or knees that might feel the draft that plagued that corner of the room. The brass horn of the gramophone was a bright reflection of sunlight from the window in front of which it rested on a Queen Anne mahogany low chest. Every chair and sofa had a Canterbury magazine rack beside it full of recent publications, and small stacks of books perched on tables or ottomans.

Upstairs the rooms were even more relaxed. Patchwork quilts covered the canopied beds, and the bed hangings were made from bright checked gingham produced from their own cotton mill. Curtains were muslin.

There was space and light and air in all rooms; it was all from North Carolina, no other place.

Dinner was served in the evening, London fashion, not in the middle of the day. And there was always wine from the cellars' generous stock. But there were only four courses, and only one dish at each course, and the food was simply prepared from locally produced ingredients.

Tea, with muffins and biscuits and cookies, was a new and enjoyable mid-meal between lunch and dinner. Chess did use the beautiful silver service made by a famous London silversmith of the previous century. But the tea leaves steeped in a fired clay pot made in Sanford, North Carolina, because no matter how beautiful it may be, a silver pot gives a metallic flavor to brewing tea.

There was always an additional small pitcher on the tea tray. This one held whiskey. Soldier preferred its "sweetening" to the sugar bowl's. The old man came for tea almost every day. His weakening heart profited from the stimulation of the tea and the affection that awaited him. Gussie usually demanded his full attention and gave him hers. It made Chess happy to see her daughter's generous, sensitive heart and Soldier's undisguised pure love for his godchild.

Chess did not want outsiders to intrude on the special intimacy of teatime, so she instituted a late breakfast hour for entertaining the ladies of Standish. Her brief view of England's Royal Family had chilled her. They were isolated and imprisoned by their rank. Now that she was home again, she was determined to destroy the "grande dame" role that she had played before. Her ego missed the respectful adulation, and that shamed her. However, she discovered at the small breakfast gatherings that there were a number of intelligent, interesting women who were willing, even eager, to be friends on an equal basis. She became less and less lonely, a problem she had not even noticed or acknowledged before. Her life became richer in humanity all the time.

The Literary Circle continued to be a pleasure, under James Dike's not-too-avant-garde guidance. Chess put the yellowing pages of *Trilby* in a glass-topped table in his bookstore, customers came from as far away as Raleigh and Winston to shop there. The membership of the Circle increased, too. The meetings had to be moved to the big room at the new Masonic Lodge on Richardson Avenue. Outvoted by the members, James and Chess went along with the change to a new name, "The Trilby Club."

"I can't believe what's happening with that book," Chess told Nathan nearly every week when newspapers reported another example of the spreading mania. Its publication in September unloosed an avalanche.

Young women in particular were caught up in the craze. Chess had to forbid Gussie's bad imitation-English accent, an American attempt at what disapproving editorials called "Trilbyismus." But she relented a little. For Christmas, one of Gussie's presents was a small silver pin of a bare foot, after Trilby. It was the latest craze.

The holidays were the best ever, with a decorated forty-foot-high pine tree in the hallway perfuming the whole house, and a succession of evening open houses where everyone sang carols around the piano to Gussie's enthusiastic, flawed accompaniment.

It would have been almost perfect, except that Nathan came home one evening smelling of Lily's rose perfume.

And on Christmas, as on every other day, the longing for Randall was a constant, aching wound in Chess' heart.

It's getting better, she told herself over and over again. It will go away in time. Edith said she recovered from her affair.

Ten years seemed a terribly long time.

Chapter Forty-One

SOLDIER DIED IN HIS SLEEP on February 10. A snowstorm began during his burial. The thick, clean, soft blanket over his grave was the angels' way of making him warm and comfortable, Chess told an inconsolable Gussie.

For the first time in years, she thought about that other grave, in Alamance County, where her tiny son lay buried, and she prayed that the quiet whiteness was blanketing him, too.

Standish's residents called it the "Invasion." The managers and office staffs of the English tobacco partners came to town en masse in March. They were all Londoners and apprehensive about their forced move to the Wilderness. But when they saw the neat prosperous little town, their fears were calmed. And when they learned how much land and how large a house their salaries would buy, the wives, at least, were overjoyed.

"None of us ever went to fancy shops or the theater or anything like that at home," one of the wives told Chess.

"Why should anyone miss them here? And a house that's not one half of another house in a dark sooty street will be so much more than we'd ever arrive at in London, it makes me fairly want to sing and dance. The kiddies don't know what it is to have a place to play in, we were that far from any park. They are like little birds let out of their cage."

These were the English that Chess had never seen in London, representatives of the on-the-rise middle class, the populace that was gradually changing the laws and attitudes of Great Britain. They felt comfortable in America, a country where change was the normal way of life.

Chess learned that much of what she thought she knew about the English was wrong. Widespread, accepted immorality was not universal. On the contrary. These Englishmen and women were as rigid about proper language and behavior as Nathan's censorious mother. One woman informed Chess that even among the titled class, there were many who patterned themselves on Queen Victoria and were horrified by her son's pleasure-loving habits and companions.

Privately, Chess was glad that she had somehow fallen into Bertie's circle and not that of his mother's. Or, in fact, the world of these newcomers to Standish. Still, she did her best to make them feel welcome. She was grateful to all the English who had been kind to her and Nathan in London. She introduced them to their neighbors, gave small break-the-ice parties, urged the grocery where she did her shopping to add imported English teas and preserves and biscuits to its regular stock. She remembered yearning for American bacon when she was feasting on Escoffier's breakfasts at the Savoy. And when she'd met Jimmy Whistler, his most plaintive complaint about being an expatriate was that he missed his mother's cornbread sticks. No Paris baker's croissants could ever take their place in his heart. Homesickness seemed to dwell in the stomach.

At the ground-breaking ceremony for the new factory in April, the Union Jack flew alongside the Stars and Stripes, and the band played "Rule Britannia" as well as "The Star Spangled Banner."

After the official celebrations, Nate and Chess had a private one at home. They opened a bottle of champagne and drank it while they took turns reading aloud the reports from the New York and Durham spies within the American Tobacco Company. Buck Duke was astounded . . . furious . . . irate. . . . He had not believed Nate could win.

But Nate had.

After that, the work began in earnest for implementing the new Anglo-American business alliance, and Nathan became increasingly short-tempered at home.

"I am infernally sick and tired of having eight committee meetings to decide every finicking little thing," he shouted one night at the dinner table.

Gussie looked up from her plate. "Why don't you just tell everybody what to do, Daddy? Aren't you the boss?"

Nate looked at Chess and burst out laughing. " 'And a little child shall lead them,' " he quoted.

"I'm not a little child," Gussie protested.

"You're King Solomon, then," said her father. "Tomorrow, I'll profit from your wisdom. Some heads are going to roll. That's better than cutting babies in half. More useful, too."

Gussie looked to her mother for clarification, but Chess was laughing too hard to speak.

She reminded Nathan of that dinner-table episode a few weeks later, but there was no laughter this time. Chess was literally screaming with rage.

To begin with, she had been quiet. The news Nathan brought her was not new to her at all.

"Chess I've got to tell you something that I'd rather cut out my tongue than say—Lily's baby is mine. I'm the father. Oh, God, Chess, I hate myself."

"I'll tell you exactly what I told Lily when she pranced in here and told me the same thing, Nathan. There is no way on earth to know for sure whether you or Gideon is the father, and the best thing for everybody is to assume it's Gideon's."

"She came here? She told you? Oh, dear sweet heaven, I'm sorry."

Chess' voice became more strident. "Stop saying that, Nathan. What you're sorry about is you're sorry for yourself. I'm sorry for you, too, but I don't want you coming to me with problems you made for yourself.

"You can't shake Lily out of your life. I know that, and she knows that, and she never lets me forget it. Do you think I enjoy those godawful dinners at your mother's every Sunday? Lily simpers at me and mealymouths at your mother until it fairly makes me sick.

"That's as much as I'm willing to do. I won't listen to your troubles and your 'sorrys.' "

Nate held his head in his hands and groaned. "It's worse than ever now. Because of the baby."

"To hell with the baby, and that's the end of it." She had to stand up and walk away from Nathan or she might hit him.

"But Chess, he's a boy."

She spun around. Her voice was quiet again, the words spoken precisely. "What . . . does . . . that . . . mean?"

Nate looked up. His eyes were red-rimmed. "Every man wants a son, Chess. Somebody to carry on his name and his work."

That made her scream. "How dare you? How dare you? Do you think that Gussie isn't the equal of any boy that was ever born? Who was it told you what to do about the new company when you were so snarled up in meetings you couldn't see it for yourself? For that matter, who was your partner when things were hard and needed the most work all day and all night? Was it a man? Was it? No, it was *me*. I made Standish Cigarettes just as much as you did. I worked just as hard as you did. And I am not a man, Nathan, not that you paid any attention to that. I am a woman. Your daughter is going to be a woman soon. And she's got more courage and more heart than any boy you'll ever know.

"How dare you go all weepy about some baby—whether you're the father or not—just because it's a boy. When all the time you're the father of a child as wonderful as Gussie, who loves you with all her heart. If you take as much as a single minute of attention away from Gussie and give it to Lily's baby, I'll kill you, Nathan. Do you hear me?"

Chess was panting from exertion, her heart was pounding, and her face was stark white. Her blazing eyes were filled with hate.

Nate looked at this stranger in front of him, and he was afraid. Chess had disappeared. He needed her; he'd never understood before how much he needed her.

"What can I do?" he asked humbly. "I was wrong."

"You can get out of my sight. You make me sick."

Head low, Nate left the room.

When he was gone, Chess sank onto the floor and wept, leaning on the seat of a delicate armchair covered in a tapestry scene of lovers in a garden.

That afternoon she drove to Nate's office and entered unannounced. "We will keep up a good front, Nathan. Gussie must not know anything about this. You owe us that."

"Of course I do."

"Also, you will not bring the smell of that woman into my house. As long as I've known you, you've washed yourself more than any man alive. Do it before you come home."

She turned and left.

She didn't cry again.

Chess and Nathan did keep up a good front. Gussie sensed that something was wrong, but she was not upset. After all, she had stopped being best friends with Barbara Beaufort at least three times, and they had always made up.

As far as the rest of the world was concerned, the Richardsons continued to be a wonderful family—"so close and they all enjoy one another more than any family in Standish."

Lily knew better. She bided her time. And she never mentioned the baby when Nate met her in the racetrack clubhouse. She whispered to him only the words that kept him under her spell. "Harder, Nathaniel, deeper, Nathaniel, tear me apart, Nathaniel, hurt me, Nathaniel, mark me, bruise me, destroy me."

On May 20, the income-tax law that Congress had passed the year before was declared unconstitutional by the Supreme Court. There was rejoicing throughout the American business world.

"Even Henry is jubilant," said Edith Horton, "although I can't imagine why. Every time he piles up anything close to four thousand dollars, he buys more horses and builds a luxury place for them to live. In the meantime, I keep buying more buckets to put under the leaks in the roof when it rains."

She peered at Chess. "You don't look like you're celebrating any."

Chess shook her head. "I read some awfully sad news in the paper. A friend of mine in London has been sent to prison."

"That's terrible. What for?"

"I don't know. I couldn't make any sense out of the article. It sounds like he sued somebody and when he lost the case, they sent him to prison."

"Maybe he didn't pay his lawyer."

"Maybe."

"Was he a *good* friend?"

Chess managed a laugh. "Edith, you're incorrigible. I told you a hundred times—no details and no names. But, in this case, no, it wasn't my lover, just someone I liked a lot. He's a writer named Oscar Wilde."

"The Dorian Gray man? I can't believe it. He's famous. He'd certainly be able to get a good lawyer, and pay him, too."

"Oh, well, there's nothing I can do about it. Let's talk about something cheerful. Have your roses started blooming yet?"

Edith rolled her eyes. "You've got to come over next week. My Gloire de Dijon is covered with buds, and the Rose of York has already got four fantastic open ones. . . ." She continued for a long time.

Chess made the right noises, but she couldn't get Oscar off her mind.

She asked several of the English women if they knew anything about it, and obviously they did, but they wouldn't say what it was that they knew, only that it was too disgusting to talk about.

She couldn't, or wouldn't, ask Nathan. Their conversations were carefully engineered by both of them to say nothing real at all.

Finally James Dike educated her. "Isn't it terrible about Oscar Wilde?" he said when she went into his shop.

Chess complained about her ignorance. James sat her down and told her the whole sad, sordid story. Oscar had fallen under the spell of a lover, and when the lover's father insulted Oscar publicly, the lover was insulted by implication. So Oscar sued the father for slander.

As a defense, the father proved that his allegations were true.

And thereby proved that Oscar had broken the law. Hence the arrest, conviction, and prison sentence.

"I still don't understand, James. I thought only Bible law applied to love affairs, unless a divorce is involved."

"Chess, Oscar was guilty of sodomy. His lover was another man, the son of the Marquess of Queensberry."

She was curious. What was sodomy, exactly? James explained, his eyes averted.

"And they've put Oscar in jail? But they've no right. Whatever he did was his private business. He didn't hurt anybody. Did he force himself on the other man?"

"Not at all. It seems the other man was proud of it. He wrote a poem that said 'I am the love that dare not speak its name.' "

"Poor Oscar. Is there anything anybody can do?"

"Nothing. His friends warned him not to sue. They offered to get him out of England when he lost the lawsuit. He wouldn't listen. He let his lover destroy him."

Chess thought of Nathan, of herself, if Randall had asked her to stay with him. She might have given up her marriage, maybe even Gussie, so totally was she possessed by him.

"Love is a fearful thing sometimes," she murmured.

"Amen to that," James said fervently.

For the first time Chess wondered about James' love life. She'd always believed he had none, because he was never seen with a girl. Now, with her new knowledge, she wondered if he had a male lover. Obviously, it had to be dangerous if he did. Poor James, then, as well as poor Oscar. It was wrong to have laws that hurt people who were doing nothing to hurt anyone else.

"Why are there laws like that, James?"

"The world punishes anyone who is different," he said with a weight of wisdom in his voice.

"Will you come to dinner Sunday, James? I've decided to stop suffering through any more meals at Nathan's mother's house."

Chess wrote a long affectionate letter to Oscar. She never heard from him, or knew whether he had received her letter.

Days and weeks and months passed, slowly and silently blurring hurts and history. When Chess and Nate went to the State Fair in Raleigh that October, a New York theatrical company was presenting a dramatization of *Trilby* at the Raleigh Opera House. They went to the play, enjoyed it, talked about it afterwards over supper at their hotel. Chess was able to talk about meeting George du Maurier at Oscar's house without getting upset about Oscar's tragedy. And she was comfortable with Nathan. Almost as much as in the time before Lily.

She believed that Randall Standish, too, had lost his power to make her miserable. He was my Svengali, she told herself, and he didn't even turn me into a great singer. She quoted herself to Edith, and they laughed together. It helped.

*   *   *

On November 7, the Vanderbilts again gladdened the hearts of the whole world by providing a spectacle that was reported for days in newspapers and magazines. Chess grabbed each new issue as soon as it was delivered. The weather was filthy—cold, constant rain and wind. It was luxurious to settle down near the fire with the paisley shawl protecting her from drafts and turn the pages, wallowing in the various stories.

Most were fulsome in their descriptions of the marriage of Consuelo Vanderbilt to the Duke of Marlborough. They talked about the eighteen-year-old bride's beauty and the Duke's noble lineage and the glories of his fantastic family home, Blenheim Castle.

Others were mean. They focused on the scandal of the recent divorce between the bride's parents and the undistinguished appearance and personal history of the bridegroom.

Some were positively nasty; they listed the details of the marriage contract, which put two and a half million dollars into trust for Marlborough, with the income to be paid to him for life, plus allowances of $100,000 a year to him and to his bride.

The *New York World* had a page with pictures of England's twenty-seven dukes. Unmarried ones of any age were circled. ATTENTION, AMERICAN HEIRESSES, blared the headline. WHAT WILL YOU BID?

For Chess, the most delightful accounts were the ones of the wedding itself. It had been so marvelously Vanderbiltish. Too much of everything. Each publication offered more details; she had only to skim over what she already knew until she came across some new description of a spectacular wedding gift or laces on the young duchess' trousseau lingerie.

Three days after the marriage, the coverage began to dwindle. On that day, only four papers put the story on the front page.

BRIDE FIFTEEN MINUTES LATE TO HER OWN WEDDING, said the Richmond *Dispatch*. Chess wiggled deeper into the cushions of the chair.

... Fifty policemen to hold back the crowd of two thousand outside the mansion ... three hundred policemen needed to control the crowds outside the church ... the church interior covered with flowers from the dome to the floor ... eighty florists ... wedding gifts including pearls that had belonged to Catherine the Great of Russia ... diamond tiara ... solid gold purse set with diamonds ... belt made of diamonds ... dozens of diamond brooches ... bracelets ... pendants ... bride's gown embroidered with pearls ... six bridesmaids ... two flower girls ... carpet of rose petals ... complete orchestra of fifty instruments ... chorus of sixty voices ... cream of society in pews ... Governor of New York ... British Ambassador ... American Ambassador to the Court of Saint James ...

Her eyes stopped, backtracked, moved slowly down the narrow column of print. There it was, she had seen correctly. "... Lord Randall Standish ..."

In New York. In America.

The newspaper fell from her hands onto the floor. What time was it? Only ten after eleven. She could be in New York tonight. It wasn't that far, the trains wouldn't be held up by the rain. She wouldn't even bother to pack; that would only slow her down. He was here. In America. So close.

Her whole self—body and soul—was aching for him, urging her to satisfy the howling need to be close, to know again the wild, consuming hunger and its appeasement.

It was as if the sixteen months without him had been obliterated. She remembered everything about him as vividly as if she had left his embrace only seconds before. Her fingers felt the crisp tangle of his hair, her lips felt the soft brush of his mustache, her mouth tasted him, her nostrils were full of the odor of his body, of their lovemaking.

"Randall," Chess moaned aloud. His name bruised her lips, echoed in the incongruous serenity of the sheltering room.

Dear God, how could she bear the agony of it? He was so near, and he was not coming to her. He had not written. He had not wanted her to meet him in New York. And it was so close.

I thought I was getting over it, she thought piteously. *I thought I was forgetting. How could anything so cruel happen? Why didn't he stay in England? Why does it still hurt so much?*

Chess pulled up the shawl to cover her. But there was no warmth for the icy despair.

Behind her the door to the morning room opened. "That fire looks good," said Nate.

"Go away," Chess whispered, but he didn't hear her.

"Lord, I'm freezing. I got the chills so bad my teeth were rattling like a trap drum." Nate spread his hands before the fire. He looked at her, and they fell to his sides.

"Are you sick? There's some flu going around. Come on, let me help you upstairs."

"No, Nathan, no, I'm fine. Just let me stay quiet for a while."

Her cold hands were in his. Nathan's were burning with heat.

From the fire, she thought, but when she saw his face, she knew that wasn't so. His skin was pasty white, the freckles stark contrast. Chess made herself stand. She pulled a hand from Nate's grasp and felt his forehead. It was hot with fever.

"You're the one with the flu, Nathan. I'll help you upstairs."

Forgive me, God, I'm glad. I'll have something I have to think about now, something else, she said to herself.

Chapter Forty-Two

THE NEXT WEEKS, Chess was in a perpetual panic of superstition. Even Nate's rugged constitution was no match for the insidious strength of the disease; crisis after crisis drew him to the edge of death. It's my fault, she was convinced. Nathan's going to die, and it's my fault because I was glad he got sick.

An experienced older doctor had moved to Standish with the English families. Chess was reassured by John Graham's silver hair and kind blue eyes and deep, confident voice. But even he could not quiet her fears.

"If I lose him, I don't know how I'll go on, Doctor," she wept.

"There's no cause for alarm, Mrs. Richardson. Your husband is in excellent general health. He won't allow this illness to defeat him. He is a fighter."

"Yes." She knew it was true. Nathan was a fighter. He would never admit he was beaten. Never before. Never, until recently. His lust for Lily had beaten him. He'd been losing

weight, looking bedeviled for months and months. Maybe he
didn't care anymore about fighting, about living.

And it was all her fault. Maybe she should have let him
go, divorced him, set him free to be with the woman he
loved. Heaven knew she could understand that all-powerful
compulsion, the heedless, cruel power of love.

No.

Her mind did not say it, it was her heart speaking. It would
not let Nathan go. Not to Lily.

She doesn't love him, she just wants to own him. And I
do love him. Ever since that first day, when he fell in the
river and laughed at his pants legs shrinking up, I have loved
Nathan.

Not always the same way. People change over fifteen years'
time. The world changes, too.

I love Nathan, though, all the same. She cannot have him.
I will fight her, and him, too, if I have to.

When he gets well. Please, God, help him get well.

It took nearly three weeks, but Nate fought and he won.
He was thin, Chess was shocked by how much he'd aged.
He was thirty-eight now; she shouldn't have been shocked
that he had lost the look of eternal boyhood. Nevertheless,
she was.

Every morning and every afternoon she carried a case of
paperwork to his room so that he could catch up on what had
happened while he'd been ill. The company managers all
wanted to talk to him themselves, but Chess wouldn't allow
them access. Their protests were unimpressive; all of them
had already learned that Mrs. Richardson was a formidable
businesswoman. During Nate's illness she had insisted on
daily reports on every aspect of every business branch, and
she had made any necessary decisions without hesitation.

Now she reported everything to Nathan. It eased his restless-
ness to know things were under control.

She went through the personal news and correspondence,
too. She even told him about Lily and Gideon's successful

fund-raising raffle for the furniture needed in the new Sunday School building.

Gussie's school play received more emphasis. She had been chosen to be Melchior, one of the Three Wise Men, and would be singing a solo verse of "We Three Kings of Orient Are." She wanted a pair of gold earrings and pierced ears for the occasion. After due deliberation Nathan reluctantly agreed. He did not like to admit that his little girl was growing up.

"I sent regrets on these," Chess said, handing him a stack of invitations, "and I accepted these, with a note saying that it depended on whether Dr. Graham gave you leave."

"Wait a minute," Nate said. "I want to go to this one. Write again and tell them we're coming."

Chess took the invitation from his hand. George Vanderbilt requested their presence at a post-Christmas house party to officially open his new house near Asheville.

"That's too long a trip in wintertime, Nathan, and too long a party. It'll be six days by the time you allow a day to get there and a day to get back."

"I want to go anyhow. All those machines of his will be hooked up, now the house is open." He looked like a weak, recently ill, stubborn boy. Youthful excitement had returned to his pallid face.

There was nothing for Chess to do but agree.

When the invitation arrived, she thought, inevitably and instantly, about Randall. Had he not been a guest at the Vanderbilt wedding? Perhaps he would be a guest at the Vanderbilt housewarming. Despite her constant worry about Nathan, her heart had leapt. But then she remembered the newspaper reports. Because of the divorce, none of the Vanderbilts associated in any way with Consuelo's mother. The entire family had arranged to be out of town for the week in which the wedding took place. George Vanderbilt had no connection to Lord Randall Standish.

The invitation on top of the "accepted" pile was for the December 18th wedding of Miss Eliza Morehead Carr to Henry Corwin Flower, Esq. It was a real plum, this invitation, much more so than the one to the opening of Tower Bridge, because Jule Carr, the bride's father, owned the Bull. And in North Carolina, despite Nate's international success, and Buck Duke's shenanigans in New York, and Dick Reynolds empire-building in Winston, the Bull was still king. If the wind was blowing from that direction, its bellows could be heard faintly in Standish.

Chess joined the other privileged ladies who were invited to come the week before to view the bride's lavish trousseau. It had been made in Paris, where Mrs. Carr and Lida—Eliza's nickname—had spent the summer.

The wedding gifts were on display, too. Chess and Nate's silver candelabra from Tiffany looked very impressive, she thought, but she had to admit that the star of the show was the antique Windsor chair sent by Adlai Stevenson, the Vice President of the United States.

The wedding ceremony and the reception took place at the Carr's big, turreted house, Somerset Villa, now five years old, but still the showplace of Durham. Ol' Jule had spent a fortune on it. The stained-glass windows alone cost $6,000.

He spared no expense on the wedding, either. A decorator came down from Philadelphia to arrange the electric lights in the grounds and the flowers inside. Also from Philadelphia was the caterer, who brought his own chefs and staff and two boxcars of imported delicacies for the wedding supper.

"I thought they'd never leave," Nate muttered to Chess when the newlyweds departed at two A.M. for their honeymoon trip. "The guests could go home, once the shower of rice and rose petals was thrown."

"Stop grumping," Chess told him. She had been making mental notes from the moment the invitation arrived, because before they knew it, Gussie would be a young lady, and after that, a bride.

Spring, Chess decided, would be a much better season than winter. She'd plant dozens and dozens of azaleas next year, then they would be perfect seven or eight years later for the wedding.

"I can practically hear the wheels turning in your head," said Nate. "What are you scheming?"

"Just gardening," said Chess, "just gardening."

The S & D locomotive hauled Nate's private car to Durham and parked it on a siding. A Vanderbilt train from New York attached it to the five private cars it already had and carried it to Asheville, then onto the spur track to Biltmore, the name of George Vanderbilt's house. At the tiny brick station all the passengers got down and were met by footmen who directed them to waiting carriages.

"This is nice," said Chess, tucking the fur lap robe over the two of them. "Foot heaters, too. Use yours, Nathan, you're still recovering from the flu, you know."

"Hogwash. Quit treating me like a cripple."

"Umm, the mountain air tastes like ice water. Isn't this gorgeous?" For the last hour, as the train wound upward into the mountains, they had been surrounded by a landscape of untouched expanses of fresh snow, punctuated by the tall jagged green exclamation points of pine trees with patches of sparkling white on their boughs. It was afternoon, and now the sinking sun was beginning to tint the snow the color of tea roses.

"A fantastic piece of engineering," Nate said in agreement. "Just wait till you see the masonry blocks and the way they fit together. The cranes were as tall as a church steeple." The light gave his skin a healthy-looking color. Or it might have been natural. He was leaning forward, wanting to get to the house and its wonders.

With two carriages ahead of them and three behind, they passed through the arched passageway that pierced the gate lodge and began the three-mile drive up to Biltmore.

"Imagine the work it takes to keep this road clear," Chess said. She was beginning to understand the meaning of "Vanderbilt."

"There's likely a shortcut in snow time," said Nathan.

If there was, Chess couldn't see it. It was purple near-dark when all the carriages came to a halt on a broad gravel area swept free of snow. Below, to their right, the peaked roofline of a French château made a mountainous zigzag line against the sky. Below it, hundreds of lighted windows beckoned a welcome. It makes Buckingham Palace look like an outbuilding, Chess thought.

"My goodness," she whispered aloud. She had never seen anything so impressive in her life. It seemed impossible that such a fantasy could be real. It had to be an illusion. Or the result of sorcery.

At a signal from the lead coachman, the carriages proceeded along the drive to the monumental tower-topped entrance. It seemed to grow and grow as they approached.

The giant front door opened when carriage wheels sounded on the gravel forecourt, and a path of light cut through the darkness. Chess looked at the huge opening and felt very small. A little bit frightened, too. Giants might live here. "His power plant must be bigger than the one for all of Standish," said Nathan, and the prosaic appreciation erased Chess' fancifulness. Suddenly she was wildly curious to see the inside. Alice in Wonderland couldn't possibly have been any stranger than this.

Chapter Forty-Three

EVERYTHING WAS HUGE. The entrance hall was larger than the ballroom at Harefields. Now that they were all under their host's roof, the guests from the other five carriages began to talk with Chess and Nate and one another; self-introductions were made all around. Three of the other couples were from New York, two from Pennsylvania.

There were children, too, six of them, all seemingly in their teens, but they were not introduced. A waiting maid and manservant whisked them off at once, into an elevator twice the size of the impressive "ascending room" at the Savoy.

The New Yorkers were already acquainted. So were the Philadelphians. They formed into two groups within minutes, leaving Chess and Nathan on their own. Until George Vanderbilt appeared. He was a thin and aesthetic-looking young man, only thirty-three. Pale of skin and very dark-haired with a rather thick mustache, he reminded Chess at first of Randall Standish. Then she recognized why. It wasn't so much a physical resemblance as the elegance that both of them displayed without trying.

Her thoughts of Randall made Chess uneasy with Vanderbilt initially. But soon she realized that the owner of this incredible intimidating castle was really quite shy, and she warmed to him.

She liked him even more when, after greeting his guests with a willed effort at warmth, he clasped Nathan's hand firmly and smiled broadly. "I am so glad you were able to come after all, Nate," he said, and he wasn't shy at all. "It's splendid. The boilers and the electric plant have been waiting for you."

Chess smiled. Boys and their toys, she thought.

A retinue of uniformed servants escorted them all to their rooms. Their clothes had already been unpacked and put away. "I knew there had to be a shortcut," said Nate. "They must have unloaded the cars and carried the luggage up here before we were a half mile along the scenic route."

The guest room assigned to Chess was oval in shape and red in color. It had bright white woodwork with classically carved trim and large panels of red damask on the walls. The furniture was covered in red damask as well. The bed was made of wood in an elaborate pattern of veneers and had a curved half-canopy with red swags and draperies. A sofa and chaise longue were gilt, and a round gilt-trimmed table with four gilt chairs centered the room. A bright fire burned in a wide fireplace.

It was lovely, Chess thought, even though it was too fancy for her taste. She dropped her coat and hat on the chaise then examined the details. Plenty of drawer space. Good reading lights. An adjoining bathroom. Chess was amazed that it was so austere. All the necessities were provided, and there was lots of room. But it had no marble tiling, like the bathroom at Harefields, and only one mirror, above the washbasin. No vanity table at all.

Nate offered an explanation. "George is a bachelor, and

his architect was a man. We men need mirrors to shave by, not for doing fancy things to our hair."

That made sense, Chess agreed. If you were a man. Nathan's bedroom was on the other side of the bathroom, with a connecting door. She noticed that there were no looking glasses at all in his room, but lots of leather upholstery on chairs and ottomans. The bed looked as if its mattress was hard.

She returned to her red damask luxury and sat on the sofa to read the leather-bound booklet that was on the table.

It contained information for guests. As she expected, a maid had been assigned to every lady who did not bring her own with her. There was a bell-pull to summon her. Laundry would be collected . . . returned . . . horses available for riding . . . bathing costumes for the heated swimming pool in the basement . . . bowling . . . billiards . . .

It sounded exciting. She had never seen a swimming pool or a bowling alley.

A loose sheet had been inserted in the front of the booklet. It announced a change in schedule for this day alone, because it was December 31st. There would be dancing in the entry hall, beginning at ten, followed by supper in the banquet hall at one A.M. From seven to ten a buffet service would offer a light meal in the second-floor Living Hall and in the ground-floor Tapestry Gallery.

Fine, Chess thought, provided we can find any of those rooms. She felt as if she could do with a ball of string to unwind as she walked through the enormous house. Otherwise, she'd never find the bedroom again.

"Where are you going, Nathan?"

"To find the boiler room. I'll be back in time to put on my dress-up suit."

"Please don't fall in the fiery furnace, and don't overdo, I beg you. All the machines will be there tomorrow, too, you know."

Chess looked at the gilt clock above the mantelpiece. Only just five. Thank goodness she'd brought something to read.

She was dying to explore, but it would have to wait for daylight.

She rang for her maid, to give instructions about her needs and to ask questions about this place and its people.

"George Vanderbilt is not even engaged," she informed Nathan when he came in. "Too bad Gussie's not a little older; I could try my hand at matchmaking."

Nathan grinned. "You'd be at the end of a long line. The poor devil practically has to beat the matchmaking mommas off with a stick. His own sisters invited some likely candidates to come visit. The place is crawling with women."

"You amaze me, Nathan. How did you find out so much when you were in the furnace room?"

"Servants know everything; you've told me that a thousand times. The basement is a lively place. I had a cup of coffee and some chicken pie in the staff dining room down there. You'll have to see it, and the kitchens, and the laundry rooms. They're bigger than the ones in a hotel. Have to be, I reckon. There are eighty servants."

"Eighty?"

"That's for the house. There's another couple of hundred for the stables and the dairy and the grounds and gardens. George grows just about everything he eats. We had hot-house grapes downstairs."

"Well, I wish you had brought me something. I'm hungry."

"There's plenty to eat just down the hall. They're starting to set up for the buffet. Come on, I'll show you."

The second-floor Living Hall was indeed just a few steps away. It was at the top of the monumental circular marble staircase, past four tall columns that formed entrance arches. Male and female servants were busy at work, arranging big silver covered serving dishes above spirit lamps. Platters and bowls of cold food were already placed, together with stacks of plates and ranks of goblets and silverware.

A great expanse of parquet floor was dotted with Oriental rugs. In any normal setting, one of the rugs would have filled the room. Here they performed as rooms within the room. Groups of chairs, tables, sofas sat on each rug.

So big. Everything was so big. Chess walked across to one of the tall windows and separated the closed velvet curtains with her fingers. If she could see sky and stars, perhaps the space she was in would feel smaller, more manageable.

Instead of sky, she saw light. The window overlooked the glass roof of an indoor garden room. It was fascinating. She could look down on people, some of them walking around, others sitting on chairs and benches amid palm trees, and still others standing in groups and talking. It was rather like being at the theater, looking at a brightly lit stage. Without sound. She could not hear what the moving lips were saying, nor the footsteps and rustle of skirts.

She saw George Vanderbilt, his back turned to her. He was facing a semicircle of women, all of them young, all of them laughing at something he had just said.

Poor George, Chess thought. Nathan was right; the man must be bedeviled by marriageable spinsters all the time.

The food smelled enticing. Chess started to turn away from the window. Then her hands tightened on the curtains. That was not George Vanderbilt down there. The back was Randall's back, the top of the dark head was Randall's. She knew it. She couldn't have said why she was so certain, she didn't have to. She knew, and she held tight to the heavy curtains to keep steady. Her blood was racing. She was giddy.

With what? Happiness? Fear? Love? Desire? All of them, and more.

"May I fill a plate for you, Madam?" One of the footmen was at her elbow.

Chess took a shuddering breath. "Yes, please," she said. "But first, will you help me to a seat. I'm a bit lightheaded. It must be the mountain altitude."

She had to compose herself. Maybe, after she could breathe again, she'd be able to think. To believe what she had seen.

* * *

Chess bent close to study her face in the large looking glass above the mantelpiece. It wasn't fair. Men could grow mustaches to hide the ugly lines from nostrils to the corners of the mouth, and beards to cover the little pouches of flesh along the jaw. Women wore their age for the world to see. Forty-five. Was this what forty-five looked like? She might look sixty, for all she knew. It wasn't something she thought about. When a woman has always been plain, she doesn't spend much time looking in mirrors.

Her hands were still pretty, weren't they? The veins showed, but they didn't stand up above the skin the way they did on very old hands.

And her hair was shinier than ever, as silver replaced the pale gold. Nonetheless, it was definitely silver, and almost half now, not simply odd strands mixed in.

I'm old, and I'm ugly, and I wish to God I'd never looked to see it. I should have exchanged rooms with Nathan. His has no mirror.

Those women Randall was charming were young. The whole world is teeming with young women and young girls.

It's been a year and a half. He probably doesn't even remember me. Why didn't I run downstairs to him at once, the way I wanted to? Why did I delude myself into supposing that I could dress up and look pretty to him?

I wonder if he knows I'm here?

There should be a list of all the guests' names in each bedroom, like the list of passengers the ships give you. This castle is like a tremendous ship, all lit up in the darkness with the mountains all around, like the sea.

"Shall I brush your hair, Madam?" the maid asked.

"No. Thank you. I can do it." Chess pulled the brush brutally through her long, heavy tresses, then formed them expertly into a thick psyche knot from the top of her head to the nape of her neck. Long steel hairpins went snugly into the places they were accustomed to.

She slid the embroidered silk combing coat off, into the

maid's waiting hands. Then she stood. Her skin was as white as the white silk of her corset cover and drawers. Her black silk stockings made shadows through the white silk. She stepped into the circle of black lace-trimmed silk on the floor and stood still while the maid pulled the petticoat up and fastened it around her laced-in waist.

Her ballgown was spread out on top of the bed. She had never worn it before. It was the one she'd had made for the Duchess of Devonshire's ball. It was the most beautiful dress she had ever owned. Or ever seen, to her way of thinking.

"Just a minute," Chess said to the maid. She'd remembered a trick Edith Horton had taught her. She wet two fingers in her mouth and bent by the chimney to cover them with black ashes. Then, very carefully, she blinked her eyelashes against the soot until they were blackened. The mirror above the mantel showed her startlingly pale silver eyes emphasized by a dark line. Chess bit her lips until they were a deep rose color.

"Now," she said, holding out her arms. The gown floated down over her head and body and settled into place around her. The maid breathed a sigh of admiration, then fastened the hooks up the back with quick, practiced fingers. She held Chess' black silk dancing pumps out, one at a time, for her to slip into.

"You look beautiful, Madam," said the young girl.

Afraid yet hopeful, Chess walked to the far wall of the room where her whole length would be reflected in the big mirror. What she saw took her breath away. Luther Witsell was truly an artist. He had made a midnight garden.

The gown was black, a stiff silk organza that looked like gathered shadows. It had the huge balloon sleeves required by fashion. They seemed suspended from the outer limit of Chess' shoulders, and their darkness made her white skin look like moonlight.

The neckline was a graceful curve, like the edge of the moon. It bared her moon white skin but modestly covered the whole curve of her small breasts. The bodice of the gown

was embroidered with scallops, like the curve of the neckline.
Each scallop was re-embroidered with tiny faceted beads of
polished jet.

The same jet made wider scallops on the silk brocade that
showed in a front panel of the skirt. The brocade was a pattern
of gold leaves outlined on a silver background.

Black organza framed the sides of the panel in jet-edged
scallops and formed the layers of wide floating skirts, pleated
in the center of the back to create a train-like fullness.

Because Luther was an artist, he had painted the gossamer
skirts in lieu of adding heavy embroidery. Delicately brushed
strokes of gilt paint made sinuous curving vines. To them he
had attached chiffon leaves painted gold and silver. The paint
stiffened them without weighting them, and they moved gently
as if touched by a breeze whenever Chess moved.

More gleaming chiffon leaves were imprisoned inside the
ballooning sleeves, discreetly shadowed by the organza.

Her silver and gold hair looked like light, her darkly outlined pale eyes were shining stars.

Chess fastened a wide band of black jet leaves around the
column of her white throat and tucked a spray of the same
leaves beside the knot of hair.

Her hand trembled when she dipped a perfume bottle's
glass wand again and again into the flowery scent that had
been part also of the soaps Randall had given her. She touched
the wand to her hair, her ears, her neck, her bared shoulders.

Then she slid her hands into the powdered, folded open
white gloves held by the maid and smoothed them over her
fingers and up her arms to the bottoms of the sleeves. The
maid buttoned the little pearls at the wrists, then presented to
Chess her large black lace fan.

Chess could hear the music beginning below. She thanked
the young maid, who curtseyed, and she went to the dance.

Nathan was waiting for her in the second-floor living hall.
"You look mighty elegant," he said.

"So do you," said she. It was true. The London tailor had
done a masterful job with Nate's dress clothes.

"Lift or stairs?" said Nate in humorous tribute to their clothing.

"Stairs," Chess replied. One lesson of her young years that she could rely on was the fearless descent of a staircase with head held high and no contact with the banister. She needed the pride-filled attitude of it right now. She was terrified of the imminent meeting with Randall.

Her full skirts trailed behind and above her several steps when she walked down the broad marble steps. Shafts of moonlight slanted through the tall leaded windows of the staircase onto her luminous hair and skin.

Those people in the hall near the foot of the staircase looked up admiringly. One of them stepped forward.

Randall put one foot on the bottom step and held up his white-gloved hand to her.

"May I have this waltz, Chess?"

Chapter Forty-Four

THEY HAD NEVER DANCED TOGETHER BEFORE. Yet, it was no surprise to Chess that they waltzed in perfect unison, with total ease, as if they had been dancing together all their lives. It had to be like this, for surely she must be dreaming. This fairy-tale castle could not really exist, this marble-floored hall-ballroom could not be real, the warmth of Randall's hand on her waist must be a fantasy. Only in dreams did a heart's wishes come true.

"Hello, my love," he had said when she stepped from the stairs into his arms.

"Hello," she had said in return.

And then he had circled, circled, circled her around the room. Neither of them had spoken again. Their embrace, wrapped in music, said all that needed saying. It was right. Meant to be. Ideal.

The waltz ended, but Chess was not sad, because this was a dream, and in dreams there were infinitudes of waltzing.

"I must go speak to Nate," Randall said, and that, too, was right. She watched him go.

A man bowed to her, held out his hand. "May I?" Chess smiled and put her hand in his, and was waltzing again. His name was Fred Vanderbilt, he said. She murmured hers. And made polite noises indicating interest in whatever he was saying, although she did not hear a word.

It was a small party, only twenty-six in all, which added intimacy to the evening. Adjoining the Hall was the Winter Garden, the glass-roofed room that Chess had looked down on. Between dances or instead of dancing, people went down the steps to the flower- and palm-filled room for champagne. Chess sat out a waltz with Nathan on one of the bamboo settees, and the normality of it helped bring her down to earth.

"I do wish you would dance," she said, as she had said a hundred times in the past.

"You'd change that tune when I stepped on your foot," Nate said, as he always did.

Neither of them mentioned that good Methodists rejected dancing as sinful. They did not need to call up the specter of Miss Mary's frown.

Nate didn't feel deprived by not dancing; there were plenty of other non-dancers to talk with at any given moment, and, as always, he was interested in what they had to say. He repeated to Chess what he'd learned about their fellow guests. George's brother Fred was not yet forty and an avid yachtsman. He regarded time spent on dry land as wasted time. His wife Louise was twelve years older than he and also an avid sailor. The two young girls were sisters, from Rhode Island. George's sister Florence was offering them as possible brides for George. Their mother was a friend of hers in Newport. Her husband, Hamilton Twombly, was a quiet man, skilled in finance and Wall Street dealings. He disapproved of George's extravagance, but could do little to stem it. Extravagance was a Vanderbilt characteristic.

The entire family had come to Biltmore for Christmas the week before; it was the first time most of them had seen

George's house, and they were still stunned by it. He had out-Vanderbilted them all. Most of the family left after the holiday. Only Florence and Fred decided to stay for the New Year celebration.

George and Randall knew each other through James Whistler. George had been an admirer and friend of the expatriate American artist for many years.

"I reckon," laughed Nate, "that George is plenty glad to have Randall around to keep the husband hunters out of his hair. It sure was a surprise to see him there at the bottom of the steps like that. Made me wonder if I was really in North Carolina at all."

"I know. It all seems unreal."

"It's real enough. The place you can prove it is the basement. The dynamo makes enough noise to blow your head open."

George overheard Nate's remark. "I warned you, Nate," he said, "but you wouldn't stuff the cotton in your ears. May I abduct your wife for the reel?"

Chess went willingly. The more she learned about George Vanderbilt, the more she liked him. "Would you be interested in joining me in making up a homesick box for Jimmy Whistler?" she asked. "I plan to ship over a ten pound sack of cornmeal."

"Splendid idea," said George.

The reel was suitably noisy and energetic. As Chess whirled and marched through the patterns of the dance, she met Randall several times. Even in a country dance, in the mountains of North Carolina, he was as elegantly composed as he had been in London's drawing rooms.

"Are you having a good time?" she asked him breathlessly when he spun her around at the center of the square.

"Now, yes," he said with the smile she remembered too well. Then the dance swept them apart.

Later, waltzing again, they made a tryst. "I'm a mile away from you, in the bachelor guests' wing," Randall said. "Meet me in the library as soon as you've dressed in the morning.

I'll be waiting. I need to hold you, not like this, as dancers, but like a man and a woman away from the rest of the world."

"I won't sleep for thinking of it."

"Nor will I."

"Liar."

"Guilty."

Chess laughed. For an instant Randall's arm tightened and crushed her to him, then all was proper again. "Be early," he murmured, "or I will go mad."

Randall managed to be dancing with her again when midnight came. His kiss looked to any observer like a cousinly salute. Chess recognized the brief brushing of lips as the same kiss that was her first, so long ago now, when they picnicked on Hampstead Heath. The sweet memory made her eyes sting.

At supper she was seated between one of the men from New York and another from Philadelphia. All three of them were skilled at social conversation, and the food was excellent, so the time passed pleasantly enough. The huge table was designed to seat sixty-four. The twenty-six guests were arranged in the center, with massive arrangements of flowers and fruit filling the empty expanses at the ends. It made the party feel cozy, and the guests feel like friends.

Afterwards, Chess asked Nate to unlace her, she hated to ring for the maid at three in the morning. "I'll be glad to do it," he said, "but she's more than likely waiting for the bell, and she can't go to bed until she's done waiting on you. It'd be kinder to get her up here and then send her off."

She was ashamed that she hadn't thought of that herself. It was all too easy to forget about other people when her mind was filled with Randall. Soon. She would be with him in only a few more hours.

The library impressed Chess more than anything she had yet seen in the magnificent house. The room was very big, but not gargantuan like the banquet hall or entrance. And it had a human element the others lacked. The walls were covered with shelves, and the shelves were full of books. Chess took one in her hands and opened it.

Randall emerged from an alcove. "I did the same thing," he said, "and yes, it has been read, perhaps more than once. Young Mr. Vanderbilt rises in my estimation with every hour that passes."

He took the book away from her, put it on a table, drew her into the shadowed alcove. "My love," he growled from an emotion-clogged throat. And then his lips found hers. Their bodies pressed together, strained to get closer. Chess was on fire.

"I can't bear this," she said, "I want all of you. Where can we go before I die from the wanting?"

Randall caught her wrist in his circled fingers and pulled her behind him through doors and halls, looking quickly from side to side, hurrying, hurrying, until at last he pushed her into a deep closet lined with shelves that were piled with towels. He closed the door behind them and they were in darkness.

"Forgive me," he said, "I cannot wait." His hands moved roughly on her breasts, her waist, his mouth covered hers, he pressed her back, back until she hit the edge of the shelves. "Lift your skirts, I must have you now."

She was as frantic as he, as desperate. In a tangle of clothes, with muffled cries of passion, they coupled standing up, clutching at the other's body to keep from falling. It was over in seconds. Then Chess began to cry, deep, shattering sobs of shame and despair. Randall held her, his fingers stroked her back. "Forgive me," he whispered again and again.

"Oh, Randall," she wept, "I do forgive you, I do. I cannot forgive myself. I was like a bitch dog in heat."

He kissed her to stop her self-damning words, and the fire was rekindled. "No," Chess moaned, "no, I don't want it to be like this."

"Wait here," he said. "I'll find a way out."

Left alone in the dark, Chess crumpled to the floor in a heap. She despised herself. What pain, what degradation there would be for Nathan if her wantonness was discovered. He would be the object of ridicule, of pity.

When the door opened she shrank away, hiding her head beneath crossed arms.

"Shhh, my darling, it is I," said Randall. "Give me your hand. You will be all right." He led her over a tortuous route of narrow hallways and stairs to a small bathroom beneath a slanted ceiling. A tiny window looked out onto miles of snow-dappled forest.

There were combs and brushes on a shelf, hot water and a basin, towels and soap. "I'll wait for you next door," Randall said. "No one will come here, I guarantee it."

When she finished washing and tidying herself as best she could, Chess tapped on the door to the next room. Randall opened it. He looked haggard. "I shall never forgive myself," he said quietly.

"Where are we?" Chess demanded. "I told Nathan I would meet him for breakfast at nine. I have to get to that indoor garden room."

"We have to talk, Chess."

"Not now, Randall, I'm too upset. And I have to meet Nathan. How do I get there?"

He led her to the staircase. At the bottom, he said, she would see the garden straight ahead. Chess began to run.

"Happy New Year." Louise Vanderbilt greeted her in the garden room. "Happy New Year," chorused several others. "Happy New Year," Chess responded.

The palm trees and tropical flowers were luxuriant in the sunlight that poured down through the glass roof. It felt like a benison of warmth on Chess' head and shoulders. She had not realized how cold she felt.

After breakfast there was a great hubbub of excitement. George had a half dozen colorful sleighs on display in an uncleared area behind the stables. Those who wanted a morning in the real mountains were invited to ride to Buckspring Lodge, his hunting cabin on Mount Pisgah, the highest peak on the nearby ridge. The route was called the "Shut-In" trail because it wound through thick forest, and the distance was seventeen miles, more than an hour going because it was uphill, and a hair-raising half hour returning, downhill.

Nate and Chess found the prospect irresistible. So did the Rhode Island girls, when they heard that George and Randall were going to go. Florence Twombly felt obliged to accompany the girls as chaperone.

After much wasted time, two sleighs finally set off. "Poor George," said Nate, looking at the first sleigh. His sister had bullied George into accompanying her and the two girls.

Randall and Nate, with Chess between them, were cradled comfortably in the second sleigh. The driver cracked his whip, and the matched pair of horses tossed their heads, then began to pull. Bells on their harnesses made a merry accompaniment.

Chess was all too aware of Randall's thigh and leg next to hers beneath the fur lap robe. She longed to run her hand along them. Instead she concentrated on the music of the bells, the squeak of runners on the snow, the beauty of the cold, bright winter day.

She'd never been in a sleigh before. The smooth glide was so different from a jolting carriage or even the rhythmic rocking of a train. It reminded her of something, but she couldn't think what. She knew only that it was excitingly strange.

So was the deep snow. Farther east, in Standish and Durham, they got snow, but it was usually only a few inches, and it melted within days. This white landscape was unreadable, there were no man-made structures to measure how deep it was: up to the step, up to the porch, up to the windowsill. It was unfathomable. Mysterious.

Ahead of them the white trail showed the thin line of runners, the blurred indentations of horses' hooves. Civilization's mark on wilderness. Chess wished that their sleigh had gone first. It would be so beautiful to look ahead and see only unbroken white.

She remembered now what the sleigh's smooth sliding reminded her of. Canoeing on the James. Skimming the surface of the unknowable depths. But, with a river, there were no marks of earlier passages. Every canoe might be the first, every journey a mapless venture.

"Bear," said Nate quietly. "To the left, in the trees."

Chess turned her head quickly, but she spied no dark form or movement. "I missed it," she said with regret.

Randall's laugh sounded strained. "By the time I recount this little adventure, the bear will have become ten feet tall and directly in our path. People do enjoy regarding America as a vast perilous land."

"I figure my chances are better with a bear in the trees than the traffic on the Strand," Nate said with a chuckle. "I always tried to find a great big fellow and dog his steps getting across the street. Reckoned the wheels could bounce off him before they got to me."

George Vanderbilt's hunting lodge was not the log cabin Chess had imagined. It was four log houses, one of them a huge dining room. Hot coffee, chilled melons, and a full array of breakfast dishes were waiting for them on tables near a wide fireplace with blazing, crackling logs almost the size of small trees. Chess carried a cup of coffee out onto the deep-roofed porch and looked at the range of mountains that stretched to the horizon. It was breathtakingly beautiful.

"This must be what an eagle sees when it flies," she said to Nate when he came up behind her.

But it was Randall, not Nathan. "My darling," he said in a low voice, "it is impossible to find any opportunity to be alone. And there is so little time before I must leave. Can you get away this afternoon? Will you meet me on the terrace outside the library? It's sheltered enough, and we can talk at least."

"Of course," Chess said without turning around. She was afraid to. He was so near. If she saw his face, she would lose herself in his goldbrown eyes, lose all control. "Go back inside, Svengali," she said, and she tried to laugh. "Or I might start peeling off my clothes and freeze to death."

She heard his footsteps and the closing door. The mountain vista had lost its power to soothe her troubled spirit.

The return to Biltmore was fast and thrilling. The horses had to race to avoid being overtaken by the plunging descent of the sleigh. Chess shrieked with excitement, Nathan bellowed encouragement to the driver, Randall's body was thrown against hers by the sharply curving trail. It was more dangerously exciting than the precipitous ride.

Chapter Forty-Five

CHESS COULDN'T FACE THE FIVE COURSES of food and conversation at the big table in the Banquet Hall. She felt as if electricity ran in her veins instead of blood, as if her skin was too tight, as if she would begin to twitch all over if she couldn't have a little time alone, a little peace.

"All that fresh mountain air got to me," she said to Nathan, "and there was that big breakfast at the Lodge, after the big breakfast here. Will you make my excuses for me? I'm going to have a nap."

"I'll pull the curtains, then. Get a good sleep. I want to try out that bowling alley after supper."

She hoped the question would sound casual. "What are you doing this afternoon, Nathan?"

"I'm headed over to Asheville. If George hasn't run up the price of mountains too high, I might be interested in buying some land."

"Nathan Richardson! I don't want to live like this. You can have all the boilers and dynamos you want in Standish."

Nate shook his head; he smiled at her alarm. "Calm down. I ain't no Vanderbilt and no prospects of being one. Or wishes, either. No, I was figuring that scatter of log-cabin lodges was real nice up there on top of the world. One of them would make a good little house for us in July and August when Standish turns to baked dust. Like the Wilsons have. Gussie got a big kick out of that time she visited them up here."

It was true. And August could be close to unbearable in the Piedmont.

Most important, he'd be gone all afternoon.

"I think that would be wonderful," Chess said.

She did actually try to sleep some. But she could not relax. Everything was wrong, and she was horribly confused.

I should be happy. I'll be with Randall soon. I know him; he'll have found us a safe place to be together, a real place for love, not some kennel of a closet. It will be like London again, the most perfect time in my life, with the whole world shut out and his arms holding me, and mine holding him.

Chess stretched luxuriously, remembering.

But her nerves knotted her muscles, and the stretching could only be half done.

I need to be with him, I need to be made love to, that's what's wrong with me. I want Randall.

She couldn't rest. She couldn't wait. She decided to go down to the rendezvous now. Even though Randall wouldn't be there, she would be in the place where soon he would be, and that would give the terrace a magic that she had to feel. Now.

The library, thank heavens, was empty. Save for the books, and books had always been her friends. She let her eyes move lovingly over the shelves as she walked with quiet careful steps to the tall french door that opened onto the terrace.

The cold air stole her breath. Chess pulled her thick cape closely around her. She had dressed to be warm out of doors, unwilling to let discomfort distract her from every precious instant with Randall.

The terrace was, like everything, oversized. It was made

of stone and sheltered by a vine-covered pergola. In winter, the vines were bare, and the sun had warmed the stones all day, so that they radiated a welcome heat. Chess relaxed her grip on the edge of her cape and lifted her face to the high blue sky and slanting rays of sunlight.

"You look like a priestess of Helios."

"Then you must be Apollo." She turned. Her eyes and Randall's met, speaking without words.

Chess' heart rejoiced, because there was something new, different in Randall's intense gaze. A hundred times or more they had looked at each other like this, and always the message had been "I want you." That was in his eyes now, and she felt herself respond as she had always done, wanting him. The other, the new, deeper, richer message was the one she had searched unavailingly to find.

He spoke it aloud. "I love you, Chess."

She trembled. "I love you, Randall."

They did not move toward each other, they did not touch. The words, and the message in their eyes, created an embrace more enfolding than any lovemaking between bodies.

It bound them for long moments, then Randall spoke. "When will you come to me?"

Chess tilted her head. "What do you mean? Is there a room?"

Randall smiled. "Greedy. I, too. Later. But now we must make our plans. How soon can you come to London?"

"I can't, Randall. I can't simply pick up and go to London for no logical reason. What would I tell Nathan?"

"My darling, you haven't understood a thing I've said. I love you, Chess. I never believed it would happen to me, but it did. I fell irrevocably in love with you. I realized it after you were gone, and I found myself looking for you on every street, listening for your laughter in every crowd. I want you for my wife. How long will it take for you to arrange the divorce?"

She was stunned. So many times she had yearned to hear "I love you" on Randall's lips. She had never thought of anything more than that. "I love you" from him was the unattainable dream. Chess wanted to hear the words a hundred times, hold them in her heart. She wanted to feel the rapture of hearing them now, not think about what might follow.

"Randall," she said, pleading. "I can't think. My mind can't take this in."

"I understand. I have been thinking for months; you need a few moments to catch up. Just tell me that you love me and will marry me. That is the first step. We'll work out the rest together."

"I love you. I do. I love you, Randall." Chess shook her head, as if to clear the confusion in it. "I don't see how I could possibly marry you, though."

Randall went to her, touched her brow with his fingers. "Erase this worried little frown." His smile was full of loving indulgence. "We'll find you a good solicitor—I mean lawyer—in America. He will know what to do. Don't worry about it." Randall's arm went around her shoulders, supporting and encouraging.

His fingers had not erased her frown. It was caused by thought, not by worry. Chess was trying to sort through the myriad disjointed thoughts careening inside her head.

"I don't know if I could live in England," she said, speaking one of them aloud so that she could examine it.

Randall laughed. "But you did, and you were a great success, and you loved it. You belong there, Chess, not here. You are a Standish, after all, not a barbarian. England is your real home now. Your Confederacy is gone." He held her closer. "And you will be with me."

Chess' gaze had been fixed on the mountains, but she found no clarification there. She turned away from the majestic view and looked into Randall's face. "I don't want to think," she said, her words hurried with urgency. "I want to feel. I want you to hold me, to make love to me. Now, Randall, I want you now."

"Yes. We'll talk later. It's all arranged. Take the lift, as if you were going to your room. Stop at the second floor, as if you were getting out, then continue to the third. I will be up there. I'll go first, by the service stair. Wait two minutes after I leave, then follow."

"Randall. Kiss me."

"Up in the room, my love. There are windows overlooking this terrace."

As soon as his hands moved across her skin, there was no need to think. She had not magnified anything in memory, there really was enchantment and ecstasy in Randall's arms. Sensation swept her to the sun, leaving the world and all its concerns far behind and forgotten. Chess loved and was loved, and nothing else mattered.

In the bliss-soaked semi-oblivion that followed, she rested her head on his broad chest and stroked the firm flesh of his muscular arm, her fingers alive to the masculine toughness of his skin. Her thoughts were lazy now, not jangled; they offered no threat.

"Randall, what do you do?" she murmured.

" 'Do?' What do you mean?"

"I wondered. What do you do? What is your life like?"

"But you already know. I collect art in a small way. I read. I go to the theater. I see my friends. I stop in at my clubs. I spend the Season in London. I stay with friends in the country for hunting. I go to the Continent occasionally."

He picked up her hand and moved it to his thigh. "Mmm, that is exceedingly nice. Use the tips of your fingernails. . . . Naturally, after we are married, we shall be expected to entertain. A bachelor has no such responsibilities. We can buy a country place with some shooting and lease a London house for the season, or the reverse, whichever you prefer. A great deal depends on the size of your settlement from your husband."

Chess' stroking stopped. She sat up. "What settlement from my husband?"

Randall pulled her back, close to him. "You will divorce him of course; these things are always managed that way.

And you'll be awarded a settlement. I dare say Nate will be more than generous; after all, he loves you. We'll buy a house and some good horses. . . ."

Chess wriggled free. She twisted, sat up on her knees, looking down at him. "You must be crazy, Randall. Do you think I'm Consuelo Vanderbilt? Just what price have you put on this marriage?"

His eyes had no affectionate indulgence in them now. "Stop being dramatic, Chess. Act your age. It takes money to live well. Only in lower-class lending library novels do men and women live on love. People in our position have certain standards to meet, or Society ignores them."

Chess looked at the handsome man who had dominated her mind and her heart for so long. She knew every inch of his strong, lithe body, every crisp curl on his head; his face was more familiar to her than her own because she had feasted her eyes on it, and the memory of it, for thousands of hours.

And yet, she saw a stranger. She knew almost nothing of his mind and his heart.

"Randall, I have to go," she said. "Nathan may come back at any minute."

He lifted his shoulders, rested on his left elbow. His right hand caressed her knees, slid to the soft, sensitive skin inside her thighs. "Stay a bit longer. You can find something to tell him."

Her back arched voluptuously, independent of her will, offering her breasts to his mouth and hands. Her body clamored for his, poured forth warm readiness.

"No," she gasped, "no, not now." She fought her own urgings, got up from the bed and stumbled into the bathroom. After she closed the door, Chess leaned against it; she felt weak.

Something deep within her, something she could not name, gave her strength to leave. And later, in her room, after the bodily weakness passed, she was able to think as well as feel.

"I love you," she had said to Randall. "I love him," she had said to herself a thousand times. How could she have been so sure that she loved a man who was—she knew now—a complete stranger?

No, that was unfair. Randall wasn't a stranger at all. He was exactly what he seemed to be, what he had always been. An English gentleman at the top reaches of Society, and bound by its structure.

It was childish of her to be offended by his talk about a settlement. It did not really mean that he wanted her for her money. Either of Florence Twombly's young protegées would do very well if Randall chose money as a reason to marry.

He did love her. Her. With lines in her face and gray in her hair.

It was cause for wonderment.

Why, then, wasn't she wild with happiness? This was what she had dreamed about, what she wanted more than anything in the world. Wasn't it? To be loved by Randall, and to love him. To make love. That's what they had done together, they had made love. They had not loved.

Love was different. It couldn't be shut up, away from the world, behind a closed bedroom door. Love was riskier than that, more exciting, love was living, learning, sharing. It was two people together making the first tracks on the unbroken snow of adventure that every new day offered.

Love was Nathan. It had been, ever since that first day when both of them had taken a great gamble on the future. Nathan—and life with Nathan—was everything she had ever wanted. Except in the bedroom.

And whose fault was that?

For a moment Chess felt all the frustration and fury that had accumulated during the fifteen years of her marriage. Nathan had not wanted her; he had made her feel like a failure; he had made her feel ugly and undesirable.

Then she began to laugh. Because she knew now that she could be desirable. And she knew also how simple it was for a man and a woman to "pleasure" one another. She did not need to wait and hope that Nathan would teach her. She might even be able to teach him a few things.

She could hardly wait to see his reaction, hear his "Great Godalmighty, Chess!"

What fun they were going to have.

The red damask room filled with the champagne sound of her delighted, delightful laughter.

When Nathan came back from Asheville, he went to his room to dress for dinner. The door between the bathroom and Chess' bedroom was open. He started to close it, then heard her voice.

"Come in here, Nathan."

She was reading, propped up against a pile of pillows on the bed. Her hair was loose on the shoulders of her eau-de-nil silk dressing gown.

"You had a long nap," said Nate. "You should have been with me, Chess. There are four parcels of land, over by a village called Brevard. The road there ain't much, but it's right along the ridge, and you can see for miles. . . ."

"Nathan." Chess dropped the book on the floor. "Nathan, will you please pay attention."

He looked at her curiously. Something was different about her, and he didn't know what to make of it.

Chess smiled. "Nathan, do you realize that we've been married for more than fifteen years and in all that time you have never once kissed me?"

"Hogwash. I must have."

"Not once, Nathan. I want you to come over here and kiss me right now."

Women! They were strange creatures. Nate shrugged and did as she asked. His kiss was emphatic, a loud smack on her cheek.

She grabbed hold of his lapel, and he couldn't straighten up.

"Not like that," she said. "You might as well be kissing a frying pan." Her hand pulled sharply on his coat; he lost his balance and fell heavily across her, his face was smothered in the pillows.

Chess lifted his head and turned it. Then she pressed her

lips to his, lightly. She moved her mouth in a circle over his lips, her teeth nipped his lower lip, her open mouth pulled insistently against his, demanding, until his tongue reached into her mouth, searching for hers and finding it.

When she drew away at last, he was short of breath.

"Now tell me you love me," she said.

"Great Godalmighty, Chess, what's come over you? What are you doing?"

"Tell me you love me, Nathan."

"You know I do."

"I don't know any such thing, because you never said so. Say so, Nathan."

"I love you. Now are you satisfied?" Nate felt like a fool. He didn't understand what was happening. He could not believe it.

Chess laughed.

"What the devil are you laughing at? Me, I reckon. You're acting mighty peculiar, Chess, now stop it."

"Oh, no. I should have done this fifteen years ago." Her fingers were busily unbuttoning his coat, his waistcoat, his collar, his shirt. "I remember when you came to see Grandfather. You washed at the pump and your bare chest made me feel funny all over." It was bare now, Chess raked it with her fingernails, with a feather touch.

Nate captured her wrists with his fingers. "Stop that. It ain't ladylike." His face was red.

Chess' eyes were bright with mischief. "You're only a man, my love. Oh, yes, I do love you too, Nathan. But you don't know one single thing about ladies, and it's high time you learned. Let go of my hands. I'm going to unbutton your pants."

"Chess!"

Her smile was demure. "Unless you can do it fast. I want my marital rights, Nathan. I want you to make love to me. I need pleasuring. Lots and lots of pleasuring. Fifteen years' worth."

He looked at her in slack-jawed amazement. And his fingers set her hands free.

Before long, Nate took control. He made love to her slowly, with lingering attention to her responses, with tenderness that delayed and heightened each explosion of passion felt. With loving discovery of what had long lay buried between them, and ultimate fusion of soul and heart and mind and flesh.

When they were finished, he held her face between his hands and kissed her gently, once. The loving sweetness of his gentleness filled her eyes with tears of love, and he kissed them away.

A gong sounded from the hall. It was time to dress for dinner.

They smiled together. It was unnecessary to say anything aloud about the comical aptness of the timing. They were both hungry for more mundane gratifications, like food. The greater hunger was satisfied for now.

Chess smiled at herself in the looking glass. It reflected a radiantly happy woman. She would not need to say anything to Randall. He would know, by looking at her, that her life no longer had room for him.

But I will tell him "thank you," she decided. Without him, I'd never have known what I wanted from Nathan, and I'd never have had the nerve to demand it if Randall had not made me feel desirable.

"You mentioned that you wanted to try out the bowling alleys, didn't you, Nate?" George Vanderbilt was a thoughtful host.

Nate looked across the dining table at his wife. Chess would have sworn that there was a flash of blue and a loud crackling noise when their eyes met. To her, the air suddenly smelled of the sharp post-lightning chemicals of ozone, rather than the perfumed flower bouquets.

"Thanks, George, I've changed my mind," Nate drawled. "I reckon I'll turn in early tonight."

Chess smiled behind her napkin.

"Checkmate, Lily," she whispered. "You lose."

This book is a work of fiction.
No one ever really beat
Buck Duke.

By the year 2000, 2 out of 3 Americans could be illiterate.

It's true.

Today, 75 million adults... about one American in three, can't read adequately. And by the year 2000, U.S. News & World Report envisions an America with a literacy rate of only 30%.

Before that America comes to be, you can stop it... by joining the fight against illiteracy today.

Call the Coalition for Literacy at toll-free **1-800-228-8813** and volunteer.

Volunteer Against Illiteracy. The only degree you need is a degree of caring.

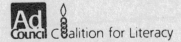

Ad Council   Coalition for Literacy